Blood of the Angels

Eugenio Fuentes was born in Montehermoso, Cáceres, Spain. His novels include *The Battles of Breda*, *The Birth of Cupid* (winner of the San Fernando Luis Berenguer International Fiction Prize), *So Many Lies* (winner of the Extramadura Creative Novel Award) and *Depths of the Forest* (Arcadia) which won the Alba/Prensa Canaria Prize in 1999.

Martin Schifino is a freelance writer and translator. He regularly contributes essays and reviews to *The Times Literary Supplement*, *Revista de Libros* and *Revista Otra Parte*, and he co-translated José Luis de Juan's *This Breathing World* (Arcadia). He lives in London.

Selina Packard is a freelance copy-editor and is co-translator of José Luis de Juan's *This Breathing World*. She has a Ph.D. in English from Goldsmiths College and lives in London.

EUGENIO FUENTES

Blood of the Angels

Translated from the Spanish by

Martin Schifino and Selina Packard

ARCADIA BOOKS

Arcadia Books Ltd
15–16 Nassau Street
London W1W 7AB

www.arcadiabooks.co.uk

First published in the United Kingdom by Arcadia Books 2007
Originally published by Alba Editorial, s.l.u., Barcelona, as *La Sangre de los ángeles* 2001
Copyright © Eugenio Fuentes 2001
This English translation from the Spanish
Copyright © Martin Schifino and Selina Packard 2007

A catalogue record for this book is available from the British Library.

ISBN 1–900850–83–4

Designed and typeset in Minion by Discript Limited, London WC2N 4BN
Printed in Finland by WS Bookwell

Arcadia Books Ltd acknowledges the financial support of la Dirección General del Libro, Archivos Bibliotecas del Ministerio de Educación, Cultura y Deporte de España.

Arcadia Books supports English PEN, the fellowship of writers who work together to promote literature and its understanding. English PEN upholds writers' freedoms in Britain and around the world, challenging political and cultural limits on free expression. To find out more, visit www.englishpen.org, or contact English PEN, 6–8 Amwell Street, London EC1R 1UQ.

Arcadia Books distributors are as follows:

in the UK and elsewhere in Europe:
Turnaround Publishers Services
Unit 3, Olympia Trading Estate
Coburg Road
London N22 6TZ

in the USA and Canada:
Independent Publishers Group
814 N. Franklin Street
Chicago, IL 60610

in Australia:
Tower Books
PO Box 213
Brookvale, NSW 2100

in New Zealand:
Addenda
Box 78224
Grey Lynn
Auckland

in South Africa:
Quartet Sales and Marketing
PO Box 1218
Northcliffe
Johannesburg 2115

Arcadia Books is the *Sunday Times* Small Publisher of the Year

To Guillermo and Jorge, in the future.

Acknowledgements

Although the teaching profession is one of the hardest-hit by depression, in which an individual suffers all the damage, few of its members have infringed the law and harmed others. By and large, teachers are peaceful people: there have been hardly any criminals among them, and they never consider using violence to achieve their ends.

With that in mind, it's almost needless to add that this novel and the characters in it do not reflect reality at all, and that all situations are only figments – accurate or not – of the author's imagination.

I am pleased to express my gratitude to Paloma and Maite Osorio, José Antonio Leal, Marciano de Hervás and Fernando Alonso, who read the manuscript and made improvements; to Miguel Costero Cortón, for his assistance with everything regarding guns; to Tomás Algre, for his patience and what he taught me about the sound of the clarinet and how it is played; and to María Antonia de Miquel, for the wisdom of her advice.

A grant from the Consejería de Cultura de la Junta de Extremadura assisted me in the writing of this novel.

1

He moved the flowers aside to look at the face hardened by death, by the blood that was already clotting under the eyelids, as if in surprise that the heart was no longer pumping it through the veins. He hadn't looked at her face for this long in twenty years. He wondered how much she had missed their talks over a cup of coffee or tea, sitting at the round table in that little drawing room of hers; he had especially avoided the place in the few months after Dulce left him. His mother's house was the last place on earth where he would come looking for comfort. But if he hadn't visited her more often, it was also to have her think that everything was fine, that her son could bear this, that he wasn't lonely and therefore that she needn't worry about him. His mother came from a generation and a country in which the word *divorce* all but signified tragedy, a devastating event that, whatever its causes, filled both spouses with pain, dishonour and shame. He had avoided her gaze in case his eyes confirmed that belief.

When he was a child and got angry over some small thing – a prohibition or a refusal to buy him a toy or clothes with the right brand name – she would find some excuse to sit next to him after a couple of hours and, smiling, say to him: 'Look at you, so handsome with that grumpy face.' It was impossible to maintain his bad mood, and he would end up laughing too, letting her kiss him, and seeking her nearness and warmth, as if to make up for those hours they'd spent apart. He remembered a time when he was going away with his class to spend a few days camping at the Paternoster reserve. He didn't have the right gear and, a week before the trip, his eye was caught by a red backpack in a shop window; it came with a cap, a canteen, a collapsible cup, a miniature first-aid kit and, best of all, a Swiss army knife with so many attachments you would have felt safe on a desert island. But it was too expensive, and his mother, constrained by her widow's pension, refused to buy it for him. Although he wasn't usually one of those people who stays angry for long, his rage this time lasted three days. Three days of barely talking to her at meals, avoiding her and slipping off to his room whenever he was free, using homework as an excuse without caring if his mother or sister believed him.

The day before the trip she came into his room to tell him dinner was on the table. As before, she bent down towards him, looked at him with a smile, lifted his chin and repeated: 'Look at you, so handsome with that grumpy face.' He'd been hoping for this for the last few hours, terrified at the possibility of going away without having made up with her. And so, despite that resistance and hardness which the onset of puberty was bringing about inside him, he smiled, too. He forgot all about the backpack and the Swiss army knife and got ready for the following day.

In the morning, when the alarm clock forced his eyes open, he saw the shiny new objects on his night table, the cap, the canteen, the collapsible cup, and the Swiss army knife bristling with attachments, displayed in the same slightly ostentatious manner as presents for Epiphany on the fifth of January. He jumped out of bed, got dressed in a rush. He ran to the kitchen, hearing noises there. His mother was packing his sandwiches and fruit. 'Put some water in your canteen,' she said casually. He turned the tap on but then turned it off again immediately; he dried his hands on her apron, as he had done as a boy, and hugged her with a childish tenderness that he was beginning to lose. They had breakfast together, and when he was about to leave, his mother gave him some pocket money. He realised it was too much, and told her: 'Half as much would be plenty.' After getting all that equipment, he would have been happy with a meagre, token amount. His mother wrapped his hand around it and replied, 'You don't need to spend it all, but you may need it if something unexpected happens. I trust you.'

Such warmth, so complete with emotion and trust, would not be repeated often after that time. Adolescence was quickly and firmly setting in, with its freight of criticism and hostility towards anyone over twenty. In order not to founder under its weight, he had to release it and move faster, like a skater who senses the thin ice of the lake beneath his feet and hurtles along at ever-greater speed to escape his fear of the depths.

It was around that time that he began to miss his father. He would ask what he'd been like, and would look at portraits both of his father alone and with the family – mostly black-

and-white pictures in which an attractive, calm-looking man carried him in his arms, or of himself with his sister, each sitting on one of his knees, and his mother beside them. They were simple pictures, undated, their edges white and neat, none of them touched up to make them seem more beautiful or colourful, but just taken for the memory or perhaps for some bureaucratic purpose, a family scrapbook or something similar. He would study his father's features and, quite often, locked in his room or in the bathroom, stand before the mirror with the portrait tucked into the corner of the frame. He would comb his hair like his father's and examine the resemblance, focusing on those features which revealed a common bone structure and in which his mother's genes had not intruded to alter the line of the cheekbone, the tilt of the nose or the width of the fore-head. Although he wouldn't dare tell anyone, at those moments – which had a clandestine air, as if he were committing a small act of treason – he missed him.

Years later he would realise that a father who dies young ends up exerting more influence than a mother who is always present, who tells you what to do and asks how school is and what you're wearing and which friends you're meeting tonight. Since she was home and alive, he did not have to wonder about her face or her personality, or worry too much about her health or all she was missing: he knew about the brutal, sudden absence at thirty-six of the man who had always been by her side. Yet up until four months ago, when Dulce had left him, he was not aware of what that meant. He was the same age now and experienced the same loneliness. For although a series of profound changes had occurred over three decades which had made the life of the previous generation nearly unrecognisable – the transition from a grotesque dictatorship to a democracy, the sexual revolution and the pill, the Internet and the bursting empire of computing, cloning and the decoding of the human genome – loneliness was still the same, having lost none of its qualities.

He wondered how many memories he had thought lost would return now his mother was dead; how many confrontations or disappointments or petty slights would gnaw at him now there was no way of rectifying them. Perhaps time heals all wounds, he thought to himself, trying hard to believe his own attempt at consolation, and so far he could stand the pain. Yet his other wound, the fact that his wife – still his wife on paper at least – had abandoned him, was still there, immune to the passage of time, the intensity of the pain barely easing. His eyes focused once again on his mother's face. It had been his sister Maria who decided that the coffin should stay open during the wake, and he was glad of a decision that allowed him to look at her a while longer. In Breda, that practice was usually reserved for men; women's corpses were never displayed, as if the rigid customs of decorum in life extended into death as well.

Fortunately she had not died from cancer or one of those long degenerative diseases that consume both the patient and those who care for her. A thrombosis had appeared as a compassionate herald to the cardiac arrest that arrived barely six hours later. Despite all the efforts of Maria and the morticians, her mouth was still slightly askew and one of her eyelids was raised higher than the other, as if her already cold muscles had put up a stubborn resistance to the final make-up. *They closed her eyes. It wasn't her; she died with her eyes open.* In contrast, her hands, crossed over her bosom, and holding an ivory crucifix, looked oddly natural, as if they could come alive at any moment. He reached out and gently caressed the distorted side of her face. It felt like a freshly unearthed mushroom, soft to the touch yet giving the impression that, if you pressed a little, your finger would sink into the flesh. Her nostrils had narrowed, tensed, as if smelling the onset of their own decay. The dim light from the bulbs in the ceiling reflected off her forehead and cheekbones, which seemed to have started giving off that phosphorescence attributed to thorns and bleached bones. *The death of one's parents is like the death of stars. Their light reaches us when they don't exist anymore*, he thought.

Without a noise, the little girl was suddenly beside him. Who had let her in? Why is there always a child near death? He noticed his eyelids and cheeks were wet with tears, and wiped them swiftly away, quietly enough so she did not notice. Her eyes looked puzzled and sad; they were brown with specks of green, like black poplar leaves just before they fall. She put out her little hand and held on to his arm, with a touch as gentle and warm as that of a bird. It was her way of telling him that she had seen him cry. He had cried at other times in the last few months, but never in front of his daughter. Julián Monasterio tried to smile; he knew that neither in the hours that had passed since the death nor in those that remained until the funeral was he to encounter a gesture of sympathy that would touch him so deeply.

'Who let you in?' he asked her after a kiss.

'No one. I was on my own.' The 's' whistled through her toothless gums: she had lost her milk teeth a few weeks ago, but the new ones had not appeared. He guessed how she had managed it. She must have remained still and silent until she became nearly invisible and the others stopped paying attention. Then she must have slipped away.

The girl stood on tiptoe and peered into the coffin. For a few seconds, she was tense with a mixture of the desire to see her grandma's face and the fear of her stillness. He hugged her: she shouldn't be there, but it was now too late to stop her.

Julián Monasterio heard a noise behind him and turned: his sister was gesturing worriedly in the direction of the girl, while making it clear that it had not been she who had brought her there or let her in.

'Come on, go with your auntie. Grandma wouldn't like you to see her like this.'

The girl nodded and took a few steps away. She stopped and turned to ask him:

'When are you coming?'

'In a minute. I won't be long.'

He was alone again. He slowly kissed his mother's forehead, and then pressed his palm against her cheek one last time.

The waiting room was humming with several conversations which were becoming increasingly loud. Perhaps everyone was getting a little restless, but at that moment he didn't care. He only cared about his daughter, the one thing he knew he had done well in his life so far. When he came out, a little dazzled by the stronger lights, some people who had just arrived offered their condolences. His daughter was sitting by his sister and looked at him in puzzlement, her eyes eager for something he could not identify nor knew how to give.

The sudden noise of the electric screwdrivers securing the lid of the coffin in the other room stopped all the whispering. As if it were a signal, María started sorting people into groups to take them to the cars, and everyone left for the cemetery. Julián Monasterio hoped that the service would not be too long or tearful; that the priest would not overuse the words heaven or hell; that there would not be too much talk of God.

↶

He waited for Alba to fasten her seatbelt before starting up the Audi he had bought the previous year. For just the two of them, the car seemed excessively big: no one ever occupied the front seat, and there was too much room in the boot. He had often thought of replacing it with a more modest one, easier to drive and less expensive to run. When Dulce had left, she had taken the small Rover that doubtless made her look like an independent woman again, without children, with little baggage. Even the bright metallic crimson of its bodywork had a youthful air about it that was a far cry from the sober blue of the Audi.

It took ten minutes to reach his sister's semi-detached house in one of the developments with which Breda, in an attempt to hide its rural origins and acquire city manners, had been expanding over the last few years. A sizeable part of the younger population preferred to live in these outskirts where the architecture was weightless and bright, the stone of the façades was mostly fake, the trees could be easily transplanted and the geometric blocks held no mysteries or secrets: every three streets, a main road. Yet the long-established coffee shops of the city centre were still the main meeting places, popular with people who liked to smoke cigars and play *mus*, their favourite card game, in which a trio of twos always trumps a pair of aces.

Alba enjoyed going to her aunt's, especially in the summer, since the development had its own swimming pool. Swimming was the only sport she had really taken to. The first few times her father saw her go underwater, swimming with the speed and ease of a frog diving away from the dangers of the surface, he watched her movements closely, a little worried when she took too long coming up for air, but amazed at her skill. He had never been a good swimmer and her talent filled him with awe and pride. He even imagined that one day, not far in the future, his own daughter – now so weak and fragile and filled with fears – would save him from drowning.

María was waiting for them and came out to say hello. She kissed the girl and asked her:

'Did you bring your swimsuit?'

'Yes,' she replied, monosyllabic as ever, hardly able to contain the impulse to go running towards the water. It was August and very hot.

'Go on, then. Luis and Pedrito are waiting for you.'

The girl looked at her father, waited for him to kiss her, and made off along the street that led to the square, the little playground and the pool. All of a sudden she stopped, came running back towards him and, unable to hide a touch of anxiety, asked him:

'Will you be long?'

'A little while. But I'll come and get you myself.'

María and Julián Monasterio got in the car. They were meeting for the first time after completing all the formalities of the funeral. At the first traffic lights, by the entrance to the old town, he looked at her profile. She was wearing a white shirt and a skirt showing her hard angular knees, which were not inviting to the touch. Her bare arms and neck gave off such a delicate scent that only now he was in the car did he notice it at all. Her face no longer showed traces of the tears she had shed a few days before, only slight rings under her eyes from lack of sleep. She seemed much better. Julián Monasterio glanced at himself in the mirror to see if he looked as well as she did. However, he found his eyes wide open and expectant, like those of a person carefully studying an abstract painting he likes but does not fully understand.

They took the lift up to the flat. Since it had been installed a few years back, when neither of them lived there anymore, the stairs were hardly ever used. But it had been on those dark wide stairs at the end of the corridor where they had played as children, scooting down when a neighbour came out on to the landing to tell them off for making a racket, and where later they had their first trysts. For years they had run down those steps to meet a man coming back from work with a leather briefcase in his hand. As they reached him, he would take sweets out of his pockets and hand them out with a smile that was to be wiped away only too soon... When Julián made for the door, he saw María's key already in the keyhole. They turned the lights on. Both had been born in that flat, with its thick walls, high yellowing ceilings and dark decor; both born in the same bed with its metal headboard and creaking springs, five years apart, a difference that had entitled María to play the role of the elder sister. He knew she would not sell her birthright for love nor money, but there had been times when he'd been grateful for that privilege which, while allowing her to impose her demands on the smallest matters, also obliged her to be protective. She had often helped him with Alba and was doing so this very afternoon.

Yet they had never been truly close. The age gap was too wide for them to have shared interests and friends in the only years when a friendship is possible, though too narrow for him to have considered her a wise, adult person he could ask for advice or comfort when in need. When he introduced her to Dulce, she had said: 'She's very pretty. I like her.' But she never did anything to demonstrate this. Of course he hadn't expected them to become best friends. María had the same friends since the start of high school: all were from Breda, girls whose parents she knew and knew her and had no objections to anything. He had always admired and found astonishing his sister's loyalty to her friends, a small, solid circle that remained unaffected by the ups and downs of work, travel, marriage, children, personal or economic differences. And Dulce had come from elsewhere, from a northern city, to work at the hospital laboratory. Julián would have been content if they had established a certain affinity to make those compulsory family gatherings – birthdays, anniversaries, Christmas – more pleasant. But they had always kept a careful distance that barely disguised their mutual dislike, as if they were both waiting for the other to make a first mistake, give offence first, and so find the perfect excuse to dispense with that studied politeness.

The musty, stuffy smell of the place seemed to be a product both of its darkness and of the million decomposing particles that were already covering walls, furniture, cupboards and picture frames, creating a layer of dust over which spiders had aggressively spun their webs.

María had already disposed of the useless things – her mother's clothes that brought back too many memories, her toiletries, her jars of mysterious medicines that hinted at problems and ailments they had never suspected. But all the rest was there.

María produced a pen and a notebook and wrote her name and Julián's on two separate sheets.

'So, how do we go about it?' she asked.

The most valuable thing was the flat itself, but they had agreed not to sell for the moment and to wait before making a decision.

'As Mum always said, we can start with the jewellery.'

'It seems right.'

María went into the bedroom and returned carrying a little box. When she opened it, they heard the tune that Julián Monasterio would always associate, not so much with the value of the jewellery, but with parties and anniversaries, for it was only when his mother dressed up for a special occasion that she would open it in front of them. He remembered her with the box on the bed, trying on a pearl necklace she was to wear to a wedding, and asking them if it suited her, as if flirting for them. Now they slowly emptied it of its contents and laid them on the table: the pearl necklace, rings, earrings, bracelets, brooches, watches, a pair of cufflinks, several tiepins and other trinkets. Nearly everything was made of antique solid gold and set with semi-precious stones. But what stood out from the rest were a pair of diamond earrings and a diamond necklace, which were concealed in the false bottom. María could not help touching them briefly, as if their intense beauty could not be taken in with the eyes alone, and the sense of touch was needed to fully appreciate the Dutch workmanship, as well as the smoothness and temperature of the stone. For a few seconds Julián Monasterio thought he saw, in an odd way, the shine of the diamonds reflected in her eyes, as in those of a hungry bird looking at its food. As if noticing her own slip, she quickly opened a cloth pouch and emptied it into her hand: thirteen gold coins that had served as *arras* for several generations. Isabel II's effigy shone on all of them, encircled by a motto and the minting date: 1845. They looked new, as if they had just left the mint, without the mixture of grime and wear which smoothes them away as they change hands.

Neither knew the details of their origin. Their mother had always been cagey about how they had come into her husband's possession, and she insisted on discretion about them. Julián and María Monasterio had grown up suspecting some shady affair in connection with the coins, a hint of theft or illegality that conferred even greater mystique on them, one of those stories of tragic love and drops of blood that sit so well with certain jewels. What they did know was that the coins were worth a lot.

'That's everything,' said María, as if inviting him to choose first.

Julián Monasterio picked up the coins. A handful of gold that barely fitted in his hand, thirteen *arras* which his father had placed between his mother's fingers and which had passed to a new generation to bear witness to a happy union. Intriguingly, the coins didn't awake any greed in him; his mind was just comparing his parents' lives to his own. They too must have had arguments, difficult moments, and perhaps they had hurt each other with petty insults and rejections. But his mother's enduring devotion to the memory of her husband, the fact that she had remained a widow with the resolve of someone who feels no remorse or desire for revenge, and the documents – a few letters and a handful of photographs – which she kept from their relationship were proof enough that neither had regretted marrying the other.

At his wedding, he had not given the *arras* to Dulce. His mother had offered them to him, but the couple had rejected them as an archaic symbol that, although they couldn't explain why, seemed to them slightly Jewish and biblical. They had only exchanged plain rings, and had even doubted that gesture and its outdated associations. Back then he believed that they would be as inseparable as the stars in a constellation, and that they had no need for symbols or vows or witnesses to go on shining together. They didn't have a church wedding, and the ceremony at the registry was quick and a little sad. When he recalled the day, Julián Monasterio didn't feel the nostalgia for a moment in which he'd been young, handsome and happy; he didn't find in it those solemn moments conferred by the organ music and the cumbersome slowness of the religious service.

He looked at his hand, hoping that María would not notice its movement and guess his train of thought. He no longer wore a ring, but his finger still had a small sign of where it had been: the skin was ever so slightly paler. A summer of a hundred days had almost wiped out that small trace of the hundred months they'd spent together.

María picked out the gold cufflinks, tiepins, a watch and a few other pieces that had belonged to their father.

'Stop worrying about it. Mum didn't want us to be sad,' she said, striving to play the role of elder sister convincingly, calm and responsible in front of her more fragile brother.

'Of course.'

She put aside the feminine pieces for herself and pushed the others towards him, and he put them into a pouch with the thirteen *arras*. That was their mother's wish and they would carry it out.

María got up and took two drawers out of a chest which contained the silver. A sudden gust of celebrations, birthdays and Christmases passed through Julián's mind. He found it odd that, precisely in these moments of sadness, every object evoked hours of pleasure and splendour, as if only to emphasise the value of what had been lost. It was the first time he had inherited something – it would also be the last – and all of a sudden, and with great surprise, he thought of people he knew who had been glad to receive the legacy of their relatives, for they had been expecting it for a long time and knew what to do with it and how to invest it. But the only thing he now felt was that, with any inheritance, the gains are always smaller than the loss which produces them.

'We haven't discussed this, but if it's all right, you can take the books and I'll keep the cutlery. You don't need it as much now,' María said.

She immediately realised her mistake. Her brother's look was very close to a reproach, but he did not voice it. Both knew her words referred not only to his loneliness since Dulce's leaving, to the pre-cooked meals in the kitchen, the nights torn by the knives of insomnia, the indifference he now felt when going past a flower or a perfume shop, the fear of finding himself ill and alone with a broken thermometer and the shards of his fever hidden between the sheets, the ease with which all the wickedness of others could one day be embodied in a laugh; María's words also seemed to suggest that – and this was the hardest thing to accept – she didn't foresee any change to his situation in the near future.

'I'm sorry, Julián, I didn't mean that.'

'It doesn't matter,' he replied, incapable of still looking offended when even a hint of an apology was offered.

Despite this conciliatory gesture, there was now a certain awkwardness between them. Suddenly they seemed in a hurry to finish, and each of them agreed without objections to the other's suggestions or requests about the distribution of the rest of the things in the house, the vast array of objects and ornaments that fill up a house in five decades of life. Then, still too hurriedly, they decided they would both come back and take their things as soon as they could.

They were about to leave when María said:

'There's one other thing.'

'What?'

'Dad's pistol. What do we do with it?'

Julián Monasterio could not answer that question immediately. If ever his father had had any need for a gun, that moment belonged in a remote past, before his marriage. Julián and María knew he didn't have a licence for it, and when he died their mother had not handed it over to the authorities for that very reason.

He had discovered it many years before, as a teenager, hidden in a book made for the purpose. He'd seen it on a top shelf when he was looking for something to read other than adventure novels, which he was beginning to find too bland. He was astonished at his discovery, for every image he had of his father was of a colourless, honest and punctual bureaucrat, who every morning for decades arrives on time at his desk in an office at the city's law courts. He kept a few pictures of his father taken in that office, surrounded by colleagues at a celebration or sitting at a typewriter that seemed prehistoric to Julián; and in all of them he looked like an obliging employee who even seems to be asking the photographer how he can be of use. A peaceful, unadventurous father who only got excited over one game, chess; who hated going out for dinner; and who had always refused to drive a car. The very opposite of an armed man.

When he mentioned his discovery to his mother, she told him it had been a sort of under-the-counter gift from a grateful superior, obtained without the regulation licence, in case his job ever brought him face to face with trouble. That must have been in the early sixties, when the dictatorship was at its most stable and the use of guns common in certain official circles, for his mother would speak of it as if there were nothing unusual or criminal about it. Giving a pistol was like giving a book or a bunch of flowers or a couple of theatre tickets.

He imagined his father's first reaction of surprise when he held in his hand that hard, beautiful object he had been given, perhaps taking it by the butt yet without daring to put his finger into the finger guard, maybe sniffing the barrel fearfully and warily before placing it back in the book. He imagined him accepting it, not daring to turn down a present from a superior who was familiar with guns and probably a little cocky or flashy, putting it into his black leather briefcase which he took home gripping the handle firmly, as if he carried diamonds or valuable documents, and then, as soon as he got in, hiding it on the top shelf of the library with the furtive manner of someone hiding poison or a pornographic novel.

That's what he imagined.

He had seen it again a few other times, when they spring-cleaned or when they had painters in the house and his mother asked him to put it away, not because it was dangerous but because it would seem awkward under the tireless curiosity of other people. Once, when his mother and María were away on a trip, he'd even tried to take it apart; he had taken out the magazine – which, as he'd imagined, was empty – and loaded it with the cartridges kept in a little box by the butt. But promptly, frightened by his own audacity, he went back and, pushing the release button, unloaded it until it was empty again.

He'd forgotten all about it a long time ago, but now María, the efficient firstborn who managed everything without leaving any loose ends, was reminding him.

'What do we do with it?' she repeated.

'I don't know. Are you sure Mum kept it?'

'Let's check.'

In the study, María mounted a little ladder to reach the shelf.

'What was the book?'

'One by Pío Baroja.'

Nothing distinguished it from the other volumes – thick old books yellowed with age, like all those books one hasn't bought, but inherited from parents or grandparents, and among which are authors so obscure and titles so mediocre that it seems strange and incredible that they ever managed to succeed, were given a print run and a renown denied to much better works at the time. María undid the strap and lifted the cover: pistol, silencer and the little box of bullets appeared before her eyes. Without touching them, she gave the book to her brother, taking care that the barrel did not point towards either of them, as if it were a small venomous animal that she was afraid of or disgusted by.

Julián Monasterio took it and weighed it in his hand as he went over those irreconcilable images: his father and the gun. A peaceful man, and a perfect, sophisticated killing device. A man who would never take advantage of his work at the law courts, a position which so easily – especially in the years of the dictatorship – could have been used as a mark of prestige, to bribe or intimidate. Julián had never heard him boast about his job, had never seen him use his proximity to the judges – and to authority, that vague, menacing word which served a bailiff as well as the governor of the province – for his own purposes or to facilitate anything. However, now, as he held the gun – inert, beautiful – so comfortably in his hand, the image of his father wielding it alone in his study did not seem so outlandish. Had he ever held it like this, as Julián did now, admiring its balance, its solid perfection? Had his hand moulded itself as closely to the butt patterned with small lozenges to stop it slipping from sweat or grease? Had his father's index finger – one he'd never seen stained with ink or lead – really resisted the temptation of slipping into the finger guard and lightly pressing the trigger? Had he not thought that a pistol is the perfect intersection of hatred and blood, that you only need a few guns for Jews and Arabs to kill each other on the terraces of Jerusalem? And had he not thought that perhaps this pistol had killed a man, as anyone who has ever held a gun thinks?

'What are you doing?' he heard his sister ask impatiently.

'I was looking at it. It's lovely.'

'Julián, please, how can you say a gun is lovely? What are we going to do with it? Shouldn't we take it to the Guardia Civil?'

'I don't think so. It would create complications. Dad never had a licence.'

'We can say we didn't know anything about it. That we found it when Mum died,' she insisted.

'Do you know if it was ever used?'

'Not by Dad, that's for sure.'

'But in the past. How can we be sure that no one ever shot someone with it?' he argued, for the possibility of danger was the only thing that would make her give up.

A few seconds beforehand he had decided not to hand it over. He would keep it in his safe-deposit box at the bank. Owning it for so many years had not been a problem for his parents and it wouldn't be a problem for him. Why should he hand over an object that at that moment seemed to him a work of art, without getting anything in exchange? Even if he gained nothing from possessing it, if he handed it over he would lose forever something he would have no chance of ever owning again.

'I'm sure the Guardia Civil can sort that out. I think they would even thank us.'

'I'll have to think about it,' he agreed. 'But for the moment I'll keep it.'

'Do what you like. But I don't want anything to do with it. As far as I'm concerned, it doesn't exist.'

When they left and got back in the car, Julián Monasterio was conscious of the weight of the pistol and the *arras* in his jacket pocket, near his heart.

Alba answered his questions with monosyllables to convey that she'd had a good time at the pool with her cousins. However much she liked the water, she was not expansive in her joy and kept that distant, glum reserve, as if she were already steeling herself for sadness and, in preparation for maturity, shedding any childish enthusiasm. Because, he thought, that frequently repeated belief that childhood ends when one first becomes conscious of mortality was not true. Childhood ends, he said to himself, when a child discovers that an adult he expected everything from – protection and nourishment, kisses and good health – can stop loving him, a possibility that had never been previously imagined. And sometimes he wondered whether his daughter had discovered it too soon. He kissed her wet, chlorine-redolent hair, and let her body press against his with her head resting on his hip, oblivious to anyone else now that he was here. He said goodbye to María and promised to speak to her soon.

2

The following morning he woke up early and called Ernesto to ask him to open the shop as he had errands to run at the bank.

He'd just hung up when the phone rang as if it had been waiting for him to finish. It was Rocío, the woman who came in every day to cook and clean and look after his daughter while he was at the shop. She'd been feverish and sick all night and couldn't come to work. She had only left her bed to let him know.

Although her absence put him out, he told her not to worry; he would take care of everything: the main thing was for her to get better. He was very grateful to her, a married woman in her mid-forties who had no kids but had shown a motherly patience and skill with Alba. He didn't want to lose her. Without Ernesto in the store and Rocío at home everything would become even more chaotic. His relationship with both went deeper than a simple work contract. He had found Rocío through his mother – whose flat she cleaned now and then – and in a way viewed her efficiency and her affection as part of his inheritance.

Unhurriedly, he made himself some toast, coffee and orange juice. Then he lit a cigarette and waited for the nicotine to take effect, making him slightly dizzy. It always seemed that the smoke from his first cigarette reached not just his lungs, but went through his whole body, numbing his eyelids, turning his stomach, making him a bit weak at the knees, but helping him put his head in order.

It was an effort for him to get up from his chair and go to his daughter's room. He trusted she had not done it again. The stress of her grandmother's death and the funeral seemed to be over, and the day before she had had a good time with her cousins at the pool.

Alba was asleep hugging her pillow with her neck slightly twisted, a habit no doll of any size had been able to check. Since she was a toddler they had bought cuddly toys for her, hoping she would attach herself to one of them, tuck it in with her under the duvet, and so curb her fear of the dark when she woke up in the middle of the night. They had given her toys of all shapes and sizes, with different textures and features, both silent and with sound, motionless and vibrating ones, but she had always left them lying in some corner or other, as if that substitute for her parents' touch was too obvious a trick for her. He had himself ended up thinking as she did: that all those compact woolly balls were in the end too ordinary, not even letting childish mischief tear them apart like dolls or articulated toys. Up to the age of four, he and Dulce had stayed with her until sleep came, and it was around that time that she took to sleeping while hugging the pillow on which he or Dulce had lain, and in which she must have found the smell and echoes of their bodies.

He watched her from the doorway, without making up his mind whether to wake her. The half-open shutters let in rays of light and the whole room was visible: the carpet with its bright reds, greens and yellows; the wicker basket that was so useful for her dolls and for playing hide and seek; the frieze decorated with teddy bears that he had used as a skirting board when Dulce brought it one day not long before she left; the long coat rack in the shape of a train, a peg on each carriage; the shelves brimming with the toys he bought her, sometimes when she didn't even ask for them, always with the excuse that no matter how many she had it would never make up for her mother's absence.

The girl was still fast asleep, deep in that sleep one finally enters in the small hours after an exhausting night of love or nightmares. Yet he had to wake her if he was to make the most of the morning. He knelt beside her and slipped his hand under the sheet, where her hips were. Again he felt the wetness, and smelled the urine immediately. What else could he do to prevent it? He had taken her to the paediatrician who had referred her to a psychologist who had recommended a small gadget that rang when it detected wetness. But this long series of measures had been for the worse: after a few nights, when Alba and he awoke in alarm at the ringing, the girl's enuresis seemed to intensify. While before she had done it occasionally, during this treatment she wet the bed more often and abundantly, as if she had decided to wage war on the detector until she drowned it and couldn't hear its warnings.

When the professionals failed, he settled on the opposite course of action: he said nothing when it happened, ignored the stain as if it were as natural as the hairs or the mark of spittle that appeared on the pillow in the morning, and pretended indifference so that his daughter did not suspect how worried he was. But that hadn't solved anything either.

With a heavy heart, he laid his head on the mattress, his eyes open in the semi-darkness. It was not he who had left, but he felt partly responsible for all this, even if he could not find words to explain his guilt, for the words he knew, had he chosen to use them, would only distort his painful and peculiar sense of responsibility. He got up from the floor and lay down next to her, hugging her and stroking her hair insistently and softly, in order to reassure her from the moment she awoke that he would not reprimand her that morning either, that he did not mind getting a bit stained, because she was his daughter and nothing of hers was alien or repellent to him or, least of all, disgusting.

The girl, feeling him by her side, turned over to hug him and kissed him on the cheek. She stayed like that for a few moments, relaxed in his presence, accepting his fingers on her sweaty hair. Then, as if she had only just noticed it, Julián Monasterio felt the sudden tension that gripped her little body, and her subtle way of moving away from him. His daughter had noticed it and she too seemed ashamed and powerless. He kissed her and held her against him once again, trying to stop her withdrawing into that distance where she hid – so much pain and resignation in such a small head – giving her time to speak first and tell him why, what nightmares, terrors or worries beset her every night to make her do that, what pursuers and with what weapons. He waited a few minutes until he realised his daughter's secretiveness was once again greater than his patience, remaining, for all his efforts, an impassable barrier.

'We have to get up,' he told her. 'Rocío can't come to work today. She's not feeling well. But we'll spend all day together.'

Obedient and silent, the girl got out of bed quickly as if fleeing from the stain and the shame, picked up the clothes Rocío had left for her the previous evening and went to the bathroom. Her slim naked little legs walking over the carpet made her look even more fragile and defenceless. Julián

Monasterio heard the noises she made in there, always the same ritual: she washed her thighs and buttocks in the bidet, flushed and came out dressed, carrying her bundled-up pyjamas to the laundry basket.

In his worst moments – when he felt really tired, when he was very busy at the store or Alba was ill – he had come to the conclusion that he was not capable of looking after her on his own, educating her, returning her to how she was two years before, when she still had parents who loved each other and her childhood was a happy one.

The problem of her teeth had also been unresolved when Dulce left. Alba had lost both her top milk incisors at the start of spring and they thought it was because her new teeth were pushing them out and were about to cut through. However, weeks and months had gone by and there was no sign of them. Now alone, he had taken her to the dentist, and Alba, in spite of the fear her eyes betrayed when she saw the shiny metal tools arranged on that sort of kitchen hob, agreed to lie down on the chair with the meekness of someone who thinks it's no worse than everything else that's happening. The doctor examined her with a spatula and a torch, and asked him if her milk teeth had come out in an accident, as the adult ones were not ready to cut through yet. He said no. Although the dentist thought it odd and didn't find any reasonable explanation, he told them they must wait, that no doubt time would solve everything, that the nature of a child doesn't always follow logical laws, that her body was full of alarms but also of wonders. He booked them for another appointment in six months, but Julián got the impression he was fobbing them off.

He had come to think that, just as the enuresis had a mental cause, so it might be with her teeth. He took good care with her diet and was sure it was not due to a lack of minerals or vitamins. Alba was a perfectly healthy girl, of normal height and weight, and her little body was fortified with vaccinations against every avoidable virus. It was as if her teeth had become stuck inside her gums due to something darker and more obscure than a mere combination of molecules. As if the girl herself had decided that they should not appear in her mouth yet, and that her pink gums should stay tender and vacant.

When Dulce came to pick her up at weekends, he had

discussed it with her several times, but she too refused to make much of it. 'They'll come out in time. Every child is different. Besides, you told me yours took a while,' she would always say, with the insistent optimism of someone immersed in an exciting adventure who rejects any minor problem that might impede her. 'Because my milk teeth took a while to come out too,' he would reply. 'You'll see, any morning now,' she would conclude in a way that made further discussion impossible.

He avoided looking at the dirty clothes Alba was carrying to the basket and asked her:

'Would you like to come with me on some errands?'

'What errands?' she said, wavering between mistrust and happiness at being with him. Julián Monasterio knew how little she liked hurrying along pavements to different places, or waiting while he handed over an invoice or went to see a client who had called him terrified by the appearance of a virus on his computer, which would take him a few moments to delete. He knew how much she hated it when the people he greeted bent down to ask her something silly that obliged her to nod or shake her head, or gave her a kiss and stroked her hair with such pity that even she felt it.

'Nothing to do with computers. I have to pop to the bank to put away some paperwork, and then we can go to the super-market to buy something nice to eat. Rocío is not here today, so we have to take care of everything.'

'OK.'

'Great!' he said, as if her company was the most important thing to him that morning. 'But first, you must finish your breakfast.'

He made her a hot chocolate and toast and stayed next to her drinking his second coffee. Then he went into his study and put the *arras*, the jewellery and his father's gun in a briefcase.

At the bank he wasn't greeted by the manager, who always gave him the second key needed to open the safe, but by a substitute he didn't know. The executive's tie and jacket meant the air conditioning was set too high for his daughter and himself in their T-shirts. The man checked his ID against the bank's database and walked him towards the vault with the second key, his decisive gestures passing for efficiency.

Julián didn't want Alba to come in with him as she might see the coins and the gun, and he'd rather she didn't get involved. Besides, the narrow, stifling, ill-lit vault was no place for a child. He asked her to sit on one of the armchairs by the door; he wouldn't be long.

It was a very small room, about seven or eight square metres, its walls covered from floor to ceiling with rows of safes, which brought about an intense feeling of claustrophobia and disquiet more fitting to caves full of mysteries and treasure. There must have been around one hundred and fifty, he reckoned – an excessive number for a small branch in a provincial city. This could only be explained by its inhabitants' malign, obsessive tendency to keep secrets and their distrust of figureheads and executors. Some were half-open, with their keys hanging from the keyholes, as they were not in use. From a corner near the ceiling, a camera could record anything that went on inside, but he presumed it was only switched on outside office hours or when an alarm went off. At that moment it certainly was off: not even the bank itself must have known what people hid in there.

The employee turned his lock, left the key in – he would come back for it later – and left. Julián Monasterio was now alone.

He opened the safe and checked its contents were in order: two million pesetas of undeclared earnings from recent sales, and a notebook and some floppy disks where he kept the rigged accounts of his business. These small scams never amounted to much and were imposed on him by his clients, always reluctant to pay any taxes. He leafed through to the last entry and wrote down the date on a piece of paper. He would have to update it soon, when it was time to do the quarterly figures.

He was taking too long and Alba was still outside, waiting for him among strangers. Remembering his promise at breakfast, he began to hurry. He opened his briefcase and took out the purse with the *arras* and the small pieces of jewellery. He counted the thirteen coins again, shiny and yellow, new in their old gold. He pushed them to the back of the safe and then took out the book. Before opening it, he turned his back to the camera even though it was off. As he had the day before, he could not help holding the gun and admiring its balance, its menacing perfection. He shut the book suddenly when he heard steps nearing the door. It must be the employee. What would he think if he saw him with a gun in his hands? Julián recognised his voice through the aperture; it was saying to someone: 'We have to wait a few minutes. There's a customer inside.'

'I'm coming,' he said out loud as he put the gun away and shut the book with a too-sonorous thud.

'Thank you. Please leave the bank's key in the safe. I'll pick it up.'

He closed the safe quickly, with trembling fingers, turning his key and thinking that even if the employee did not lock it right away with the bank's key, still, no one could open it.

Julián came out of the vault taking no notice of who was waiting, because he saw at the end of the passage that Alba had stood up and seemed nervous and disconcerted at how long he'd taken. He murmured a hurried goodbye and quickly took his daughter's outstretched hand.

They went back home and from there to the supermarket in the car. Now that he had put away those last remnants of his inheritance, he felt calmer, like someone ready to enjoy his free time after leaving a beautiful, delicate dog at a kennel, a dog of a rare breed and high pedigree, but one which can turn ferocious when threatened.

He didn't realise at what point he'd moved away from Alba as he pushed the trolley, but when he heard her cry he quickly went back, even before seeing where she was or what happened. Alba, distracted or hindered by someone – one of those types you sometimes see in big supermarkets, ramming their trolleys painfully into others' ankles without even apologising, their minds befuddled by the special offers or the tacky displays, eager people who stock up on supplies as if a war had broken out – had lagged behind and, anxious to reach him, had tried taking a shortcut up a moving ramp that went the wrong way. Realising the ramp was taking her further away she'd shouted. People nearby glanced at her, not understanding the reason for her shouts. Julián Monasterio got there in a few seconds, but knew that it would be some time before he'd be able to forget the terror on her face. He picked her up, kissed her and wiped the sudden scalding tears from her cheeks, feeling that that hug, although the result of a painful event, brought him closer to her than thousands of protective or loving words. He took her back to where he'd abandoned the trolley, and the whole time they were shopping she did not let go of his hand.

꒰

That night in bed, trying to fall asleep, he thought that life is just like that: a series of moving ramps which never stop and which are controlled no one knows by whom or from where, though it seems certain that it is done without love, pity, logic or purpose. Sometimes they carry us in the right direction and we are happy for a while. But on other occasions, because we make the wrong choice, or because someone pushes us, or simply by chance, we take the one that carries us away from where we wanted to go. Life then becomes a hopeless struggle not to descend to the basement, as had happened to his daughter that afternoon: it is like the attempt to run against the conveyor belt while getting no faster; the anxiety of trying to hold on to the handrail and realising it too recedes backwards; the hope of finding a resting place where one might correct one's course; and the discovery, on reaching it, that it is only a mirage.

Unable to sleep, he got up and went to his daughter's room. Alba was sleeping as she usually did, slightly sprawled across the bed, her head touching the wall, as if she still had that instinct babies have of resting against the cervix. He slipped a hand under the sheets, but the bed was dry. For now.

He lit up a cigarette in the living room without turning on the lights. In that semi-darkness everything looked tidy, clean, despite the fact that Rocío had been off that day. Well, it was easy to keep things tidy in an empty house missing half its adult occupants. When Dulce still lived there, the large living room was the centre of the home, the place where Alba would bring her toys and where he would read the paper or a book with the TV on. But now he would retire to his study and turn the computer on to finish some task or other, or just to play solitaire, while Alba played in her room or there with him, at his feet, as if they were both avoiding the spaciousness of a room that seemed to emphasise Dulce's absence. He barely watched TV anymore, and some nights, once his daughter was asleep, he would go online and chat with women who were as sad and lonely as he, or look for erotic contacts that might not be too disappointing.

He put his cigarette out in the ashtray. On his way back to bed, he thought that if there was a way he could remedy his daughter's sadness, perhaps he wouldn't mind his own so much.

⤶

The following morning when he was in the shower Rocío knocked on the bathroom door.

'You've got a phone call.'

'Who is it?'

'I don't know. They asked for Mr Julián Monasterio. A man's voice. It sounds important.'

Worried by that 'Mr' and the use of his surname, he promptly put on a bathrobe and opened the door a crack for Rocío to pass him the phone.

'Hello.'

'Good morning. I'm sorry to disturb you so early. I'm calling from the bank. You were here yesterday, using your safe, and we think you left it open. You turned the key, but the lock didn't catch.'

'What?' he asked. He didn't quite understand what he was being told.

'We think you left your safe open when you came in to use it. We think you turned the key when the door was off the frame.'

Comprehension dawned as he recognised the employee's voice.

'But didn't you use your key afterwards? Didn't you check?'

'No, I'm afraid I didn't. It's a lamentable error, and we're terribly sorry,' he heard a voice well-trained in its dealings with clients, one of those voices as apt to be docile as firm, depending on whom they are addressing. 'Two things occurred by chance at the same time. It seems unlikely, but that's how it happened. You may remember there was another client waiting. As there are empty safes with their keys in, I must have mistaken yours for one of them. And then I'm afraid I forgot. We didn't notice until this morning when we were doing our daily check. I couldn't be more sorry,' he insisted. 'The best thing would be for you to come here as soon as possible, although I can assure you we believe these unfortunate coincidences have had no unpleasant consequences for you: your safe is not empty. We could see some papers, a small leather wallet and a little cloth bag. Naturally, we haven't touched anything.'

And the gun? he wondered, reluctant to share the optimism of the voice. And the gun? Yet he seemed to remember he'd put the book under the accounts documents; if it was true they hadn't touched anything, they couldn't have seen that, either.

He dressed hurriedly, told Rocío the call wasn't important and, skipping breakfast, went straight to the bank. It was still closed to the public, but they were waiting for him, and the employee who had served him the previous day came to the door. He pretended to be calm and his words sounded as firm as over the phone, but his face betrayed worry and anxiety: his restless eyes were not as efficiently trained as his voice. The employee seemed to hope nothing was missing as much as Julián Monasterio himself.

He followed him into the vault, and the employee showed him the catch that had not found its home. He should have locked it afterwards, but as there were people waiting he put it off so as to lock both safes at the same time. And then he forgot about the first one. He was there as acting director for this hot August, he didn't know all the routines well and everything seemed doubly difficult, he added, by way of a tepid excuse.

The man left him to check the contents. Julián Monasterio looked towards the security camera near the ceiling: it was already off. Without further ado, he lifted the accounts papers and saw nothing but the metal bottom of the safe. The book had disappeared. Everything else was there: the small leather wallet with the two million and the purse containing his father's jewels and the thirteen gold coins which, when he re-counted them with his trembling fingers, in the silence of that small strongroom, jingled outrageously. They had taken the gun but had left things that were fifty or a hundred times more valuable! Unable to believe his eyes, he reached into the very back and tried to dislodge the safe to see if the book had fallen out the back, as happens in some chests of drawers. But each safe was built into a separate compartment with an iron bottom that left no space, not a crack. His heart was a breathless colt in his chest. Why? And who? Who, in a quiet city and in peaceful times, was more interested in a gun than money and jewels?

Unless, he told himself with stubborn optimism, desperately trying to keep on top of things, unless the person who took the book didn't know it contained a pistol. Of course. That must be it. It wasn't a professional thief or anyone familiar with crime – such a person would have left a Baroja, and even the most valuable codex – but a devoted reader who might have been afraid of stealing the *arras* and the money, and getting tangled up in a police investigation. But a book! In grabbing it he would have thought that no one would report the theft of a book; almost no one read anymore. Julián Monasterio himself had not opened a book for weeks, not even one of those second-rate noir novels, which were nothing much more than a puzzle to be solved, and which Dulce had bought every week for a collection that soon bored her.

When the thief opened the book and saw its contents, no doubt he would dispose of it, perhaps terrified at what he had done. Among the few book-lovers he knew, none were violent or capable of doing any harm. They were quiet, amiable people, who moved unhurriedly and had myopic gazes, and in some cases were quite prone to melancholy. They wouldn't know what to do with a pistol.

It was the only reasonable explanation he could think of and with it he managed to calm down. He heard the employee's voice behind the door.

'Is everything all right?'

He hesitated for a moment. If he said something was missing, he would immediately have to specify what, and although this would mean he might find out who was waiting behind him the previous morning, he could not be sure it was that person who had taken it, for several other people might have entered the vault over the course of the morning. He had nothing to gain, so he lied, trying to hide the presentiment of some inevitable, imminent misfortune in his voice.

'It's all here.'

'Are you sure?'

'Of course.'

The employee came in and they both turned their keys and made doubly sure the safe was locked. Then each pocketed his key. The man apologised again, walked him to the door and shook his hand, relieved that nothing irreparable had happened.

Julián Monasterio went to a cafe and ordered breakfast. As it was being served, he impatiently lit up the first cigarette of the day. Once again he had doubts; the explanation he had given himself a few minutes ago, of a possible bibliophile-thief, now seemed weak and forced, a naive theory formed so as not to feel disheartened. Fortified by his coffee he wondered whether to go over to the Guardia Civil station and tell them everything. He had ignored María's advice, the efficient older sibling María, and had put the pistol in his safe in the bank. But now it could be counterproductive to report its disappearance, for anyone might suspect dark motives and intentions in a series of actions which ran counter to logic and any sense of civic responsibility. It would lead to questions he would not know how to answer. Whose weapon was it? How had he come by it? Why hadn't he handed it over earlier? What was his intention in keeping it in a safe? Who else knew about it?

He had got up from his stool, but sat down again. Breda, he told himself, looking for another way to avoid doing anything, was a quiet place – the capital of malice, but a quiet place nevertheless – not a city given to violence. No one went into the street with a loaded pistol in his pocket. As soon as the thief discovered the contents of the book they would surely have thrown it into the Lebrón or buried it. What would anyone want a pistol for?

He arrived at the shop determined to work, as there was much to do and Ernesto didn't make important decisions without consulting him.

Ernesto was a good assistant with whom he had an excellent working relationship. He was twenty-five and had been with Julián for two years. He was rather plump, tall and dark, and had a premature bald patch that was about to spread over the top of his head. His sedentary job with computers had made him gain a bit more weight, and he sweated whenever physical exertion was required. But he was very good with software, better than anyone might have guessed from his mediocre student record. Julián Monasterio had hired him not long after he had finished his computing studies, and sometimes prayed that he wouldn't leave, that he wouldn't embark on the adventure of setting up his own company just yet, as commonly occurred when technicians realised they knew more than those who paid their wages. No other business evolved and generated its own archaeology at such a speed. Two years was enough for software that was once thought a brilliant, lasting solution to become obsolete. And two months away from work was enough to turn an expert into someone needing urgent retraining.

He greeted Ernesto warmly, left his briefcase on the desk and asked him about urgent matters. He had not been in the previous day. After Alba's scare on the supermarket ramp, he had devoted the whole afternoon to her: he had taken her to the swimming pool and then they'd gone to the cinema to see a *Manolito Gafotas* film.

Ernesto, without looking up from the computer he was repairing, pointed at his in-tray on the desk.

He went through it, still disconcerted by what had happened that morning, and unable to concentrate. He was too troubled and his eyes skimmed the notes until they stumbled on one of the words Ernesto had written several times: PC.

Unexpectedly, those two letters opened up a path in his mind which gave him a means to cross from his confusion to his work. He began thinking how in a few years their meaning, if not their sound, had, without his being conscious of the shift, radically changed. When he started seeing Dulce, he was a member of the Communist Party, something he had always kept from his mother. He was not one of those prominent activists who spent half their spare time at Party headquarters; nor did he speak out at the meetings he attended now and then, or had folders covered with political stickers, or jumpers pinned with Party badges, and his relationship with the local leaders went no further than a warm yet polite greeting. He had always refused to add himself to any list and the most he had done was put up posters during electoral campaigns when all hands were needed. He had been a faithful and quiet activist, until little by little he felt too sceptical and disenchanted to keep his membership without a feeling of incoherence. For all those years, PC had only one meaning in Spanish which everyone used and recognised without hesitation: *Partido Comunista*. However, he was sure that to most people now it meant *Personal Computer*. And this new meaning revealed what was happening on the street, what people cared and knew about and what they ignored or despised: technology before politics;

virtual games from the comfort of one's home before contact with the outside world, which was often difficult and bore the risk of infection; the simulacrum before the stone; individualism before any old collective engagement. Paradoxically, the global village was increasingly composed of individuals who were more and more alone.

Ernesto had finished with his computer and was looking at him, awaiting his instructions. He went over the pending list: some computer repairs, a company asking for a quote for the renovation and maintenance of its hardware, several requests for an Internet connection. Nothing so difficult that he wouldn't be able to catch up by putting in some extra time.

When evening came he was exhausted, but at least work had made him forget the pistol from time to time; now, while tumbling into bed, he thought it was also a matter of time, and until it disappeared into the flow of days he could bear it. He would forget it in the same way that, more and more frequently, hours went by without his thinking of Dulce; in the way that weeks would go by and he would eventually forget – or remember, but without pain – his mother's death.

As he waited for sleep to come, he reflected that he would, without hesitation, exchange all the advantages of the world and the time he lived in for a measure of order. Many years before, another Party member had asked him: 'If you absolutely had to, what would you choose, chaos or injustice?' He'd tried to slip away and not answer, for of course it was a trick question. But his friend had insisted and he had ended up giving the answer expected of him: chaos was preferable. Sometimes he would remember his answer and knew he had lied. Times were different back then, but even then he would have preferred injustice, for the unjust is a clear-cut moral category that one can fight against, whereas with chaos he had never known which are the right weapons, or where the enemy lies, or whether continued disorder does not in the end generate a greater injustice than that which it is supposed to prevent in the first place.

Now, however, he wouldn't have lied. Now, he would exchange long life expectancy, entertainment, computers, medicines, anaesthesia, household appliances, old-age security, travel... for a little more order in his life. For a logical world – not necessarily a happy world or a paradise, just a coherent and logical one – in which his daughter's bed was dry every morning, the woman he loved had not left him without reason, roses smelled nice and fruit tasted good, and no one needed a pistol.

⸮

A few days later he went back to his mother's house. It was the last Sunday in August.

Ever since he'd left the safe open he had become intensely aware of opening or closing doors. Such a simple action, repeated so many times a day, a week, a year, he said to himself, ends up being a reflex; it's one of those movements that, precisely because they pass into the unconscious, leave us free to think and allow us to concern ourselves with more important things, which would be impossible if we paid attention to every step we take or every gesture of our hands. But now he noted this action every time he made it, sometimes to an obsessive extent. There were a few times when he had retraced his steps to make sure that a door had been properly locked, for his mind had not retained the moment when he turned the key and made sure the door was secure. It was such a simple action, he thought, and yet there was so much to gain or lose by it: leaving a door locked or unlocked in a house which holds fifty-years' worth of a life; locking or unlocking a small safe where one keeps a gun.

And so he unlocked the door knowing he was unlocking it and that he had to turn the key three times to disengage it fully. María had phoned him to say she had taken what was hers, so he could take his share. They would leave the rest there, until they decided what to do with the flat: rent it out, perhaps sell it.

He went through the half-empty rooms strangely disquieted, unable to stop anywhere, or to sit on one of the remaining chairs. There was something holding him there but also driving him out, as if the sparse furniture, the ceilings bereft of the lampshades María had taken, leaving the sadness of bare dirty bulbs hanging from wires, the old, efficient appliances, the absence of paintings on the walls, as if all this were shouting: *This place is no longer yours.*

When he opened a wardrobe he saw a few of his mother's

dresses still on their hangers. He could not stop himself touching them, in spite of the pain conveyed by the empty cloth:
whereas other objects only evoked use or physical contact, those
dresses ruthlessly emphasised the void of the human shape that
had inhabited them, what had been and was no more. His
fingers found the zip of a blue blouse, and he remembered it
had been he who had sometimes helped her fasten it. Now all
those buttons, fasteners and clasps with which her hands had
struggled to cover her body were useless.

He took an old suitcase and went round the rooms once
again, throwing into it those things he would take away: books
– though none hollowed out to contain a pistol – photos, ornaments, old papers and documents, letters – some he himself
had written to his mother – old vinyl records he wouldn't listen
to again, some childhood toys that Alba would regard with
lukewarm curiosity before dumping them indifferently in a
corner.

There were still some paintings and the odd small piece of
furniture, but he didn't have the strength necessary to move
them.

3

On the evening he would be killed, Gustavo Larrey was the first person to arrive at the school. He believed punctuality was not just a matter of politeness or good manners, but a necessary act of solidarity towards others. He was an early riser, and even during the two months of summer holidays he had not fallen into habits of laziness, into staying in bed when the noise of the cars and the footsteps of passers-by began to sound outside. He did not smoke. As a PE teacher he kept in good shape, and this, as well as a certain inner energy, got him out of bed even if he'd stayed up late, not as part of a health routine, but because his body seemed to demand a measure of activity that his mind welcomed. Before breakfast, he often went for a run of a few miles towards the Fuente de Chico Cabrera, nearly always along the same route. He knew the distances between each of its landmarks, the ascents and descents, the potholes and stones that could trip him.

He had been up early that morning too. He cleaned the house, did the shopping and prepared some food, so that when his wife came home from the hospital at about two, she found the table laid, fragrant smells of cooking, and a red rose in a vase. They ate, put things away, and had some coffee in the kitchen. It was a delicious moment they loved to share, even more so in those weeks when she was on night duty at the hospital and they had less time to be together. Then they went to bed, as she had to be back in the hospital that night for another twelve-hour shift. They made love and he got up afterwards, while his wife dozed off listening to the afternoon news shows on the radio – in which guest speakers twisted the noble art of conversation in pursuit of wisdom into a base trade in pursuit of slander.

Gustavo Larrey was careful not to make any noise opening doors or in the shower in case he woke his wife, and got ready to leave the house. He always wore a tracksuit to school, which his job made necessary, but on this last day before the start of term he dressed casually in dark trousers and a pale-coloured shirt. The School Council was meeting at six and, although he didn't mind his appearance in front of his colleagues, a track-suit would have shown poor taste, if not disrespect, in front of the parents.

When he arrived at the school, the gate was open, but not the door into the building. He used his key and went to the PE teacher's office, a small room adjacent to the shed where the sports equipment was kept. He sat at the table and leafed unhurriedly through the local newspaper he bought every day. He paused at the culture and sports pages, and spent some time reading a few articles.

He folded the newspaper and put it on the table. From a drawer, he took out a folder with the time table for his subject, which he ought to take home later; he placed it on top of the newspaper so as not to forget it. Then he reread the notice of the meeting of the School Council, which specified only one item on that day's agenda: the election of a headmaster for the next four-year term, since the previous mandate had ended. There were two candidates: Jaime de Molinos, who had held the position for eight years and wanted to retain it until he retired, with all the administrative and economic advantages that entailed, and Nelson. Continuity versus renovation, thought Gustavo Larrey. At least, that was the way they had presented things in their proposals.

But he had read them carefully and there really wasn't that much to choose between them. Whoever was elected, nothing much would change at the school. Hence the difficulties in the election. Both candidates had an equal number of supporters, and only those like himself who were undecided could tip things one way or the other. He still hadn't decided who to vote for. He was exasperated by De Molinos's habitual author-itarian attitude, but neither had he any confidence in Nelson's management skills, or in his ability to make decisions before the inspectors or in the face of the parents' occasional unrea-sonableness; nor in his motivation to resolve those matters which seem almost domestic but which can have such an influ-ence on the normal running of classes: repairs and mainte-nance, the selection of publishers and materials, quality control of school meals, extracurricular activities.

People had started arriving; he heard the murmur of conver-sation that seemed amplified in the empty building. From his office he recognised Rita's voice. She was the newest member of staff, a speech therapist with whom he had found an affinity from the beginning. Her voice now, after the summer, had regained its pleasant tone, and seemed rid of that sadness it had had during the final term last year.

He grabbed the Council agenda and notes and went to say hello. As he turned into the corridor, he saw her go into the headmaster's office and followed her, as he wanted to sit next to her at the meeting. She was making some photocopies. Larrey realised that when he'd picked up the agenda he had also taken the newspaper and his folder, but decided to leave them there in the headmaster's office and come back for them later.

Rita finished her copies and they left for the staffroom. They were nearly all there. Jaime de Molinos was talking to the secretary, Julita Guzmán, and to Corona, the director of studies. Nelson was chatting to the parents.

Rita looked particularly attractive. Her summer tan had not yet faded, and freckles on her nose and cheeks gave her a fresh, almost childlike look.

'Do you know who you're going to vote for yet?' he asked her, but not really interested in forcing the confidence. He suspected she would vote for Nelson, but they were close enough for both to know he was not asking her for a name.

'Yes. Blank.'

'No. Please. We have to do this as quickly as possible. It's going to be so close, it's better we decide it once and for all.'

They fell silent, for at that moment, as if the bell which would summon the pupils the next day had rung, the remaining members of the School Council walked in.

Normally, De Molinos had to call for silence before starting any meeting, as conversations and trivial asides would carry on, refusing to die out. But this time it wasn't necessary. Soon there was an expectant silence, broken only by the noise of chairs being pulled nearer to the large rectangular table, or by the soft tapping of a pen or a lighter lighting a cigarette.

No one made objections to the minutes of the previous meeting, as if reading them were a boring and unnecessary prologue that, however, had to be carried out in order to confer some order and legality on the next item. Even the secretary's voice, flat and dry, cold, devoid of nuance, seemed to discourage any comments.

As she was reading, Larrey studied her face, trying once again to detect the contours of her thin lips or some emotion in her lightless eyes. She was a grey figure no one would notice outside the school, a spinster who was, as far as anyone knew, irreversibly a virgin at fifty-five. She was one of those women who, by being chaste, end up idealising their own chastity. But she didn't occupy her post solely because of her sympathy with Jaime De Molinos's rigid ideas; her efficiency and her obsession with order also made her the ideal person for the job. She managed the school's budget as thoroughly as she did her own money. She would watch over the number of personal photocopies each teacher made and the time they spent on the phone, charging them for their calls as precisely as the telephone company. She handed out school materials impartially, so that every classroom had what was needed and nothing more. She dealt with all correspondence, pupil records, teacher's absences and documentation without errors, and according to a strict order that was absolutely necessary if one was not to drown in a sea of paper. For this reason she didn't take well to others' errors, such as erasures in a school report, or a mistake in the minutes. A few teachers harboured a lingering hatred for her, and they often blamed her, rather than De Molinos, for any upset that some trivial demand had caused. Rita, with whom she had occasionally been intransigent, and whose work she didn't understand, had once said to Larrey: 'She hates children. She hates the fact that every day they grow stronger, more independent and wiser, while she only grows older, clumsier and weaker.'

The secretary was a very different person from Manuel Corona. Although everyone who knew him thought his character was the opposite of what was required in a director of studies – that is, someone dynamic and creative, skilful and open-minded, who could function as a bridge between the authorities and the teaching staff – he'd occupied his position for years, and there had never been a powerful reason for anyone to raise objections. His way of dealing with academic matters – which tended to *laissez faire* and sanctifying every teacher's right to do whatever they liked in class – did not really agree with De Molinos's disciplinarian ideas. However, the latter had included him on his team right from the start, like a leader who cedes a piece of political territory to an opponent, and in doing so, not only seems generous and understanding of those who think differently, but also sends out a warning that if this is not accepted, there will be no other concessions.

Corona was nearly obese, something rare in a profession dominated by lean people whose daily exertions with the children, the constant bending to their level, and their state of permanent stress prevents them from gaining weight. It was easy to imagine him as the potential victim of a massive stroke. He had the kind of shape that makes it difficult to buy clothes in the right size and to tie his shoelaces. His double chin wobbled like a frog's. He always came to school wearing a jacket and tie, which meant that he could avoid all physical contact with pupils. Obsessed with cleanliness, he was always washing his hands or, when circumstances did not permit it, used the wipes he kept in a drawer of his desk. He wore thinly-rimmed glasses and was always clean-shaven, which made his lower lip more prominent, as if flattened out by the weight of the upper lip and his shiny cheeks.

'If there is no other business, we'll press on to the last item today: the election of the headmaster for the next four years,' said the secretary.

She read out both candidates' names in full – Mr Jaime De Molinos Díaz, Mr Luis García Nelson – and mentioned their proposals, which it was quite likely many people had not read. Then she handed out the ballot papers and explained the procedure.

They had to vote twice. At the second ballot, the secretary's voice trembled with disquiet as she read the name on the last ballot paper, and she proclaimed that Luis García Nelson had been elected as headmaster for a period of four years.

Larrey looked at Rita and found surprise in her eyes, too. Both had voted for him in the second round, but they still hadn't expected him to win. The way the election worked made it very difficult for a headmaster to be ousted from his post, and he could very easily remain in it until retirement, provided he didn't make any serious mistakes and kept away from scandal. Even if the teachers were against him, he could be elected on the strength of the votes of the parents, who lacked detailed information about internal matters and tended to be swayed by even the weakest display of authority in such a position. Unlike the kind of power held in politics, in which any decisions taken gradually erode it, in a school, the way someone carries out his duties actually consolidates his position, confers on it a certain prestige and a place in the hierarchy that guarantee its continuation.

Larrey and Rita saw Jaime De Molinos get up to shake the victor's hand, murmuring congratulations with barely parted lips. Presently the secretary brought the proceedings to a close. She must have been thinking it was her last such meeting, and her voice, when reading the minutes of the election, had the ceremonial tone of a farewell.

Everyone stood up, talking about what had just happened. As he left, Larrey heard De Molinos say to Nelson:

'I guess you can wait a day for the office. I'll have to take some things away.'

'Of course, take as long as you need,' he replied. 'But now we should all go for a beer. We've had enough talk.'

They left the building. The sun had gone down, but the floodlights over the main schoolyard diminished the darkness of the sky. De Molinos locked the door and, a little later all the members of the School Council were at the bar where the teachers went for coffee every day when they were not on duty during breaks. Nelson felt the need to buy drinks for everyone, perhaps a little surprised by his victory, but also enjoying a measure of revenge towards someone who had stood in the way of every opportunity for change and development in the past few years.

Indeed, there was not much left to say, and Julita Guzmán, who never usually took part in those celebrations anyway, was the first to leave. The rest followed suit not long after. The next day was the first day of school and they had to be punctual. The parents, however, stayed at the bar, except for one who left, claiming urgent business to attend to.

Larrey walked Rita to her car, and for a few minutes they discussed the election results, what Nelson could do if he really put his mind to it, and the pity they felt for De Molinos.

'I'll give you a lift if you like,' Rita said.

He usually walked home, but was about to accept when he remembered something.

'I have to go back in. I left my newspaper and folder in the headmaster's office.'

'I can wait.'

'No, don't worry about it.'

He retraced his steps to the school for some eighty metres. The gate was still open and, rather oddly, so was the main door of the building, even though De Molinos had closed it half an hour before. Someone had mentioned that the caretaker was not in that evening; he'd had to take an ill relative to hospital. Larrey envied him slightly, for he may come across his wife along a corridor or tending to a patient. He missed her. They'd been married for eight years and he was as much in love as he had been at the start. Those nights she was on duty seemed long and tedious to him. He didn't know what to do with himself, and when he was in bed he longed for her touch, warm, intimate and slightly perfumed. The memory of her brought a flood of well-being that made him forget the stress of the meeting. He reflected that classes started the next day and he would be a happy man this term, too.

He went in, not bothering to turn on the fluorescent tubes in the corridor, which in the darkness of the building would seem scandalously bright, guiding himself only by the emergency exits and the light coming in from the schoolyard. He moved towards the headmaster's office. In a place which was usually so noisy the silence seemed deeper and, in a way, sadder. The key was hanging from a nail behind the noticeboard. All teachers knew this, for any of them might be the first to arrive or the last to leave, due to a meeting or preparation of lessons. He opened the door. The blinds were open and he didn't need to turn the lights on to be able to see his folder and the newspaper on the desk where he'd left them. He moved forward, reached out to take them, and at that moment felt a blow on the back of his neck. Everything turned blindingly white.

⌐

He was usually the first one to arrive in the office. But that morning he was only a teacher, and so he lingered in the hall with the rest of them, trying hard not to show how frustrated he felt at having lost his post. He would respond to any expression of condolence or solidarity with a mask of scorn and indifference; no one, not even the best-intentioned, would have the pleasure of seeing him hurt, tense or shaken. *Power, how satisfying it is,* he thought, *that small degree of power that allows you to be the first and last to speak while others listen and obey your decisions, power whose benefits lie not so much in the paltry privileges given as in the pleasure itself of granting or denying them For the satisfaction that comes from being at the top does not so much depend on how great one's reach is, whether it encompasses forty people or forty million, but on its very nature.* How he hated, not only Nelson, but now all those who had fuelled his expectations and his confidence in his own triumph! And how he despised those who, even while they were close to him, like Corona or Julita Guzmán, had failed to foresee the danger drawing near, and to help him form a plan to avoid it! It would have been so easy to tear the other candidate apart by spreading that rumour among the parents of the School Council!

Although it was almost nine, Nelson had not yet arrived. De Molinos said nothing in response to someone's comment about Nelson's lateness on the first day of his new job. This was the first piece of criticism – light, smiling, yet poisonous, too – against Nelson; similar, to be sure, to what he would have received for various things over the past eight years.

Then someone else observed that it was strange that Larrey, who was always very punctual, had not arrived yet, either.

De Molinos had to collect some personal effects from the office, the spoils of the battle, but he would not go in before Nelson arrived. He had lost, but he wouldn't make things easy for the other man by falling into the kind of camaraderie everyone else would realise was false and that, far from concealing his humiliation, would only add to it. Someone who has not considered defeat is never a good loser. Nelson would come to him with his worries, and he would answer them, or not, feigning ignorance, and then Nelson would have to discover for himself all the ploys that were necessary to make the parents happy or expedite the bureaucracy he and Julita had perfected over eight years. It wouldn't be easy for him: like anyone who has a blind faith in his powers of improvisation, he wasn't particularly organised. The very fact that he hadn't arrived yet, on the first day of classes and in his new post, while the school-yard was heaving with parents and children excited at being back at school, was symptomatic of his disordered life.

He saw the caretaker ring the bell for the pupils to get into lines, one for each class; then they would go in with their teacher, who would take them to their classroom.

As the bell was ringing De Molinos saw Nelson coming through the door, in a state of agitation, as if he'd been running. *By one second,* he thought, *you've managed not to be late on your first day as headmaster by one second. I bet we both know who you were celebrating with last night.*

Nelson was congratulated by those who had not telephoned or seen him yet. He was dressed less casually than normally, and De Molinos, leaning against the banister of the staircase, had to admit his new post suited him: a man nearly twenty years his junior, sporting a tan from the long summer on his face and hands, with a physical allure that was only enhanced by the small power he had just taken on. His left-handedness even gave him an added originality, as well as proving his strength of character and his resistance to external pressure.

The children had started going in, youngest first, and were walking to their classrooms preceded by their teachers. Rita, who, as a speech therapist, was not in charge of a class, was amazed once again at the value of education, not just for the knowledge it imparted, but for all those details that showed children from the first moment that the chaos of the world could be ordered: six hundred pupils who only a minute ago were greeting, running, colliding, screaming, crying and fighting noisily in the motley confusion of the schoolyard were now settling without fuss into their classrooms, taking their places and becoming relatively quiet in a way that would have seemed impossible from their previous excitement. As for the little ones, it was the first time they'd left their homes on their own. School, thought Rita, is the first environment where the child is left alone and obliged to work without their parents' protection, without familiar faces to turn to for help or comfort after a painful fall or after the first blow from someone stronger. And if that first step into the world, at age three, is painful for a prolonged period, there is a possibility that the child will always see the world as inhospitable and full of enemies.

Nelson approached Corona and De Molinos:

'Shall we go to the office?'

'Yes, I was waiting for you,' said the former headmaster.

Nelson called Rita. 'If you don't have a lesson now, could you come with us for a moment, please?'

'Sure,' she replied. She guessed what was about to happen, the proposal to which she would, without arrogance and disdain, say no, a calm, convincing no, immune to insistence or appeals.

They walked along the corridor and De Molinos waited for Nelson to retrieve the key from behind the noticeboard, like the guest who, despite feeling his host's welcoming hand on his shoulder, refuses to be the first to turn the door handle.

'The key's gone,' said Nelson, perplexed.

'It's in the keyhole,' Corona observed.

The door was closed but not locked, as if left by someone who plans to come back in a moment. Nelson pushed it open and took two steps before freezing in astonishment. Only astonishment at first; understanding and shock and fear would come later.

'Oh my God!' shouted De Molinos from behind him, also frozen in astonishment, and then suddenly overcome by a dark feeling of having been avenged, as if that body sprawling at his old desk was, in spite of everything over the last eight years, his first payment: *This is your welcome for daring to take what wasn't yours, this is what awaits you: chaos and confusion.*

'Gustavo!' screamed Rita from behind them.

Before any of the three men, she bent over the body, as if she could still help him, though everyone had guessed immediately that such immobility was permanent. It wasn't necessary to have seen a corpse to know that blood clots in a matter of minutes, that the stain on the floor that had come from the wound on the neck must have been red at some point but had taken a few hours to dry and turn that dirty brownish colour, to pass from the condition of sap to that of excrement. Underneath his right arm were yesterday's paper and his folder. He'd come back for them and hadn't wanted her to wait for him in the car. Bewildered by that detail, she touched his forehead and noticed its coldness. Then she withdrew her hand, as if she had noticed she shouldn't have done it. Yet she still bent lower to look at the back of his neck.

'How could this happen?' she asked, almost inaudibly. She did not address the others, who stared at her paralysed, but seemed to be asking the body itself, as if searching for an explanation which would refute that the wound before her, black and round, with some hairs encrusted at its edges, had been caused by a bullet.

Nelson seemed to emerge from his stupor, picked up the phone and called the hospital for an ambulance.

'I think you should also call the Guardia Civil,' said De Molinos.

Nelson glanced at him and, not saying a word, looked up the number in the directory. He had to repeat what had happened and where he was calling from twice for the person at the other end to understand it wasn't a joke. In a small provincial city that hadn't quite got used to the idea that it was no longer a town, and in which only eight or ten deaths from unnatural causes occurred every year – all of them due to accidents, suicides or drug overdoses – a call like this one, reporting a homicide at a school on the first day of term, sounded like a pupil's practical joke.

'I think we should send everyone home,' said De Molinos.

'Who?' asked Nelson, failing again to understand.

'The children. The older ones can go home on their own. I'm sure there are a few of the little ones' mothers still in the playground. The others must be notified. Whatever happens, it'll only be a few minutes before the whole city knows.'

↝

A magistrate, Lieutenant Gallardo, and two civil guards – a man and a woman – were waiting in the corridor for the three special agents to finish their job in the office. They were forensics experts, another of the departments that had multiplied in the police force in its efforts to modernise, become self-sufficient and not depend on other branches of the civil service: there were now experts in computer crime, ecological crime, domestic violence, immigration, fiscal fraud, genetics, tourist protection. They were agents dedicated to only one field, young specialists with brilliant student records who knew more and more about less and less.

The lieutenant knew he couldn't take a look at anything

before those inside were done. He wasn't impatient. Besides, the new instructions concerning his involvement were very clear: in such cases as this one – sensitive, high-profile – local agents shouldn't touch anything unless it was strictly necessary. It just took a phone call to Madrid for that select brigade of technicians to turn up a couple of hours later. They were not terribly popular among the others, for even when equal in rank, they adopted a superiority that older officers, for whom only the stripes counted, found difficult to stomach. They were never armed and never dirty, as if weapons and sweat were the barbaric vestiges of a bygone era; they never made hurried hypotheses, or gave out details of what they were doing; they were reluctant to enter into amicable relations with other officers or to spend the night at the station, even if that meant paying for a hotel out of their own pockets; they seemed to have as much difficulty dealing with people as they had ease interacting with objects or detritus: a minute scrap of paper, a semen stain on the headboard of a bed, a hair in a plughole; and they didn't hide how eager they were to leave those provincial cities that so oppressed them. *The Wise Men Brigade,* the others called them, feigning disdain, but in reality acknowledging their rigor and efficiency, and how essential their tasks were.

He had asked the young female teacher and the three men only a few routine questions: whether, when they found the body, everything was as it had been the day before, and whether they had touched anything other than the phone. He confirmed that *rigor mortis* had spread throughout the limbs and, therefore, that the body had not been moved after the shooting.

While taking a look around, during the first visual inspection, the female officer had spotted a shiny object between two piles of children's books and had studied it without touching it: a shell from a pistol, 7.65 mm calibre, the make, FN.

There were no other signs of violence or disorder in the room: books and papers, the photocopier, the filing cabinet and the computer had that solid calm characteristic of bureaucratic objects at rest, and were unaffected by the grisly image of the corpse among them. She had closed the door and waited for the others.

The flashes that repeatedly lit up the room and the corridor were no longer in the service of a celluloid negative, but of sophisticated digital cameras that would later allow for any detail to be quickly and clearly enlarged. Fingerprints, traces of hair and eyelashes, or even a speck of dandruff or skin attached to the shell would not only be studied later under the microscope, but also analysed in a genetic laboratory. In the last four years, techniques had completely changed, but the lieutenant was still a little distrustful of the final results. Although science might help in some cases, he was very sceptical about this one. Whoever had shot the man now lying on the floor would probably know as well as they did what he should and shouldn't do, what traces not to leave, what resources they had to hand and, therefore, how to evade them. In the end, the lieutenant told himself, only determination, intelligence and carefully chosen words could help clear up this mess.

4

Perhaps if his father hadn't died when Julián was only eleven, none of this would have happened. But it's very difficult to forget the legacy of a father who dies when the son has only just entered adolescence. To reject any object or memory would have seemed like a kind of betrayal.

Those times had been quite different for many of his classmates and friends. They were sons of men who'd had a measure of power or influence during the dictatorship and suspected they had not always exercised it in the cleanest manner. For them it would probably have been easy to get rid of an inherited relic that turns up one day, stuffed into a book by Baroja; easy to condemn that unjustifiable slap they received once, to condemn it emphatically so that years later it would not be inflicted on the son's son. But he had not been granted the period during which confrontation facilitates rejection, and keeping that dark portion of his inheritance in check had proved a lot harder. How could he spit on the grave of someone who had only been good to him?

Sometimes, many years ago, he'd envied his friends when they spoke of their difficulties at home, of their arguments with their parents over a longer curfew, or getting more pocket money or evading punishment for their poor marks. These friends of his almost always argued with their fathers, seldom with their mothers, who were prone to harmony and forgiveness. When one of them said, 'You're really lucky, not having an old man who gives you a hard time,' Julián Monasterio nodded and half-smiled, thinking that some nights he'd rather come home an hour late and engage in some kind of confrontation with a father than find his mother's perpetual trust and understanding. He was a good son and a good student, and didn't squander his money. She knew it, and in exchange for that, never restricted his freedom, only allowing herself to give him advice that never amounted to an order.

Because of this, he had to set his own boundaries when drinking, or when driving with someone who was barely sober; it was he himself – at an age when the normal state is confusion and turmoil – who had imposed order on the world around him.

He would sometimes imagine himself as the protagonist of an Oriental tale, not knowing whether he'd read it or dreamed it: he was a man crossing a desert, carrying treasure that does not belong to him, unable to make use of it because one day someone he doesn't know will come, demanding a final reckoning. That was what his freedom felt like, a boon he'd been granted without doing anything to deserve it, and that, therefore, he could not waste. He would then remember his mother's distant words, when she had put too much money in his hands: 'You don't need to spend it all, but you may need it for something unexpected. I trust you.' He'd come back from his camping trip with almost all the coins. It was some time before he understood that his mother, with those words, had forever instilled in him a deep sense of reserve and responsibility towards what he was given, and this had an effect less on material things than on his very character: *Even if you have it, don't spend it all, keep some of it in case someone comes asking for it.*

As time went by, he got to know other boys who'd been orphaned at a similar age. And by observing them he reached the conclusion that the premature absence of a parent brings about two very different types of behaviour, with almost no happy medium: those who turned their lives into a disorderly merry-go-round, giving in to any stimulus or temptation, and those who operate their own brakes in an excessively responsible manner. He belonged to the second group. True, a couple of times he'd given in to the impulse of running off and had done a few stupid things, both outlandish and harmless, but even at his most reckless he had kept the point of return in sight. On very few occasions had he dared go beyond the city walls to bury his brother's body, contravening the laws of the city. All in all, he'd been a quiet teenager, and only later did he realise that quiet teenagers become insecure adults.

He only remembered one period when he had disrespected his father's memory. It was the time when, without his mother's knowledge, he had become a member of the Communist Party, not long after the death of Franco. He always kept it from his comrades that his father had worked at the Courts of Justice, as if that building where all protest demonstrations ended up, and which for them symbolised the most stubborn opposition to the coming of democracy, had secreted a fluid that contaminated all who had worked in it. He only told Dulce of his father's occupation, convincing himself that if he could not entrust his past – with its teenage embarrassments and complexes, the petty evils of childhood and the most absurd fears – to the woman he loved, and be sure to find understanding and kindness in her, then not even love was worth his while. But back then she was so in love with him that no matter what he said her love could only grow. She was so different from all the rest!

From the first moment, she had seemed exceptional. Most of the girls he knew back then looked as if they were in uniform. Their individual features were flattened out by their generational trademarks: long, often dishevelled hair; thick eyebrows; equally hairy legs and armpits; no make-up, flat shoes, loose-fitting skirts or jeans, and jumpers vaguely redolent of curry or henna. Yet Dulce, although she shared their environment and many of their features, was marked out by her immaculate appearance which could even seem refined, and she firmly refused to be pigeonholed with the rest.

However, despite her confessions, Dulce had never given herself to him in the same way, like someone jumping into the void. Although she had told him everything about her happy and fulfilled life in the present, she'd been very careful when dealing with the past. After she left, Julián Monasterio finally understood that she had always kept deep reserves of privacy, which he was never allowed near. Since about a year before, when she began to be a stranger, when he sensed something was going on yet was unable to broach the subject, they'd had only one long conversation: the one in which she said she was leaving the following morning. In the last months, not only had their kisses stopped – they'd had sex without kissing, like those animals that copulate without once looking into each other's eyes – but words too had slowly become covered in ashes. Their conversations were limited to Alba and her school, their respective jobs, and the odd interesting TV programme, as if they were two strangers on a long train journey, obliged to talk out of politeness. The two or three times he asked her what was wrong, Dulce responded with evasions and became almost aggressive, as if he had no right to ask such a question. Only on the last night did she reveal a whole range of reasons for leaving, the kind of reasons those who leave always make sure they are well-provided with. Until a few days later, when he finally came to accept he was alone, he didn't understand the trap her silence had laid for him: how often some well-organised half-truths can amount to the crudest lie! Because without being entirely false, her reasons – lack of enthusiasm, monotony, the need to find out whether she was in love with another man – had drawn a bleak prospect that strayed further from truth than from lies.

He turned the computer off. He'd had it on without knowing what he was doing; looking at the screen and typing was the best way of not being interrupted by Ernesto. He suddenly stood up and grabbed his coat.

'I've got to go out for a minute,' he said. 'Won't be long.'

The September morning was clear and cool. He walked for a bit, bought the local newspaper at a news-stand and went into a cafe. After four days, the story of the murder was no longer on the front page and had been relegated to one column on the accidents and crimes page. As no new information had been made public, the story only repeated what was known: that the bullet was a 7.65 calibre, the make was FN, made in Belgium in 1958. They had even published a drawing of the casing which had all that information stamped on it. But the pistol or revolver that had fired it had not yet turned up and Breda's Guardia Civil, working with a team of experts, was still investigating.

What could he do? he wondered. Four weeks ago he'd had a box of that same ammunition in his hands. Too many coincidences. He could not keep burying his head in the sand, waiting for his problems to solve themselves. Even if it turned out not to be his gun, eliminating that possibility would help him calm down. He had no conclusive evidence, but every day that went by, every hour, every minute convinced him further that the projectile and the gun were his own. And in that case, every minute, every hour and every day spent in silence had made him a little more guilty, until now, when he could no longer go and confess to the lieutenant of the Guardia Civil that it was he who owned the pistol of unknown origin that had been stolen, and that he had, furthermore, remained quiet about for four days after the murder, if a murder it was, as everything seemed to indicate. It was quite possible they wouldn't believe him, and then, he thought, he could spend half his life in prison.

He folded the newspaper and considered the worry of the last four days, irritated with himself for his continuing inability to make a decision. He couldn't predict the consequences of notifying the authorities, but couldn't guess what would happen if he kept silent. A year ago he would have gone straight from the bank to the police station; he would have solved that unexpected problem as soon as it arose. But all the misfortunes of the last few months were turning him into an insecure, hesitant man, who weighed his every decision, fearing that in any of them there might lurk a new trap. Only at the shop and when operating computers did he still feel on firm ground.

Suddenly he remembered that one of his clients, the owner of an estate agency, had once hired a detective to find out which member of his staff was amusing himself by downloading viruses on to the company's computers. He didn't remember the detective's name, but it was an unusual surname that had caught his attention. The man had solved the problem quietly and without much trouble, and it was all sorted out with a dismissal. His client hadn't wanted the law involved as he didn't want too many questions asked and people poking about inside his computers; buying and selling property was a speculative business in which undeclared money played too powerful a role.

Julián Monasterio hesitated for a few moments, as he gulped down his coffee. He lived in a developed country, with a police force that was in theory reliable, and at the service of its citizens. When he'd discovered detectives existed, he'd found it odd; odd too that some people should trust them. But now he understood the need for them. One turned to a detective when the ineffectiveness of the law, one's shame or a shady affair made it impossible to go before a judge. He imagined it must be a murky world; coming into contact with it might have unpleasant consequences. But wasn't the situation he was involved in murky, too? He made a decision, and asked for the yellow pages. There was only one name listed under Private Investigators: Cupido, R. He dialled the number and made an appointment for fifteen minutes later.

His first surprise was that the man did not have proper work premises. His office was in his own home, like some doctors' surgeries, which could give the impression of amateurism, but could also be a guarantee of safety and discretion. He discarded the first possibility as he sat on a chair at a desk. The detective sat opposite him.

His second surprise was that he could not see a computer anywhere, when it was surely just the place to have one. The large office desk, the metal filing cabinet, the phone, a closed wardrobe, a calendar with the dates in large numbers and some pictures indicated that this was his regular place of work. *Here's a man,* he thought, *who has resisted the end-of-the-century mania for computers. He's not one of those people who think that anyone without a computer in their pocket won't survive in the new millennium.* Although it was strange, he liked that absence. It seemed to him that the man's disdain revealed great confidence in his own ability to acquire and process the necessary information, without relying on computer databases.

As for Cupido, he waited for the first wave of confusion and suspicion to pass. His clients usually felt like that, as if they expected to find a guy with a gun next to his sweaty armpit, in a hot, chaotic office, with a fan hanging from the ceiling and the blinds filtering just enough light to favour intrigue and secrets. But the man he had in front of him now didn't seem concerned with the decor, but with something deeper and more distant and more pitiful.

'I don't really know what I want you to do yet, if anything. Maybe I just need your advice, to explain what the law says, what the punishment is for something that just started out as recklessness.'

The detective nodded in sympathy, looking him in the eye. With their first words, his clients always had to make a special effort to get over the humiliation and embarrassment of turning to a stranger to solve an often deeply private problem, to confront their own inadequacy. Their first words were hesitant, threaded with fear and mistrust. He tried to make it easier for his clients to express themselves.

'Why don't you tell me everything from the beginning?'

Julián Monasterio hesitated, as if he still regretted having come. But before him was a quiet man, whose calm voice was neither calculating nor patronising, and who seemed ready to solve any problem: not just routine petty scams or the heart-breaks of adultery, but more unexpected offences too, things that weren't even seen as offences. He didn't give the impression that he was doing this because he hadn't found anything better to do.

'Would you... I mean...' Julián paused, looking for words that wouldn't compromise him and would be easily forgotten, 'would you have to report something if you thought it was serious?'

'You mean you want to tell me something and swear me to secrecy?'

'Yes, something like that. A sort of confession.'

Cupido looked at him wondering how much he could hear without compromising himself.

'Is it a crime?'

'No,' he answered emphatically. At least he was sure of that. In moral terms, anyway. It was all because he happened to be at the centre of a number of coincidences. He was sure that if all the hidden weapons in Spain suddenly turned up, they would form a veritable arsenal. If they were melted down, there would be enough metal for a statue in every square in Madrid. But the others were still hidden. Only his had disappeared. Why had everything been slipping out of his control over the last few months?

'You can count on my silence.'

'It all started with my mother's death, a month ago.'

He paused and took out a pack of cigarettes, as if he needed the help of that simple gesture to put his story in order. He offered one to Cupido, who shook his head. He lit up with a disposable lighter, taking his time to choose the right words so that nothing was left out. He told Cupido everything that had happened, repeating certain pieces of information he thought important, as if he wasn't sure the detective would understand, and carefully glossing over the most difficult parts, as he didn't know if his own criteria for innocence and guilt were the same as Cupido's.

He felt better when he finished talking. The detective had barely interrupted him, and hadn't once expressed incredulity or doubt. Julián Monasterio was beginning to feel he could trust Cupido, from the signs the latter gave that he still followed him, even as the story became more complicated.

'Why are you so sure they shot him with your gun?'

'Have you been following the news?'

'I have.'

'Then you'll know the case is a 7.65 calibre, quite rare, the make is FN, and that it was manufactured in 1958, the same year as my father's. I don't think there are many others like that around Breda.'

'Let's say that's the case. How can I help you?'

Julián Monasterio opened his arms in a small gesture of hopelessness, as if his empty hands showed he had nothing else to hold on to, and that was why he was there.

'I told you at the start. I don't even know if you can do anything. If you can still do something,' he corrected himself. 'To put it briefly: I want to solve this problem.'

Deep in thought, the detective looked at him, trying to gauge his despair, his pessimistic refusal to believe in chance, coincidence or the possibility that the bullet may have been fired with another gun, his certainty in misfortune, that kind of misfortune that makes people irreparably unhappy even as it corrodes any faith in the future.

'I'd like to help you if you're sure you need me,' he said. 'But my advice is you go and tell everything to the Guardia Civil. The lieutenant is a more understanding man than he's given credit for by this city. Perhaps he'd make you sweat for a few hours, but he'd have no doubt you're telling the truth.'

Julián Monasterio shook his head several times, with a certainty that indicated he had long ago discarded that option.

'No, I don't want my name cropping up anywhere. I've got a six-year-old daughter and she's got enough troubles as it is. I don't want her father's mistake to hurt her even more.'

He lit up another cigarette and inhaled the smoke with the greed of the addict who uses nicotine to calm some greater anxiety. The tip crackled for a few moments, and receded towards the filter like a fuse. Unhurriedly, almost whispering, he started telling Cupido in detail about his wife leaving him, his daughter's enuresis, and her refuge in a muteness that he found desolating.

Once he finished talking, Cupido understood why he'd had that distressed, suffocated look when he'd come in, like an aquatic animal that's spent too long out of the water.

'You're asking me to recover the gun and give it back to you with maximum discretion, so that you can put it back in the safe it was stolen from.'

'That's right.'

'In order to find it I have to find the person who has it, and who may also be the one who fired it.'

'Find him. I don't care what happens to him afterwards,' he said, adding: 'If you want, we can discuss money.'

～

Cupido had taken the job without a clear idea of how to tackle it. What should he do? Find the thief and confiscate the gun from him, of course. And then? Keep the name quiet, even if it was the person who had shot that teacher? Because if he revealed it, the name of the real owner of the gun would also come to light. It was a complicated business, and its difficulties both seduced and disquieted him in a personal way, as if he'd taken on the surplus of anxiety emanating from his client. Few people who knew the nature of his job would believe him, but he still felt a kind of moral obligation in those cases in which innocent blood was spilled and ended up implicating those who were not guilty. It was a personal challenge to solve them. Many would not believe him, but he still thought that the world rotted a little more every time a man died violently and prematurely.

There was a possibility that the thief was not the murderer, but he had to discount that and be prepared for the worst. He had a gun himself, a Glock 19 he'd never had to use. He hid it in the hollow behind a shutter, where he could access it easily with the slightest pressure from his fingers, and he thought of it as one more of those tools kept in a toolbox, bought ages ago for a particular purpose and then not used for so long that the fact that it even existed has been forgotten. After Julián Monasterio's visit he remembered it. He then checked the date on his licence and realised it had expired several months before. His best, most effective weapon had always been words. There might have been a time and a place where a different kind of private detective lived, tough and cynical and bitter, almost primitive in his readiness to use violence in a violent environment. But his work in the city where he lived didn't demand those kinds of skills.

Although it was going to be difficult, Cupido was sure he would once again find a solution. His job was about exploding the complex system of lies behind which the culprit takes cover. If you have the strength to rummage through other people's miseries and face the occasional risk, if you have the stamina to keep trying even when all questions and answers seem exhausted and there is no way out, an investigation will always end up bearing fruit, just as fertile ground, after tilling, will push the crop towards the surface despite drought and intensive farming. You only had to say the right word or ask the right question at the right time, with the same faith and confidence as the farmer scattering seed.

5

The school building was prematurely run-down by the eroding force of six hundred children stampeding in and out of it four times a day. Although its walls were painted halfway up in an ugly brown colour in the hope that this would conceal the dirt, sundry prints of hands and shoes had made blackish streaks that Cupido noticed as he followed the caretaker along the corridor. They came to a door where a metal plate stated 'Principal'. It was ajar, and the man knocked and pushed on it slightly to announce:

'There's someone here to see you.'

'Come on in.'

The caretaker stepped aside to let him through, closed the door behind him and left the detective with the headmaster. He was a man in his early forties who seemed to take care of his attractive appearance in order to keep looking forty for as long as possible.

He got up from his chair, walked round the desk that was covered in papers and small writing implements and approached to shake his hand. He studied Cupido for a few moments, wondering who he might be, as his appearance – jeans and a plain shirt – did not suggest a school materials salesman or someone from the education department. Nor did he have that responsible, alert air of parents who are bringing their children to school for the first time and cannot hide their suspicion and worry at leaving them among strangers for so long.

'What can I do for you?'

'My name's Ricardo Cupido,' he introduced himself, trying to sound neutral and polite. 'I'm a private investigator. I'd like to ask you a few questions in connection with your colleague's death.' The beginning was always difficult, because his presence stirred memories of conflict or pain when many of the people he saw only wanted to forget.

'A private investigator?' the headmaster repeated in surprise, as if it were a non-existent profession, whose place was only in books or films, fantasies or dreams. 'We've already told the

Guardia Civil everything we know. I'm not sure whether...
Who's hired you?'

'The father of one of your pupils,' he replied, avoiding the
lie.

The reference to a parent puzzled the headmaster even more.
After everything that had happened, he knew he was in their
hands and should listen and attend to any of their suggestions.
Larrey's death had had a cruel and paradoxical effect: instead of
extending the status of victim to the rest of the teachers, it had
made them all suspects. In the eyes of the press and of public
opinion, the only victims were the pupils, who'd had to go back
a week later to a school tainted by violence.

Nelson had heard the wildest theories coming out of Breda
to explain the tragedy, and in most of them the finger pointed,
not at someone from outside the institution, as he had always
maintained, but at those inside, at any teacher who'd been seen
exchanging whispers with Larrey. Elaborating on words or half-
phrases they'd heard, the children's imaginations fed the most
peculiar rumours, apportioning blame absurdly and disconcert-
ingly. The teachers were all suspects. And the longer it took to
solve the case, the more outrageous the different theories would
become. There were too many people listening to and greedily
swallowing any story, as if nourished by them. There was no
sense in remaining silent.

'What would you like to know?' Nelson asked, his voice firm
again, but his eyes still betraying mistrust.

Not many questions were necessary to complete the picture.
Nelson repeated the same account he'd given several times in the
past few days: the decisive School Council meeting, the members it comprised, the election's result and the drinks to which
he'd later treated everyone. Except Larrey, everyone claimed to
have gone home afterwards. Nelson, at least, had done so.

'Was there anything odd about the meeting, anything that
didn't normally happen?'

'Odd? Everything was odd that evening,' he replied, his eyes
lost on some spot on the wall over Cupido's right shoulder,
with that gaze that, by staying unfocused, seems to will away
the present in order to concentrate better on memories. 'Odd
that after eight years in charge De Molinos was defeated at a
School Council, when not even I thought the others would vote

for me. Odd that after his defeat he didn't seem angry and managed to control the disappointment he surely felt. Odd that Julita Guzmán stayed for a beer, when she never goes into a bar. Odd that Larrey went back for a folder he'd left behind. Odd that the caretaker was away precisely that evening, visiting someone in hospital... If a couple of those coincidences had not taken place, that death wouldn't have happened.'

'Who could have wanted his death?' Cupido asked, spurred by the confidences Nelson had slipped into, as if the headmaster, by adding that conditional to the objective account of the events, had given him permission to approach the more personal side of the mystery, not just the circumstances: the place and time, everyone's absence or presence, the easy recourse to alibis.

'But that's what's so strange, too! Honestly, if there was someone at the school who had no enemies, not even enmities, it was Larrey,' he said. Then he reflected for a few moments, as if calling to mind everyone else's grievances and grudges, and added: 'The awful thing about death is, not that it happens, but that it never happens to the people we'd wish it on.'

He remained motionless, his mouth slightly open, staring vacantly out of the window overlooking the playground where the PE teacher's whistle and the children's races could no longer be heard; he seemed surprised and frightened at the words he'd just uttered, their full meaning only revealing itself after he had spoken them.

Cupido waited in silence for him to go on talking, but instead Nelson bent to read some papers on his desk.

'Could I see your colleagues, the others who also found the body?'

'Two male teachers and a female one. Corona and Jaime De Molinos are now in class; they'll be out in fifteen minutes. Rita is in the speech therapy office. But they'll decide whether they want to speak to you or not.'

He pressed a button on his intercom and leaned over the speaker.

'Rita?'

'Yes?' answered a pleasant voice.

'There's a... private investigator here, who's come to talk to us. He'd like a word with you.'

At the other end there were a few moments of silence.

'Tell him to come up.'

As he said goodbye, Nelson added:

'I don't think these interviews will be much help. The murderer came from outside, as I keep saying. The main door was open when the caretaker came back at about twelve. He thought one of us had forgotten to close it and didn't look in the office.'

He peered out into the corridor and called out:

'Moisés!'

From the caretaker's booth, a young man stepped out and came towards them. He must have been twenty-two or twenty-three; he had very short clean hair and long, narrow sideburns. When he was closer, Cupido noticed the glint of an earring. His face was attractive, and his head seemed supported not by the bones of his spine but by the thick tendons which shaped his neck, giving a clear image of strength. The boy did not fit the stern and rather dilapidated atmosphere of the school. He dressed like one of the older pupils, but could no longer be one; he was old enough to be a precocious, energetic young teacher just out of teaching college; but then what didn't fit was his place in the caretaker's glass booth, his indifferent yet mocking expression, the spark of disdain, and the almost martial-looking tilt of his chin.

'Could you take the gentleman to the speech therapy office, please?'

The lad nodded, but Cupido noticed his grim expression, that of someone whose free time has been interrupted for some thankless task. He guessed he was someone who didn't like taking orders. The detective parted from the headmaster with some words of thanks, and started up the stairs.

'Do you work here?' he asked.

'Here? No way. I'd go crazy with all those kids always screaming. And it's not a lot better with the teachers, you know?'

'No?'

'No,' he replied curtly.

'So what do you do here?' he insisted, perplexed.

'I'm a conscientious objector. I'm doing alternative service. But if I'd thought about it properly, I probably would've chosen the army. There'd be less people giving orders and trying to meddle with everything.'

'You don't like the new headmaster?' suggested Cupido.

'No. At least you knew where you stood with the one before. He didn't like objectors and he told me once, right at the start, that I'd work harder here than in the army. Sometimes he acted like a sergeant, but then he'd forget I existed for a week. The new one seemed different, but he's turned out to be worse. He's a control freak.'

'Did you know Larrey?'

'Sure. He was a good guy.'

'Did you see him that evening?'

'No, I only come here in the mornings, until full days start. Then I'll be on an afternoon shift, as well,' he explained. Suddenly cautious, he stopped in the middle of the corridor for a moment. 'You're a journalist, right?'

'No, I'm a private investigator.'

He looked up warily, as if regretting having talked so much. That week there had been a constant stream of reporters, of nosy, worried parents, and school authorities asking about the news that had so shaken the life of the school, as if they'd all been paid to find out the murderer's identity. But the presence of a private investigator was quite unexpected, and he had to be as careful as he'd been with that lieutenant. He'd treated him almost mockingly, not bothering to hide how much he despised his status as an objector – making some joke about his appearance and the barracks, the cropped hair and the sweat, his earring and discipline.

They were presently at the door, and he knocked.

'Come in,' they heard.

Cupido walked into a pleasant room with a cosy, homely feel; it had a table with chairs around it, a bookcase full of books and educational games, several flourishing pot plants, a lamp in the shape of Pinocchio and a full-length mirror reaching the floor, which was fitted with a green carpet. Tacked on the walls were photos of children, ABCs, and health or community-awareness campaign posters, all in cheerful, bright colours. The room didn't seem part of the school. The decor had a personal, almost family feel which invited you to sit on the carpet, take off your shoes and look at yourself in the mirror.

The teacher, he reckoned, might not yet be thirty. She was wearing jeans and a pale short-sleeved shirt. Cupido thought her beauty would have been conventional had it not been for her mouth, a mouth you wanted to kiss, with full, striated lips that became smooth and pliant when she smiled. 'I'm Rita,' she said, proffering her hand.

'I think I was the last person he spoke to,' she started telling him after Moisés closed the door and Cupido asked the first questions. 'Unless the person who shot him said something first, which doesn't seem very likely given the way it was done. And although everyone looked at me strangely for a few days, as if I still had his image in my eyes, I'm glad it was me. Gustavo was nice to everyone, but we were friends.' She stopped for a few seconds, as if looking for adjectives that sounded neither clichéd nor conceited, and then added: 'By that I mean something less simple than having a coffee, laughing at the same jokes and sharing similar ideas about work and colleagues.'

She rested her elbows on the table and covered her face, pressing against her eyes with her index and middle fingers, as if she wanted to wipe away a painful image: the bloody neck, the hair matted around the wound, the brown stain on the office tiles.

'That evening when we left the bar, I offered him a lift. He liked walking, and he always went about on foot.'

'Why didn't he go with you?'

'He'd forgotten his newspaper and his folder at school and had to go back for them. I said I'd wait, but he didn't want me to.'

'Didn't you think that was odd? Couldn't he have left them there till the following day?'

'No, I didn't think it was odd, because he was very careful with his things. I guess he must have needed the folder. Term was starting the following morning,' she explained. However, she had the feeling that anything she might say to this tall, attractive man would be of no use, just as it hadn't been for the lieutenant conducting the investigation. But it felt good to talk, she found a kind of consolation in going over the same details, the same story, making it seem more ordinary, to share and appease the pain and to feel less lonely. And this man before her, seated on a child's chair which only reached halfway up his legs, listened to her without impatience, looking her straight in the eyes with the kind of polite, warm attention that invited her to go on.

'I've heard everyone liked Larrey, that he didn't arouse any ill will,' risked Cupido.

'And it's true. Not because everyone speaks well of him now he's not here, with that indulgence and compassion we deny the living, the ones who really need it, and which we only grant the dead. He was just like that. He didn't have any enemies, he couldn't have any,' she said emphatically. 'I think he was happy, a man contented with his work and his family. Have you met his wife?'

'No.'

'You'll see what I mean when you do. And he really enjoyed his classes,' she added. She looked out of the window and listened, as if expecting to hear echoes of his whistle and the children's shouts in the now empty playground. 'He wasn't frustrated or bitter, even though frustration and bitterness are all-too-common in our profession. I often heard him say that the world we've been destroying for two thousand years could be put right in two decades by the kids entrusted to us, if we only knew how to educate them properly. He was a good teacher, a job that women are usually more successful at, perhaps because we're more patient or because we can hide our moods better, and so our weaknesses. But Gustavo... when a man is a good teacher, he's better than us.'

'Why did all four of you go to the office that morning?'

'Of the four of us, I was the only one without any administrative position. I suppose Nelson was going to ask me to take over the job of school secretary. When the previous headmaster left his job, his team left, too. Out of politeness, maybe Nelson didn't want Julita to be present.'

'Did he ask you, eventually?'

'There wasn't time. Then... he hasn't mentioned it, and we haven't discussed it. I guess what's happened made him change his mind. Or maybe he realised I wasn't going to accept.'

'And who...?'

'The previous secretary is staying on,' she cut in. 'She's very experienced, meticulous and organised, and, in that respect, is the best choice.'

The bell rang throughout the building indicating breaktime.

Presently they heard the powerful clamour of chairs being pushed back, children's voices and shouts, and headlong races along the corridors towards the freedom and sunshine of the playground.

'I'm on duty,' said Rita getting up from her chair. 'I don't think I've been very helpful.'

6

Jaime De Molinos waited in his seat for the last of his pupils to go out into the playground. He was exhausted. The two hours in class had tired him more than an entire morning in the headmaster's office answering phone calls, doing paperwork and speaking to the agitated, insolent mothers who came to see him. He was fifty-eight and sighed with fatigue and tedium when considering the two years he still had to put in before taking early retirement. At the age when his strength was beginning to flag, Nelson had kicked him straight back into the classroom. You needed inexhaustible energy to control and teach anything to those thirty little brutes; they sometimes seemed to be looking at him from their desks with mocking, malicious smirks. He tried not to, but he couldn't help thinking that from the moment he lost his position, his pupils saw him differently; they no longer fell silent when he passed them in the playground or shied away from him, as if the aura that had once given him their respect, fear and obedience had disappeared. Previously, when a teacher came to his office with the most disobedient and recalcitrant children, even the cockiest ones would bow their heads, well aware that in there punishments were severe, and that it was he, the supreme judge, who administered them. In his office it wasn't what you were accused of that mattered, so much as who accused you. Although he was conscious that it was an unfair situation, he had done nothing to change it.

De Molinos looked around, gathering strength to start the tidying he'd put off in his first few days. The previous year the classroom had been occupied by a supply teacher who'd had some rather insubordinate ideas. At the end of the term, she had left those ridiculous, idiotic, brightly coloured decorations all over the furniture and walls. *Flowers*, he whispered with disdain, *flowers in a classroom!* She'd left a bunch of roses on top of a cupboard, perhaps a thank-you gift from a parent for a report with no black marks, which was only to postpone failure until it became irreparable. *A stupid gesture. Once, no one would have given flowers. If anything, a book, a pen and inkwell, a box of chocolates.* After the summer, all that was left were the dry stalks, their thorns toughened by the heat, and a heap of brownish petals around the vase. He stood up and emptied it into the bin. He put the vase away in a drawer: it was of no use to him.

Also on top of the wardrobe was a globe. He set it spinning with a sharp slap. His vision became blurred by the rapid gyre of bright solid colours and suddenly he felt a little dizzy. He stopped it dead, with the feeling that the whole world, not just the globe, spun in space in a disorderly manner, afloat in an unfathomable, incomprehensible void, kept in motion by the occasional blows of an angry hand. For a moment it seemed to him that the cardinal points, the tropics and meridians, the poles and the equator, which once seemed inflexible reference points, could be turned upside-down, and this filled him with puzzlement and pain. He felt like a medieval friar who, after a whole life spent believing in the fixedness of the earth and contemplating the carousel of the sun and the stars, finds out that it is in fact he who is moving, that he is wrong, and everything is a mirage.

In front of him now was the map of Spain and the continent of Africa. Suddenly, still dazed, he felt distant and indifferent to the whole world and its fate, its inhabitants, and the miseries, wars and catastrophes he watched everyday on TV. Now he cared about nothing, felt no solidarity or compassion towards the human race, as if the offence committed against him by one of their number had contaminated the rest of them. His emotional life occupied only two places: home, where he always deferred to his wife; and school, where he had been ousted from the most senior position. His dismissal felt like a mutilation and, just like amputees and their phantom limbs, he felt a puzzling physical pain that he wasn't always able to locate in a precise part of his body.

He left the globe in its place, afraid of touching it again, and he went to the cork panelling on the wall to continue tidying. He ripped down the drawings, and tacked up the class time table and the ten basic rules of correct behaviour. He had drawn these up himself a few years previously – when that pupil had hanged the dog belonging to the director of studies – to contain the increasing breach of order in the school. He had decreed that those tablets of law should be visible in all classrooms and that pupils should be reminded of them every so often. The previous teacher had failed to comply with this. Very well, at least in his classroom he would make sure that everyone observed those ten commandments.

Without stopping to rest, moved by a spirit of cleanliness that, as it grows, turns voracious and purifying until it becomes almost destructive, he continued tearing down the pictures and posters about oral hygiene or racism or the benefits of reading. He crumpled everything and put it in the wastepaper bin, crushing it down with his foot when it was full, until he saw that the classroom was once again a spartan place where nothing invited distraction. He still had to empty the drawers in the desk and the cupboard, get rid of anything superfluous, leave nothing but the basic tools for work: pencils, ballpoint pens, geometric shapes, rulers and set squares, the globe, the blackboard rubber, and the piece of chalk whose squeaking he had once found unbearable but which he ended up getting used to. But he'd leave that for another time. He deserved a rest during breaktime, too. He sat exhausted at his desk and, although it was forbidden to smoke in classrooms, lit a cigarette and inhaled deeply.

As he smoked, he pulled out the handbook he'd brought from home, his beloved old canvas-covered folder, which he kept as if it were a relic, and hadn't used since his first years in the profession. In its yellowish pages were written all the things a teacher needed to have at his fingertips: the rule of three, fractions, the value of pi up to the eighth decimal point, the metric system and other measuring and conversion tables, maps of Spain and the world, the basic spelling rules, the ten commandments... Therein was the essential trinity: alphabet, number and law. Everything else was dispensable. He stroked the covers again. Their smell was reassuring, evoking a time long past when he was still young and strong and almost happy. Of course, the new classroom wouldn't be complete without the dais. The dais made of dry, hard wood, on which the master stood in order to be better seen and heard by the students. It was also the scaffold where, as an example to others, the one about to be punished was displayed. But to dream of reinstating it was going too far.

He looked at the classroom again, its desks in rows. Each pupil would gain what he could earn with his effort or intelligence, nothing else. He hadn't taught for eight years, but that was one thing that hadn't changed for him. He would teach his lessons as he always had, and his pupils would once again listen in silence and bend their heads over their books as if about to lick them. None of that trendy 'assisted learning' or 'individual attention'. No explaining a point or a problem at least three times and in different ways so that everyone had a chance to take it in. No dumbing down so that no one lagged behind. Life was unfair from birth in its distribution of talents, and the pupil who didn't learn that at school would learn it later at work in a much more painful way – through dismissal, unemployment and alienation. He would set an equal rhythm for everyone from the start and those who didn't want to get left behind would have to work hard to keep up, for he was not prepared to slow down or help anyone. As if teaching was somehow in his hands, when no one can teach anyone who is not willing or able to learn!

He stubbed the cigarette out and put the ashtray away in a drawer. Then, walking with his hands behind his back, in an attitude reminiscent of the clergy, he went to the window and opened it to air the room. He did not lean out, but remained in a semi-dark spot from where he could survey the playground without being seen.

Outside, male and female teachers formed two separate groups, as if even after thirty years of coexistence the division of the sexes could not be overcome, and the same old provincial prudery remained, with its stale and poisonous secrets on one side, and crudely obscene jokes on the other. As it was a pleasant morning, it was not only those on duty who were outside, but other teachers too, who preferred the fresh air to the staffroom.

Among the women was his wife, Matilde Cuaresma. He watched her strong, arrogant, no longer attractive figure. She had once driven him crazy in bed, but little by little she too had become colourless, under the pressure of years, the monotony, or dressing in those dun-coloured clothes that hid the grime pupils brought in from the playground, their hands covered in dirt, or sticky with the remains of sweets and sandwiches. Her upright gait had lost its confidence, her head hung forward from so many hours bent over exercise books and files. He saw her stop in her tracks to make herself better heard, gesturing in irritation, and confirmed once more that the one thing she had not lost – and would never lose – was her family pride, the arrogance of the Cuaresma name. While it conferred on her the prestige of rural wealth, it also obliged her to defend it constantly from the destructive irreverence of the times.

He guessed they'd be talking about the new headmaster, about his victory by two votes, and the reforms he'd promised. He had noticed that, a week later, all of them were more concerned with the planned changes – and the difficulties brought about by change – than about the death of their colleague. Even he had begun to forget the murder in the face of his loss of the headship. He had no reason to miss Larrey. True, Larrey had been a good teacher, and he'd never had any trouble with him; he did his job well, didn't absent himself without notice, and ran his classes in the best possible way: one which never required the head's intervention. But he couldn't say he missed him. By contrast, any mundane detail could remind him of his expulsion from office. He would not get the head's extra pay – some fifty thousand pesetas – in his next pay cheque, which, if he'd held the position for ten years, he would have continued to receive permanently. Nelson knew that, just as he knew that he was only two years away from the protection of retirement, and had still dared snatch away a supplementary wage that he had come to consider his due. Why hadn't he waited, why the hurry? If Nelson had come to talk to him, they could have reached an agreement, they could have put both integrity and shame to one side, and secretly shared the advantages of power. He would have disregarded all the promises of succession made to Corona, and instead ensured that Nelson took over from him in exchange for that last prerogative.

He looked at his wife again. In the last week, Matilde had often reproached him for his stubborn complacency in assuming that Nelson posed no threat, when she had repeatedly warned him. He had admitted his mistake to her, his overconfidence, his naivety in not recognising the kind of temptation that power, however small, awakens in ambitious people. And that admission, far from being a relief, made him all the more irritated with Nelson.

To Matilde, being the headmaster's wife meant as much as the headship had meant to him. He knew it would take a long time to forget the words she'd uttered the evening he came home and confessed his defeat: 'I should've run for it myself. I would never have let that good-for-nothing make off with the votes.' He now wondered how many things he'd done at her instigation that he would never have dared on his own. Of course, many had been satisfying, but others had borne scant fruit that hardly made up for the great efforts he had exerted. It had always been she who'd forced him to scale greater heights, occupy new territories, keep making fresh efforts to right the initial imbalance between them: to show the gratitude of a man with nothing taken as a husband by one of the wealthiest young ladies in town.

However, he couldn't say he hadn't been happy. With her he'd come to feel that warm marital joy that stems from a long, steady intimacy. They'd married young, and during their first years together they'd enjoyed themselves in bed and had four children, now all grown and left home. They probably would have had a couple more if he hadn't convinced her it wasn't a good idea. After many nights talking softly and persuasively, Matilde had agreed to contraception. Eventually, her religious convictions had given way before his insistence and the painful memory of a tragic family precedent. Many years before, her own mother, prompted by the family doctor, had written to Rome requesting the Pope's permission for a tubal ligation, as the practice was then. There had been complications with her fifth child and the doctor didn't want her to risk another. The Vatican's permission, however, was not forthcoming, and her mother had died giving birth to her sixth child. It was a girl: Matilde.

A few soft knocks interrupted his train of thought. He moved away from the window and called:

'Come in.'

A tall man came towards him. He didn't look like a police officer, or someone from the Ministry of Education. De Molinos's eight years dealing with the latter meant he could identify them instantly: they wore suits and ties, carried black briefcases full of papers and tried to pretend they felt completely at home in the school. But it was a futile pretence, as even the inspectors were bewildered by so many laws and reforms and Ministry regulations, and after a few minutes, doubt appeared on their faces and they would wonder what line they should take: whether they should sternly check that schedules and programmes were adhered to and penalise any possible deviations, or whether they should chum up to the teachers.

'Jaime Molinos?' asked Cupido, offering his hand.

'De Molinos, Jaime *De* Molinos, with a capital letter,' he corrected firmly. That particle was the only valuable antique he had inherited from a family of peasants and he never allowed its omission.

'Ricardo Cupido. I'm a private investigator.'

'Investigator,' he repeated in surprise. It had never occurred to him that Larrey's death would be investigated through any channels other than the official ones. And private investigators were something exotic and distant, part of the fictional world he watched on TV in the evening while dozing off in his armchair. He would never have thought a job like that would fit in Breda, a small city where a detective seemed as out of place as a stockbroker or a sea captain. His presence there, however, introduced a new and disturbing element into the school order. And he was suddenly delighted about this new development, as it meant more difficulty and worry for Nelson.

'Who's hired you?'

Cupido expected the question. It was always like this, and the name of his client often determined whether his interlocutors would cooperate or not, as well as the nature of their replies: hostility and indifference if it was an enemy, kindness if his client was someone powerful or a friend.

'The father of a pupil who doesn't want to be named. I've already told the headmaster.'

'Have you spoken with him?'

'With him and another teacher, Rita. She told me you and the director of studies were present when the body was found in the office.'

'And why do you want to speak to me? I'm sure she and Nelson have already told you everything in painstaking detail,' he said in an ironic tone. 'And, of course, I bet their versions match up to the last word.'

The innuendo was too obvious not to be intentional, and

Cupido realised that for the first time he was hearing something new and damaging, different to the routine account of events. It was one of those pieces of information that could be very revealing, for although they often stray from the objective truth, they cast light on the speaker's conscience. He could not ignore that invitation to confidence.

'Do you mean they...?'

'I don't mean anything,' De Molinos cut in, 'although everyone says so. Those two don't exactly set a good example for many people. Just imagine what parents and pupils would think if the rumour spread. Imagine.'

You do nothing to silence it, thought Cupido. He instinctively hated such veiled insinuations, made by people never brave enough to put their own name to them, but who knew with a malicious certainty that there was always someone ready to believe certain things said about a woman. He wondered why, if this rumour was so important, De Molinos hadn't spread it before the election. Perhaps because he was sure of victory.

'I'm under no obligation to tell anything to a private detective,' he went on. 'I've told everything to the lieutenant from the Guardia Civil. But if the present headmaster has done so, I'd better give you my version, too. I suppose you want to know what I did after leaving the bar.'

'Yes, I do.'

'I went straight home. Corona, the director of studies, and I walked together part of the way. I didn't really need to start emptying my office that night, did I?'

'Could it have been a burglar?'

'A burglar in the school? No. We've had a few burglaries, petty thefts, rather – possibly carried out by former pupils who thought that by taking away a stereo or a VCR they were avenging some old punishment. Once, a computer was stolen. But it wasn't a burglar this time. If they'd got as far as the office, they would have searched it. It's easy enough to find a petty-cash box in a cupboard. Besides, a burglar, if they'd seen anyone inside, would have run off or hidden. It's not as if Larrey caught them by surprise. From the way he was shot and fell, it looked like Larrey was there first.'

'Were the lights on when you got there in the morning?'

'Yes. They must have been like that all night. The blinds

were down and you couldn't have seen anything from the outside.'

Some shouting from the playground attracted De Molinos's attention, and Cupido approached the window to take a look. Two of the older pupils, about fourteen or fifteen, were fighting, punching each other with the fury of adults. Others had formed a circle around them, and for a moment, the school playground, with its high metal fence behind, looked just like a prison. Presently three or four other students jumped into the melee and the fight turned into a frenzied mass of bodies rolling on the floor. A few teachers ran quickly towards them and managed to separate them with some effort.

'This school is descending into chaos,' said De Molinos.

'We all fought as children. And sometimes we did each other a lot of harm.'

'A fight like that, almost collective, has never happened in that playground before,' he insisted in a severe voice. 'Nelson is not the right headmaster for this institution. He won't be able to maintain the necessary discipline. He didn't even know how to maintain it in his own classroom. Right now, he should be down there dragging the culprits off by their ears. Can you see him anywhere?'

'No.'

'He's probably in his office waiting for someone to bring them in for a lecture about peace and harmony. As if words were enough to deal with those little brutes.'

Possibly more than with punishment alone, thought the detective. Any punishment he had ever received only made him hate school. And it wouldn't be easy to stop boys fighting in the playground when they saw the adults engaged in a different kind of violence, harsher and more single-minded.

De Molinos left the window and returned to his desk. From his chair he surveyed the empty classroom as if it were a distant, uncomfortable and unknown place. His gaze attracted Cupido's, and the detective thought that, just as a house reveals its owner's character, so does a classroom its teacher's. Each desk was set in regimented lines, the walls were bare, and there was no decoration that might distract the children's attention. It was a marked contrast to the speech-therapy room he'd just left, and he found it odd that worlds so dramatically different could coexist in the same school, as if the teachers shared no common educational project or even an attempt to appear coherent, so that the children had consistent standards to learn by. He imagined De Molinos giving his classes from the chair, no doubt longing for the good old days and the high wooden platform that was no longer in use; quieting any noise, convinced that the only road to learning is total silence; explaining something with the authority of one accustomed to giving orders without raising his voice or leaving his seat. From what he knew of Larrey, he and De Molinos must have been very different.

Cupido waited a few moments before asking his last, possibly pointless but nevertheless unavoidable question:

'Did Larrey have enemies?'

'Enemies? You'll find people who make all kinds of enemies in this place. But Larrey was the only one everyone liked.'

'And him? Did he hate anyone?'

'I'm afraid we'll never know that now.'

Cupido said his goodbyes and left the classroom as he heard the strident bell marking the end of recess. From a window he saw the swarm of children miraculously sorting themselves into lines. The teachers stood at the front, waiting. Most of them looked nondescript: not in immaculate uniforms, like bank clerks, nor unclean either, like mechanics or manual workers, with that dirt that goes with the job and which confers dignity even as it stains. Instead, they looked grey, as if dust – from chalk, from the playground – made them dull and neutral; they weren't repellent, but they had no elegance or seductive appeal either. Their jumpers, trousers and skirts were of those colours that can resist dirt and barely show it. Not even their shoes – the women's flat – had that just-polished shine that can divert attention from the shabbiness of an outfit. Cupido thought that if any of them had walked through the streets after firing the gun, no one would have noticed, as if their very ordinariness made them invisible. And yet, their profession was one of the most honourable, and within them beat the same passions, fears, desires and joys as in people of any other profession. He'd known for a long time that a person can be profoundly good or evil without giving any outward sign of it, without being either brilliant or original or eccentric. Often, both the finest talents and the worst monsters had hidden their exceptional qualities beneath an unremarkable appearance that protected them from other people's interest and curiosity.

The pupils had gone in and the group of teachers was lingering by the door, deep in conversation, and no doubt reluctant to face the intense effort of teaching and keeping three dozen energetic children in order in a confined space while also holding their attention

He left the window and walked along the corridor, looking for the gym to speak to Corona. As he went down the stairs he came face to face with the group of teachers. They all fell silent. They must already know who he was and what he was doing there. As he passed them and said hello, Cupido felt an echo of the fear and respect he'd felt as a child, when he met teachers in the street. Today they still had the same smell he remembered from his childhood, a mixture of chalk, sweat and pencil-shavings. And although their faces, close to, had diverse features, these men were very similar in the way they dressed, moved, cut their hair (neither cropped nor long) and looked at him, as if trying not to stand out. For a moment they seemed identical to the teachers of his childhood. A particular subspecies within the human species which never modernised, or changed, or learned more than was strictly necessary; people who remained separate from the rest of evolution, unchanging in their tastes, opinions and beliefs and who never established friendships outside their own profession; a group whose essence remained unaffected by history; grey people clinging to their comfortable routine and reluctant to accept the responsibility they'd been handed. Hence, perhaps, the failure of all educational reforms, which never engaged the enthusiasm of the very people who should have been their principal agents.

At the bottom of the stairs he saw the open door of a large room. An enormous rectangular table stood in the middle, around which were dozens of cushioned chairs. It was the staffroom, but Cupido thought it could have done with a lick of paint along with the classrooms. Its dull, unwelcoming decor consisted of an electric coffee machine with some coffee left in the pot, a small fridge, a TV on top of a low, long table, and some dull landscape paintings of mountains and trees.

A woman of about fifty-five, thin, with grey hair, and dressed in a thick grey suit, was poring over some papers; she had a red pencil in her hand, and was scoring things out at intervals, fiercely correcting mistakes. He guessed it must be the secretary, whose position freed her for some teaching hours, and decided to talk to her.

'Julita Guzmán?' he asked, trying to sound amiable.

'Yes!' the woman replied, startled. She hadn't heard him come in, but her disturbed expression betrayed more than surprise. The sudden movement of her body revealed she was so tense she would jump at anything.

Cupido introduced himself for the fifth time in little over an hour. When the woman learned his job, she refused to go on talking to him, on the grounds that she'd already told everything to the relevant authorities.

'It's not you I'd like to speak about, but Larrey,' explained the detective, although he was extremely curious about why she'd stayed for a couple of drinks that evening, given that she never set foot in a bar. 'Some information about his family.'

His words seemed to reassure her, as she said:

'His parents were dead and he had no siblings. He was married. I visited his widow after the funeral and she's devastated. I don't think it's a good idea to go and speak to her.'

'I won't,' he assured her.

And he would try not to unless it was absolutely necessary. Before coming to the school he had thought about it, and had decided against it. He didn't expect to find any momentous or vital information. A precipitous visit would probably only increase her pain unnecessarily.

'It's not here, in the school, where you need to be looking for the...' She hesitated, afraid of the correct word. 'It's outside, among the thieves, the madmen, among the pupils' parents.'

'Why among the parents?'

But apparently the secretary didn't hear him, and she went back to the papers she was reading and marking. A blurred figure, well wrapped up and fearful of winter.

7

When Nelson told him a private detective wanted a word, Manuel Corona went to find him immediately, to demonstrate that he was not afraid and had nothing to hide. Nevertheless, when he spotted the detective at the end of the corridor, entering the classroom where De Molinos must have been, shut away, brooding over his failure, not emerging to the playground or for coffee, he decided to wait. He was sure he was right in imagining De Molinos pacing between the straight rows of desks, his head bowed and hands clasped at his back, muttering angry, bitter words. Corona would have felt some pity if the other's failure had not also meant his own, in a way that only the two of them knew. In private, he'd been told several times that he'd be next, that after two years he'd only have to step forward to take the position De Molinos would hand over after a splendid leaving dinner. All the current teachers would attend, as would those who had worked at the school in previous years and were still alive; after dinner, over coffee and liqueurs, the men smoking cigars and the women cigarettes, as they do at weddings, thank-you telegrams from the municipal and provincial authorities would be read out, and finally, after a champagne toast, De Molinos would be presented with a pair of gold cufflinks and a silver plate engraved with his name and the dates of the forty-two years he had dedicated to teaching.

Corona had first viewed these promises with scepticism: it was all a long way off. But returning after the holiday he'd realised it was the old man's penultimate year at the school. The prospect of replacing De Molinos and giving up his own difficult, tiring classes had gone from being a distant possibility to a comfortable, proximate certainty. He'd already pictured himself in the office, his hands chalk-free, his white collar clear of the dust kicked up by the constant whirl of pupils, and the peace of being away from kids who never spoke if they could shout in his ear. He imagined himself leaning back in his chair answering the phone, or dealing on equal terms with the inspectors, who always dressed so neatly and elegantly. He even imagined the looks he would get from colleagues and parents, filled with the respect that power, however small, inspires.

And now the old man's defeat had wiped out a future that had been almost tangible. Nelson would remain headmaster for at least four years, and Corona knew that, all things being equal, he'd never be able to compete with him. He didn't have his eloquence, or his repertoire of anecdotes for every occasion, or his good looks, or his way of smiling seductively for an instant before saying hello, or that confidence in public speaking which had been so effective in gaining the parents' votes. And even if Nelson's skills one day exhausted themselves and he was no longer able to bamboozle those around him, Corona would be too old to replace him. He couldn't wait that long, he wouldn't make it. With his obesity, his heart had to work like a slave to pump his blood into each and every one of the cells that made up his nineteen-stone body; old age would arrive ten or fifteen years early, and soon there would come a time when, on going to bed at night, he wouldn't know for certain whether he'd wake up in the morning or remain asleep for ever.

Unlike Nelson, he had no adventurous past to bring on nostalgia, nor even memories of pain or misfortune that, as they move further into the past, are always better than emptiness. His life amounted to a childhood with a dog as his only friend; the humdrum, painful adolescence of a fat, graceless boy who often had to suffer others' mockery; and a youth spent travelling between ten different towns without finding affection or a reason to stay in any of them. Every school year he was sent to a different village, and his memories of them became increasingly confused as time went by. Looking back, he felt like one of those travellers who, on returning from a long journey (undertaken not for pleasure, but from sheer necessity), cannot quite recall what he saw in each city, where that cathedral was which he liked so much, or where he spoke to that woman one night, even though he knows he will never revisit the city or see the cathedral or talk to the woman again. His past was a muddled, tangled skein in which now and again he pricked himself on a hidden needle. The names of his former pupils, the colleagues he shared his working hours with, the boarding houses or sparsely furnished apartments he'd lived in, the narrow roads that took him there, the look of the classrooms, the dates... everything blurred into a murky whirlpool from which he couldn't salvage any accurate details that might help him feel his life was a product of his own will and not of chance.

And when he looked forward, now that his succession had been thwarted, the prospect of a future decided and planned by him seemed unlikely. He could guess what his last years would be like, for little would change. He'd carry on looking after his father until the illness gnawing away at him finally entered its final stages; he'd remain at that school, in the job that exhausted him and made him constantly dirty. He had no faith in the supposed birth-rate crisis that might let him retire early: every year, children registered in hordes, as if they'd come into the world by spontaneous generation, not from the union of a man and a woman. He'd go on living alone, without a woman by his side who was not disgusted or repelled by him and his misshapen body whose hormones had always been unbalanced; he'd go on cheating his solitude with sporadic visits to brothels from which he always left disappointed, the intensity of his desire never matching the satisfaction he received; he'd go on living in the same dark, run-down house, and he'd die in the bed he slept in now.

He retraced his steps and went into the staffroom, where a young female teacher was waiting for him; the local authorities had sent her to replace Larrey. She was alone – Nelson must have gone out to the playground or the cafe – leafing through one of the education magazines the school subscribed to and no one ever read.

A few minutes before, when Nelson asked him to show her the playing fields and give her her time table, he was surprised to learn that the new teacher was a young woman. Even if the supply teachers who covered short periods were little more than twenty, which cruelly accentuated the average age of the permanent staff, he hadn't imagined that they'd send a girl for that subject. PE had always seemed to him a subject in which strength, speed, energy and the ability to control a large outdoor space all called for a masculine temperament. She was very pretty, too. She had blonde bobbed hair, and a face that was attractively tanned but neither from rural hardship nor a sunbed, something he could never achieve. He went from pallid to sunburned with no transitional stage. She embodied all the delicacy he admired, and was a far cry from the stereotypical female PE teacher – butch, powerful, hoarse-voiced, with big wide feet that would never fit into a pair of high heels.

'You're Violeta, aren't you?' he asked, although he remembered her name perfectly well.

'That's right.'

'If you like, I can show you to your office. It's by the gym, where we keep what's now going to be your stuff.'

'OK,' she said. She bent to pick up a little sports bag that was at her feet, and followed him.

'We hadn't imagined they'd send a young woman as a PE teacher,' he said amiably.

'Why not?'

Immediately, he realised his mistake. The comment, which he intended as an expression of pleasant surprise, sounded in his mouth like a criticism, a sign of disdain or what women called machismo but was in fact just a habit. It was often like this with young people: he found it hard to understand them and to make himself understood, as if they spoke different languages, each riddled with traps for the other; or perhaps as if they spoke the same language, but one which an evolution of five hundred years had laden with nuances unknown to him. He was only trying to be friendly, not even daring flattery, as he was aware of what he represented for a girl like this: ugliness and all its complexes and attendant small obscenities. Often, when he happened to find himself in front of one of these kittenish girls for a few moments, he imagined them wondering what it would be like to spend a night with a man like him: the mattress dipping from his weight, his sweat, his fat, his smell, and his loud, laboured breathing.

'Well, it's not often you see girls teaching this subject,' he explained.

'You'd be surprised, Manuel,' she replied familiarly. 'It's all changed a lot. Today no one associates PE with uniformed children in a line, like the army. It's quite different now.'

'Of course, of course it's changed, like everything else. I didn't mean that. But I've always heard your colleagues complaining how tough it was out there on the track, so cold in the winter and hot in the summer. Not to mention how difficult it is to control kids out in the open.'

'But if you're prepared to work harder than them, to tire them out, they calm down soon enough. In the end, it's like any other subject: a matter of burning calories, not sitting still in an armchair.'

He couldn't tell if those words were directed at him, at his double chin and his stomach directly neighbouring his thighs. But he was annoyed by them, as well as by the overwhelming confidence of an inexperienced supply teacher who might never have a steady job. But he wasn't going to argue, or get carried away by sudden hatred.

They reached the little office that had been Larrey's, and he unlocked the door. Although the Guardia Civil had gone through everything, nothing was out of place. The table and cupboard were tidy and the hangers from the changing rooms empty; and in the adjoining room, all the sports equipment – mats, ropes, a vaulting horse, boxes, hoops, hockey sticks, balls, rackets, skittles, nets and shooting-targets – lay with the disquieting calm of toys belonging to a child who had suddenly died or disappeared.

He noticed Violeta hug herself, as if she felt cold all of a sudden. For the first time, her gaze had lost some of that confidence, so hurtful in its capability and charm.

'I'm not afraid of the children or the playing fields,' she said. 'I'm afraid... The last teacher, why was he killed?'

He was somewhat taken aback by this question, for on the girl's young lips it took on a brutality it didn't have in the mouths of his other school colleagues. To anyone else he could have said it was an accident, a coincidence, a mistake or a burglar that had broken in, but with her those answers were not enough, for her mouth was also asking: Could it happen again? What am I doing here filling the gap he left? What am I doing here?

'The guy they called before me turned this job down. He was scared of replacing someone who'd died like that.'

'You needn't worry,' he replied, though he felt a peculiar satisfaction at seeing her confidence and control disappear. 'It was too strange for there to be any reason behind it, but we're all positive that neither the killer nor the motive is to be found in the school.'

The girl nodded a few times and seemed to accept his words;

for a moment he enjoyed his protective role. He opened the folder and showed her the time table, the classes she would teach, the materials available and the meticulous fortnightly programme Larrey had drawn up.

'When do I start?'

'Ideally now, after break. But if you're tired you can start tomorrow.'

'No. The sooner, the better. I've brought my gear,' she said bending down to pick up her sports bag.

She went to the changing rooms and reappeared a few minutes later. She was wearing an elegant red and grey track-suit, and had tied her hair up in a ponytail that made her look even prettier and fresher and cleaner. Corona felt that the fleeting minutes in which he'd held her attention with his words and helpful information had disappeared like a breath of air. The girl probably saw him once more as an older colleague, fat and dull, who had nothing else interesting to say. Now, dressed in her tracksuit and white trainers, she seemed impatient to be gone, to leave the office and leap on to the track like a beautiful young animal, to run around with the children. He had the sudden thought that the age gap between her and the pupils was smaller than between him and her. The appearance of this girl, just graduated from teacher-training college, had been enough to remind him of what he often forgot among his colleagues every day: how old they all were.

He almost jumped when the bell marked the end of the break. The girl came up to the desk to check the time table.

'3A. Better get out and start.'

'Of course.'

He sat still in his chair, unable to move. His hands felt soiled with a mixture of his own sweat and the dust that had already settled in the closed room. He missed the wipes he kept in his desk. It was always the same, an endless personal struggle against the filth of the world, while all around him some people were strangely happy living in the mire. He'd always felt a kind of disbelief seeing TV images of Third World children playing by thatched-roofed huts, surrounded by flies and scabby dogs, excrement and rubbish, and who nevertheless seemed happy, and smiled with such white teeth and such honest laughter that it couldn't have been faked for the camera. As if the misery and filth around them were harmless and could not sully their innocence. Seeing Larrey, and the girl who'd just gone out – in a tracksuit and trainers, she seemed even lovelier than in street clothes – he'd also wondered, slightly enviously, how they managed to be clean and happy despite their close contact with so many sweaty, dirty and unhappy people.

Perhaps the others weren't lying; perhaps he was the only one who'd hated Larrey. A controlled, healthy hatred that kept him alive, an intense hatred: the hatred of the deformed for the beautiful, the hatred of the solitary man for the one who lives close to happiness – for no one is so hateful as the person who embodies an ideal to which we aspire and can never attain. Larrey's quiet work routine, free of both laziness and ambition; the domestic happiness that surrounded him like a halo when he arrived at school in the mornings; his physical magnificence – the kind that is all the more enviable because its beneficiary does nothing to preserve it – were qualities that were necessarily painful to someone, like himself, who would never achieve them. He had often compared Larrey's glorious abundance to his own dull life, and it made him feel unpleasantly dirty. Larrey never looked dirty despite his many hours on the track, the sweat from his exertions, and his contact with the children. Watching him, Corona had come to think that cleanliness doesn't so much depend on how often you wash your hands as on some kind of internal, untransferable quality, like hair strength or metabolism. Some people would always appear neat, even if they didn't shower every day, as if their bodies did not emit humours and excrescences. In contrast, there were others, among whom he could not help but include himself, who looked dirty as soon as they got out of the bath: their hair became lank and greasy, their nose was promptly covered in blackheads, their skin shone as they expelled all the surplus grease, and their clothes seemed to attract flies and dust.

He heard footsteps approaching along the corridor and knew they were for him, their slow, tentative pace suggesting someone unfamiliar with the layout of the school, someone who had to stop and read the sign on every door. He opened a folder and pretended to be reading: this was not his office and he didn't want to seem as if he was loitering. Because, truth be told, he was stalling. Although half an hour before he'd been willing to meet Cupido straight away, now, after the conversation with the girl, he'd lost that first impulse. He wanted to stay there for a while, in silence, with no one else around, alone with his apathy and his poverty of soul, away from the conflict that always seemed to come from contact with others.

Why did he want to talk to the four of them? It wasn't as if they were like those concierges who love to repeat the story of some tragic event they've witnessed. The fact that he had found Larrey's body was simply a coincidence that couldn't help any investigation. And now the steps were coming closer he feared the way the tall man was walking towards him, the tone of his questions, and the insistence of his gaze. He imagined his colleagues' reaction to the interrogation, if that was the word for it. He saw Nelson being amicable but careful, wriggling away with characteristic skill as soon as the man touched on any thorny detail. He saw De Molinos answering tersely, or perhaps refusing to speak to someone not in uniform. And what about Rita, who'd been so close to Larrey? The detective was surely one of those guys who treats a man and a beautiful woman differently, who avoids tough words with women, as if words might injure them. But he was here now. There were two soft knocks, and a voice asked, 'May I?' while a face half-showed itself through the crack in the door.

'Come in,' Corona replied, without lifting his eyes from the papers he wasn't reading. He took a few seconds to close the folder and look at the man who had approached the desk and now stood at the centre of the room, introducing himself and mentioning his dubious profession.

'I was waiting for you. Although I don't think I can help you. I didn't know Larrey very well,' he added, thinking that it was not just Larrey, but that he barely knew the passions, desires or misfortunes of any of the colleagues he'd lived with for ten years.

'But as director of studies you would have formed a professional opinion of him,' ventured the detective.

'Yes, of course. Professionally, yes. He was a good teacher. He never missed a class, was never off sick, was never late. Although his subject was 'soft', he was well regarded by all of us. And by the parents.'

'Was this his office?' asked the detective taking a look at the grilled window and the shelves, the almost paper-free desk, the equipment room, as if, from the decor and dimensions, he could deduce information unimaginable to others.

'Yes, it was.'

'That morning when you found him, Nelson asked the three of you to come with him to the office.'

'Yes.'

'It makes sense that he asked De Molinos, whom he was succeeding, and yourself as the director of studies, but why Rita?'

So you've guessed already. So soon, he thought. Only someone from outside would realise that if Nelson was thinking of making Rita secretary, then it was Julita Guzmán who was missing from that group. But it wasn't the secretary whom he would be replacing; she was too efficient for Nelson – and his lack of organisational skills – to give up. No one had mentioned it, and after Larrey's murder everything had remained the same, but Corona was positive it was he who was to be replaced by Rita, as director of studies.

'I don't know. I suppose he had his reasons,' he replied, trying for insolence. He fell silent, fearing the next question might put him in a tight spot, steeling himself to seem bold enough to hide his weakness; but the detective simply retained his words, as if filing them away for another time.

'The day before, at the meeting, did anything strange happen with Larrey?'

'No, not with him. The only strange thing was that Nelson had been elected. But no one complained or contested the result of a legitimate election. We live in a democracy, don't we?'

'Of course.'

'Then we had a few drinks at the bar and everything was perfectly normal. Nelson didn't brag about his victory, and De Molinos didn't seem terribly affected by his defeat. Julita Guzmán was the first to leave, and after that we all left gradually. There was nothing strange, no sign that anything unfortunate was about to happen,' he insisted, pleased with his explanation. Everything would be all right if it ended there with no further questions.

'Did you walk home with De Molinos?'

He knew what he meant: a mutual alibi. He guessed he'd asked the same question of the old man.

'Only for a few minutes, the part of the route we share. The next day was the start of term, and our job, contrary to popular perception, is a hard one. Possibly harder than ever now. The authorities send us endless regulations, memos and circulars obliging us to take on tasks that used to be carried out by doctors, the media or social services. Even servants: some people want us to change the children's clothes when they wet themselves. Parents no longer wait respectfully at the gate; they stride along the corridors and barge into classrooms without even knocking, as if they owned them, and they're more and more demanding, as if their kids were all geniuses. And the pupils are losing what remains of discipline. Have you seen the graffiti on the back wall?'

'No, I haven't.'

'A mural of offensive and disrespectful language. That's what we've taught them to write for.'

He could go on listing the assaults against his profession, but he realised the detective didn't seem disposed to listen to his litany of complaints. As if he had no other questions, the detective thanked him and took his leave, giving no sign of disappointment.

Before returning to his office Corona popped into the teachers' toilets to wash his hands. He felt old and tired, and noticed the sweat beginning to make itself visible at his armpits and around his neck; his tie pressed hotly under his double chin, hindering his breathing. Later he dallied at his desk, going through his paperwork but unable to concentrate, anxiously waiting for the bell that would bring the morning to a close.

~

He opened the door of his house and, while taking his coat off, took a look around the living room. A quick glance was enough to tell if Petra had done her job properly in the morning or if she was late finishing her chores with the excuse that his father had needed her constantly. He hated coming home at noon and finding his lunch uncooked, clothes sitting in the washing machine, the beds unmade in the bedrooms. But now it all seemed in order: the floor sparkled in the light from the window, there was no smell of stuffiness, and the cushions on the armchairs and the sofa were fluffed out, even if the sofa had, under his weight, given way in the middle and looked oddly like a canoe.

The shining floor, or perhaps the detective's visit, which he still felt agitated about, made him think suddenly of Bruno, the King Charles spaniel he'd had until three years before. He stared down at the tiles, as if the dog was still there, looking up at him and wagging his tail in welcome. With greater tenderness than he felt for any person, he recalled that soft, warm ball of fur that followed him wherever he went, pursuing him until he let him lick his fingers. The mutt didn't mind his fatness, his sweat or the dust he brought in from school, didn't care what the hand he was licking had done in the last few hours.

Bruno had captivated him from the very first with his unconditional love and fidelity. When he sat, Bruno sat at his feet and lifted his head at the slightest movement, fell silent when he did, whined when he had to go out and lock him in, spun like a top with happiness when he heard his steps coming up the stairs, and hurled himself on him as soon as he came through the door.

And yet, it wasn't he who had brought the dog into the house. Bruno had been a retirement present for his father when he left the nuclear plant. One of his colleagues thought that now his father had nothing to do, the young animal, only just weaned, placid, friendly and of good pedigree, would make better company than a silver tray – the directors' present – or the clock the staff had bought for him. The dog would get him out of the house and keep to a fixed schedule that would stop him losing track of time; it would force him to be responsible for a task, and this would make the transition between full-time employment at the power station and the long hours he now had at his disposal easier. His father had put the silver tray in a corner, visible but out of the way, and muttered: 'A clock. It's always a clock for someone retiring, so he doesn't forget he's only got a few years left.' As for the dog, he'd liked it even less, but didn't dare refuse it in front of everyone, unable to tell if it was a joke or only a well-intentioned mistake. He'd looked forward to his retirement precisely because he would have nothing to do, he'd be able to waste his time without feeling guilty, staying in, smoking and maybe drinking, lying in bed or watching the sci-fi or futuristic disaster movies he liked so much. He told his son how, as he was coming home after the retirement party, he had been going to throw the puppy out of the car window when it managed to get from the back seat to the front, tangled itself round his feet on the brake and nearly made him come off the road. But he brought it home, in the same bag as the tray, ready to give it away or abandon it near the Paternoster reserve, at the mercy of the wild boars.

It took three days for Manuel Corona to become completely attached to the puppy and decide to keep it, despite his father's reluctance and his warnings that he would get tired of looking after it. He couldn't get rid of a creature that, from the moment he came into the house, had sought his contact and his smell with such innocence and trust as no living thing had ever shown him. He willingly took care of him, and fought his embarrassment the first few days he walked him in the street: a tall, fat man with a little dog on a lead, patiently and ridiculously stopping by a tree as the puppy lifted a leg, or smiling awkwardly to the owners of other animals that came to sniff him, at times speaking to him in mock reproach with too high-pitched a voice. And all of this in Breda, a small provincial town that had not yet cast off its rural origins, and where a dog was often a parasite no worthier of affection than a lizard.

Soon after came the search for a name, the need to differentiate him from all the other dogs in the street. It wasn't easy to find, as none accurately summed up that warm, greedy, furry form without being bland or corny. For days he tried out pleasant-sounding combinations of syllables, even if they made no sense, Spanish and foreign words, rude and refined names, of trees and animals, weather conditions and planets, heroes from myth or film, minerals and exotic places, and of other well-known dogs. Sometimes he would call him by a name he liked at first, but which he would rule out a little later. Finally, all of a sudden, the name appeared to him and seemed so obvious that he wondered how he hadn't thought of it before. He called the dog Bruno, for the words evoked the black and russet-speckled colour of his pelt and was playful, cheerful and affectionate, like his character.

And as if the name had made him an adult, Bruno began to

submit to some basic rules and become house-trained. His lively learning intelligence was another reason to love him. Corona would never have thought that an animal could have such an ability to listen, lifting his head and staring at him till he finished talking, as if he understood each and every one of his words. There were pupils at school, he told himself, who could not match Bruno's memory and reasoning powers.

For four years – only four years, too short a life even for a dog – Bruno was both a small child to be cared for and a companion to alleviate his loneliness and the arid absence of emotions. Then not long after, all *that* had happened, with the hanged body and that boy.

He walked along the hallway, said hello to Petra, who had nearly finished preparing lunch in the kitchen, and went into his father's room.

'How are you today? You were asleep when I left.'

'A bit sleepy after a whole night without a wink,' he corrected. He was one of those invalids who are always reluctant to recognise any improvement in their condition, any spell of physical well-being. 'But Petra woke me up soon enough with her door-bangings and noises. I think she does it on purpose.'

'No, Dad. She has to clean and tidy the house and she's bound to make some noise.'

'But she doesn't have to turn the radio on and play that horrible music.'

'I'll ask her to turn the volume down.'

'She won't listen to you. It's as if she's in charge here, not us.'

He clicked his tongue in annoyance. The same unending conversation every day. He had told Petra himself that she should wake his father everyday at ten to give him his medication, but if his father found out he would refuse to take it. Besides, the only way to make him sleep at night was by keeping him awake during the day. At first he had let him sleep in and then, in the middle of the night, his father would get up and move around the house like a ghost, flush the toilet repeatedly, turn on the TV, eat in the hallway and finally, once he realised his son was not going to get up, would come into his room and tell him he couldn't sleep because something or other hurt.

Perhaps Petra used his instructions for her own benefit, but he and his father couldn't have done without her. She'd been with them several years, and by now was like one of those English butlers who plan the shopping, clean, iron, let visitors in or turn them away, remember dates and domestic deadlines, know the best repairmen for the appliances and run the household in such a way that they become indispensable to their employers. She lived in the same building, in a dark flat on the lower-ground floor, so they could count on her for any unforeseen event at any time. On top of that, she was an excellent cook.

'Did you take your tablets?' he asked. His night table was covered in bottles of Nembutal, Zantac, Prednisona, painkillers...

'Yes.'

'Let's eat, then. I'll help you up.'

Corona took his father by the arm to the dining room. Through the pyjamas he could feel his father's thinness from the pain and chemotherapy. He could feel the bones that were still held together by tendons which became surprisingly tough when they tensed, and betrayed the strength with which his father was delaying the inevitable. A bird hanging on to the branch of a tree amidst the systematic destruction of a hurricane.

They sat at the table Petra had set, and his father looked impatiently at the steaming casserole, a drop of spittle shining on his lip. His tongue and taste buds gave him the only pleasure he could still allow himself, as they still sent and received accurate brain signals better than any other part of his body. The doctor had said that one of the most common side effects of the chemo was a reduction in the sense of taste, and possibly a loss of appetite, as everything would taste metallic. However, that hadn't been the case with his father. At the table, his face became visibly happier.

His father served himself plenty of vegetables, and didn't wait for Corona to be seated to start chewing, making dull clicking noises like the sound of a frog diving into a pond. Manuel Corona was still surprised at his father's appetite, a hunger unaffected by discomfort or medication, as if food was the best antidote against the spread of the cancer. He'd often wondered whether his father's illness was a consequence of having worked at the power station for thirty years, even if doctors denied any direct, provable link.

Some days his father spent the moments they were together enumerating all his complaints about his pain, the way Petra treated him or the state of the world according to the TV news. But this was one of those meals during which they barely talked, both opening their mouths only to swallow with their customary greed. They both finished the vegetables at the same time, and Corona got up to fetch the second course.

When he came back with the roast, he stopped for a moment, surprised at how violently his father's skull – hairless from the chemotherapy – moved, as his jaws chewed on a piece of bread. No other part of his body gave such a clear omen of death. His pale, yellow skin, lined with dark veins, lacking the healthy sheen of ordinary baldness, and the clarity of the joins between the bones of the cranium, formed the exact model of a skull.

He felt such a burst of pity that the tray with the roast shook in his hands. Pity for his father and also for himself, for he foresaw an imminent future in which he would be alone, seated at that same table, with the same yellowish tablecloth and the same cutlery, his feet on the same carpet that was beginning to fray and show bald patches. He let his father serve himself first and he disguised his trembling by drinking a glass of water, carefully wiping his mouth and meticulously placing the utensils back in front of him. Then he cut a piece of meat and put it in his mouth. But although he usually came home from school with a voracious appetite, he was no longer hungry. The meat seemed tough and gristly and became a ball between his teeth that he couldn't swallow despite the eighteen times he had chewed it. When he looked at his father, who was wolfing down the meat with a satisfaction that seemed almost trance-like, he realised it wasn't the toughness of the meat that was stopping him eating, but the complete absence of saliva in his mouth.

⌒

'I think we've got something, Lieutenant,' said Ortega, one of the young officers he had assigned to the case. He had also assigned a female officer, the first woman he'd had under his direct command.

'Give me the details.'

'The only FN 1900 we have proof of in Breda was registered at the law courts. It was confiscated from a coffee smuggler in 1962, with bullets and a silencer.'

'Silencer as well?'

'Oh yes.'

'That would explain the fact that no one around heard the shot. And the date fits the manufacture date for the bullet casing.'

'But that's all we've got. The following year it still shows up in the inventory, but it's not there in '64. We had a look and it wasn't put up for sale at the public auction of weapons that year, either.'

'So?'

'We think someone on the inside must have taken it. A gun like that is a jewel. It has incredible accuracy for its size, a collector's piece,' he said with a connoisseur's enthusiasm. Gallardo glanced at the woman and noticed the hint of an ironic smile at her partner's fervour. 'We've talked to one of the two judges who worked there at the time. The other died seven years ago. He told us something that may be of interest.'

He looked at his partner for a moment. He seemed to hesitate whether to let her carry on with the explanation, but as she remained silent, he continued:

'It seems that a colleague, someone who was really into guns, wasn't very scrupulous about this sort of stuff. He knows that, on more than one occasion, this colleague let people he trusted keep particularly good pieces. He said that they signed a paper as a procedure, and the gun magically had a new owner. But none of those papers are left.'

'The old methods, then?' Gallardo confirmed. He wanted to make it quite clear, in front of this officer, and especially in front of the woman (neither being over twenty-eight, and neither having been born when the pistol was confiscated) that even though he was fifteen years older than them, he had no connection with the era they were discussing.

'Yes, the old methods.'

'And there's no chance of finding those papers?'

'We don't think so. The present judge assured us. If you like, we can investigate further, but there's probably nothing left in the archives,' the woman put in.

'Yeah, let's keep on looking a bit longer. But I'll send some-one else. You two have got enough on your plate.'

He leaned back in his chair and looked at the two officers, so different from each other, in a way that resisted the homogeni-sation imposed by their uniforms and their milieu. Whereas Ortega was one of those men, indifferent to the cold, who wore his sleeves rolled up all year round to show off his biceps, and had a tendency to violence that would make him dangerous without the self-discipline and honesty, Andrea was quite slim, and the lieutenant wondered what qualities had compensated for her physical fragility when she entered the force.

'You've done a good job. Hopefully it'll lead us somewhere, because when we find the owner of the pistol, we'll probably have found the one who shot it. You'll need to draw up a list of all the people who worked at the law courts in '63 and '64. We'll have to talk to all of them. The ones who are still alive.'

'We've got one already, Lieutenant. While we were there we thought it might be useful,' the woman said, pushing a printed sheet of paper towards him.

'Thanks,' he said, bending towards her to take it: a dozen names with their addresses at the time and the years they'd worked there.

Andrea was closer now, next to his desk, her hips almost touching the edge, and while the lieutenant examined the sheet he was aware of her proximity. At first, when she was posted at the station, he didn't like the fact that a woman had been assigned to him, for he could foresee a source of conflict and tension with the other officers, all of them men. But in the few months he'd seen her at work, her willingness to work hard both during training and while on duty, her vigilance and her organisational skills had caught his eye. He liked how seriously she took her tasks, even the most trivial ones; he liked the emphatic, energetic way she read suspects their rights, so differ-ent from the tired routine of the veterans; he even liked the way she drove, attentive to every movement, and he often let her drive the car he was using, not something he let anyone else do. Besides, in civilian clothes, which were less coarsely-cut than the uniform, she became an attractive woman. He'd seen her talking to Ortega a few times outside the station. Although they were so different, he wondered if there might be something other than camaraderie between them, and he was surprised to find that he didn't like that possibility at all. Perhaps it had been a mistake to assign them together so often: a young man and woman on the beat at night, along lonely roads. Once this job was over he would have to review the situation.

8

He was drinking his second cup of coffee at the kitchen table, waiting until it was time to open the shop. Rocío had just taken Alba to school, and he'd stayed home on his own, smoking and going over the day's work, and trying to forget that his daughter had wet her bed again that night. Once again he told himself that her disorder was not necessarily linked to the separation, that this relapse was due to her first tense days at school with a new teacher – how difficult it was for Alba to like a stranger! – and that it would all pass as soon as she got used to the new routine. As a child, he too would feel weak at the knees at the start of term; he was almost forced to school by his mother and María, had to be torn from his mother's skirt, and took quite a while to get over his fear of the new teacher, who invariably seemed an ogre every year. Besides, many children of separated parents were strong, cheerful, brilliant in their studies, calmer and more responsible than those parents who had conceived them, as if to teach them a lesson through their early stability.

But he knew the whole morning had been disturbed by the image of the stained sheets; the memory would appear before him at any moment no matter what he was doing. And it was always associated with Dulce's absence, so insistently that longing was beginning to turn to anger, as every time it happened it was he who had to deal with it alone, without any help. On those mornings, any hint of nostalgia or understanding disappeared, and he only felt a repressed rage towards his ex-wife which he couldn't share with anyone. He felt like the first man to test a parachute, pushed from a plane into the void. He tried to persuade himself that, here at the beginning of the twenty-first century, humanity should offer ways to overcome all difficulties, or if not, at least the pleasures to help forget them. But as he fell he found nothing to hold on to.

He longed for the moment when peace would come. As with many other broken marriages he had known, he expected that the old troubles would be forgotten one day, and that they would be able to see each other without hatred or reproach, like two old comrades who hide the depth of their wounds and salvage their friendship by blaming whatever made them enemies on others, or on chance.

The bell rang and he went to open the door, thinking that Alba or Rocío must have forgotten something. It was neither of them.

On the landing, two officers of the Guardia Civil, a man and a woman, both very young, asked him his name and whether they could have a word with him. They had a bureaucratic neutrality that was neither kind nor intimidating, while a firm, smooth pressure emanated more from their uniforms than their manner.

'What's happened?' he asked them once they were in the living room.

'Nothing serious, don't worry,' said the woman. 'We'd just like to ask you some questions about your father, about his job.'

'My father ... my father died many years ago,' he said, unable to conceal a tremor in his voice. They were finally there. Despite his concealment, they had found him out.

'We know. That's why we're coming to talk to you,' said the man, moving his shoulders inside his shirt, as if he felt uncomfortable inside it, or was too hot in this house with its closed windows, and where the smell of biscuits and baby soap lingered, even a hint of urine, typical of households with children.

'What would you like to know?'

'I assume you've heard about the murder last week at the school.'

'Of course, hasn't everyone? No one talks about anything else in Breda.'

'We believe the weapon they used came from the courts where your father worked.' It was now the woman's turn, while the man looked at him. They didn't interrupt each other or cut into the other's questions, as if they took turns when speaking according to a strategy whose rules he was unable to guess. 'A rare make, and a bullet from the year it was manufactured.'

'And?'

'Did your father have a gun?'

'No,' he lied. Both looked at him in silence, neither disappointed nor pleased. The woman made a note of something and then they both let a few seconds pass, as if they didn't know how to continue, the woman glancing at the decor of the living room, while the man fidgeted inside his greenish uniform, showing an expansive strength that contrasted with the woman's femininity.

'Are you sure?' asked the man, with an insistence that was perhaps just his way of warning that the first time round they never believed anything they were told.

'My father died when I was twelve. If he'd had... a gun,' he said, quickly correcting himself, well aware of how close he'd come to making a definitive mistake: just one word could save him or damn him, 'he wouldn't have told me. My mother died a month ago. She'd kept many of his things, but there wasn't a gun among them.'

'And you never heard him talk about guns? About a collector or someone who liked them?'

'I don't remember. Besides, wouldn't you need a licence? I'm pretty sure my father didn't have one. And we didn't find any documents like that among his papers.'

'Times were different. What we're looking for left the court depot in a way that wasn't very... orthodox,' explained the woman vaguely. And with that hint of a confidence Julián Monasterio realised that their visit was part of a routine investigation and that he was not implicated to a greater degree than anyone else.

'I don't think it would have ended up in my father's hands. He was a quiet man, a grey bureaucrat and, I've always thought, an honest and efficient one. He was never into that kind of thing. He didn't even like hunting.'

He fell silent, wary of getting carried away and giving more explanations than he was being asked for. Presently both officers shook his hand and began moving towards the door.

'I'm sorry I couldn't be of more help.'

The man turned to add:

'What we've just told you is confidential. Please don't share it with anyone.'

'Of course. I'll bear that in mind.'

He closed the door behind them, listened to the noise of the lift, and went to the window to watch them from behind the curtain. He saw them get into a car and drive off. Relieved, but moving swiftly, he phoned María and explained the visit and everything that had been said. They would probably come and talk to her, and she should tell them the same thing.

'I told you we should've handed it over to the Guardia Civil, even if that meant being fined,' she replied in that older-sister tone she still couldn't help.

'I know, and you're right. But we couldn't have foreseen a coincidence like this. Now there's no turning back. I'm only asking you, if they come and see you, to tell them you've never heard a gun mentioned at home. Oh, and don't say pistol or revolver, just gun, as they haven't specified which it is.'

There was a long silence at the other end. María, who was always good at predicting problems, but not so good at thinking up solutions, must have been gauging the risks and consequences of agreeing to her younger brother's whim. Like anyone with a strong, methodical personality, she was convinced that chance kept its darkest moves for the weak, the careless and the unhappy.

'It's the best we can do,' he insisted.

'Where do you have it now?'

'In the deposit box at the bank, with the *arras*, Dad's jewellery and some paperwork,' he replied. That was the hardest lie. When he decided to keep the gun, he guessed he'd have to deceive some people, but he wouldn't have thought his own sister would be one of them. He thought of the detective he'd just hired and quietly prayed he did something to ease the pressure soon. What would his sister do if she found out that the gun had been taken from his safe and had probably been used to shoot a man in the back of the neck? He wasn't sure she would agree to hide that.

'Are you sure?'

'I told you. Two days ago I went to put some papers away. The gun was still there, in the book.'

'Fine,' he heard her accept with a resigned sigh. 'If they come to ask me, I'll tell them I've never heard of any pistol.'

'Gun,' he corrected.

'Gun. But if things get complicated, I'll stick to that version. I told you before that it was better to hand it over and that I didn't want anything to do with it.'

'Thanks, María. Don't worry about it anymore, it's not worth it.'

He had hardly hung up and was trying to calm himself when the phone rang next to his ear, like a released animal jumping relentlessly up into his face. He didn't dare answer it straight away, fearing more bad news. All around him lived happy people who'd never felt tempted to smash their fists into the phone, to shoot the messenger. All around him lived happy people who received congratulations for no particular reason, invitations to parties they'd never consider going to, calls from women ready to share a few hours of laughter and pleasure, requests from friends to watch a film or a football match or to chat about nothing for a while. Yet in the last few weeks, the phone had been for him nothing but a direct link to misfortune. And so he picked up with the suspicion of one who expects nothing good.

'Good morning, could I speak to Julián Monasterio, please?' It was a man's voice.

'Speaking.'

'I'm calling from your daughter's school.'

What now? he thought. He was still so caught up in the previous two conversations that he immediately thought the call would bring some further complication regarding the gun, some loose end linking him to the teacher's death. And it wouldn't just link him. If there was one thing he'd feared from the start, it was any possible consequences for his daughter, the drain water from the storm he'd unleashed, which would stain her with its filthy silt. No, he could not allow anything else to weigh on Alba, he could not allow her to think that the happy years granted to any child of her age no longer existed for her. Her sadness was already excessive, and she had an adult's gaze in a six-year-old body. He couldn't bear that his daughter was more miserable than himself.

'Is anything wrong?'

'Nothing serious, don't worry,' said the man. He must have noticed the anxiety in his voice, and quickly reassured him. 'I was only calling to ask you to come to the school to talk about Alba.'

'But is anything wrong?'

'No. I'm the director of studies. Her tutor and the speech therapist think Alba would profit from some individual support lessons. At least for a while. It seems she's acting a bit oddly in class.'

'Oddly?'

'A little. Yesterday the caretaker surprised her outside the school, trying to go home during school hours. She won't respond to the teacher and apparently doesn't talk to her classmates either. We think it would be good to take her away from class for some time every week, in order to help her. But we'd rather explain all this here, not on the phone. Do you think you could come over?'

'Of course, what time?'

'Classes finish at one.'

'All right. I'll be there at one.'

He dialled the shop and told Ernesto he'd be a bit late. His employee didn't say anything, but judging by his bluntness when he rang off he wasn't too thrilled. There were several jobs pending and Ernesto would have to be in two places at once. Julián Monasterio knew that sometimes he was exceeding the terms of Ernesto's contract, and that, if he went on doing so, the lad would leave; but in the last couple of weeks he couldn't help it. Everything seemed to conspire against him: he had never liked others doing his share of the work, yet now he did nothing but request it; he liked doing things calmly but now everything moved too fast. Words he had barely heard in his life – pistol, murder, robbery, abandonment, separation – were now being repeated so often that soon they would be painfully familiar to him.

He lay down on the sofa and lit another cigarette. It was barely two hours since he'd jumped out of bed, but he'd been through so much that he felt tired already. He tried to isolate each problem – the civil guards' questions, his sister's reluctance to become his accomplice, the calls from the school and to the store – and to work out if he had done or said anything wrong that could be set straight. But he was unable to separate them in his mind. They were all overshadowed by his daily unhappiness, Dulce's absence and the dull pain he still felt. And all that sorrow kept him in a state of constant indecision, stopped him gaining the lucidity he needed to gauge the rightness or wrongness of his actions.

Everything had collapsed in on him at the same time, a weight greater than he could support. Again, he told himself that he must endure it until it faded or until he became indifferent. Every misfortune and every intense joy are ephemeral intervals in the daily routine, he told himself, and one can only wait with patience for pain or pleasure to run their course. Yet for the first time he feared that if he repeated these words too often, there would come a time when he wouldn't find in them the strength or the consolation or the hope that had so far allowed him to carry on.

Little by little, cigarette after cigarette, the problem of his daughter prevailed over the rest. Now he realised he'd overlooked it for too long, adopting the same attitude as his ex-wife, the same lame excuse for not facing it: 'You weren't very talkative either, when I first met you.' He felt a pang of remorse: he knew next to nothing about five hours a day in the life of his daughter. In fact, he didn't even remember the name of her new teacher. Alba had told him, but he didn't pay enough attention to retain it. Although he knew he gave her care and protection, he was positive he had not involved himself enough in her education. Where school was concerned, he only asked her routine questions about what she'd done that day and told her to work hard and be a good girl to her teacher and classmates. True, he promptly bought her all the materials she needed, signed any authorisation for a school trip, and paid the parents' association fees on time, but not much else. So far he hadn't taken a single look at her textbooks or exercise books, and he hadn't asked if she needed any help.

He would be there at one to talk to the teacher.

Once he had decided that, he went back to the phone and dialled the detective's number to tell him about the Guardia Civil's visit. What they had discovered might make complications if they found someone who remembered and could prove that his father had been given that gun. There was no answer, and he left a message on Cupido's voicemail saying he needed to speak to him urgently.

9

I know I'm not to blame for everything that's happened. So why can't I get rid of this sense of guilt? she whispered as she looked at herself in the office mirror. She was sitting on the carpet, leaning back against the table, already tired of her work although term had only just begun. Since Larrey's death she hadn't been sleeping well. She arrived at school tired, and found it hard to go over exercises repeatedly with the children.

She had never felt so bored with her job before; she wasn't like so many of her colleagues, who watched the clock from the moment they arrived at school and counted the hours until the end of the day, the days until the next holiday, the years until retirement.

She didn't think she'd done too badly up to now. If there was something her specialism demanded, it was patience. The patience to get wary, mistrustful children to trust her; the patience to get them to open mouths that were often almost hermetically sealed, to get them to talk, so that their tongues would loosen and they would learn to articulate every word they were capable of thinking. She knew that any pupil, no matter how high his marks, would never achieve much socially without being able to express himself so that others would not make jokes or mock him. She knew intelligent students who had dropped out after compulsory education because of their inability to overcome a speech defect. Ashamed and insecure, they looked on as their phonatory system lagged far behind the speed of their minds. It was curious, she thought, that while her colleagues constantly struggled to keep pupils quiet, her job was precisely the opposite: to make them talk.

Although the contrast made some people – Julita Guzmán, Jaime De Molinos – view her specialism with some disdain, she knew she was a good teacher: patient, efficient, affectionate, and loved by the children. The pride and self-esteem she felt in this gave her the strength to continue as she was. Her job was more to her than a means to a monthly pay cheque, as it might be for a bank clerk or a plumber, who works with inanimate materials – money or water – which are immune to pain. The teaching profession demanded a special sensitivity, for the material one worked with was childhood dreams, and she wanted more than anything for those dreams to play out as long as possible without the inevitable monsters. No one should be denied the only brief period in their lives when it's possible to be happy, when a rubber ball, a windmill, a bag of sweets or a hug and a kiss are enough to create joy in its purest form.

She had to admit she was sometimes a little conceited about her professional skills. She liked the recognition of others, and to make a good impression on her pupils. She'd never been able to curb that expression of her vanity, although she knew that the best education is one in which teaching occurs without leaving a trace. A sapling grows to be a tall, strong tree and the hole it was planted in is no longer visible, nor is the harsh pruning that helped form its shapely crown, nor the cuts where grafts were inserted, nor the place where the surface roots were ploughed up, and nor is the name of the gardener cut into its bark; and so the best education is one that makes a child a relaxed, independent adult who carries no scars of punishments or humiliation, nor too strong a stamp from any particular teacher.

Three years ago, as any inexperienced newcomer in a job would, she had tried to deal with her insecurities by seeking out those colleagues whose ideas, interests and tastes had most in common with her own. The average age of the teaching staff was quite high, and many were nearing retirement: the school was situated at the centre of Breda, and was a coveted posting because of its accessibility and the high academic standard of its pupils, who came from middle-class homes that valued a good education. By and large, the school didn't have any of the serious disciplinary problems of the institutions on the outskirts. In provincial towns like Breda, people still lived around the main square, and old families who had always occupied the historic centre had not yet disappeared, nor given way to that powerful, prolific and unstoppable influx of immigrants and the disenfranchised, who always seemed to be lying in wait for the big houses at the heart of a city to fall into ruin. She had secured the post despite her lack of experience because her specialism was one in which competition wasn't as fierce as among general teachers.

She'd found a common bond with Larrey and Nelson almost immediately, not so much because they were the youngest members of staff – even if they were pushing forty – as because they too seemed to like their work and didn't discuss it only to complain. She wasn't so sure about the others. True, there were some who were professional, but most put up with their jobs as a more or less tiresome way of making money that didn't require too much effort and had long holidays.

Last year, she had found out too late that she had been deceived in Nelson, and that he too was one of those who see their profession, not as part of themselves, but as tedious labour to which they give only their time. Why had she let things go so far with him, why hadn't she stopped before it became a dangerous game?

It took her several months to find an answer that was not very reassuring, to understand that a secret relationship like theirs – between a young female teacher and an attractive, married male teacher, one that is based on concealment, on the stimulus of risk, on kissing in secret, on their hands brushing past when they met in a corridor, on discovering that caution can be as exciting as a caress, on looking at each other in a staff meeting knowing that the forty faces around suspect nothing of your secret – cannot stop halfway, but has to go further than any union sanctified by ceremony and habit. In a secret relationship, the lovers have to reinvent the wheel: what is already known of love and pleasure will not do. In a secret relationship the lovers can barely tell the difference between the lips and the teeth, a kiss and a bite, tenderness and fierceness. And if one day it becomes routine, that is the moment it will begin to die. The lover who already has some domestic stability – monotonous perhaps, but not so unsatisfying or unhappy as to destroy it – will always choose, faced with two similar options, the one most likely to give him social acceptance, comfort and peace.

And she thought then that she was in love with Nelson, and followed his every whim. Yet she would never play the victim; with him she had reached the kind of fulfilment and intensity she'd almost never experienced before. And although it was he who had initiated each risk, all their decisions had been taken together, accepted by both, so she felt she could not really blame him. Only when she became pregnant did she discover how, when things go wrong, it is the woman who has more to lose; how much more easily and quickly the man withdraws into the shade in the face of the sudden explosion and stench of firedamp.

Nelson had refused to accept any other solution than abortion. When she told him that she was in two minds, that she didn't know whether to keep the child, without asking anything of him – neither help, nor company, nor a name, and least of all money – he used arguments that appealed to her well-being as a woman, as if she was his only concern, and not because he was terrified of confronting his wife, his colleagues, everyone around him. He barely referred to himself, as if it was she who would be the worst affected if she did go ahead with it. He knew that if he had used any typically masculine argument – calling the child's paternity into doubt, or blaming her for not preventing it – she would never have listened and would have seen it through to the end.

Once there were no more doubts – the most painful of her life – she planned the Easter holidays around it: she made an appointment at the clinic on the first day so she would have the rest of the holiday to weather the pain she imagined would follow, to cry and to wipe away the traces of tears.

In the end, it turned out not to be necessary. She always thought it was the stress of those two weeks of waiting that did it, as if her body had ignored its own metabolism and instead had decided to obey the dictates of her will. And although one morning, waking up to intense pain, and seeing the stained sheets, she thought that the dark clot on the white linen would spare her the days of anxiety, depression and tears, a few hours later she knew that this painful episode wasn't over. The loss of that minute follicle, that didn't even look like flesh, that was barely a membrane like a small brownish vegetable, left her with a sense of emptiness that seemed disproportionate to its size. Sometimes she would remain immobile for no reason, sensing her blood circulating, rushing through her veins in search of a lost pearl. At other times, while walking down the street, or queuing at the supermarket, she felt that other women knew, just by looking at her, what had happened, and she only just managed to fight back the tears when given kind words or a pleasant smile that, in her imagination, negated all accusation, all harshness.

She spent the following weeks in a daze, like a freshwater fish thrown into the sea, for whom the fluid seems the same – it has been returned to the water and can swim – but whose gills become hardened by salt and cannot breathe properly. Every time she saw a mother with a pushchair she was overwhelmed by an odd mixture of tenderness and shame which she found difficult to shake off. Then she tried not to think, often unsuccessfully. She pictured herself pregnant: her belly would bump into the kitchen surfaces as she did the dishes; she wouldn't be able to sit so easily on the carpet of her office and would have to walk very carefully across the playground where the kids were playing with balls; she would wear maternity clothes, non-elasticated tights and flat, comfortable shoes; her lips would be a little sensitive, as if chapped by the cold; her freckles would turn a deeper colour.

Going back to work helped her out of her depression. The only person who knew and could have helped her too, Nelson, had no more than kind words for her, almost always rushed, as if now that it was all over, he were afraid of her, of seeing her alone, of looking her in the eye. All his confidence, brilliance and wit disappeared when she was present.

As for Gustavo, she never knew if he suspected anything, but judging from his behaviour he must have done. In his free time he would come to her office for a chat, telling her inconsequential stories about his classes and the little accidents on the playing field that worried him. He took her for coffee on their breaks and sometimes waited for her after school, and on one occasion even took her on one of his bike rides. He was like a doctor who gives the patient a placebo and lets time heal an illness for which there is no other cure.

One May morning two months later, she looked at herself in the mirror before leaving for work, and was surprised at the assertive, attractive image she saw, all the more so because she hadn't been aware of the change or of having done anything to bring it about. She was wearing a short-sleeved shirt and a skirt just above her knees which gave her a buoyant, youthful look, and a feeling of optimism. Suddenly she realised it was possible to endure a painful illness, a mutilation or the death of a loved one, and a few weeks later to smile again as happily as before. As she put on her low heels, she momentarily felt the old painful memories, but cast them off by looking at herself in the mirror again. She knew she was attractive and all that remained was to see if her body would respond to another's touch with the same ease and intensity as before. At a certain point, she'd come to feel that what had happened to her might wither and shrivel her irreparably, in the same way that some African women have their ability to feel pleasure removed along with their clitoris. She knew that every wound left a scar, every accident made one more cautious; she knew that pain generated the fear of reliving it, and suspected that she wouldn't escape this unharmed. In the first weeks she had sworn never to sleep with a man again. Yet now, at the height of spring, she doubted the wisdom of that vow: she needed to know that everything in her body still functioned, that the blood flowed to every crevice. She felt like a little girl who falls painfully while running, looks at and cleans her wounds, but then stretches her legs to make sure she can still run.

It was the beginning of June. Two colleagues retiring at the end of that year threw a party for everyone. She hadn't gone out since everything had happened, and though this time she drank more than usual, alcohol was not the only reason why she accepted Moisés's offer to walk her home at the end of the evening, albeit keeping it hidden from the others. When she opened the door and let him in she was fully aware of what she was doing. That night she liked Momo, she liked him a lot. Ever since he'd arrived at the school she had noticed his glances, his desire to talk to her and be with her, and on two occasions she had kindly turned down his invitations to go out. At first because of Nelson, and later because of the bad memories. But as she closed the door she knew very well what was going to happen.

She wanted to spend the night with him. They'd danced to a few songs and she'd been attracted by his strong shoulders, by the warm, clean feeling of him and by his fresh youthfulness – he was six years younger than her – which was an almost insulting contrast to the general decrepitude of the party that was celebrating two retirements amidst envious congratulations. Next to him, even Larrey and Nelson seemed slightly worn, older and a little faded, as if they'd stayed up all night.

But it was not all about physical attraction. Thinking about it later, she reasoned that in her impulse towards Momo there was also a need to go back to her own youth, to the Rita of five years ago, and to forget about the thorny present that gave her no pleasure.

In contrast to Nelson's allure, his neat skilful hands and his experience, Moisés had the flexibility and innocence of those bodies which have not yet acquired the unnecessary accretions of time. His cropped hair, longish sideburns and silver earring were charming and fresh, nothing like the grey, standardised elegance of the other guests. She suspected he was at the party because of her, as he didn't really know anyone else. Maybe he had been invited formally or casually, like any other staff member at the school, without being expected to turn up, and he had taken the opportunity to be near her for an evening, somewhere that wasn't the school, surrounded by children and shouting.

He didn't fit in with any group of people, and barely spoke as they were eating, but he seemed to be listening attentively and she saw him trying hard to laugh at the old jokes, hiding his boredom. He sat near her at the long table, and she noticed that he drank hardly any wine and behaved with such restraint that at times it seemed fake, though doubtless convincing to the older teachers nearby: a strong lad with hair cropped like a prison inmate who nevertheless didn't look threatening; who wore an earring but was not effeminate. He was discreet, and showed no interest in her that could be observed by the others.

In bed everything had gone well. She had no problems becoming aroused and following the pace set almost entirely by him: quite fast, and again half an hour later. Even at dawn, before he left, she had come intensely one last time on the receding tide of her previous pleasure, although she'd never liked this moment much, as it deprived her of the deep, restorative sleep that always overwhelmed her afterwards. So, everything had gone well, but once her body had passed the test she didn't particularly want to repeat it on another night. Compared to her, Momo was almost a child, and she was aware that this fleeting adventure would never bear fruit in her heart. It wasn't so much the difference in age as one of beliefs, ideas, habits, culture, disappointments, morals and ambitions. Momo could live ten years while she lay in a coma and the difference would still be there on waking.

A few days later, when he insisted on seeing her again, she told him there would be no second time. She felt she didn't owe him anything: she had asked for nothing she herself hadn't given. Momo resisted at first, but seemed resigned when he said goodbye with one last hug.

There was a knock at the door and Rita stood up before calling, 'Come in'. Matilde Cuaresma was bringing a girl whom the director of studies had mentioned before. She was expecting her. The girl looked up with big fearful eyes, and took in the room, so different from the classrooms, the carpet on the floor, the full-length mirror, the lamp in the shape of Pinocchio, the bright, lively decor. A room so different from the rest of the school it seemed as if it had been stolen from the home of some happy children and transplanted wholesale.

'She's the pupil I told you about. You have to see her.' The teacher urged the girl forward a little, firmly but cautiously, as you urge a dog about to be abandoned, or a seemingly docile cat that might arch its back, ruffle its fur and show its claws and needle-sharp teeth. 'I don't know what's wrong with her, but she doesn't speak.'

'Well, it's early days. Term has only just begun,' Rita replied, a little annoyed at this habit some of her colleagues had of bringing kids to her office at the slightest sign of a problem, as if incapable of solving it themselves, and never willing to give the children any time in the classroom to break through their shyness or uneasiness.

'Corona agrees that you should see her,' she replied. 'She was very quiet in kindergarten, but now she seems to have fallen completely silent.'

Rita bent towards the girl smiling, took her hands and asked her:

'What's your name?'

The girl kept her eyes on the floor, her long eyelashes almost hiding the honey-coloured, green-speckled irises, refusing to look at her, with the kind of obstinacy which Rita knew well and which, after a few weeks, she nearly always conquered.

'I'm Rita, I've got a very ugly name. Don't you want to tell me yours?'

'She's called Alba Monasterio,' replied the teacher impatiently.

'Alba. That's a very pretty name. I think I'll have it for myself. I'd like to be called that.' She touched her hair.

The girl looked up for the first time, to see whether her face bore out the kindness of her words.

'She seems autistic,' put in Matilde Cuaresma.

Rita looked at the teacher from below, not hiding her irritation at the fact that such a serious diagnosis had been made in front of the girl with no thought given to all the implications.

'And what's she like with the other children?' Rita asked.

'Doesn't talk either. During breaks she's mostly on her own. And yesterday the caretaker saw her on the other side of the fence, trying to go home.'

She may not talk, thought Rita, *but she's listening to everything we say now, and who could reply to those kinds of comments?*

'It'd be best if she came to see you now, at the start of term, before any more time goes by and there's nothing we can do,' she said in a softer tone, simulating concern. Yet when she tried to be kind, her scorn for the girl, her hatred for the fact that she had the courage to remain alone and in silence, without needing anyone, seemed to grow worse. 'Her parents are separated, you know,' she added.

'That has nothing to do with it,' replied Rita, standing up.

'We've told the father. He's coming to see you. At one o'clock.'

She took a deep breath when Matilde Cuaresma left the office. It seemed that Nelson's new regime had changed nothing.

She sat down on the carpet beside the girl and began talking to her, using her name – Alba, Alba, Alba – every time she said anything to her, asking her how old she was, what she liked, what were the names of her friends. The girl did not utter one word in reply and only nodded or shook her head, her calm eyes fixed on the colour of the carpet, those brown eyes with green specks, like black poplar leaves just before they fall. *What are you afraid of?* she asked herself. *How can I convince you that once you've told me, whatever it is will start to disappear?* She touched her head again and, since half an hour had already gone by, walked her to her classroom. She would speak to the father and find room for her in her schedule.

When she returned to the office she saw Moisés waiting for her by the door. He had some papers in his hand and gave her one. It called for a staff meeting, but when she read the agenda she saw that it contained none of the issues that, in his proposals, Nelson had said he would address.

Moisés entered the office after her and closed the door behind him. Rita repressed a gesture of irritation. She had not spoken to him alone since the start of term, and had no intention of doing so now. They'd had a fling, but she'd made it clear before the summer that it was finished and there was no point in bringing it up again.

'Rita.'

'Yes?' she replied. The way he said her name, softly, as if trying to wake someone, she guessed what was coming.

'Would you like to go out tonight?' he asked, with the smile that was so successful with the fourteen and fifteen-year-old girls who sought him out at breaktime. It was his first question, totally direct, and with that slightly harassing tone that comes when love and desire are displayed openly. But he wasn't aware of the nuance: he was still too naive for that, too young to have a pleasurable adventure without turning it into an infatuation.

'No, Momo. It's not a good idea. We've already talked about it.'

'Are you busy? I can give you a hand at home if you need anything.'

Once he had helped her hang some paintings and move furniture, and he'd been happy to share those small domestic tasks with her. She liked keeping her flat clean and tidy, and changing the decor perhaps too often; but such a naive way of trying to win her over, even though she might have liked it in the past, now, after what had happened, seemed to her clumsy and slightly irritating.

'No, I don't need anything at home. It's not that. I just don't want us to see each other any more. There's no point,' she replied, trying to rein in the increasing irritation she was feeling at everyone that morning.

'There is to me.'

His imploring, watery gaze, helpless and freighted with innocence, might have convinced any woman over thirty to hold him to her breast and caress his clean, cropped hair. But she realised that her maternal instincts, if she had recovered them after what had happened, could not be awakened by anyone who already had teeth and knew how to talk and walk. Suddenly, unable to move, she saw him in a new light. She knew him well enough to suspect that he was dissembling and that, beneath his sincere wish to be with her, there was something calculated about his behaviour, the way he poured all this effort into an adult desire. *Why is he a conscientious objector?* she suddenly wondered. *Is it because he has genuine moral objections to carrying a gun, or was it simply convenient, to avoid the stress of discipline, military hardship and a few nights on the watch?* And just as she did with some of her pupils, when she drew out from their most trivial phrases those sounds that were the key to their diction problems, so she drew out from her own thoughts those three words – *carrying a gun* – which all of a sudden, like a magnet placed under a sheet of paper that shaped iron filings, brought back the image of Gustavo Larrey dead in the office, lying by the table, with that small bullet wound in the back of his neck that had barely bled. Could it be possible that a lad of just over twenty had killed a man, and that his voice was steady as he smiled and asked a woman to go out with him and embrace him?

But what's wrong with me? she thought, rejecting a mental picture that seemed so repulsive that she had to close her eyes and rub them to erase any sign that it had been there. *Is it possible that my ability to trust has died, and that I see no one as guiltless except the children who come here for me to put a pebble on their tongues?*

'No, Momo,' she repeated, unable to find better words, reflecting that between a man and a woman there are many ways of indicating attraction and sexual desire, but very few ways of refusing that will not hurt the other and also close off all doubt and possibility of reply.

'It's because of Nelson, right?'

'What do you mean?' she almost shouted. The sympathy she'd tried hard to maintain disappeared, giving way to blind anger. She would not allow an insolent kid to invade her privacy, to throw stones into the water just to see what monsters they could raise. Because he couldn't know anything. Nelson and she had always been very careful, and even if someone might have been suspicious, no one could know for sure.

'Have you gone back to him?' he insisted. His tone had changed too, as if her anger was contagious, and now he sounded like a jealous boyfriend demanding an explanation.

'I haven't gone back to him because I've never been *with* him. Is that clear? And if I do get together with someone in the future, it's certainly none of *your* business. Who do you think you are? Now please, get out.'

He hesitated before her for a few seconds, as if he still had something to say and, like her pupils, couldn't find the right words. Then, finally, he dropped his head and left, closing the door behind him.

Her legs were trembling and she had to lean against the table so as not to fall. The bell that marked the end of the day sounded very distant, the children's voices coming to her like an unreal echo of runaway horses. She sat in the armchair, waiting for everyone to leave and for the school to fall silent. She was not afraid of large, resonant spaces; on the contrary, it was in small enclosed rooms that she was more likely to feel uncomfortable.

She didn't want to see anyone or to say goodbye with the routine 'see you tomorrow' as her colleagues rushed off, relieved that work and the children's ceaseless demands were over for the day. She realised she had no one to talk to, no one to confide in, no shoulder to cry on. Her parents lived in another city – though she couldn't have told them anything anyway – and the two or three friends she usually went out with wouldn't have understood; they would have been surprised and a little offended at her for keeping so many secrets from them for so long, and perhaps even a bit annoyed for not having worked it out themselves. They would have comforted and reproached her – none would ask her if she'd been happy while it lasted, or if there was something they could do – and she needed neither of these. If only Gustavo was there, on the track or in his office by the gym, to tell her some old story, and watch over her with that kindness and indulgence he always showed. She missed him unbearably.

There was a knock at the door. She feared it might be Moisés again; before he left she'd noticed him hesitate over whether to say something more. But the man who came in was about thirty-five, dark, of medium height. There was something familiar about him, not so much in his features, but in the cautious way he looked around the room before moving towards the desk, as if he was entering a workshop where dangerous or fragile materials were handled. Then he looked down at the carpet, and she recognised the gesture. His daughter had done the same half an hour before.

'I'm Alba Monasterio's father. I got a call this morning, asking me to come and talk to you. I hope I didn't keep you waiting.'

'Do sit down, please. I'm Rita. I'd rather be on first name terms, if that's OK with you.'

'Fine. Great,' he accepted. Then he added: 'What's going on with Alba?'

His voice betrayed an anxiety that bordered on physical pain. He'd sat on the edge of the chair, as if he was afraid of hearing something so terrible he would have to run out. *He too is afraid. Like his daughter. Like me*, she thought, suddenly overwhelmed by sympathy.

'Alba was here with me this morning. I'm the school speech therapist. Her tutor is a bit worried because she doesn't talk in class. She doesn't volunteer any comments, or ask for anything, or answer when spoken to. She doesn't seem too comfortable with her classmates, either.'

The man nodded, his gaze sunk on the carpet, his head tilted sideways in a gesture very much like his daughter's.

'She's always been very quiet. But now...'

His hesitation made Rita ask the most delicate question. Not all parents reacted well to it; some refused to answer it or lied, for it meant venturing into difficult, sometimes moral terrain, and this was, after all, only a school, not a church. But she knew it was easier for them to open up to her – whom they saw as someone halfway between a teacher and a therapist – than to the teachers, who were always more concerned about pressing on with the academic programme than with the personal circumstances of the pupils who held it up, always trying too hard to make the class contained and homogeneous, when it was impossible for any group larger than four children to be so.

'Has anything happened at home?'

The man lifted his head and looked her straight in the eye.

'Yes. In the last four months, too much. The two of us live alone now. Her mother left. And a few weeks ago her grandmother died; they were very close. I guess it's too many changes not to feel a bit lost. But at home she does talk, though sometimes she finds it difficult to explain things. I mean, it's not a physical impediment, or autism, or anything of that sort.'

'Of course not.' She was glad that terrifying word had crossed his lips. And she was grateful for the rest of the information, well aware of how hard it had been for him not to hide it. 'Of course it's not autism. I actually don't think it's anything serious. From what you tell me, it's not surprising that Alba has withdrawn into herself. But for her own good, we have to draw her back out.'

'How?'

'By talking. Talking to her a lot. In class, with a new teacher she doesn't know and all the other children looking at her, one can expect her to be shy. Here, it will just be the two of us. We'll work together for half an hour a day. You may have to help her at home if she falls behind with her school work.'

'Fine, whatever's best for her,' he said after a few seconds.

'I think it's for the best. And at home you should keep on talking to her, asking her about her friends at school, what she does in class, if she's being good. Talk to her about things she knows and keep her from those she cannot understand yet. It's so obvious that we sometimes forget it: Alba, all children, need good, conflict-free role models during these years when they are learning about emotions for the first time.'

She stopped, worried that she'd started using the kind of jargon she was always careful to avoid when talking to someone from outside the profession. But the girl's father – he hadn't given his name – was gently nodding his head.

'Keep on talking to her,' he repeated. He got up with a gesture of relief, as if he'd feared something much worse before he arrived. 'I don't know how to thank you for your concern.'

'Not at all. It's my job. But I'd like you to come back if you notice any change in her. For better or worse.'

'I will.'

From the door, as he was about to leave, he turned to ask her, in the same anxious tone as he had used at first:

'Is there any news about the... death?' he said, choosing the least harsh word.

Rita didn't find the question strange as people she knew asked her the same thing every day. A violent death was still the most interesting piece of news in the city, news that had turned the school into a breeding ground for rumour, to the despair of the teachers and in particular the senior team, who in every official statement maintained that the murder was a tragic event that had come from outside the school, and would, of course, not be repeated. Nevertheless, the mothers didn't seem convinced and stayed near the playground after dropping off their children, as if they wanted to extend their protective presence. Rita had even seen some of them come into the building and, unsettled and curious, stop in front of the sealed-off office in the same morbid spirit as people drive slowly by a fatal road accident, staring at the crushed car and the bodies, not fully covered, lying on the road.

'Nothing,' she replied. 'Everyone's at a loss. A private detective was even here the day before yesterday. But no one seems to know anything.'

'Hopefully it will be solved soon.'

'Hopefully. For all our sakes.'

When the noise of his footsteps disappeared down the stairs she realised everyone must have gone and she was alone. She picked up her folder and, on the way out, bumped into Nelson at the door. In spite of herself she gave a little shout and jumped.

'You scared me!'

'I'm sorry. I popped round before, but I heard you talking to someone and I waited till you were alone.'

'Come in. What is it you wanted?'

'Nothing to do with school. Just a chat.'

She could barely suppress a smile thinking about all the visitors she'd had that morning. Everyone came looking for her company, her help or her comfort, without taking into account what she might need. All these visits – Matilde Cuaresma entrusting her with a six-year-old girl as if she were a dangerous little animal she didn't know what to with, Momo begging for a date, and now Nelson – couldn't help but seem to her a bit of an invasion.

'What is it?'

Nelson closed the door behind him for greater privacy, or as if he feared that someone – although the building must have been empty by then – might hear them.

'I've been watching you these last few days and you seem very tense. And worried. We all are, and I understand why you should be even more so. I know you and Gustavo were very close.'

'We were.'

'If there's anything I can do ...'

In spite of his kind tone, Rita felt that his words were for form's sake, and that he was not coming to offer anything, but to ask. A certain sadness broke through the smile until it took over his whole mouth and his eyes veiled by half-closed lids. She wondered if she presented such a helpless image to him; if men's tendency to approach women who they sensed as fragile or unhappy was a purely masculine instinct, as if they knew in a primal, animal way that happy women are also unavailable.

'If you like, we could meet up one afternoon. To talk.'

She remembered that Moisés had used almost the same words, and once again replied in the negative, now with caustic irony.

'No. I don't think it's a good idea.'

'What's wrong, Rita? You talk to me as if I were your enemy.'

'You know what's wrong. What went wrong. I don't want to find myself in a situation like that ever again. And now leave, please. It's pointless talking about this stuff anymore.'

Nelson strode towards the door, offended, and from there said:

'You're not the same Rita I knew.'

'Of course I'm not the same. All of you changed me,' she replied. The way she'd just presented herself made her suddenly want to cry.

'All of us? Is there someone else?'

Her eyes were filling uncontrollably, and a couple of tears rolled down her cheeks.

'It's always the same with you men. You can forgive a woman anything: wasting your money and your time, drinking, being stupid or capricious. But you'll never forgive her for hurting your pride. It's always the same. You'd kill to find out things that do you much more damage once they're known.'

She wiped away her tears as the door slammed shut.

10

He put on his helmet and started pedalling towards the Mayorga road. He'd been told where Saldaña lived, the only parent on the School Council who had left the bar at the same time as the teachers on the evening of the meeting, and could therefore have gone back to the school.

He didn't know what he might get from this interview. Instead of the controlled, precise, cautious words of the teachers, he suspected that, in someone who lives off the land, the brutal and solitary struggle without guarantee of results might produce a manner of expression limited mainly to monosyllables, energetic nods or headshakes, repetitions of the other person's suggestions, and no personal opinions: a mixture of mole-like caution and the cunning usually seen in rural comedy sketches.

He pedalled in a leisurely manner for ten kilometres to the area on the other side of the Lebrón where family homes were scattered in eight- or ten-hectare parcels, most of the land given over to growing sweetcorn, tobacco, tomatoes, fruit trees and pastureland – perennially thirsty crops that up until thirty years before, when the reservoir was built, had been unknown in Breda, but that exploded into growth on the irrigated land, as if for centuries the ground itself had been storing a food that only needed water to make an opulent harvest.

You couldn't miss Saldaña's house by the road; it was a carefully built structure in two units, with a porch and terraces, a lightning conductor and a satellite dish, in permanent use as a house, and which stood out among the more basic, solid and dark structures that had been built as storage spaces and places of rest after work rather than as personal homes. In addition, the patch of land between the house and the road, though it was now neglected, had been a garden not long ago, something that any other farmer in Breda would have considered a ridiculous extravagance. Its spaciousness was unusual in a property given over solely to agriculture, and could still be seen in the design and breadth of its ruined flowerbeds. A few trees for shade, skeletal rosebushes, unpruned lilacs, the remains of some geraniums and decorative plants that had toughened and refused to die – as obstinately as a beautiful woman might endure the privations of a shipwreck, hoping to recover her lost glamour as soon as another ship rescued her and she was asked to dine at the captain's table – made the house look more like a cottage than a farmstead. At the back, there was also a dirty swimming pool, on whose surface fallen leaves shone in the sun like little shavings of gold that refused to sink. Cupido noticed that half of the large back field was planted with sweetcorn, which was beginning to shed its ears and turn that brownish-grey colour that makes its leaves look like swords; on the other half stood fruitless apple, pear and peach trees.

The whole place seemed to belong to a man who draws everything he can from the land, but also knows how to enjoy urban comforts: hence the pool and the garden, the satellite dish and the lightning conductor, the air conditioning, the landscaping, the silence and the independence. A combination of rural labour and civilisation that, although it was no longer strange elsewhere, was still unusual here in Breda, a village built from its foundations in a spirit of defensiveness, toughness and austerity. The farmers Cupido knew were still taciturn, stubborn and unsociable men who boasted of being able to crush a bee-hive between their calloused hands without feeling the stings, to strike a calf dead with a blow to the head, or eat a kilo of cured meat without troubling their bowels.

He got off the bicycle and called from the gate. Presently a man came out on to the porch; he was of indeterminate age, common in those who have a full head of prematurely grey hair. He invited Cupido in, and the detective crossed the thirty metres that separated them. Saldaña was wearing those blue overalls that until two decades before had exclusively been the attire of factory and construction workers, but had found their real practical home amongst rural workers. Yet there was something that didn't fit, as if his strong, yet clean hands, or his close-shaven face, somehow gave the lie to those coarse clothes.

The detective gave his name and the business that brought him there. He was still propping up his bike and Saldaña listened to him from the top of the porch. Hanging down by one of the pillars, swinging in the breeze, was the loose cable from the lightning conductor.

'Who's paying you?' he asked finally. 'The schoolteachers?'

'No, one of the pupils' parents.'

'But it wasn't a pupil who was killed.'

Cupido looked at him, disconcerted, not exactly sure what Saldaña meant by that reply, though aware that it made sense in a way.

'Come in,' Saldaña said suddenly. He opened the front door and gestured him inside.

The detective left the bike leaning against the porch and followed him. He accepted a beer and, while Saldaña fetched it from the kitchen, took a look around. Against his expectations, it contained none of those rural knick-knacks – antique windmills, sets of rusty keys, still lifes depicting the kill or the kitchen, tools of long-forgotten use, wooden yokes, yellowish ceramic plates – with which many country houses hark back nostalgically to an archaic way of life that, nevertheless, the owners have been trying hard to leave behind. In a bookcase by the chimney were at least a hundred books and Cupido scanned the titles; many of them were by authors he would not have expected to find there: Tolstoy, Cervantes, Euripides, García Márquez. He took down a volume of Kafka's letters and, when he opened it on a page with the corner turned down, he noticed some underlined sentences. He read: 'But it's as if I were at school, the master walking up and down, the whole class having finished their work and gone home, except for me, here, flagging, my mistakes in maths getting worse, making the master wait. Naturally, you end up having to atone for something like that, as for all offences made against teachers.' He closed it and replaced it as he heard footsteps returning. His eye was caught just then by a photograph, framed and under glass, placed on the mantelpiece, in which Saldaña himself and, he supposed, his two sons were smiling: they were a boy of four or five and a teenager.

'My wife's out. She works in Breda and will pick up our son from school later,' he said as he came back, noticing his curiosity.

Cupido didn't want to start the conversation as an interrogation or use his ability to make people talk even when they intended to skirt the issue. He knew that his curiosity to learn something was often less intense than the other's curiosity in what he was going to ask. So he didn't really need to behave like a grand inquisitor. Of course, some people refused to give him any answers, but very few refused to listen to his questions, if only to find out the extent of his ignorance. Besides, he was careful to hide that sense of superiority inevitably given off by the person conducting an interrogation, the person deciding which pieces of information matter and which he can do without, and determining the route of the conversation.

With Saldaña he suspected that those basic strategies would be of little use. The man before him seemed indifferent. Neither suspicious nor intrigued, just indifferent.

'What did you want to talk to me about?'

'That evening after the meeting, you left the bar at the same time as the teachers. You didn't want to stay with the other parents on the School Council.'

'True. I left very early. There wasn't a lot left to talk about with the parents. And I'm not that fond of the teachers, either.'

'But you're a member of the School Council. And you volunteer for that.'

'Yes, of course. What better way of being on the inside to check they're doing their job properly?'

Again, Cupido looked at him in surprise. It wasn't often that such scorn was expressed for a profession that was generally valued and praised for its importance by the media, even if neither the state nor society did much to dignify it or give it any prestige or respect. Public praise, private censure. The contradiction remained unresolved: just when the idea that extending education to the whole population was the best tool for their redemption and well-being had finally triumphed, the social standing of its chief practitioners had reached an all-time low.

'What have you got against the school?'

'Has no one told you?'

'No.'

'Between them, they killed my son.'

'The school?' he asked, again surprised.

'You don't have any children.'

'No,' replied Cupido.

Saldaña looked at him as if he was still at the top of the porch, perhaps regretting having invited him in, perhaps wondering if the serious accusation he'd just uttered would have any effect on a man without family, who'd come to his house in a cycling jersey and who was paid precisely to doubt anything he might hear. However, he started talking:

'I know my son was a difficult lad. Ever since he was little he had been lively. The kind of boy who wants to touch and taste everything, who drags chairs over to the window so he can lean out, and who stares at electric plugs as if treasure was hidden inside them. The kind of boy who terrorises your hosts when you visit someone. I had my difficulties with him, but he always listened if you spoke to him calmly.'

He looked at Cupido to make sure he understood what he was saying. The detective nodded briefly for him to go on.

'At school he got through the first years with some difficulty. He repeated a year. But when he got to the higher classes, the problems got worse. He didn't like to study and no one there was able to explain to him that we all need to do things we don't like. His marks went down, and he started being sent out, a punishment that first he found humiliating and painful, but soon became a sort of liberation, because outside in the corridors, no one controlled him. He ended up provoking his teachers so that they would send him out. The first time he was suspended from school it was because he insulted a teacher who, it seems, had once humiliated him. Don't get me wrong, I'm not trying to excuse him. I only want to balance the blame. The next term, he was as keen to leave as his teachers were to throw him out. From outside, I felt powerless to control the situation, and although I urged him to work hard and be patient, I knew his disenchantment was permanent. One day...' he paused, hesitating to go on.

'Yes?' prompted Cupido.

'One day, in class, with the director of studies, something happened that I'll never forget. My son had taken a centipede to school. Alive, but trapped in a jar. He'd always been curious about those kinds of creatures. Somehow, Corona got wind of it, and said that if anyone had any insects hidden in class they should go and flush them down the toilet. Have you ever been bitten by a centipede?'

'No.'

'It hurts a lot. And it leaves a scar like the ones you get from an operation.' He fell silent for a few seconds. 'My son hid it in the pocket of his trousers. He took the pain rather than give in to the teacher. He came home with his thigh all red and swollen, but I didn't hear him complain once.'

Saldaña looked at the picture on the mantelpiece and went on:

'A little later he was expelled, and, by law, a new school had to be found for him. Every school where he might have been more or less OK shut their doors to him. I guess they made calls and inquiries, asked what kind of pupil he was, got all the inside information. A pupil with a file stamped 'Expelled' in the education system is like a man with a criminal record in society at large: he's marked and no one will take him on. I'm sure you know that as well as me.'

Cupido ignored the allusion to himself and remained silent. But of course he knew it. He had a file with his fingerprints on it in the archives of the courts of Breda and knew how difficult it had been to settle back into society. And how many people still expected him to go and find somewhere else to live?

'At school they suggested I take him to a boarding school away from here: an isolated place deep in the country, run with the kind of discipline you get in the army or in a young-offenders' institution where they put unruly boys. I refused: it couldn't be the solution. The other alternatives were the old schools near the cemetery, the only place in Breda where he was admitted. Do you know them?'

'Yes,' he replied. They were in Casas del Obispo, an outlying area of Breda. Eight classrooms had been built there. No one bothered to maintain them and they had become run-down and damp. It was an old, small school, its windows systematically broken by stones, walls filthy with graffiti and insults, a porch sometimes soiled with excrement, and a reduced staff undermined by depression. They couldn't bear the stress of the students and parents living in a ghetto of miserable subsidised housing, to which Breda had abandoned everyone that didn't fit on its well-established scale of social acceptability. A large part of its population had at one point in their lives known either imprisonment or prostitution.

'Although he had only one year left, maybe I shouldn't have let him go there. But I thought it might do him good to see other people who had a lot less than him, who didn't have such an easy life. Besides, it was only for the rest of the year. The following year he was going to college.'

He stopped and took a long swallow of beer. He seemed to be steeling himself to face the most painful part of his story.

'But my son was too young to learn that kind of lesson. For the first few months we asked him how things were going. He didn't complain as much, seemed to have calmed down a bit, the transfer seemed to be doing some good. We were a bit surprised at his calmness, but fooled ourselves, saying that was how teenagers were: they feel miserable when we think they ought to be happy, and seem happy among ruins. When we realised, it was too late. We'd misjudged the reason for his apparent quietness. We didn't suspect it at first, as we always gave him a little money and it wasn't until later that he started stealing from the house. But he was already stealing produce from our plot: kilos or crates of fruit or other things we grew. When he told us, we were amazed that he could have kept the secret so cleverly. Later he began to steal openly, and valuable objects – things that were so well hidden you didn't realise for a while that they were missing – began to disappear. It was a devastating process. Sixteen years old and within a few months he couldn't stop shooting up. He always had a lighter, a spoon and a little syringe in his pocket. My wife and I desperately tried to get him off the stuff. We watched him, stayed with him at all times, never left him on his own. We told him over and over that he was harming himself, and all we managed to do was make him feel even more restless and guilty, and at the same time, make him want another fix. I even shut him downstairs, in the cellar, and it sounded like he was going to headbutt the wall down. Finally we admitted defeat, and sent him to a rehabilitation centre. And to stop him hating us so much. But, again, it was too late. It was a disease. Perhaps now he could have lived in a more or less tolerable way, but four years ago no proper therapy existed.'

Again he stopped for a few seconds, to finish his beer and carry on with this confession that must have been both painful and beneficial to him. The tale of how unhappiness had broken into his house and ruined his dreams of an idyllic life, destroying any aspirations he might have had to being something other than a simple peasant covered in dirt and sweat, who supplies the city with food in exchange for a few coins he guards jealously under a stone. He started talking in the neutral tone of someone who assumes his listener won't understand him or his reasons, but Cupido's silent attention lent weight to his words. He was not only telling his story now: he seemed to be reliving it.

'At first, after his death, we were so dazed we couldn't think. The empty space in the household, at the table where we ate, in his room, was only too obvious. It was such a painful absence it swallowed up any attempt to rationalise it. But given time you start understanding the reasons and sharing out the blame. I know what part is mine. I also know that if his first school had treated him differently and he hadn't been expelled, the rest would never have happened. I know that as well. I've been mourning my son for four years now and I still can't forgive myself, so no one can ask me to forgive them. No one can ask me to forget when I've not even come to resignation. De Molinos, Nelson, Larrey and a few others were on the School Council that decided on his expulsion. But don't jump to conclusions. I found out that Larrey was the only one, out of all of them, who suggested giving my son another chance. I only feel gratitude towards him.'

⤺

As he'd planned, he took the southbound road when he left Saldaña's farm, ignoring the protests of his legs and lungs, which always advised him against the steep slopes of Yunque and Volcán, where nature had not been tamed by the hand of man. The climb demanded all his strength and the kind of concentration that prevented any thought except the preserving of his strength. But he needed to shake off Saldaña's words and analyse the links between the schoolteachers and the only parent who had had any chance of seeing the back of Larrey's neck that night.

He had finished the first part of his investigation, which always consisted of speaking to those involved in the case, like a doctor who, before he even gets the results of analyses, scans and X-rays, investigates his patient's symptoms and his own suspicions, lifestyle, allergies, operations, his record of health and illness. And, just like a good doctor, he was careful not to make an early diagnosis just in case he recommended the wrong therapy, whose side effects might delay the return to health.

The fact was, he was a little confused and didn't know where to go from here. He couldn't imagine the motive, the culprit, or the reason for the shot. He'd seen enough crimes, of all sorts, to know that no two of them were identical, and that no rule could be abstracted from them all. Each was different from the last, every impulse seeking a particular kind of damage or a distinctive type of execution. Sometimes he'd found it easy to uncover the motive; at others the easy part had been finding the murderer, not the motive. But this time the mystery was twofold: no one seemed to have had any reason to shoot Larrey. Sure enough, those implicated had spoken at their leisure against those they hated – giving them less time to praise those they liked, as if hatred took up more of their time than friendship – but no one had said anything against Larrey.

However, his job was about distrusting appearances. He knew that life was too long never to have made a mistake or caused harm; he knew there was not a single person alive who wasn't hiding a shameful secret, and that many would do anything to keep it. His profession, unlike most others, had shown him the various forces that move men to harm other men, and had made him ask himself a crucial question: how to carry on practising it without losing the shreds of hope which are essential to believing in good? Looking into so many dark hearts had revealed to him that, at certain times, the limits of evil were easily crossed, even by the most ordinary and peaceful, by the most unassuming human beings. He sometimes recalled Warhol's assertion that one day everyone would be famous for fifteen minutes. He didn't believe in this assertion. However, he did believe that everyone, if they were sure of impunity, would use fifteen minutes to cause irreparable harm. You'd better not have a gun to hand if you wanted to live through those minutes and remain innocent.

In the job he was on now, someone had been offered that opportunity, and had not hesitated in taking it. Everything suggested that this person could have any one of these faces: Nelson's attractive face, Rita's emotional and frightened one, or the expression of the former headmaster, De Molinos, victim of wounded pride; Julita Guzmán's distrust or Saldaña's sadness and lifelessness; Corona's neatness and calm or Moisés's energy. Except for the conscientious objector, whose presence at the school was unexpected, anachronistic and rather odd, the other six had left the bar before the rest, and each had ended up – as they all said – going home. Any one of the seven might have followed Larrey back to the office.

He'd reached one of those interminably straight stretches of road that hardly seems to ascend as the distance makes the inclination seem gentle, but it had exhausted him on previous occasions; its deceptive appearance meant he kept no strength in reserve. For speed, he'd never liked straight roads: they emphasised the solitude of the country, eliminated the surprise of bends and dangerously numbed both the cyclist's and the driver's concentration.

He cycled along it without rising off his seat, his head lowered, a gentle wind at his back. Even so, he was breathless when he got to the top, and had to stop for a rest. The slope fell away steeply at the other side, so much so, that when you picked up speed going down it, it felt as if you might take off and fly over the fields of grain. The irrigated land was behind him now, and the waters of the Lebrón which dispersed into the swamp had died out a few miles back, in the last irrigation channels that nourished the grass fields and less thirsty crops like sunflower and soy. This marked the transition to the poorer and drier soils that extended over the undulating land, made by the same geological forces that had also pushed up the almost twin masses of Volcán and Yunque, twenty miles to the north. He rested at the top for a few moments, by the ditch, contemplating the fallow fields in the distance, the greenish blots of bushes that were rougher and hardier than any tree, and the village bearing the name he used to like and fear so much as a child: *Silencio*. Then he turned and dropped back towards Breda.

He didn't know how to progress. The only lead was Julián Monasterio's bank; he could check if any one of the seven faces had hired a safe there. If a name turned up, perhaps the view might clear. But he needed a warrant to get that information from the bank and, as a detective with no other connections to the law than his friendship with the lieutenant, Gallardo, he was stalled. Only Gallardo could get a warrant. And for that Cupido would have to tell him how he knew where the gun had come from, and thus implicate his client, when secrecy had been the first condition stipulated when he had been hired. There were too many obstacles. Unless, he thought, the lieutenant agreed to keep the identity of the owner of the gun strictly confidential, a price Gallardo would only pay if he was confident he would find the culprit by that route. He might as well try it, he said to himself eventually, as he neared the first houses of Breda. He just had to convince his client to let him initiate the negotiations.

Tired, he dismounted inside the garage, looked at the meter on the handlebars and saw he'd done almost seventy kilometres. Not bad, even if he felt at that moment that his legs would come off at the hips if he took one step.

He went up to his flat, had a shower and heated up one of the ready meals he was eating more and more frequently. Before dialling Julián Monasterio's number he checked the messages on his voicemail. His client had beaten him to it. He wanted to talk to him as soon as possible.

Monasterio picked up after one ring. His voice betrayed impatience when he said:

'We have to talk soon. Something's happened. Could you come to the shop?'

'I'll be there in ten minutes.'

He left his dirty plate on the table and went to meet his client. The door was shut, but Julián Monasterio was waiting inside and opened it as soon as he saw him through the window.

Behind the counter there were two desks overflowing with computers, some of them with their covers off; although it was a shop that sold the most sophisticated technology, it still looked like a workshop in which mechanical labour was still innate in man. A pile of old hardware was accumulating in a corner, perhaps in perfect working order, but already obsolete, with insufficient memory and speed to run new and demanding programmes. Cupido thought fleetingly that there was no way around it: the road ahead was necessarily littered with waste. Civilisation perfects itself at the same speed and ratio that junk proliferates. Rubbish is the ultimate price of success.

'The Guardia Civil came to my house this morning. A man and a woman, very young. They know the gun left the courts irregularly, but they don't know who ended up with it. They're asking everyone who worked there forty years ago. And their children.'

'What did you tell them?'

'The only thing I could. That I didn't know anything, that I'd never heard my father say he had a gun.'

'Do you think they believed you?'

'I think so.'

Cupido nodded gently, trying to calm him. However, he doubted that Gallardo would leave it at that. He knew him and knew that if he didn't find any answers he'd go back and start over, again and again.

'I carried on thinking, afterwards. I'm not sure that some of my father's colleagues or someone who worked there might not know who took it. Some must have died and others perhaps don't know a thing. But what if they find someone who remembers?'

The detective guessed they both had the same image in mind, whose apparent fragility and innocence did not neutralise the threat it posed: one of those doddering elderly people who hardly ever leaves the house or, when they do, it's always to walk the same route; who forgets to take their medicines and the name of the person they're talking to. One of those people who never remembers what happened or what they saw the previous day, but whose memories are writ in stone when it comes to anecdotes and details from several decades in the past: the ray of sunlight that fell in their distant office; the defendant whose name they took one day and they knew, despite everything, to be innocent; the final recipient of a gun hidden in a book.

'If someone remembers,' he replied, 'it won't be easy to convince the police that you didn't know anything about it. I know the lieutenant. They wouldn't let you go.'

Julián Monasterio hung his head, and once again the detective felt a pang of sympathy towards him, his pitiful inability to face a problem that should never have been a problem, the fragile state in which any news was a fright.

'So what can I do?'

'Negotiate,' Cupido said, although he feared he'd be misinterpreted. His client was asking for salvation and his only suggestion was an honourable defeat.

'I haven't a lot to offer.'

'I think you have as much as they do.'

'What?' he opened his empty hands, to show there was nothing left in them, not even the ring on the finger where a band
of whiter skin remained.

'You told me that the day you left the safe open there was
someone waiting outside the vault, but that you didn't look
back and don't know who it was or what they looked like.'

'Yes.'

'The lieutenant would give anything to know where the gun
came from. Because the person who took it must also have a
safe there. That information would make things a lot easier for
him. There aren't a lot of people who might have shot Larrey.
If one of them also had a safe in the bank, it would be a revealing coincidence, wouldn't it?'

'But they would also see my name on the list. After this
morning's visit, they'd know who the owner was. And they'd
wonder why I didn't come forward before, as soon as I knew of
the theft. I don't think they'd be very well-disposed towards me
after what's happened.'

'But that's exactly what I'm suggesting: negotiation. A deal
outside the station, without any witnesses, or any signed papers.
We tell him we know where the gun came from, although we
don't know who did it. He can find that out himself and get all
the credit for it. In return, we ask that the name of the true
owner be left out of the business.'

'Without my name even being made public?'

'Without your name even being made public.'

'Would he agree to that? Would the law agree to that?' he
asked with the same distrust as on the first day, when he
thought that luck might be on his side.

'The law makes deals with people a lot less clean than you,'
said Cupido.

He sometimes had to take jobs from people he disliked, who
kept information from him and treated him as disdainfully as
you would a pest exterminator or a dog, ashamed at having to
talk to him and impatient for their relationship to be over. But

Julián Monasterio had from the start awakened in him the kind of sympathy he felt towards helpless people. Without knowing him well, Cupido could gauge from his manner that his problems went well beyond the loss of the gun, and that the punishment he was getting was far harsher than he deserved.

'Are you sure they'd leave me out of it?' he insisted.

'I'm sure the lieutenant would cut you a deal. You run the risk of them getting to you by some other route anyway.'

Julián Monasterio got up from his chair and stared out of the window. The street was empty. A few passers-by hurried along. He thought of his daughter. If he didn't hurry, he wouldn't get home in time to see her, and ask her about her new teacher and kiss her before she went back to school.

'I'll think about it,' he said, turning to Cupido. 'Give me a day to think about it and I'll give you my answer tomorrow.'

11

He took all the pieces out of the case. It was a small case of soft black leather like the one a rent collector or a bureaucrat might carry everywhere without anyone guessing at its contents. He put them on the table and started assembling them, in the same ritual order as always, which to him was as fixed as the sections of a mass to a priest; the bell, the lower and upper joint, the barrel and the mouthpiece. Once complete, he caressed it lovingly and fitted the reed into the mouthpiece without tightening it too much.

He could do without many things in life: a house of his own, a woman, a car, money and a job, that long list which so many men he knew used to achieve happiness, lying to themselves and believing the lie. But he couldn't do without the object he now had in his hands: a piece of hollow ebony, drilled with seventeen holes.

This was the best part of the day, an hour before sunset. He'd come back from school and had coffee with his wife, hiding his impatience, pretending he was listening to her routine complaints or gossip, made her believe that he too cared about what was happening on TV, in one of those stupid daytime shows she liked so much, where ordinary people came to speak of their most intimate misfortunes so openly that he couldn't help feeling a little embarrassed. Once he estimated enough time had gone by for him not to incur her reproachful looks, he went to the soundproofed study. He left her barefoot on the sofa, chain-smoking with such indolence that the greatest effort she seemed capable of was lifting the cup of coffee to her lips. But a woman's indolence requires style – he would think as he walked up the corridor and spotted her shoes on the carpet – and has its time: the years elapsing over her thirties, when a mature woman, although lacking the energy of youth, can still raise her head and be active, indeed very active when stirred by the incentive of generosity or the promise of pleasure. Before those years, indolence bespeaks bitterness; afterwards it loses all power of seduction and only indicates laziness.

Once the door was shut, he would take out the parts of his

clarinet, assemble it, caress it for a few moments and tune it to B. Always the same ritual. Only then did he start to relax, well-being taking possession of him. The outside world of the school, with the children's shrill shouting, the teachers' petty envy and apathy, as well as the private world of his home, on the other side of the wall, slowly faded away. The notes rising up acted like the filaments of a brush, which effortlessly but relentlessly swept away all the sad vulgarity that surrounded him. Compared to the warm, velvet music, all other human sounds seemed harsh and dispensable; not only the coarse noises made by an imperfect body as it expels everything it cannot process, but also the human voice, which has a lamentable phonic poverty. Even the sounds of nature, like water or wind, couldn't compare to the adagio with which Mozart had proven to every generation, both before him and after, that this underestimated wind instrument could be a match for the clavichord. That brief piece of music filled him with a kind of contentment he hadn't found in any other activity, enveloped him in a soothing bubble of sound where his headache and neck pain disappeared, as did the stress of having to maintain his façade of importance, and hide the unhappiness he was obviously resigned to. As they flew from the bell, the notes of the adagio pushed against the walls and lifted the ceiling, expanding the room and wiping out the entire world with their powerful momentum, until only an infinite prism remained, devoid of everything outside the melody, at whose centre he was blowing, blowing, blowing until he felt his jaws would dislocate and his lips could no longer meet.

He'd learned to play at a very early age. His father played in the municipal band of a town in the Levante region, where he himself had only returned for fleeting family visits. His father had started him off on an old C clarinet, with barely any technique, and had given him some advice he still remembered fondly. He insisted that you should start by caressing the clarinet as if it were a woman, and end up handling it like a sailboat. You had to put it in your mouth as if you were kissing it, gently yet firmly, pressing the reed to lips that should be moist but not covered in saliva. Then, as the instrument itself became bolder, you should follow it, let it sound and give it as much wind as it asked for, a breeze or a hurricane, sunshine or rain for the afternoon of a *corrida* or a concert.

Once he'd learned the basics he'd started playing in an amateur jazz band. Twenty years ago that was the music of choice for the enlightened liberals who treated the brass and percussion repertoire of municipal bands with Olympic disdain, and only barely tolerated, with a supercilious look, the rock bands that were also rife in those days before heroin had taken its toll. Every season, he and his three companions went up to the San Sebastián or Vitoria festivals, hoping to learn, and to close the distance between themselves and Paquito d'Rivera or Perry Robinson. Those had been years of constant rehearsals and blind faith in possibilities.

And yet his enthusiasm didn't last long – just long enough for him to realise that with his puny lungs and scant talent he'd never go very far. The band dissolved after three years; they were all bored with how little progress they made, how little success and prestige they had with girls, and with their inability to put together four vibrant, original chords that got feet tapping.

It was during that time, however, that he discovered the richness of classical music, as if Bessie Smith, Duke Ellington or Charlie Parker had been springboards that sent him back to the deep, ancient roots of each instrument. He started to go further back in time and, perhaps because he was no longer trying for anything that wasn't on the stave, he found in the classics a more intense pleasure than in jazz. Mozart, Schubert, Schumann or Brahms were like immense rivers, the secrets of whose basin, current and banks could never be known; next to them, Goodman or Armstrong were mere babbling brooks, certainly rich in clarity, vitality and nuance, but which would never reach the sea.

One day on the radio, he heard the adagio of Mozart's clarinet concerto. For the duration of the piece he thought he was surrounded by angels. Those seven minutes struck him as the most sublime created by any musician. The melodic interplay between clarinet and violins, the way the former began a phrase to cede it to the strings, reached an ineffable perfection. But even when the clarinet took its leave it seemed to remain in the background, lying in wait, watching over the playing of the other members of the orchestra. And that whole game of challenge, of call and response, happened in the first part, in less than three minutes. After that, the clarinet took control of the piece again, as if it was dissatisfied with the others' work and hushed them so it could be alone for its glorious outburst, allowing the violins to return only at the very end.

He studied it so intently that he'd never forgotten it; he didn't need to look at the score to tell if he'd made a mistake. Nearly every day when he shut himself up in the study he began with the adagio. The first notes of the arpeggio – C F A, A F G – were like a swing that suddenly swept him off his feet and lifted him into the air, without any intervening steps. Now, too, he began with it.

But tonight he could find neither the right rhythm nor that feeling of well-being. Trying to relax, he clenched and unclenched his fists, and flexed his abdominal muscles before continuing.

Ten minutes later he still felt tense and clumsy. His fingers pressed against the keys and holes routinely, more like a typist's than a musician's.

As he forced a chord, he felt the reed crack between his teeth, and a splinter of bamboo stuck painfully into his tongue. He moved the mouthpiece away and spat into his hand: the saliva was laced with red. He placed the clarinet on the table with some surprise – that had never happened to him before – and went to lie down on the chaise longue, to close his eyes for a few moments and think of nothing.

It was impossible, he couldn't forget school. Ever since he'd taken over the headmastership he'd worked tirelessly, carefully answering official letters, sorting documentation, exams statistics and attendance sheets, calculating the calories in the school menu, worrying over the tiniest details. When he came home, his head was still buzzing with half-finished tasks, business pending and calls. He drank a cup of coffee with his wife and half-heartedly told her some anecdote about the school, trying to hide the fact that, deep down, he didn't care so much about keeping the institution in order as about his right to demand that the others were as equally active as himself. Having presented his proposals to the School Council and been elected, he couldn't now leave everything as it was before. For some time he would have to carry out at least a part of what he'd promised. But he didn't have the courage to undertake the reforms he had announced and face a large part of the teaching staff, who tended towards laziness. In fact, continuity drove his behaviour, and he hadn't even replaced any of the previous senior team. His nervousness and bad conscience came from that immobility. Besides, since the death of Larrey everyone seemed to be scrutinising every move he made, ready to pounce on any mistake. He was terrified of the possibility of some other misfortune – an accident in the playground, or an increase in the failure rate – which would drive people to believe that, since he had taken over, everything led to disaster.

He had turned forty and he wasn't going to move cities. He would wait until retirement and grow old in Breda. It was too late to look for another position and start afresh, closer to what he'd always thought was happiness. For years he'd tried to get a transfer to Madrid or one of the big, bright cities in his home region. Back then, his length of service was insufficient. Now it wasn't, but what was the point? Why did good things always come too late, he wondered. He recalled with hatred all the obstacles De Molinos had set before him over his decade as headmaster, with a persistence that couldn't be anything but a deliberate attempt to stop him gaining the necessary points and merit. It was as if De Molinos had seen in him, from the moment he came to the school, the possibility of damage, the presence of an enemy. Now they *were* enemies, of course, and he had never pretended that his efforts to oust De Molinos were less about money or power than about revenge and his growing rancour. For without those obstacles he might have obtained a transfer through retraining. English as a subject had reached saturation point, there were no new vacancies and competition was fierce. But he could have retrained as a music teacher with little trouble. And then he could have gone anywhere he liked. Twice he had asked De Molinos to send him on a course, and both times De Molinos, using his prerogative as headmaster, had put forward incompetents close to himself, who couldn't tell the difference between a crotchet and a quaver, couldn't play an instrument and probably knew nothing of Mozart except what they'd seen in *Amadeus*.

Why then did the old man dare show surprise and scorn when, with the two of them alone in the office, he'd told him he was going to run in the election? Why that mocking frown that actually clinched a decision he might still have gone back on? Was he so sure of his citadel that he didn't take a challenge seriously?

But the worst thing was coming to such a deep hatred from such petty causes, having been invaded by bitterness without a grand, compelling reason, some passion justifying its intensity. The fact that work differences had nourished so much spite showed unquestionably that his life was driven by mediocrity.

He stood up suddenly to shake off the image of Rita, which was where these thoughts always ended up; he couldn't stop them before they reached and contaminated her. He pressed the tips of his fingers against the edge of the table and forced them backwards until he felt the pain extending to his wrists. Then he opened and closed his fists several times and took up the clarinet again. When he spat into his hand the saliva was no longer red with blood, as if the bitterness of his thoughts had also gone to work on his tongue, cauterising the wound. He picked up a new, softer reed and fitted it into the mouthpiece. He opened the score on the music stand at the first page and sat straight on his stool, right in the middle of the sound-proofed room, ready to persevere until he drew out the music's wonderful capacity to engross him.

At first the notes were loath to come out, they had to be forced. He felt he didn't have the breath to keep up the pressure during the crescendo, as if a wide belt compressed his dia-phragm and restricted him from taking in enough oxygen. He slowed down the rhythm until, little by little, he found it satis-factory. Only then did he go back to the beginning, to the simple primordial notes – C F A, A F G – and just as every finger was hitting the keys at the right time and his nostrils were dilating greedily to breathe in and he was feeling the first waves of contentment reaching his feet, he heard the door open and saw his wife pop her head in to ask him:

'What do you want for dinner?'

He removed the mouthpiece from his lips, irritated but hid-ing it, as he'd learned to do in the last few years, having accep-ted that the girl he had dreamed or invented was gone for good; the girl who, when she came back from a trip, put her arms around his neck and kissed him on the lips and always brought him a foreign record or a score; the girl with whom, long ago, sharing tears over naked skin, he had wept for so much pleasure and happiness. Now, slowly, without his realising how or even beginning to understand it, she had become the woman he turned his back on in bed, and in whom he had lost all interest due to the same relentless wear that made him lose his hair and gain a bit of weight and get the white hairs that had been unthinkable a few months ago.

'Anything. I'm not hungry.'

He saw her turn, without closing the door, in her elegant orange bathrobe that didn't hide the beginning of the curve of her back, the way her neck drooped slightly, the stoop of her shoulders; she had lost that angular freshness he'd liked so much, her head now bending forward as if the cloth rubbed against a wound in the back of her neck. Last year everything had finally gone completely cold between them. They hardly ever talked about important things, for they were afraid of finding in them references to themselves and their miseries; they barely told each other about what they read or dreamt, their comings and goings, their daily plans, for they shared none. They'd turned their backs to each other, and even in bed it had been some time since he had crossed to the left-hand side she occupied. Maybe if they'd had children... But also that chance of joy and warmth had come too late. When Rita told him she was pregnant he couldn't believe it. He recalled all those doctor's appointments fifteen years before, at first hopeful, then increasingly brief and dismal, the consultations with gynaecologists who studied them and asked questions no one else would ask, made them undress, and carried out tests on their blood and semen. He recalled the rather humiliating feeling of being like guinea pigs in their hands, as after several years of pleasure and happiness she still wasn't pregnant. A tedious series of analyses and tests, statistics and graphs, led to one conclusion: it would be hard for them to have children, although perhaps in a few years, with the advances in medicine... They were young – every doctor had told them – very young, and hormonal levels varied mysteriously with time. Any metabolic change, any wayward hidden gland that one day starts functioning at full capacity for unknown reasons, might change things. Best not to become obsessed – they insisted – to keep on trying, enjoy youth and happiness, and wait to see their bodies' reactions. If in three or four years nothing changed, they might be able to try chemical treatment. In America and Italy, they were having amazing results with infertile couples...

They'd left their first consultations surprised and disconcerted. As soon as they were out on the street, they would kiss and desire each other desperately, unable to understand why two beautiful bodies seemingly created for pleasure were barred from procreation. And so they waited for those years and, contrary to their expectations, their mutual sterility didn't turn into an obsession but was forgotten, or at least silenced. They still loved each other, had a good life, seldom went a day without making love and never had to go without anything that made them feel good. And now, now, how was it possible for such unspoken hostility to come about between a man and a woman who fifteen years ago had loved and desired and admired each other to the point that they felt their love would be for ever and needed nothing to keep it so, not even a child? Where had the trap lain? What had happened so that a man and a woman who, fifteen years ago, would have laughed at all external threats and bad omens, now avoided each other and put the lights out and turned their backs in order not to see the other? His relationship with Rita had not been the cause, but the inevitable consequence of a weariness that had started way back – as smoke is of fire and pain is of a blow to the face. Of course it was too late, and when he told her he didn't like children, she replied with a question that still buzzed in his ears: 'Then why the bloody hell are you a teacher?'

He put the dismantled clarinet away in the case and went to the kitchen. His wife was washing some lettuce, and he took a stick of celery and a leek out of the fridge. On the ashtray by the sink, a cigarette gave off blackish smoke that no doubt prickled her eyes and made her half-close them, hardening her expression. In the last few months she had put on too much weight, even more than those few extra pounds that are not only acceptable in a woman of forty, but also become one of her most attractive features. Her large breasts no longer awakened in him the greed he'd felt during their first years together. Now they looked like two large cakes a bit past their sell-by date that would only give indigestion. Every year she became weaker, every year she had more aches and pains, more melodramatic illnesses that required more medication, although her body was the kind that while getting relief from a medicine also suffers its side effects, so that it was never entirely healthy.

In contrast, he couldn't help thinking that Rita would still be a beautiful woman at forty. She'd never look that age before she turned it. Why hadn't he dared leave his wife? Not now, sunk as they were in indifference; but then, during those years when she went through that furiously jealous period, and he first realised the inevitability of his infidelity to this person who was clinging to him so tightly that she was becoming his shadow.

'Do you want to lay the table? I can finish this up,' she said indicating the vegetables.

He took the tablecloth into the dining room, almost relieved not to be near her, and laid it over the table. These were the only words they had left, niceties about the domestic routine, the shopping or money, and half-hearted anecdotes about people they knew or small incidents at work. There would come a time, he thought, when neither of them would be able to endure the pretence that words and mundane tasks were necessary and sufficient any longer: washing lettuce, sewing on a button, going to the occasional mediocre provincial concert. For a moment he stared at the red and green lines in the cloth, amazed again at the fact that he had become a different man, a parody of who he used to be, the remainder of something that once had been clean and honest and now was shabby and a bit dirty, a jumble of effective phrases with which he had managed to deceive a young girl for a few months.

12

'Another one of your chats, is it?' asked Gallardo, offering his hand.

'As you can see. It seems inevitable that we talk every now and then,' replied Cupido.

They had arranged to meet on neutral ground, the cafe of the Europa hotel. Three years had passed since the events at El Paternoster reserve, and the hotel was once again full at weekends and listed in Michelin. Cupido didn't want to go to the station. He'd even dared suggest to Gallardo that he not wear a uniform, as what he was going to propose ran counter to the strict military rules that Gallardo was so fond of.

'But I can't say I'm glad to see you. Every time you show up like this it means extra work for us,' he said in a forced ironic tone that didn't hide his curiosity and impatience.

'You know how much you need me, Lieutenant.'

Gallardo smiled sideways, without showing his teeth, as he sat down in one of the deep armchairs of the cafe.

'Not for long. You private detectives don't have a lot of options left. Just as your disgusting profession was born a century ago when the army stopped taking care of civilian offences, it'll die out in a few years, when we lose that function, too. If it's any consolation, we'll both have to look for a job at the same time.'

'I don't think they'll retire you. You're the only civil servants that people are happy to pay more to when you have less to do.'

'You're wrong. The future is in the lab. It's all about satellites and DNA and GPS, all those shitty acronyms that aren't even proper names.'

A waiter approached them and they ordered coffee. Gallardo waited for him to move away and continued:

'We'll end up directing traffic, going on the beat and being used as security guards. When there's a mystery, they barely let us get involved. The instruction we most often get from Madrid is: "Don't touch anything." Now the lab technicians run the show: they find a sample and a few hours later they tell you whose it is, how old, what sex, what they eat, what they do, what their parents were like and what their children will be like. It's a disgrace. All that's left for us is to go and arrest people. Deduction and mystery are becoming history. Though I reckon there'll still be some murky cases they'll need us for. Anyway, what did you want to see me about?'

'That teacher that was killed at the school.'

'You've stuck your nose into that, too?' he asked, caught between irritation at the intrusion and curiosity about what Cupido knew.

'Yes.'

'And?'

'I've got some information and I'd like to make a deal.'

The lieutenant shook his head, as if his fears had been realised.

'I thought as much. All that discretion about meeting here could only mean one thing.'

'What did you want me to do, put it in writing?'

'Don't screw me around, Cupido. You're more like a salesman than a detective. And what's worse is you're always peddling someone else's stuff. What old shit do you have for sale now?'

'Something that might earn you another stripe,' Cupido replied with a smile, ignoring his remarks. Like so many officers he had known, Gallardo went from one extreme to the other without transition: he either forced himself to speak like a minister, quoting rules and regulations, or swore like a convict, giving full rein to the perennial military fondness for coarse language.

'Stop talking drivel. What do you know?'

'I won't tell you anything without one condition.'

'You know perfectly well that some things are non-negotiable.'

'And you know that I serve whoever's paying me before anyone else. And I'm sure he's innocent in all of this,' he replied. He was aware that his words sounded excessively solemn, but he also knew that this kind of language, based on rules of conduct as traditional as they were firm, were his best bet for persuading Gallardo.

The lieutenant looked him in the eye for what seemed too long a time to Cupido.

'In the last few years,' he said at last, 'everyone in this country has come to think they can make a deal with the law and change the rules. But make no mistake, I'll only give you as much as you can give me. This had better be worth it. What's the condition?'

'His name must not come out. No leaks to the press. There are people who would have a harder time than himself. Children. My client,' he said, although the word always sounded strange to him, 'will take personal responsibility for a mistake that shouldn't have had consequences. That should have had no consequences,' he emphasised.

'Was there a criminal offence?'

'No,' he lied, for he knew that hiding a gun without a licence constituted one. For those with a licence, it was a bureaucratic mistake. But right now that wasn't a very important distinction.

'I'll do everything within my power.'

Cupido nodded slightly. That was all he needed.

'I know where the gun came from. A Belgian FN, model 1900. With silencer.'

A spark of wiliness and delight flared up in the lieutenant's eye. With all the trails in a muddle, no leads to act on, and the investigation at a standstill, that piece of news was more than he'd hoped for.

'Where from?'

'A safe-deposit box in a bank, where it was kept. My client made the mistake of leaving it open, or not properly locked. A coincidence in a thousand or in a million, but it happened. And someone took it before the bank staff realised the safe was open. It was possibly someone who was waiting behind my client to go into the vault. But he didn't notice who it was. He didn't look back.'

The detective went on to give all the details he knew – the mother's death and the legacy, the gun hidden in the book, the date of the theft, the name of the bank – and tried to explain why he had not reported the loss:

'He couldn't have imagined someone would use it for that. He's not one of those men who expects the worst from humanity and, therefore, lives on the defensive. He's not one of those men who never forgets to lock every door,' he finished.

'What's his name?'

'Julián Monasterio. His father worked at the courts until his death, many years ago. It seems someone there gave him the gun, which from then on became part of the family inheritance. To Monasterio, it was only a memento. His name must be familiar: two of your officers interrogated him a few days ago.'

'And he kept silent then, too.'

'Of course he kept silent! He'd gone too far to simply back down. After everything that had happened, who would believe his story: that he'd failed to lock his safe at the bank and that someone had stolen a pistol hidden in a book, leaving behind everything else, including money and a bag containing coins and jewels? No one would believe it. And yet, it may well be the truest part of the whole story. Besides, he's a confused man who hesitates over every step he takes. His wife left him a few months ago. He's in sole charge of his six-year-old daughter.'

'All right, all right... A sad, disturbed and fearful father trying to protect his daughter. Like thousands of other fathers, since women found out they too can leave home without being returned to their husbands in handcuffs. But you're not offering much. It still doesn't solve anything,' he bargained.

'It might help. The person who stole the gun has a safe at the same bank. You could check if any of the clients is also one of the suspects at the school.'

The lieutenant finally leaned back in the deep leather armchair. The lamplight bounced off the skin of his head, with its implacable horseshoe of receding hair, on which Cupido found it hard to picture the three-cornered hat that the Guardia Civil used to wear. Gallardo had adjusted to a new Guardia Civil purged of its obscure and bloody associations. His face was now lit with a sort of calculation and satisfaction, and the detective knew he was going to accept everything he had proposed.

'Only a judge can ask for that sort of information. I'll need a couple of days to draw up a report and persuade him to demand a list. There's nothing worse than a bank for releasing information about their clients. Actually, there is: you.'

'You can't complain. I always offer you more than I ask for.'

༄

He'd worked without a break all morning and had completed a lot of his smaller jobs. It was coming up to one o'clock, the time Alba finished school, and he'd promised to go and pick her up in place of Rocío. He asked Ernesto to close the shop and walked the few streets to the school.

Several parents were waiting for their children outside the playground. Although there were some men, most were women, as if looking after children was still a fundamentally feminine responsibility. Nearly all young, they chatted away in groups, and seemed cheerful and happy. And perhaps they were, perhaps they felt satisfied with that quiet existence in which their children were the central protagonists and determined their time tables and the shape of their lives.

In previous years, on the few occasions he'd picked up Alba, the walk home had been very pleasant. His daughter, happy to have him there, would tell him what had happened that day, whether she was pleased with a word of praise she'd had from the teacher for one of her drawings, or annoyed with a classmate. Now it was only the two of them, he thought he ought to repeat these walks more often.

The bell rang and presently the children appeared. The little ones came out first, in a bit of a daze, looking around like someone who exits a cinema or a theatre on to an unknown street. But as soon as they spotted the familiar face among the adults waiting for them, they shed all insecurities and ran towards it to receive a kiss and a hug, a smile, the little intimacies. Soon, as the age of the classes went up, the pupils' attitudes changed. They came out talking to each other, oblivious to the rest, looking with a certain disdain at the little ones who still needed their parents to get back home.

Alba was among the first in her class to come out, and Julián Monasterio chose to believe that it was because he was waiting for her. He bent down to kiss her, took her heavy rucksack which must have been killing her fragile back, and left the playground with her hand in his.

'How was school?'

'Fine,' she replied, in that laconic manner she took shelter in when asked anything involving her emotions or experiences.

'Were you with Rita again today?'

The girl looked up with her big eyes – long eyelashes he often praised, saying they were like fans, the irises the colour of black poplar leaves about to fall – as if asking him what he knew

145

about her new teacher to call her by her name, what kind of bond he had established with her, when in previous years it had always been her mother who knew the teachers and came to talk to them.

'Yes.' Again the one syllable.

'And what did you do?' he went on, trying to sound interested but not vigilant or worried or pushy.

'We talked a bit.'

Good, very good, he told himself, feeling a wave of gratitude towards the teacher. He hesitated to ask what they'd talked about, for he was curious to know how Rita had managed to topple his daughter's walls so soon, but he held back. He didn't want to pressure her.

'I think she's sort of my friend,' Alba added all of a sudden, the words still cautious and qualifying, still suspicious of good faith. But that little step forward was already a triumphant advance.

'Excellent!' he exclaimed, and suggested: 'Before going home to see Rocío, let's have a snack, shall we?'

'OK.'

They sat at a terrace table and he ordered a vermouth, a soft drink and a plate of olives. Julián Monasterio saw his daughter eat with appetite, staining her fingers and lips with oil as she watched some girls playing in a park across the street.

'Do you want to go and play with them?' he asked.

Alba shook her head in silence.

'Go on,' he insisted. 'I'll watch you from here.'

'I don't know them.'

'So what? You can make friends.'

'No,' she said firmly.

He was thinking of paying and going over to the shop before Ernesto closed up when he saw Rita walking down the street towards them. She was carrying a blue folder, and seeing them, stopped to say hello.

'How's it going, Alba?' She touched her hair.

'Fine,' the girl murmured.

'Are you having a drink?'

The girl nodded without looking up or speaking. Julián Monasterio waited a few seconds before cutting in.

'Would you like a vermouth, or a beer?'

Rita started to demur, fearing that he'd misinterpreted her previous comment, and said something about being in a hurry, but Julián Monasterio had already got to his feet and pulled up a chair for her.

'I bet a drink would do you good after all those hours talking to the children at school,' he said, a little surprised at how decisive he had been.

'All right.'

She sat down and, while the waiter brought the order, said some pleasant thing to Alba which the girl barely replied to, as if now that her father was there, it was he who was responsible for keeping the conversation going and answering all the questions.

Rita, however, didn't look disappointed. She kept treating her kindly and patiently, accepting her nods and headshakes as no less worthy of consideration than the most elaborate sentence.

Julián Monasterio leaned back and observed them. He remembered her words during their interview: 'And at home you should keep on talking to her, asking her what friends she's got at school, what she does in class, whether she's being good.' He got the impression that the teacher treated his daughter in a helpful or healing manner and that she did this so effortlessly that it couldn't just be part of her professional remit. Sometimes when he'd had to be friendly to a child with Down's syndrome, or some other disability, he'd always felt his kindness was an imposture, a fiction, and that everyone – including those he was paying attention to – knew he wasn't acting naturally. In front of those children he'd always felt awkward. In contrast, Rita's attitude to his daughter didn't seem at all forced.

'You're sure you don't want to go and play for a bit?' he insisted again when the waiter came back with their drinks.

Alba accepted the invitation now, as if she understood they both had to talk about something she shouldn't hear. He took her across the street and came back to the terrace. She stopped by the group of girls playing in the sandpit and crouched near them, burying her hands in the sand like them, but not daring to approach them, waiting in vain for them to come and ask her to play. Julián Monasterio thought at that moment that she acted like someone who's decided not to ask the world for anything so as not be refused, only taking what was offered.

'How's she doing?' he asked.

'It's not easy,' Rita said watching her, alone across the street, hopelessly waiting for an invitation. 'We talked a bit today. About her games. She told me she really likes swimming in the pool and the sea.'

'It's true. It's like she feels safer floating in the water than treading on firm ground. We used to go to the beach in the summer for a month. But this year, as we were alone, I didn't think it was a good idea,' he added, well aware that he was venturing on to difficult terrain he didn't let many people into.

'Was it during those months when Alba started talking less?'

'She'd never been one of those chatty girls that get a smile in supermarket queues or in waiting rooms. But, yes, when her mother left,' he went on, and realised that he hadn't mentioned her name, Dulce, or any of those words prefixed *ex* which still suggested some kind of bond, 'her tendency to silence got worse. I guess we're both guilty of not knowing how to stop it.'

'Her mother, does she live in Breda?'

'No, she moved to another town. She comes to see her two weekends a month.'

His answer surprised her, for normally it was the men who pack up one day and leave the women in charge of the children. She felt the same flow of kindness and desire to help as when they'd met at the school, and it was this that made her say:

'I suppose it's not easy. It must be hard sometimes.'

'Hard? It's always hard,' he said, averting his gaze and looking at his daughter, who was still playing alone in the sandpit. 'But it's bearable. You feel like a piece of wood half-submerged in water. You look at it from above and it looks broken in the middle, and yet it's in one piece. Sodden, but in one piece. I can't remember what that's called. You must know.'

'I think it's called refraction.'

'Refraction,' he repeated slowly. 'You look at yourself and you see you're broken, or twisted. Then you put your hand on the place where the wound is supposed to be and with some scepticism realise that, in spite of it all, you're still in one piece, that it's all there, your entrails and your organs, your heart and your bones.'

He stopped, surprised that he was talking like this, at how soon he had moved out of the area of discretion and wariness that separates a man and a woman who hardly know each other. He picked up his glass, less out of thirst than to help disguise his surprise at the intimacy they'd developed in such a casual encounter. It was empty.

Since Dulce had left it was the first time he had spoken to someone in this way, intimately and calmly, without seeking comfort or compassion, trying not to seem a wounded animal whining to be stroked, but also avoiding the frivolity he'd often noticed in separated men and women who joked about their failed marriages and related intimate anecdotes with a forced cheerfulness that verged on the ridiculous. It was the first time he had spoken of his ex-wife with someone who didn't know her and, therefore, took the past as he told it, without correcting him; the first time that the past seemed behind him, buried in the unbearable heat of those summer months, and didn't jump forward to contaminate the future like a rabid dog.

For a moment, though, he wondered whether the intimacy that the conversation had led to was not simply grounded in physical attraction. He liked Rita, he liked her a lot, from her unpainted fingernails to the freckles on her nose and cheeks, from the way she held her glass to the shape of her mouth: although her lips gave the impression of being frozen, the tongue that could be glimpsed through them every now and again was a promise of warmth and sweetness that made you want to kiss them even more. But for her part, why did she listen to him so attentively? He couldn't tell if it was her good nature or her sense of duty that had kept her with him for half an hour, but he felt that the way she looked at him, listened and talked to him, and the lack of caution in her questions, denoted an interest that went beyond simple professional curiosity.

⌒

Rita had listened to him at first with surprise; it was strange to be there all of a sudden, sitting on a terrace and having a drink with a man she barely knew. In fact, she didn't even remember his name, only Alba's surname, and although she tried to recall it in the half hour they were together – she'd read it on his daughter's school report – she still didn't know it when they said goodbye. But what was really strange, and also comforting, was the dignity with which he told her about his complex personal life. His confidences had emerged in a natural way, without either of them forcing them. And despite its sadness, his story had not been depressing, for he told it so honestly and delicately that he neutralised any awkwardness she might have felt otherwise.

She was all the more surprised, too, because the conversation was the polar opposite of her daily routine. At the school there was a tacit agreement not to go into colleagues' private lives – and this included anything touching on sentimental, ideological or family matters, that is, almost everything that mattered. It wasn't allowed to ask any questions that might even hint at a personal problem or at one's mood. Conversation was restricted to the weather and sport, aches and pains, to how slowly the term seemed to be going, how undisciplined some students were, how lamentable was their parents' influence, even if most really participated very little in their school life. So, with exceptions, no true friendships developed at school. Gustavo Larrey had been her only friend, but now he was dead. For a while she'd felt – wrongly, as it turned out – that she was Nelson's friend, for until then she thought it was inevitable to grow fond of people you spend many hours with every day. But it wasn't. At the school she'd learned that forty people can live together for twenty or thirty years without building a relationship that extends beyond politeness. So she too had ended up accepting that it simply wasn't the right place for expansive sentiments. Only with the children, the almost terrified pupils who came to her office, was she able to let her affections free without getting surprised looks, to express the brief and comforting physical contact she was used to: touching an arm when saying hello, stroking their hair when they did well, leaning on someone's shoulder when she felt tired or laughed too hard. At first, when she'd done it spontaneously with her colleagues, she'd noticed how the arm tensed up or the shoulder perceptibly moved away, as if her gestures were inappropriately extravagant for this place. And so she had learned to rein in her demonstrations of affection, and now she knew that she too was beginning to be accepted as another member of the Very Serious and Respectable Society of Moderation.

It was also because of this contrast between the dry protocol of the school and the intimacy of their conversation that she had enjoyed the chat with Alba's father so much. They'd said goodbye agreeably and when, before leaving, she kissed the girl, who had come back to them after getting tired of waiting for an invitation, he'd said:

'I'll come and pick up Alba from school again one of these days. I'll probably see you there.'

'Sure. That'd be nice.'

Before they parted, neither had mentioned the possibility of fixing a date, but she had the intimate feeling that they would soon meet again and that such an encounter would amount to more than a simple greeting.

Later, as she walked away along the pavement, she felt a sort of lightness that was not solely the effect of the two vermouths. She was surprised when she arrived at the door of her flat so soon. She didn't remember her walk home, lost as she was in his words and gestures. Somehow it was as if the extent of her loneliness had been reduced during that half-hour of conversation. Since Gustavo's death she'd been sad and she discovered – not without recognising the flash of egotism this revealed – that finding a sadness different from her own helped her a lot. In a way, during that talk she'd felt like a blind person who, sitting on a bench in the street, hears the tap of another's cane drawing close along the pavement. It was as if they'd recognised each other and had started talking. She was twenty-eight years old, and in her professional environment – where everyone thought that the giving of a confidence always preceded the request for a favour – it wouldn't be long, if she wasn't careful, before she succumbed to scepticism and suspicion in the face of such confessions.

She changed her clothes, washed her hands and, looking in the mirror, discovered she felt grateful to him and would like to do something in return. For the first time in her life she was attracted to a man who seemed lost, less well grounded than she was. She sensed her own frailty and problems could bring him a bit of security and consolation. *Perhaps I'm getting old and I'm starting to feel a maternal instinct*, she said to the mirror with a flirty smile.

These words immediately evoked her painful episode and her

mouth closed over her teeth. What kind of wound was it that, when remembered, did not seem to have lost its depth or virulence and refused to be cauterised by the passing of time? *Don't think,* she repeated, *don't think about it.* Once again she tried to recall his name, unable to evoke the sounds or syllables that matched his face. She knew it was a simple name, easy to say, but not very common. She tried a few out loud, in vain. She lived alone and no one could hear her.

13

Her eyes took a while to adjust to the sudden darkness of the church, a moment which always made her feel briefly yet intensely afraid: she could no longer see what was happening in the light of the street, but neither could she make out anything inside the church. At that moment of transition, she felt like a blind person on the edge of a cliff, at the mercy of anyone who might want to push her into the void. Every month she felt clumsier, more fragile and slower in all her reactions; every term she found it more difficult to control the frantic rhythms of her pupils, who day by day grew quicker, tougher, stronger, and more independent.

At that time of the evening, half past six, the sun sank below the stained-glass windows, and the small church withdrew its bell-tower and curled up into the dark like a snail. Only the rose window let in a little of the increasingly faint twilight over the atrium like a dense, slow fog that made the temperature drop several degrees.

Julita Guzmán shivered and approached the basin of holy water built into one of the columns. One of the last rays of light reflected from somewhere and rippled strangely in the water, as if butterflies flew over the basin. She touched her heart and crossed herself slowly, leaving small wet patches on her forehead and lips.

The church was nearly empty. Only a few dark, kneeling figures seemed to be praying or begging something of the cross or the saints, who looked on indifferently from their alcoves. Without looking their way, she went to her usual place, at the end of a pew towards the front, a piece of worn-down wood she considered almost her own. From there she could easily slip out into the street on the rare occasions when it got too crowded. This was almost always during funeral services for a dead colleague, but also, on one occasion, for a former pupil of the school, the one who had been expelled and ended up dying a couple of years later, from one of those illnesses she would never suffer from and was ashamed to name. This seat was also very close to the confessional and she was able to see if Father

Lucas was inside. She liked to go to confession on days like this, weekdays, when she didn't have to wait and she could be sure that the priest would listen attentively to her small sins, which she listed rigorously according to the catechism. At weekends it was too crowded: there were many lax people who thought they'd earn salvation simply with their Sunday visit, as well as half-dressed tourists, garish and disrespectful. She suspected the priest got impatient with her on public holidays, bored as he was of always hearing the same story. Julita Guzmán told herself that, since all her sins were venial, Father Lucas didn't want to busy himself with her at weekends, when so many people came to the church, their souls unquiet with offences, slights, thefts, lies and the guilty pleasures of the flesh. Yet at other times, while she waited from her pew, she saw how long he took with girls or young women, and she couldn't help having her doubts and even thought that he disregarded her in order to listen to stories and secrets that were more... After all, the priest was a man too. And she was positive there was no man on earth who was chaste and disciplined enough to refuse to listen to confessions like that falling from the lips of a woman.

The woman who was nodding now in front of the grille was very old. She wouldn't be long. Julita Guzmán started saying the Lord's Prayer, concentrating on the changes in the text she was still unable to internalise, bound as she was to the old words, which seemed to her more solemn and effective. Nevertheless, before she had finished, her attention had already dissolved into the tranquillity afforded by the almost empty church, the only public space where she felt safe and at peace.

The particular kind of agoraphobia she'd always suffered from had got worse with age, and any place with more than thirty people in it terrified her, made her feel like a feather at the mercy of a stampede of buffalo. When she couldn't avoid being in a crowd, she looked for a wall to lean her back against, stayed near the exit and avoided all physical contact. Women like her, who had never loved, who had never been touched by the rough hand of a man, found such proximity unbearable. She'd come to the conclusion that the world was overpopulated: that was the reason people had to squeeze together – mouths too close, breath and saliva, hips brushing past in teeming streets, bottoms and stomachs bumping in queues – causing so much promiscuity and violence, which could be avoided by maintaining a safe distance from each other. Proximity, she thought, is the first condition of contagion, and since there are viruses, both moral and physical, inside every human being, the best prophylaxis, when total isolation is not possible, is distance.

And so she preferred the smaller, older churches to the most solemn and ostentatious cathedral, where she felt oppressed by the number of tombs and the height and grandiosity of the domes, altarpieces, chapels, columns, organs, choir stalls and grilles. Churches were perfect in size and decor, for at the other extreme she despised those modern suburban parish churches built with cement, tiles and bricks which had none of the nobility of the bare stone. *And I say also unto thee, that thou art Peter, and upon this rock I will build my church.*

The old lady finally left the confessional and Julita Guzmán went over to take her place. She hitched her grey skirt up a little so as to kneel more comfortably on the worn velveteen of the prie-dieu, and repeated the same words as always. Through the grille she heard the tired voice of the priest responding; after a very long pause, she thought she noticed the tail end of a yawn in his last sentence.

She always confessed in the same order, going through each of the ten commandments to make sure she didn't forget anything. *Thou shalt have none other gods before me*, and she didn't, and she loved Him and, had she been able, would have instituted His rules upon the face of the earth aided only by a legion of sexless angels, armed with the holy oils and sacrificial knives. *Thou shall not take the name of the Lord in vain*, and her lipless mouth only dared utter it during prayers and the catechism, with such piety that at times, in doing so, she felt like a burning bush. *Keep the Sabbath day to sanctify it*, and not only on the Sabbath, often turned by a noisy, perfumed crowd into a Sunday carnival, but nearly every evening she heard Mass at her church, and had done so for decades, during which she had also acquired a full list of bulls, jubilees and indulgences with which, nevertheless, she was not wholly sure of attaining salvation. *Honour thy father and thy mother*, and although they were dead, on every All Soul's day she evoked them, and her powers of memory had so far never failed to recall their faces and their stern moral legacy. *Thou shalt not kill*, and she feared the colour of blood, feared even coming into contact with that of the purest children, and had killed no one, although at times her turbulent hatred surprised her and she wanted some of her fellow men to die. *Thou shalt not commit adultery*, and not even in her youth had she opened her thighs or her mouth, a chaste woman in a lecherous city. *Thou shalt not steal*, and she had never stolen, not a pin nor an orange: not even in her job as secretary managing the school's funds had she pocketed one peseta or kept one gift, when she could have done so with total impunity. *Thou shalt not bear false witness against thy neighbour*, and she never lied deliberately, although she had to admit she didn't always tell the whole truth, everything she knew. *Thou shalt not have impure thoughts or desires*, and everything she considered impure had gone from her nightmares, whether the desires of the she-wolves or the wetness of pigs. *Thou shalt not covet thy neighbour's house*, and she also abided by this rule, not so much because over the last years she had saved everything that she needed for her present and future material well-being, as because what she needed for her spiritual well-being – not to feel so immensely alone and so afraid – were not objects and, therefore, she couldn't take them from anyone without their substance changing.

Her confession, then, was a victory march along the road of virtue. The few obstacles she found were only venial faults, like not having been charitable, or not having resisted sloth. So she didn't stay long on the hassock. What would have created a genuinely impossible conflict for Father Lucas would have been an examination of her conscience regarding the eleventh commandment not listed on Moses's tablets: *Thou shalt love thy neighbour as thyself*. Sometimes, Julita Guzmán wondered why Jesus had added those words, when no doubt He knew that some neighbours are impossible to love. She would go further, and say it's impossible not to hate them. Even though she accepted the passages from both testaments to the letter, in those words she sought an allegory that might be interpreted in a hidden or figurative sense. For it was too demanding a precept, an impossible one to fulfil: if it was already difficult to love one human being, how much more to love an entire community!

But soon she would chastise herself for her lack of faith, her weakness, her arrogance in doubting the accuracy of the sacred texts, precisely when it was so necessary to follow their doctrine, in these times when everyone dared to decide for themselves what was or wasn't a sin.

She ignored again that last commandment and waited for the priest's routine absolution. Her penance was also the usual.

Father Lucas drew aside the maroon curtain and came out of the confessional. She saw him go up the altar steps with a slow, effortful gait. Some more people had arrived to hear Mass, but Julita Guzmán thought they were still too few. The murmurs that came after the priest's first few words did not fill the church: they were hushed voices that contrasted bleakly with the children's shouts outside, with the horns of cars that penetrated into the intimacy of the sacred in a powerful tide, indifferent to the solemnity of the liturgy.

The altar boy opened the book to the page marked, and Father Lucas, bending closely over it, started reading the day's parable. *They brought even infants to him that he might touch them; and when the disciples saw it, they rebuked them. But Jesus called them to him, saying, 'Suffer the children to come unto me, and do not hinder them; for to such belongs the kingdom of God.'*

Julita Guzmán shifted a little in her seat, uncomfortable, for there were too many disquieting details that afternoon. And she still had to teach the catechism! She had promised to do it because willing, well-educated people were needed, and Father Lucas had asked her so insistently that she could not have kept on refusing without revealing that she didn't like children, that, like the disciples in the biblical parable, she'd rather keep them away for as long as possible. How could she tell the priest that because of her dislike and fear of them she had sold herself to Nelson when he proposed that she continue as a secretary, thus betraying two decades of friendship and comradeship with the previous headmaster? How could she tell anyone? Children were diabolic beings whose faces had more in common with gargoyles on the cornices than with the rosy angels fluttering around the Virgin in the glorious paintings of the altar piece. The first artist who painted them in that way must have been unaware of their cruelty, stubbornness and clumsiness; she was sure he had never been trapped for five hours with twenty-five children, frenzied by games, fights and contact with each other.

Perhaps they had been different, more docile and respectful in the past, at a time when they could be caned – not viciously, but firmly – without their parents' complaining as if caned themselves, threatening to report the teacher to the police and put his picture in the papers as if he were a criminal. But that time was long gone, a golden age in which there wasn't a single more morally respectable word in the pedagogical lexicon than *discipline.*

And how could she fight the present, against children and parents who were conspiring in the same rebellion?

Father Lucas was already giving Communion. She hadn't noticed and quickly left her pew to take it before he finished with the three or four other communicants. The priest's trembling hand put the consecrated wafer on her tongue and Julita Guzmán slowly took her leave, her head bowed, feeling the unleavened bread stick to her palate which was dry and worn and did not have enough saliva to moisten it.

She remained alone in the church once Mass was over. The children wouldn't be long. Sitting on the pew she thought of what she was going to teach them that day. Sometimes, before Nelson had taken over the office, she would bring copies of biblical texts, religious poems or lives of the saints, which she made on the school photocopier. That small infraction was not a problem for De Molinos, or for her conscience, as she didn't do it for her own benefit but for that of the flock. But now she didn't dare. Although Nelson had asked her to continue her work as autonomously as before, she couldn't allow herself those liberties. It was not a matter of economics, as the amount of public funds she channelled to the service of religion was insignificant, but of convenience. The last time she'd gone to a shop to photocopy one of her old yellowing prayer books or her saints' lives, she'd caught the mocking expressions exchanged by the employees; the girls behind the counter, all red lips and painted nails, were indifferent to her, but friendly to the male customers, and so smiley that she'd come to wonder why people smile so much, what reasons for laughter they saw around them.

Father Lucas came back in through the vestry door. He approached her and handed her the key. Julita Guzmán guessed his next words.

'I have to go now. I'm very tired today. Please lock the door. You can return the key tomorrow.'

It wasn't the first time it had happened, but she couldn't refuse. Although at first she'd been grateful for the privilege – to guard the house of God – now she didn't like to remain alone in the church at all. When she had to, she grew increasingly afraid of the damp silence of the stones as she was turning the lights off, the bones buried under the tombstones, the smell of extinguished candles, the bleeding scars of the old statues.

'Are the classes going well?' asked the priest, in a way that made it clear he only wanted an affirmative answer that would not disturb his rest.

'Yes. Though it would be better if the children were a bit more interested.'

'A sign of the times,' he replied. A routine phrase of resignation and farewell he used when he had nothing else to say or didn't wish to continue talking.

Julita Guzmán turned to watch him walk to the door, shadowed and stooped, on the way to the room he had in the parish house. At moments like that he looked terribly old, and she lamented that the paucity of new priests forced the church to keep decrepit old men in service. Because young people still felt a radical disdain of churches and sacristies. And if any of them heard the inner call to help others, they channelled their impulses to NGOs that were in fact damaging the ministry, taking over areas that had traditionally been managed by the Vatican's agents.

Suddenly, the children's lateness made her impatient. The darkness had become denser, and she went over into the vestry to turn some lights on. There were not many bulbs, and they were not very powerful, but their brightness instantly comforted her. She put some coins in the collection box and lit several candles on an old stand left in a corner among the new electric light panels. She still liked the stale smells of incense and wax, although they barely existed anymore. They were being displaced by the aggressive smells of cleaning products and the mixture of perfumes all the women wore, from the youngest just out of school to the oldest whose make-up could not hide the fact that they were old enough to be grandmothers. She put out the match as she heard the steps of the first children. At last they were there.

She waited for them to be seated and stop talking. For her the church was, even more than the classroom, a place to keep silent; but it wasn't easy to shut them up even there. She was about to cross herself to start the class when she noticed the absence of Marta, the girl who always listened to her the most attentively. At nine years she showed such goodness, intelligence and faith in God that Julita Guzmán had talked of her to Father Lucas as an uncut gem whom they must take care to destine to the future service of the Church.

'Where's Marta?' she asked. 'Is she ill?'

The children looked at one another, not daring to answer.

'Beatriz,' Julita asked one of her friends. 'Where's Marta?'

'She said she's not coming anymore,' the girl replied quietly.

'She's not coming... anymore?' she asked carefully, fearful of what her question might unleash.

'No.'

'But why? What's happened?'

'Her parents have become Jehovah's Witnesses.'

'What, just like that, all of a sudden?'

'Yes,' several of them repeated, almost vehemently, as if once the news was out all were impatient to share the details.

Her legs were shaking so much she had to sit on the chair placed in front of the pews. She had been shown once again that, one way or another, in spite of her age, her rank and the knowledge she'd amassed over thirty years of trying not to let them get round her, she always ended up losing in her relationship with children.

The pupils fell silent when they saw a disappointment and pain in her face that went beyond the usual impatience she displayed over their mistakes or bad behaviour. As if they'd been accomplices in Marta's desertion, they remained still and quiet, a little afraid of the way the catechist was looking at them, as if they were all members of a sect. A minute later, however, they saw the teacher pick herself up from her chair, make a space next to them at the end of the pew and kneel down facing the altar. Then they heard her words: 'Let us all say the Lord's Prayer so that Marta returns to the way of truth.'

The children had left. She straightened the chair and, as she went past the altar, kneeled down and crossed herself slowly. She felt very tired. She turned off the lights in the vestry before proceeding to the exit through the semi-darkness that bats like so much.

Once outside, she turned the key in the heavy door four times. The street was very dark, as if the granite walls soaked up all the light coming from the lamps. She quickened her steps towards the main road, where many people were still walking, despite the cold weather that had arrived early that September. She went across the road at the traffic lights and, as she reached the other side, saw Moisés passing by with a girl. They were walking hand in hand. He seemed not to notice her, and, uncharacteristically, Julita Guzmán looked back for a few seconds to see whether it was the same girlfriend he'd had two years before. It was. The girl lived in a building opposite hers, and, a few months ago, when she was doing some shopping, she had heard her say that she and her boyfriend had broken up. Julita Guzmán was happy everything was fine again.

She had distrusted Moises from the moment he arrived at the school. Of course, that was her attitude towards any human being capable of talking or moving quickly, but she had good reason to be afraid. She knew his parents and knew that from an early age he'd spent long hours at home on his own, as they devoted almost all their time and attention to the bar they owned. To her, who thought a child's education must be based on control, discipline and order, so much independence so soon was a time bomb. However, so far, Moisés didn't seem a lad prone to recklessness or scandal. True, she didn't like his clothes, or his cropped hair, or that earring he wore; still less the fact that he was a conscientious objector. But despite all that, it had not been long before he gained her respect through his work at the school. At least with her, he wasn't lazy and carried out the small tasks she set him without complaint, even those the permanent staff ought to have done, like making photocopies or stamping six hundred school reports. At break-times, when a child was crying or had hurt himself, Moisés – she wouldn't call him Momo, his biblical name was too beautiful to contaminate it with such an ugly nickname – had no problem looking after them, staining himself with their blood, something that repelled the teachers. He was very clean, and his neatness had impressed her too, for she had always associated leather clothing and men's earrings with a lack of personal hygiene that, at least in him, was not the case at all. So it hadn't taken her long to accept his presence in her office and she knew she would miss him when he left in a couple of months.

She was also glad he was seeing his girlfriend again; she was a bit older than him and perhaps could curb his youthful faults. At the end of the previous term, after she heard a rumour in the neighbourhood, she'd suspected there was something between him and Rita.

She never usually went to her colleagues' work gatherings, and only attended farewell dinners for those about to retire, as they were almost solemn occasions one could not miss without offending the guest of honour. The hours at the restaurant always seemed long. She didn't feel at home amongst the festive shouts and slightly drunken joy. She couldn't laugh at the coarse jokes that were told, and didn't dare raise her voice with witty comments, as she could never think of anything to say. She ate little and didn't touch any alcohol. Although she tried not to leave her place, if she absolutely had to, she tiptoed. No one noticed her and she noticed everyone.

At the last retirement dinner, Moisés and Rita had sat nearby, and, from her corner, she had seen them laugh together and caught their occasional conspiratorial glances over the glasses of wine, red meat and the open eyes of the fish; they barely managed to hide the intensity and intimacy of their glances, which seemed rather inappropriate between a teacher and a young conscientious objector. In the following weeks, until the end of term, if she ever ran into them along a corridor or found herself in the same office as them, she attended to the tone of their voices and the kinds of glances they might dart at each other. And although she never noticed anything special, she'd suspected they were... She couldn't say it. That word was so vexing and painful to her: lovers! It burned her mouth, each syllable like a hot red iron placed between her lips.

She had eventually given up her suspicions, but the shadow

of doubt had lingered. The joined hands of the couple walking away along the pavement seemed to dispel it forever.

As if encouraged by that small revelation, she left the main road and took a shortcut through a narrow dark alley that cut between workshops and backyards. Cars didn't usually pass through there.

She soon regretted having taken the route. Some of the streetlights were broken, and the shadowy, deserted pavement, without the doorways of inhabited houses, was frightening. She didn't want to look back. Pressing her bag to her side, she quickened her pace. Her tiredness seemed to have disappeared, but when she reached the end of the road and the junction where her neighbourhood began, the lights of some bars spilling into the street and the cars noisily going in both directions, she felt exhausted, like an old horse forced to run a race for which it no longer has the speed or stamina.

She went into her flat, bolted the door twice, chained it and, for the first time that autumn, turned on the heating to get rid of the chill that was making her shiver.

14

It was the first day of afternoon classes, and Alba was sitting very close to her. As they were both tired in that final hour, she had given Alba a sheet of paper and asked her to draw anything she wanted, suggesting that she might like to do a drawing of her family. At first, the girl had hesitated, immobile in front of the white paper, as if there were an internal resistance in her muscles and tendons, and her hand was not free to move over the sheet; as if she sensed a trap in this attempt to make her express with a pencil what she refused to express in words.

Rita wondered if she hadn't been a little hasty requesting something that would only interest Rita herself. Since the day she had talked to Julián Monasterio on the terrace, while Alba played alone in the sandpit in the park, he had been on her mind; she had forgotten his name that time around, but it had appeared on the tip of her tongue the following morning, with that resounding second syllable that, although a little rough at first, acquired an unsuspected sweetness when repeated. Not that he was on her mind all the time or obtrusively; it was more like a light and pleasant shade, or one of those delicate scents that become noticeable when a chance movement brings it closer to your sense of smell. She didn't know what prompted his image to drift in and out of her mind, but she did know that he always appeared in areas of light, openly and transparently, showing what was in his hands, unlike Nelson or Moisés when she'd thought of them in the past, who were always slipping along shadowed walls and giving the impression – it seemed to her now – that they were carrying sharp objects.

And so she couldn't help but be curious about him. Their – what was the word... 'encounter' seemed too little, and 'friendship' too much – had started rather strangely, almost intimately, or if not intimately, at least trustingly, when it would have been more normal for two adults to start talking about trivial things and let more delicate matters come out little by little, if at all. But their conversation – and she didn't know how this had happened either – had gone straight to the heart of their concerns and problems. So the next day she wanted to know simple details of his daily life, as if to make up for that first imbalance. She hardly knew anything about him, his work, his home, his tastes, or the places he went to when he wasn't at work or with his daughter. She felt she had come to know the interior of a complex piece of architecture, but without having seen its simplest and most visible parts: the façade, the doors and the windows.

She guessed that, after those confidences, he might feel a bit awkward, like someone who talks too much over an evening of drink and high spirits, and the next morning worries how other people might use what was revealed. She hadn't seen him again in the six days since then. It was always the woman who looked after Alba – her name was Rocío, Alba said – who came to pick her up.

And so she'd decided to ask for a drawing of her family or her house, and while Rita opened a book and pretended to read, the girl had finally started on it.

In the foreground, at the centre of the sheet, she had drawn a rectangular swimming pool enclosed with a double line, as if she feared that the water might spill out. Inside it, surfacing, was an image of herself. The limited skill of her fingers had not hindered her from capturing an expression of well-being, the hint of a smile on her face, amid a halo of water droplets dripping from her hair.

Rita watched her without saying a word, waiting for Alba's father to appear on the paper, confident that the drawing would illustrate the idea she had of Julián Monasterio's relationship with his daughter: very close, perhaps excessively so, and for that reason not conducive to the peace of mind of either. A relationship like a wall erected against the outside world. Sure enough, his picture was the next to appear: standing near the pool, facing forward and looking at the water. Alba wrote DAD underneath it, as if she were aware that other people found it difficult to recognise him and wanted to make it absolutely clear who the person near her was. The face of the figure was not smiling, but neither was it threatening or unpleasant. It was calm, motionless, neutral, and was remarkably well-balanced and symmetrical. However, Rita noticed that at the inner corners of his eyes, Alba had put in some odd semicircles, like swollen tear ducts. Unable to overcome her curiosity, Rita had stopped her to ask her what they were, and Alba replied that they were the tiny holes that tears come from.

Carefully, Rita moved her finger away from the painting, as if she had touched blood, as if her curiosity had taken her too far. She was moved by that detail: it revealed a side of the father that had clearly made a strong impression on the daughter. Those two swollen tear ducts sounded a note of sadness, but didn't fill the whole picture with sorrow. She was glad the picture didn't show him as one of those men who are so crushed by failure that they're no longer able to believe in happiness. Yet she couldn't help wondering how many times Alba had seen him cry.

At the top of the sheet, in the background, appeared two boys with a red and green ball between them, playing football, quite oblivious to the appeal of the pool. She asked her who they were and Alba told her the names of her two cousins.

It wasn't surprising that she should draw her mother last. Rita guessed that deciding how to draw her – in how much or how little detail, what size, where to put her – would be the hardest part of the task. Alba hesitated for a moment and turned her head towards Rita, as if she were about to say she'd finished or didn't want to add anything more.

But Rita kept her eyes fixed on the unread book, pretending not to notice Alba's doubts, and forcing her to make a decision. The girl placed the pencil at the left side of the sheet for a few seconds without moving it. She lifted it up again. On the paper was only a black dot. Alba could draw very well, and Rita guessed it wasn't the technical difficulty of capturing her mother – if it was her mother – that held her back, but doubts over whether to include her in a drawing where she'd already put her father. In the end, with determination, she outlined a torso which sprouted legs, arms – from one of them hung a parcel which looked like a present – and a head. Alba didn't write anything underneath it.

'I'm tired,' she said when she had finished.

'That's fine. Why don't you tell me what you've drawn there?'

'My dad,' she pointed with her pencil. 'Me. My cousins. My mum.'

'And the pool, do you have a pool at home?'

'No, it's at my cousins' house.'

'Do they invite you over?'

'Sometimes.'

'Does your mum bring you presents?' She pointed at the figure.

'Yes.'

She looked at the drawing of the woman. Alba had placed her very far from her father, by the left margin of the piece of paper, so close to the edge that her right arm barely fitted in. Her hair was long and she was wearing a short skirt. Although Alba hadn't drawn her any smaller than the others and had not neglected the details, she looked like an afterthought on the scene, far from the centre of gravity that pulled the other figures together, looking off the page as if there were something there that interested her more.

'It's very pretty. Can I have it?'

'Yes.'

'I'll put it on the noticeboard, so everyone can see it.' She stood up and tacked it on to the cork panel.

Alba smiled faintly and started putting her pencils away in their box, carefully placing each one in the right place according to the chromatic scale. The bell rang. Rita touched her hair and let her out.

She lit a cigarette and smoked it slowly, gathering the strength she needed to attend the staff meeting. Smoking was forbidden in the classrooms, but she only flouted the rule at the end of the day, when no more children would be coming in, not long before the cleaning ladies came round to open the windows, sweep and hoover.

She went downstairs and into the staffroom. They were nearly all there already, silent or chatting in small groups. It was the first staff meeting called since Larrey's death, and although for days everyone had talked and speculated about him, no one said his name out loud now. The large rectangular table forced them to meet each other's eyes at precisely the time everyone was trying to tiptoe about and not come under general scrutiny. The suspicion that there among them, right beside them even, might be someone whose hands were stained with blood – as well as the possibility that others think the same – made the meeting strained.

Nelson, Julita Guzmán and the small group of stragglers in the corridor soon came in. If in previous meetings someone had to insist on silence, now everyone seemed impatient to listen to Nelson. Any decision he made would be carefully analysed, in so much as it would reveal what kind of decisions he might make in the future – in the same way that, after general elections, the measures taken by the first ministerial meeting reveal the intentions of the government more clearly than the whole electoral campaign.

Julita Guzmán opened the minutes of the previous meeting, intending to read them whether they were approved or not, but Nelson gestured her to wait.

'Before we start, the board would like to thank you all for your cooperation and presence of mind over the last two weeks, and for the dignity with which you've born the tragedy that has affected us all. I believe I'm speaking for all of us when I say once again that it's been a matter of civil disobedience, caused by someone from outside the school. We've also thanked the lieutenant for the discretion with which he's doing his job, and managing to avoid the presence of officers at the school, and we have said so in a letter that is available for anyone who may wish to see it.'

He paused and his eyes scanned the staff, as if to make sure that he not only had their attention, but that their attention was closer than usual because of the new way he was conducting the meeting, solemnly and ceremoniously, with an elaborate delivery and a care for detail that was substantially different from De Molinos's style. Indeed De Molinos had been coarser, more authoritative, briefer and more averse to rhetoric, and had resolved disputes in a more straightforward manner.

'I know we've all been affected by Larrey's death, and that we shall remain so for some time. But a school must put its pupils first, and it is vital that they notice the consequences of what has happened as little as possible. The best way to achieve this is by making sure everything goes back to normal. Let the lieutenant do his job well while we do ours. Let classes go on in the most efficient way, and let's keep to the schedule. It's the best we can do for them. And so, although we won't in any way forget it, the board will not speak in an official way of this death again, unless some news emerges from the investigation. I think Larrey himself, who cared so much about his pupils, would approve.'

Rita saw everyone nod, in a wave of agreement that, like the waves of applause in football stadiums, started from Nelson's right, went past her and round the table until it stopped with Julita Guzmán. They all seemed to share the sentiment of the headmaster's careful words, which they would be able to repeat later, away from the school, perhaps because they expressed their wishes better than they themselves could.

The secretary started reading the minutes of the last meeting, but Rita could not concentrate. She was still thinking that Nelson's words were an official invitation to forget Larrey, in a polite and compassionate manner that was even a tribute, but that nonetheless encouraged an act of forgetting that everyone seemed to agree on. If his death had at first been a painful and brutal event, now the pain and brutality had passed and there were still no signs of the murderer, it had become a cause for awkward disquiet that was best set aside until others – the lieutenant or the tall detective who had come to the school – came to solve it. Larrey was dead and one had to feel sorry for his family, but there was no point in mourning him when they were all still alive. She looked around and reflected that her colleagues were not as affected as Nelson had said. In a few weeks' time no one would remember Larrey, the way he died, that he would never see his hair turn grey. They listened to Julita Guzmán read the minutes, and Rita was sure that none of them even contemplated the possibility of asking for a transfer to somewhere that wasn't tainted with blood. They were comfortable there, in a quiet, monotonous posting where they could await retirement. And if any of them, late one evening, when classes were over, felt a little afraid walking along one of the dark and deserted corridors of the school, their disquiet was no doubt less intense than their laziness.

Julita Guzmán was still monotonously reading the minutes whose points no one would remember. Rita knew there would be no objections, as everyone wanted to finish and leave as soon as possible. At that moment she decided she would ask for a transfer. She couldn't remain there, overshadowed by such an anomaly. She would move to the outskirts of any large, distant city, or perhaps to a town on the coast where the sun shone in the summer, where tall, blonde-haired people who loved the sea and spoke in another language came for the holidays, and where a strong, salty wind aired the classrooms of the school in winter ...

Beside her she heard the voice of Matilde Cuaresma telling a younger colleague about a problem she'd had with some students. The minutes were not interesting and some murmurs were already rising. Among Matilde's words she made out some phrases that, spoken in the staffroom – the place that should have been the backbone of the school, from where all the beneficial fluid flowed – seemed almost obscene:

'With those kinds of kids, it's best to stand them in a corner, facing the wall. That really gets them.'

Rita too stopped listening to the secretary. That whispered comment next to her had increased her sense of unease. If children were regarded as annoying enemies who had to be subdued no matter what, then all decisions taken in that room were worth nothing. Just pieces of paper for appearances' sake in front of the inspectors and which would be ignored as soon as the teachers closed their classroom doors. She told herself that not all her colleagues were like that, and it would be unfair not to acknowledge that. But her mood was too low for her to be equitable. As Julita Guzmán read the last lines of the minutes, Rita glanced at the faces around the rectangular table, their expressions barely hiding boredom and impatience. These were the pillars of the state school system. As a group, they were so sure of being right, that none of them knew more in their fifties about their profession than they had know in their twenties; so satisfied were they with their efficiency, training, dedication and results that most of them sent their children to private schools. With a sudden revelation she understood why teachers' children rarely chose to follow in their parents' footsteps. Apart from the lack of social recognition, they would have heard, from an early age, the complaints about work, the thankless environment, the daily malaise that borders on bitterness. Given such messages, it was understandable that none of her colleagues had a child who wanted to make a family tradition of teaching, unlike so many lawyers, doctors or architects, those inherited professions whose prestige increases in direct proportion to how many generations continue its practice.

Nelson was talking again. He was tackling the issues of the day: informative meetings with the parents, extracurricular activities, details of internal organisation, and small administrative and management changes.

Rita was waiting for something else, but he was done in fifteen minutes. Was that all he had to say? Were those the improvements that sometimes, when he was not yet headmaster, he had deemed necessary? She looked around expecting a comment, a question, a suggestion, a hint of disappointment that might confirm her own and imply she wasn't alone, but they were all silent, as if pleased that nothing important had changed. Only De Molinos seemed a bit surprised that, deep down, the staff meeting was so similar to the ones he had presided over until a few weeks ago.

As he was talking, Nelson had not looked at her once, as if he were afraid to meet her eyes and see the disappointment in them.

Everything was going according to the plan dictated by inertia, when under the title of 'Other Business' the last item on the agenda arose. Corona, the director of studies, spoke to remind everyone of the dates of the school festivals and highlighted some information and announcements they had received.

'The fluoride has arrived, as well,' Nelson added. 'May I remind you it should be given to the children once a week? The caretaker will deliver a bottle to each classroom.'

'He needn't deliver one to mine. I'm not going to bother with it. The children's health is their parents' responsibility and they should do it.'

It was the first time De Molinos had spoken and everyone looked at him, surprised at the harshness of his tone over such a trivial matter. Rita thought this interruption was less to do with the small task of making the children rinse their mouths with fluoride for a minute, than the need to reject some of Nelson's proposals, and resist his new subordinate state.

'Someone from the Department of Health can come and hand it out. It's not our responsibility if a child has a cavity. It may be their parents' or a dentist's, but not ours. We've got enough to do teaching them maths, grammar and religion without having to worry about their hygiene on top of that.'

Rita expected Nelson to come back with a quick and brilliant response that would rebut De Molinos's opposition. His last few words had been deeply exasperating to her. Due to the nature of her work, which was often close to therapy, she took them personally. Sometimes she had held that teaching respect for others, rejecting violence, and maintaining a minimum of hygiene were not only as important as a physical law or a geographical concept, but that both kinds of knowledge could not be separated. She doubted anyone could love science, or maths, or language without at the same time loving cleanliness, or valuing words over force, or the peace that comes from giving order to the world so that every thing and every living creature have their place. And Nelson had always agreed with her. That's why she thought the conciliatory and craven reply he was giving now so strange:

'There should be a way to work it out.'

She sat up in her seat, curious to know what arrangement he would suggest. She looked at Manuel Corona. But neither did he seem prepared to put in a word, although he always insisted on the need to maintain hygiene in the school and set an example with his neatness.

'We have enough fluoride for every child. We can notify the parents. If they want some, they can bring a container. We give each pupil the stipulated dose and let them take it at home,' Nelson suggested.

'That seems better. We can't be expected to do these things,' someone else said.

She was listening to all this in surprise and feeling intensely ashamed. Maybe they couldn't be expected to do this particular thing, but they could be expected to help their pupils form healthy habits. They weren't officially required to tie a three-year-old pupil's shoelaces before going down a twenty-five step staircase, and yet they did it. But what really irritated her was that it was Nelson himself who had suggested this... con. She couldn't find a better word for it.

'Fine. We'll do it that way. We'll give the fluoride to whoever asks for it and then forget about it.'

'I don't think we should forget about it,' she heard herself contradict him and tried to curb the antagonism she felt towards most of the forty faces looking at her in surprise. 'How long has this health programme been running?'

BLOOD OF THE ANGELS

'Ten or twelve years,' replied Manuel Corona.

'And so far it's been carried out.'

'Yes.'

'Well I don't think it's such a good idea to abandon one of the few healthy habits we've instilled in our pupils.'

'I don't think ten or twelve years is enough to instil any habit in them,' replied one of those voices incapable of separating humour from malice or sarcasm.

'On the other hand, we know those children who need it most won't come to get it, those children whose parents have never bought them a toothbrush,' she added, ignoring the comment. At any other time she would have been embarrassed to utter such words in front of so many people watching her, but in her exalted state they seemed to cohere with what she'd said before.

Nelson fixed his eyes on her as if he were calculating the shortest way across the woods, unsure of which path to take.

'You can come to my class and give it to them,' she heard De Molinos say. He had waited for everyone to fall silent before delivering one of those malign responses that always left her speechless.

'OK, OK,' put in Nelson, the conciliator. 'Each of you can do what you think best. Give it in class or hand it out to be taken at home.'

Distracted and drained, she remained silent for the rest of the meeting, not listening to the rest of the discussion. Soon afterwards she saw everyone get up and leave. She hadn't written anything in her meeting notes, a blank sheet of paper that could have been no better a reflection of how empty she felt inside. No one had raised their voice to back her up, and that general indifference reminded her that there was more than one way to hurt her. She closed her folder without looking at anyone, telling herself she was making too much of a trivial matter that was irritating her unnecessarily. But she couldn't get it off her mind. Fine, she thought, she would ask for a transfer in a few weeks, as soon as the opportunity arose.

Back in her office, she was picking up her bag when there was a knock on the door and Nelson came in, closing the door behind him.

'What do you want?'

'You left very upset.'

'Of course I did, and you've come here to tell me not to worry.'

'Yes, that is why I came, actually.'

She looked him in the eye, searching for the words she couldn't speak during the meeting.

'I can't believe how much you've changed. If I'd been told a few weeks ago that you would defend De Molinos in a meeting, that you'd side with his laziness and his ideas of what a child and a school are, I wouldn't have believed it.'

'It's not like that, Rita. You know it's not. A school is not a battlefield where you have to crush your enemy. Sometimes you have to give in on small matters so you don't have to on more important ones.'

'I've heard that one before, and better put. But it's exactly those seemingly small matters that make all the difference between a pleasant, well-run school, and a kindergarten or a reformatory. I thought I heard you say that once.'

'All I know is it's not worth getting so upset about such a small thing. Fluoride hasn't even been proven to be effective.'

'No, of course not. Not even in children that will only get to see a dentist when their mouth is rotten and it's untreatable. This is a state school, not a luxury boarding school. Some kids will get the fluoride here or nothing at all. Go on, tell me now that it's none of your business if a group of pupils have cavities or not.'

She felt so certain, so confident about what she was saying, that a little exaggeration hardly seemed important. She made for the door to leave, but Nelson didn't move. She saw his hand – the left hand she'd once found so attractive – move up and softly take her arm.

'I think you're exaggerating and none of this is doing you any good. You can't be harsher on your colleagues than on your pupils.'

'Of course I can. I have no reason to be harsh on my pupils.' She shook off his hand. 'Let me by, please.'

'Rita, I understand that you're a little tense. Larrey was a close friend of yours and I know how much you liked him. But I see no reason why you should take it out on me. I didn't kill him and it's not my fault that he was killed.'

'It's never your fault, Nelson. Ever!' she hissed, feeling suddenly very tired of fighting alone against a sense of unease that
must have been obvious and yet no one did anything to
assuage. She pushed him gently aside and left.

It was already getting dark and even those children who usually stayed behind in the playground had gone home, leaving
the grounds deserted. She walked alone, remembering De
Molinos's caustic comment inviting her to come to his class to
do his job. Why did she always meet hurtful people everywhere? Why did she always run into trouble with those around
her simply because she tried to be honest and run her classes
well, when those were the very things that should make her
appreciated? Since Larrey's death she knew she wouldn't find
the same kind of affection at the school, but she expected
people to be at least polite. She'd come to Breda to work, without knowing a soul. She'd left behind her family, her city and a
circle of friends, some of whom had let her down. By and large
she was sure that everything would be fine in the new place and
she would hurt no one and no one would hurt her. But one
fine day you find out, she told herself, that evil and the impulse
to do harm for no reason and without provocation can come
from anywhere.

She was passing the terrace opposite the park where she had
sat with Julián Monasterio six days before and suddenly
remembered him with unexpected intensity. So much so, that
she stopped on the pavement for a few seconds, thinking it
would be nice to meet him there and then, and chat for a while
about anything, sitting in one of those white chairs with a drink
in her hand. She was sure – without any concrete evidence –
that he would never, no matter what happened, speak against
her to make others laugh at her.

Instead of going straight home, she walked towards his store,
in one of the high streets near the square. She saw him through
the window sitting in front of a computer. There was a younger
man at a desk beside him, and she guessed it must be his
employee.

She had no reason to keep on staring and was about to walk
on when he, standing to get something, saw her in the street
through the window. He went towards her, opened the door
and came out, as if he'd guessed Rita's being there had nothing

to do with computers and as if he didn't want his employee to hear them talk. On his face, a first fleeting expression of happiness at seeing her gave way to a questioning, almost concerned look, the same vulnerable gesture she'd seen at some point in their two previous encounters and which made her want to reassure him. She realised he was waiting for her to say something about Alba, that classes were not going well, or no progress was being made. They said hello and then Rita was quick to say:

'I was passing and stopped for a moment to take a look. And then I saw you were in.'

'Are you just off from work?' he asked, pointing at her folder.

'Yes.'

'It's late.'

'Oh, we had a meeting.'

Julián Monasterio looked back inside, where Ernesto was typing at a computer. His own computer was on, too.

'I've got to go back and finish up, and then go home to check on Alba. Do you fancy meeting up later for a drink? Or dinner?'

'Yes,' she agreed.

They arranged a time and a place and parted with a 'see you later' that was both promising and reassuring.

15

In the first weeks after the separation, if you could call being deserted a separation, Julián Monasterio would imagine the places Dulce might be without him: countries they'd once wanted to explore together, mountains and beaches, trains and ships they'd dreamed of travelling on and never had. He imagined her strolling along a beach, her arm around the waist of a man who rested his forearm against the small of her back, on the sensual machinery of her hips; or smiling for the camera amongst sunlit ancient stones; or sleeping in the front seat of a car driven by the man, on a long journey to one of those foreign cities he should have taken her to: Paris, Venice, Prague, Budapest, Istanbul.

He felt he still loved her even as he cursed her, as he said *whore, whore, whore, whore* over and over again, until those words he wouldn't have dared speak to the dirtiest woman scorched his lips. Then he retreated, afraid of his own despair, and fell silent and numb out of rage and pain and a sense of shame. But two hours later, when the alarm clock went off and he had to gather all his strength to get out of bed, even before he started worrying about the sheets he knew Alba had wetted, his first thoughts were of his ex-wife. Sunk in exhaustion, his eyes still closed, he would imagine Dulce turning up unannounced right then, carrying the suitcases with everything she had taken in them, and putting everything back in the cupboards as if she'd never left. And he didn't know whether he'd forgive her, or shut the door in her face with words of contempt, those very words that had burned his lips a few hours before.

But as the day dawned, his pain eased, as if it were a kind of secretion made in the darkness of the night. Then he told himself that, if she came back, he'd be able to compromise and forget the months when she'd made him so miserable, as she had made him happy for a much longer time, a whole decade in fact. Take those ten years away, he would say, and Alba's bed would still be a tree. He would get to the shop and immerse himself in his work, fuelled by coffee and cigarettes – he barely ate, his mouth felt full of ashes – and made himself sit in front of the computers, repairing them or loading them with programmes. He took care of delivering hardware himself in his car, sweating along the glaring streets of Breda, which, at the height of that whitish, somnambulant summer, were reminiscent of an overexposed photograph. With soaking neck and armpits, he would appear on the doorsteps of astonished clients who had placed an order only a few hours earlier. Those who knew him and had heard about his wife – with a speed perfected in Breda over centuries of spreading trivial gossip as well as the most damaging slanders – must have thought that by overworking he was punishing himself for some fault that led to the break-up, but their sympathetic or amused looks had no effect on him. He noticed how quickly everyone paid him, without bargaining, as if they were trying to get the awkward transaction over as soon as possible, as if they could compensate him for the weight he carried.

He would take the cheque or the notes and go back out into the heat of the scorching streets, under a clear hard sky. Storks were drawn like magnets to the iron steeples of the churches. Now that autumn was starting and everything had turned golden, he realised to what extent, during that summer, Breda had seemed to him a pale, silent, half-asleep place, crushed under the weight of the broad vertical sunlight. Once, he had stopped to wipe his brow in front of a bookshop window, and through the glass he'd seen several pictures of the town's most colourful places: the church and the tower with its large stone pendulum clock, the palace of the De las Hoces family, a balcony covered with geraniums, some pieces of craftwork... It took him quite a few moments to recognise it as Breda, astonished at the photographs, so much brighter and more colourful than a reality he saw as mediocre, impoverished and fragmented.

Another time he came across a dead donkey. He'd seen it the previous afternoon as it walked aimlessly around the market, oblivious to the horns of the cars that had to stop to let it go by, with that slow, noble, almost majestic gait which imminent death sometimes confers even on the least graceful animals. It wasn't branded and it wore no tack other than a sweated band of leather around its neck, broad and dark as a barber's strop. The appearance of a donkey in the middle of the city seemed to him an anachronism at the beginning of the third millennium, an animal which was starting to look almost prehistoric next to the computers that stored the whole world's knowledge.

It was lying on its side in the alleyway where lorries went into the market, blocking the way, an army of flies shared between its anus and its half-open mouth, which revealed yellowish teeth as big as dominoes. The firemen had taken a long time to arrive and remove the carcass. He didn't know why he remembered the tale of the musicians of Bremen, and imagined that the cock, the cat and the dog had abandoned their clumsier and more naive companion to the mercy of the robbers, so they could continue their adventure without the donkey which was just a hindrance.

And when his working day was over and night fell, he lay awake and wondered what it was that Dulce had needed and he hadn't managed to give her. He revisited memories looking for telltale details he should have noticed before she left, but he couldn't find any moments of cruelty or periods of sadness that might have justified her actions.

At other times he wondered what the man she'd left with might be like. He'd only seen him once, from the balcony of the flat, when Dulce came to pick up Alba and the man waited in the car for them to come down. Through the windshield Julián Monasterio made out a dark face, but he couldn't see any other details of body, age or demeanour. However, he clearly imagined her lying beside the man, naked and in the same positions she'd adopted with him. The more arousing the positions and movements had been, the more painful and unbearable the images were, but then, the more difficult they were not to imagine.

And so, night after night, he ended up falling asleep just before dawn, not having found a satisfactory answer in a whole gamut of speculations, all equally bitter; not having found out whether the failure of his marriage was due to a lack of tenderness, or to a lack of obscene words that might, more often and more decisively, have broken through their recent bourgeois decorum in bed.

On another night spent searching obsessively for mistakes, he had remembered a small incident from many years before, when they were not yet married, just after they'd started seeing each other. A small incident that, along with everything that had happened a decade later, he didn't know whether to characterise as an involuntary indiscretion – as he had then – or as dust she'd thrown into his eyes to check the speed and intensity of his reflexes. But you don't always close your eyes in time, he told himself, and eyelashes don't always keep out dust. It had happened like this. They hadn't seen each other for a few days, as she'd been up north visiting her family. When she came back, he went over to the flat she shared with some friends – a place covered in tapestries, cushions and posters on the walls, with wicker furniture and a see-through bath curtain. They locked themselves in her room and took their clothes off impatiently. As they made love, Dulce must have come without his noticing, and he remembered her whispering in his ear, so casually that he was taken completely by surprise: 'You can come now, if you want.' It was the first time she had used that word, which still had awkward, almost obscene overtones. Up until then, when they talked about sex – and they didn't talk much, they just had a lot of it – they did so in a roundabout way, using the sort of private, metaphorical language that every couple elaborates in secret, like an intimate rite that no one else has access to. But now Dulce had said the word so casually that he thought it couldn't be the first time she'd used it, even if it was the first time he had heard it from her. It didn't take much to work out that a different language implied a different listener. But even then he had learned not to trust women who reached maturity without ever making a mistake, and by mistakes he meant, with that confidence his love for her gave him, all her previous relationships before him. He would tell himself that she too had a past life in which he didn't exist, and that he couldn't erase it without also erasing some of the qualities that had made him fall in love with her. Nevertheless, and in spite of all these reflections, he'd felt a pang of jealousy so intense that he still remembered it ten years later.

Details like that, distant and half-forgotten, haunted his memory on those summer nights, as he drifted drunk and hungry around a city that was as hot as a tin roof, or as he tossed and turned in bed enduring the heat, and changing positions in a vain attempt to stop sweating. He came to think that there had always been a hidden side to Dulce which he'd never had access to, like one of those monasteries where tourists can see the brightest and most attractive parts of the architecture but are not allowed inside the cloisters or the basements which permit a hidden view of the building and without which the curious traveller cannot really claim to know everything about the place.

However, Julián Monasterio couldn't have stated categorically that he had never suspected its existence. Sometimes he had imagined the possibility of turbulence, although he didn't imagine when or in what way it would manifest itself. Sometimes he had glimpsed Dulce's unknown side when she went through one of her neurotic phases, when she was equally prone to depression and moodiness as to enthusiasm. During those phases, there was no happy medium for her: she went from thinking herself the most miserable woman in the world to thinking herself the happiest; she didn't like anything around her, even if it was beautiful, good or wonderful, and only the distant and obscure seemed attractive; she would get up in the morning strong enough to take on the most demanding projects, and feel crushed by fatigue in the evening... But as soon as she went back to normal, and they made love during a night full of kisses, he would forget those hints of disaster.

↩

He hadn't been on a date since she'd left, and the one with Rita in an hour made him a little afraid. He feared he may have become one of those men who, after a failed relationship, cannot see the difference between the woman who betrayed him and all the rest.

After shaving he got in the shower and let the hot water ease the tension in the muscles of his shoulders and neck, cramped after so many hours in front of the computer. He scrubbed until he felt very clean. After Dulce left him he had vowed to take care of his body, stop smoking, do sports and travel more, telling himself that if good habits had been beneficial while he was happy, they should be all the more so when he was miserable. But he hadn't fulfilled his own promises. He was aware that in only a few months he had started giving in to the dangers of solitude: neglecting his personal hygiene, becoming slovenly, eating badly and hurriedly, acquiring idiosyncrasies and egotistical habits that aren't possible when living with others.

As he put on his deodorant he told himself he would have taken as much personal care if he were having dinner with friends or with his sister, but he knew that in his meticulous attention to his appearance was the wish that Rita would like him, would find him pleasant and attractive. That would be enough for the night. Any greater goal he saw as not only impossible, but also presumptuous. Whatever would be, would be, and rushing would not make things better. How long would it be until he made love again, he wondered once more, with a surprising lack of anxiety for a man accustomed to sleeping with a woman for over a decade, who had now been living alone for several months. How long until he kissed and was kissed, caressed and was caressed, seduced someone instead of renting a mouth and a pair of open legs? Not just fucking: he could do that any time.

Once, on one of those summer nights, he had left Alba at his sister's, taken the car and gone far away, hoping that someone else's caresses might make him forget who he still wanted. After driving for a couple of hours, he stopped at a colourfully lit roadside bar: a place away from the world. He hesitated for a moment, without getting out of the car, parked in a shadowy corner. There, so close, with the engine and the lights turned off, his loneliness and what he was about to do weren't so obviously connected. But he hadn't come that far only to go home straight away, and so he went into the bar, trying to muster an expression of confidence and indifference he imagined any regular would have.

The decor, the furniture that didn't look as if it had been salvaged from a flea market, the at least surface cleanliness, the bright lights, and even the look of the women, who were quite young, all surprised him; he had imagined somewhere dark and sordid, almost illegal. Neither could he see any threatening men who looked like bouncers or pimps. The girls who were free waited at the bar or by the jukebox, and didn't approach him with aggressive or obscene proposals as he had feared. They didn't even look at him much. They kept their distance, as if they guessed he needed some time to drink a whiskey and slow his galloping heart. About ten minutes later, when he'd started to wonder if he should make the first move, a young woman with blonde hair, possibly dyed, whom he thought quite attractive – though it could have been the whiskey, or the excitement the place was beginning to exercise in him, or the short skirt and low-cut blouse – approached, greeted him with a kiss on the cheek, and asked him his name. He was about to tell her when a certain caution sparked a lie; he was sure she would be expecting a lie anyway. She repeated it and smiled, and he was surprised at how convincing her smile was, for a woman who let ten or fifteen men fuck her every night, he thought, could only be full of loathing. And you had to be very skilled to hide it that well.

He paid what she asked, without considering whether it was too little or too much, not knowing what he was buying, and followed her up a staircase and into a nondescript room. While the woman did something in the bathroom, he took off his clothes. He folded everything on a chair and, barefoot, tiptoed over to the bed. The bedclothes seemed clean and he sat on them, waiting patiently, while his sex, oblivious to any sense of unease, and to the strange place and its inhabitant, started to harden.

Naked, the woman lost much of the voluptuousness she'd displayed in the bar, and seemed defenceless, almost vulnerable. Perhaps it was set up like that as part of an age-old scenario perfected from the dawn of time to please the client: boldness and the promise of pleasure downstairs, and submissiveness and gentleness upstairs. With a smile she lay at his side and without even asking what he wanted, taking for granted that this was what was expected of her, took hold of his sex at the base, unrolled a condom over it and, just as some animals moisten their food before swallowing it, started licking him and covering him with saliva before voraciously taking him in her mouth, as if she were hungry or thirsty.

The kiss she'd greeted him with was the only one of the night. It was later, when he was drying himself, hurrying to leave, that he wondered how long it would be before he made love again. Not fuck: he could do that any time. To hold a woman in his arms, slowly kiss her, naked for the whole night until dawn. As he drove back he thought that, of course, there were lots of things a man living alone can do, but at that moment he knew he preferred the disadvantages of sharing one's life to even the most promising prospects of solitude.

He heard the door open and presently Rocío saying hello to Alba, who was in the front room finishing her dinner. He'd called Rocío from the shop to ask her if she could babysit, and she'd agreed without a murmur.

Julián Monasterio came out of the bedroom, dressed and showered, and Rocío looked him over, barely hiding her curiosity. It was the first time since Dulce had left that he had put on a new shirt and dressed to go out; but she didn't say a word. She picked up Alba's empty plate and took it to the kitchen.

'I have to go if I'm not going to be late. Give me a kiss,' he bent down to his daughter.

'Are you going to have dinner?' she asked again. It was evident that she didn't like it.

'Yes.'

'Are you going alone?'

'No, with some friends,' he lied, not because Rocío was listening but because he didn't know how Alba would react if he told her he was going out with her teacher. Once again he realised how difficult it was to talk to her, to draw a line between caution and lies. He was wiping some ketchup from the corners of her mouth with a napkin, and at that moment he would have liked to have Rita beside him to tell him what to do. He stilled suddenly, napkin in the air, surprised at this impulse. He realised it was the first time he hadn't thought of Dulce in a matter relating to their daughter, when she had always been his guide until then. In moments of doubt over everyday problems he always wondered what his ex-wife would do in his place, and took her agreement or disagreement into account in any decision he made. But this time it was Rita's image that had spontaneously appeared in front of him.

'Will you be late?'

'A bit. But Rocío will sleep over with you, just in case.'

Alba didn't reply and it was obvious that, although she loved Rocío and felt safe with her, she was in no way a substitute for her father. Julián Monasterio shook off the image of damp sheets the next morning, kissed her and went out.

The bar where they'd arranged to meet wasn't far and he

walked there. It was unusually cold for the first days of October and the pavements were nearly deserted. A fresh, sharp wind swept through the narrow streets downtown, and already carried the breath and smells of autumn, as if it had picked them up through Paternoster woods and, laden with imminent decay, came into Breda to remind everyone that summer was over and settled weather was not to be expected in the following months.

As the shop was almost on the way, he took a one-street detour to check that everything was all right. He did that sometimes: he liked to look in the window from the outside when it was shut, like any other passer-by stopping for a moment to look at prices and items. The lights were on. At the back were his desk and chair. From that position, two hours before, Rita had watched him working, perhaps had watched him with curiosity for a few seconds until he saw her. What had she seen, he wondered. He'd put up a mirror to hide an ugly column that was in the middle of the window display, and he moved to look at himself in it now. Over the last few months, the look of fear and confusion he encountered whenever he chanced upon a mirror was so intense that he could no longer see the man he had been, like an explorer lost among savages for many years, who is rescued and is horrified at the face he sees in the looking glass presented to him. Yet now, in the face emerging from the stiff collar of his new shirt, he saw restlessness, not fear. And that was exactly what Rita must have seen: a thirty-six year old man, a little round-shouldered from all those hours in front of the computer, but still strong, with thick hair cut short, as only men who don't have to worry about incipient baldness can. No part of his face was particularly attractive – the lips were too thin, and the nose a touch too big – but it had that appeal some men manage to derive from pain and asceticism, and which shows through as leanness and in lines that seem not so much signs of age as fruit of a life's efforts, self-sacrifice and a surplus of emotion. But he also saw in those twenty square centimetres of skin a lack of vitality and optimism he didn't like at all. With his eyes closed, he rubbed his hands over his face as if he wanted to erase his features and rebuild his entire face from its outline. But when he opened them nothing had changed. He said to himself: *That's me. I'm thirty-six years old and I'm still learning to be happy. Not to be too unhappy.*

He came to the bar and ordered a beer. When he saw her come in he noticed she too had dressed up for the date. Not as if she was going to a party, but her skin glowed slightly, and she wore a pale lipstick that softened the lines that were like tiny incisions around her mouth and disappeared when she smiled, as if trying to show that she had dressed up for him but at the same time had wanted to hide that she had. He liked that discretion: heavy make-up and elaborate dresses, no matter how prestigious the designer, had always seemed forced and uncomfortable to him.

From the moment they arranged to meet, Julián Monasterio had felt nervous: it had been many years since he'd gone out with a woman other than Dulce, and he was afraid he would be boring or uninteresting, or act as awkwardly as he had on his first dates as a young man, when his eagerness to be funny had made him utter banalities that he regretted later.

Besides, he'd never been witty or talkative. He'd never been the kind of man who could make others' amusing anecdotes or adventures his own. He laughed at jokes, but never remembered them and couldn't get the funny bits right. He'd always had good friends who took that role with such wit that he was allowed to remain in the background, which was where he liked to be. And in his last few months alone he'd seen this tendency to silence grow, replying tersely to greetings and remarks from people he knew, as if his daughter's silence was linked to some dark, long-buried inclination of his own that had reappeared.

But when Rita appeared in the bar he forgot all his fears. He was a little surprised to realise that he felt comfortable with her immediately, and that relaxed feeling made everything else easier. After a couple of minutes he realised that he didn't have to think twice before he spoke and that he was saying anything that came into his head. They finished their beer and he suggested getting the car to have dinner away from Breda, in a little restaurant by El Paternoster. Although it was frequented by hikers and passers-by and was too crowded during the day, in the evening it settled into a strange bucolic peace, accentuated by the silence and the solitude of the reserve. It wasn't too far, about eight kilometres, a distance that meant they would leave the city behind, and this relative remoteness gave them the feeling they wouldn't encounter any familiar faces that evening they'd rather not.

For Julián Monasterio it was a little disturbing to have her there by his side in the dark interior of the car. He'd forgotten that its small space, so everyday and mechanical, could bring together two strangers, intensify their perfume, and enclose them in an atmosphere of intimacy. In the eight or ten minutes the journey took he noticed how the anxiety, the emotion, the slight nervousness, the flirting, doubts and boldness of his first dates as a young man came back to life, although so did the caution, fear and cowardliness of the last few months. In those moments, Julián Monasterio felt both younger and older, and had anyone asked him to explain it better he wouldn't have known how.

'I've never been here before,' said Rita, when they arrived.

'I think you'll like it.'

They got out of the car, and she stood motionless, looking at the broken line that separated the sky from the tops of the Volcán and the Yunque mountains. Every now and again a shooting star appeared, like the surplus of the incandescent stuff that stars are made of. The wind shook the branches of the oaks and the pine trees in the quiet night, and it was as if their movement made the cold more noticeable. Rita folded her arms against the wind that tugged at her hair with awkward insistence. In no hurry to go into the restaurant, which looked silent and lonely, Julián Monasterio offered her his jacket. He was fine where he was, watching her look at the mountains, confident in the man waiting behind her, and oblivious to the tiny threats of a million animals that live under stones during daylight but now had surely left their dens.

When they finally entered the restaurant, there was no one else in the small dining room, and as some of the lights were off and several chairs were on tables, they thought it might be closed. The place gave the impression of the simultaneous order and chaos of a house the day before a move. They called out, and a woman came into the room to welcome them, surprised.

'I didn't hear you,' she said.

'We were hoping to have dinner,' said Julián Monasterio.

The woman looked questioningly over her shoulder towards

the kitchen, where a man in chef's clothes appeared and nodded.

'We were about to close. We didn't really expect anyone. But do sit down,' she said, pulling up two chairs. 'You'll be our last customers this season.'

'Isn't it a bit early for that?' asked Rita.

'Not really. From early October on, not many people come up here. But don't worry,' she added when she saw them hesitate. She took a lighter from her pocket and lit the candle on the table, as warmly as a good host would light the chimney for her finest guests. There was no breeze, and the flame grew straight, without flickering. 'You're our last customers this year and it wouldn't be right for you to leave on an empty stomach. It would bring us bad luck. We'll make something special, even if we don't have everything on the menu.'

⤶

It was colder when they left the little restaurant. But they felt happy, filled with that slight euphoria brought on by the conjunction of wine, food and good conversation. And no doubt the solitude of the restaurant had contributed to this feeling; they were the only guests, served by the chef who came to ask them at one point how everything was, and by the woman who tended to them as if they were nobles from a bygone age, seeming to understand their need for everything that evening to go without a hitch.

As they reached the car, Rita turned her back to him and stood motionless once again, in the same manner and in the same place as before, contemplating the play of light on the peaks that stretched to the heavens, and now seemed taller and more vertical than before. The wind still whistled between the branches of the oak trees, and as they moved they cast blurred, animal-like shadows in the moonlight, which reached up from the crater of the volcano towards the sharp October stars.

For a few seconds Julián Monasterio stood there looking at her. He was aware that if he stepped forward he could embrace her, and the possibility excited more desire than he'd expected when he'd left the house. He felt that every circumstance, every chance the night had presented them with – dinner in a deserted restaurant, the moon and the mountains, the wondrous chlorophyll wall of the nature reserve, the remoteness – conspired to create only two alternatives for that moment: the first was to stay where he was and wait for Rita to go to the car; the second was to move, but if he did that it would have to be to embrace her. Without hesitating any longer, he took off his jacket and stepped towards her, put it over her shoulders and left his hands there, feeling her wind-tossed hair caressing his knuckles.

Touching the unknown, mysterious territory of another's body, he felt as ambiguously as the conqueror, who, setting foot on new land, expects to find a paradise to colonise, and realises that he is, in a way, betraying the motherland he's left behind. For a moment, Dulce's memory was very real. But it drew away as soon as Rita leaned back to rest against him.

'Thanks,' she said, as she felt the jacket on her shoulders.

'Everything seems a little unreal tonight,' he whispered in her ear.

'It's a strange and wonderful night,' she replied quietly, turning her face to him.

Julián Monasterio knew those words referred to him. During dinner he'd felt the distance between them get smaller. But now that they were outside, without the man and the woman from the restaurant close by, everything confirmed just how close they had become. He no longer doubted that before him was a woman he could make fall in love with him – in another time he would have said seduce – and that if he set his mind to it, he would. Although it would be risky, it was worth it: he was seeing everything he'd hoped to find in the last few months now in Rita's eyes.

They kissed slowly, embracing and barely speaking, every now and then separating their mouths to press their cold cheeks together, to touch the other's hair or the back of their neck, or to look at the lips they'd just kissed as if to find a visible sweetness.

'Let's go,' he said, all of a sudden. Now he'd come to a decision he was surprisingly certain of what he should do next. As if things he had forgotten were coming back to him, he suddenly knew that he had to respond to those kisses and his overwhelming emotion decisively, intimately, deeply. He couldn't let them fade away, disappear without delivering what they promised, no matter how afraid he may be of emotional entanglements and the fact that it may all prove a pale imitation of his life with Dulce. If they didn't spend the night together, he knew these wonderful moments might never come back, might dissolve into nothingness. Perhaps his timidity would never grant him another chance, her offer slipping away as he hesitated over whether to take it. He felt this was one of those moments in which passion will only accept advance or retreat, with no option of remaining still and picking up later where one left off, in the same place, under the same conditions.

'We could go to a hotel,' he suggested, wanting to find neutral territory. He imagined four or five reasons why Rita would not want to take him straight to her flat, but none of them worried him or made him feel inadequate. But he heard her say:

'I'd rather we went to my place.'

They got in the car and returned to Breda along the almost empty road, sometimes holding hands and letting them lie interlaced against their legs.

Once in the flat, they kissed and helped each other out of their clothes, pausing each time a garment revealed an area that deserved kissing or caressing for its beauty or its tenderness, as if they wanted to enjoy everything without haste. They had the whole night to themselves, sure that in the city that slept around them no one was asking for them.

Julián Monasterio had almost never given in to sudden or intense emotions; often, when something made a strong impression on him, he stopped and had to wait until he could regain his emotional balance before carrying on. Now, however, following his decision at the restaurant, he let himself go completely. They were both naked now and Rita's body, far from making him nervous, gave him a strange sensation of peace.

Their caresses were different. His were cautious: he touched her still unknown body, surprised by joy and gratefulness, without yet daring to give his mouth as important a role as his hands. Rita's caresses, on the other hand, while not obviously bold, were the kind that incite and encourage the other's boldness: the barely suggested parting of her thighs when his hand paused at her knees, or the way the tip of her tongue slipped into his mouth, that first, simple penetration, seemingly of no consequence but which clearly shows how far the rest of the body is available.

Everything went well, well enough for the second time to be better than the first. When they made love again, they had both let themselves go without holding back, without that initial caution which is concerned with the other's pleasure and stops one giving free rein to one's own. And so once the whispers and the moans died away, they felt they knew each other intimately, in body and temperament; for any act of love in which two people give themselves over to each other's will, naked and unarmed, innocently and without shame, also reveals their souls.

Julián Monasterio came back from the bathroom and lay next to her. The blood that had engorged his sex was returning to his heart, and with it a peace he had thought lost forever. Taken by surprise, he began, in those moments, to believe that the word *happiness* might have real meaning again, that it wasn't simply a false conjunction of three syllables that a man strives pointlessly after just so he can forget sorrow and stay on his feet. He lit two cigarettes and passed one to Rita. Outside there were no more sounds of cars, and the streets seemed deserted, as if all the inhabitants of Breda were fast asleep. Only the murmur of the wind sounded at the window behind the curtains. And they were already talking of what had happened that night, making sure that not a word or a gesture would bring them down from the place where the tenderness of their bodies had taken them, from the blind trust that allows someone to open themselves to another. Sunk in that pleasant tiredness that is not fatigue, they talked and touched each other still, looked at their nakedness, pointed out what was missing or excessive, expecting the other to contradict them and kiss the flesh where the defect was. In those moments of slow and indolent touches, no longer keen with desire, of contentment, lying on a bed warmed by their bodies, they tried to make everything that was imperfect, or vulgar, or ordinary, beautiful.

16

Cupido took the gun out of its holster and lifted it to his nose. It smelled of slightly stale grease, and iron or steel, the smell from the depths of the earth all heavy metals preserve no matter how much they are treated or cleaned. There was no smell of gunpowder, though, as it had been a long while since he had fired it. Only very occasionally did he practise shooting against a black silhouette at one of the ranges in the capital. He'd never fired it at a man, and was fairly sure he never would, so he sometimes wondered what he still wanted it for.

He kept it on top of a cupboard, without many precautions; he'd never imagined anyone would break into his place, and there were no children in his flat who might be curious about it. One night he'd met a dubious woman – women were to him exactly like the air he breathed: he couldn't live without them, but couldn't hold them too long either – who asked him if, in his particular line of work, he always carried a gun. He replied he never did, but that he had one at home. Although he thought for a moment she might refuse to come home with him, it was that very factor that seemed to convince her, as if the gun itself was capable of awakening the kind of desire it seemed at first unconnected to. And so they'd got to his flat, and without much preamble went to bed. Although Cupido thought she'd forgotten, at one point the woman – a beautiful young woman, who was no longer hesitant and knew exactly what she wanted – asked him to show her the gun. He refused, as if she had been joking, but the woman insisted, while looking at him in such a way as to suggest that, in exchange, she would do anything he wanted. Cupido, who had known for a long time that things work out a lot better in bed when everybody's happy, eventually gave in, even if he felt a bit awkward, and had to tell himself that where love and sex were concerned, he'd never know every fetish and would always be taken by surprise.

Sometimes he'd noticed how people's faces change when they hold a gun in their hands. How fear and aggression, nervousness and occasionally violence, rise to the surface. The woman had weighed the unloaded gun in her hand, smelled it and praised its beauty, and had caressed the dense, dark bluish metal slowly and suggestively: the detective became so aroused he had no trouble accepting everything else she suggested. The woman asked him to hold the gun while they had sex, as if the gun – with the aura of threat and power it had, even unloaded – was the third essential member in that peculiar ménage. And he had to admit it hadn't been bad that night, excited as he'd been by the contrast between the cold metal and their inflamed bodies, by the obscene words made by the double intention of language, by the shameless way the woman kept every one of her silent promises.

He placed it on the table and looked for the licence in the metal filing cabinet. It had expired almost five months ago. He took the forms he'd requested out of an envelope and started filling them in, feeling that it was all a bit superfluous and dispensable, because if something couldn't be solved with thoughts and words, then it couldn't be solved with a gun.

That bit of rubber-stamping made him go through a procedure that bored him intensely, a series of requirements drawn up to dissuade people from acquiring a gun, to prevent someone in the grip of rage from obtaining one before their rage had passed: certificates of psychological and physical fitness, others ensuring one knew how to store, maintain and handle it, and a copy of one's criminal record. The latter had made things particularly difficult the last time he'd requested a licence and he managed to get one only after a few months, basing his application on work purposes which, fortunately, had never justified it. He filled in the bank details for the taxes and attached everything to the manual for the pistol, which contained details of the brand, model, calibre and serial number: it was surprisingly similar to the registration card of a car. All this, along with the gun to be licensed, he would take to Lieutenant Gallardo, who would make the whole process easier. He'd also use the visit to ask him about the investigation at the bank.

When he was working on a difficult case, Cupido tried to dedicate himself entirely to it, as he did now over the business of Julián Monasterio's gun. He put everything he had into solving it, with as much dedication as a parent whose child has been kidnapped: he thought of nothing else, spared no phone calls, covered miles if necessary, and knocked on every door.

However, sometimes the very nature of an investigation – during which periods of intense activity involving two or three nights without sleep might be followed by dead days of waiting – meant he worked in the same way as self-employed professionals like builders, plumbers and repairmen. Their jobs are irregular and they can't turn anything down, since a busy spell can be followed by one of unemployment. So they can have several jobs on the go at once, often to their customers' irritation. Every so often, Cupido took on an easy case that could be solved in one or two nights, hidden in a dark corner or in his car, on duty while everyone else around him slept, had fun or made love. During the lull while the bank's clients were being investigated, he solved a simple case of bookshop thefts. The owner was baffled, as she hadn't managed to stop them in spite of the constant watch she and her staff kept on their customers. For a few days Cupido turned into a reader and bibliophile with a strong interest in new titles, facsimiles, literary prizes, best-seller lists and the marketing ploys used by publishing houses to get their books into windows and prime space. He'd always liked reading and still read a lot when his work permitted, so he didn't mind spending a few hours there, among so many writers he admired. Browsing through the books he encountered phrases or lines that raised a smile and made him think: 'Crime is not profitable,' he read in one of Euripides's tragedies. And then, in a poetry collection by Francisco Brines: 'Questions / Without answers are sterile.' As often happened with poems, he felt that this one spoke directly to him. The deadlock he'd reached in the Julián Monasterio case, not knowing how to continue, still waiting for results dependent on a third party, made him wonder whether he'd approached it correctly, whether he was not asking unanswerable questions and, therefore, whether he needed to ask different questions of different people. For so far he only had unconnected pieces of information that did not lead anywhere: a man shot dead on the one day he was not wearing a tracksuit, a pistol stolen from a bank safe which had probably been used to fire the shot, and a small network of hatred and ambition. These pieces of information seemed to obscure the whole inquiry, in the same way that the weak streetlights of his childhood, lighting only a small spot on street corners, made the surrounding area look darker.

This was always the worst moment of an investigation, when he had several clues in his hand and was incapable of interpreting and extracting a hypothesis from them. It made him feel stupid.

One afternoon he'd seen a woman hide a book under her jumper; on the way out, he bumped into her in such a way as to make it fall out. She was a relative of the owner and often popped in to say hello. They hadn't even thought of her as a possible thief. A few moments of general embarrassment followed and, as so often happened, he got caught in the backwash and ended up hating his job as a detective.

The doorbell rang and for a few seconds he put off answering it, not wanting to listen to a new problem from a man or a woman who'd end up involving him in their misery. When he finally made up his mind, he saw Lieutenant Gallardo in the doorway, in civilian clothes and carrying a briefcase.

'Come in,' Cupido said.

But Gallardo was already stepping into the flat, looking around with the open curiosity of someone who's used to gaining access everywhere without much resistance. He sat in the armchair for clients and waited for Cupido to do the same on the other side of the desk.

'So this is where you work?'

'Yes. Did you expect something different?' he replied, seeing that the lieutenant too seemed prepared to find a less domestic place, with more signs of his job: a room with a big fan hanging from the ceiling and a coatstand with a raincoat and a gun holster hanging on it. And in an adjoining room, a secretary with a fake air of sensuality and innocence. 'You don't need a lot more to do this job.'

'You reckon? You wouldn't get very far without us. You think a bank would give you a customer report?'

'You've got it?'

'Yes.'

'And?'

'No one from the school, or their spouses, or a close relative has a safe in that bank.'

The news made Cupido feel, once again, very uncertain about this case, fearing he was entering into a disappointing and idle phase when days would go by without a single step forward. *One never gets entirely used to disappointments*, he thought. If he didn't find out anything else, he would wait a few days before telling Julián Monasterio that he couldn't progress, that all his inquiries had come to closed doors that themselves didn't even seem to hide any mysteries.

'But we've got a name,' the lieutenant added with a half-smile that wasn't quite as ironic as he'd hoped.

Cupido understood the joke was a bit of payback and curbed his impatience. Now he knew why the lieutenant hadn't seemed angry at any point since he'd come through the door. After ten years dealing with the police, he could tell just by looking at them when an investigation was not going well at the station. They were no philosophers, and couldn't bear living with questions that had no answers. When things were going badly, their inner unease ended up affecting the civilian population as well: an inflexible approach to traffic incursions, all the officers swamped with work in foul moods, official vehicles patrolling over the speed limit and ablaze with lights and sirens. It was only Cupido's anxiety that had stopped him guessing Gallardo had something and that this was the reason for his visit.

'Saldaña has a safe in the same bank, under the same conditions as your client. A farmer with a safe,' he repeated, noting the strangeness of the fact.

Cupido felt the same: it was the last name he would have expected to find on the list. But if Saldaña had shot Larrey, that would explain why the school gate – which he didn't have keys to – was still open when the caretaker, back from the hospital, closed it, thinking someone must have forgotten to do it.

'And the bank, don't they have a record of when people access their safes?' he asked, looking at every possible angle.

'No, they're just the guardians of the treasure. A customer comes in, presents ID, asks for the key, and they give it to him. That's all. The very game of concealment demands it. Have you never been in one of those places?'

'No.'

'It might seem hard to believe, but neither had I until now. They even disconnect the video camera on the inside during working hours. I'd really like to see what's inside those safes, how many millions in undeclared cash, how many compromising documents, how many obviously illegal products, how many traps.'

'And the staff who were there that day, they don't remember anything?'

'Not a thing. It's been a month and a half. Besides, it was August and there was an acting manager who doesn't know the regulars. He does remember our man, though, Julián Monasterio, and he's confirmed the incident: his safe remained open until the next day. At least we know he wasn't lying.'

'I always knew he was telling the truth. The story is too absurd for anyone to make it up expecting to be believed.'

But at that point it wasn't Julián Monasterio who mattered, but Saldaña. His name on the list seemed to evoke his presence between Cupido and the lieutenant: the image of a dark, saddened man with coarse hands, but who displayed that beginning of refinement in looks and habits that the use of technology was imparting some country people, whose skins no longer seemed several centimetres thick and whose hair no longer seemed closely related to that of their horses; they still had very strong arms, though, and while moving and doing physical work they acquired a kind of dignity and nobility that they lost when they were still, when they seemed to shrink and become insignificant.

'So now what?' asked Cupido.

'I'll go and talk to him. I've got a warrant for his arrest.'

He got up and they said goodbye. The detective would have liked to go with him, to hear from Saldaña's own lips his confession or his denial, but he knew that the lieutenant would not ask him along on official business, nor could he request it. He walked Gallardo to the door and watched him take the stairs, ignoring the lift. Everything seemed to be coming to an end without him having played any notable role, yet that filled him with calm. For a moment he felt like the stagehand of a provincial theatre company on tour, who knows he will have to start packing up the set when the curtains are drawn one last time.

He went back inside, phoned Julián Monasterio, and told him how far the information from the bank had taken them.

⌒

Alba was visiting her cousins for one of their birthdays, and Julián Monasterio was at home alone. He had a headache, but even so lit a cigarette and went out on to the balcony. A cold, unpleasant wind swept in between the buildings and quickly carried off the smoke towards some birds flying nervously back to the sheltering trees. Down in the street, drivers were starting to turn on their headlights, no doubt surprised at how quickly the autumn swallowed up the sunset.

Cupido's call had calmed him down, tipped him towards a sort of optimism that was nevertheless not quite complete. When he thought of Cupido's words he could see that not everything was solved, and an undertone of suspicion and impatience to get things over with prevented him from relaxing fully.

He stubbed out the cigarette in one of the remaining pots on the balcony, which were filled with earth but no plants. Dulce had always taken care of them, and he sometimes recalled her figure crouching over the roses, geraniums, ox-eye daisies, the rubber plant, the yucca that wouldn't stop growing in its big flowerpot, and a plant whose name he didn't remember that had blue flowers with petals so fragile they looked like butterfly wings. He remembered her with a bag of black earth for repotting, a watering can in which she had poured a bit of liquid fertiliser, and secateurs she used to cut off dead leaves and twigs which she then put into rubbish bags. When she was finished, he liked to hug her and kiss and smell her fingers, on which the humble, hairy leaves of the geraniums had left an intoxicating fragrance that mixed with the smell of her body.

Looking after the plants was one of the few household chores she liked doing; she was always reluctant to do the dishes, pick up after Alba, make the beds or sweep, even if only at weekends, since during the week it was Rocío who took care of all that. But he saw her put something else into the flowers, a personal touch that wasn't simply a physical activity. Between the moment when she crouched over the first flowerpot with her secateurs and the moment when she calmly and contentedly smoked a cigarette a couple of hours later, looking at the loose black earth, the plants free from parasites and excrescences as if purified, her face showed disappointment, sorrow, enthusiasm, doubt, suspicion, shrewdness, illusion and hope. For several days afterwards she would go out on to the balcony and look at the results of her efforts, but little by little the plants started to lose the glory brought by the fertiliser and the pruning and she stopped looking at them until the next time. In a way, her interest in plants, like all her personal interests – and more accurately than her work, her clothes or the house – faithfully reflected her personality.

When she'd moved out, she'd left most of the pots, even suspecting that he would neglect them and that those miniature gardens that had flowered on the balcony would wither away.

And that's exactly what had happened. He had watered and fertilised them a few times, in the days after she left, when he still believed she was having a moment of madness and would be back before long. She would find her house just as she'd left it, with her favourite fruit in the fridge, the day's newspaper in its wicker basket, the pots blazing with flowers and greenery on the balcony, the two pillows on the made bed, and the sheet so clean and taut that you could roll an apple on it without making creases. But later, as the days went by and he realised she wasn't coming back, he gave up on that too, just as his hair had started to grow over his ears, he didn't buy any clothes and hardly ever polished his shoes. In abandoning the plants, in the smell of the dying flowers, he found some revenge. 'Look what I've done to the stuff you liked so much,' he would sometimes murmur when he went out on the balcony for a smoke. Furiously, he would crush his cigarette out into the dry earth, imagining it was her skin, the same skin he'd kissed and caressed so passionately in the dreams of the previous night. Then he was suddenly scared by his reaction and went quickly back inside, regretting having given in to a violent impulse that was not like him at all, and embarrassed that anyone might have seen him from a window and read his mind from his movements.

On one of the weekends Dulce came to pick up Alba, back when she still came up to the flat instead of staying downstairs with the excuse of parking difficulties, she had seen from the living room the neglected pots in which there were only stalks and dry leaves. For a moment she stared at them with an expression that was closer to a botanist's interest in the effects of a drought on a field than to their owner's sadness. He stood next to her, waiting for a complaint, or any comment that might warrant an aggressive reply. He had imagined that situation and prepared a reply that would show her some of his pain. But Dulce had looked away, as if that abandonment was exactly what she expected of him. Her indifference had been more painful than any protest or censure, because it implied that now she no longer cared at all for the house where she'd once lived.

And the house where she'd lived, little by little, lost all traces of her. If one day it was the plants, then another it was the tray on which she liked to have dinner sitting on the sofa, when its presence by the TV had become unbearable to him. Yet another day it was a hairpin found under a cushion, or a framed photograph there was no point keeping now, or the business letters and bills in her name that, little by little, stopped coming.

Julián Monasterio noticed that, although the pain had not entirely disappeared, at least it had stilled a little. He wondered how much influence Rita had on the calm and hope he now glimpsed in the future. After a few days of seeing each other, with all that that expression implied, she had gone away for the weekend to visit her parents, and they had both agreed to speak when she came back on the Monday. But most of the evening had gone by and she hadn't phoned and he hadn't moved to either. The days he hadn't seen her had made him cautious, and he couldn't stop thinking about the downside of too hasty a relationship, before he'd had time to protect himself against its risks. He feared he'd jumped in at the deep end too soon, when only a few months ago he had still lived with another woman whom he loved and with whom he had a daughter. Maybe it was the age gap of eight years, maybe Rita was used to quick, uncomplicated relationships, he told himself, trying to avoid the unease he felt at the idea, as he imagined younger men beside her. Perhaps, he even thought, that trip to see her parents was only an excuse to meet up with a male friend from her home town.

But he soon rejected the idea, thinking he must do something to keep his lack of trust and suspicions at bay, which were always so ready to cling to him and whisper their poisonous words.

All this was what stopped him calling her now. It wouldn't be enough to ask her how the journey and the holiday at her parents' had gone. They'd have to talk about themselves, mention how they missed each other during her absence, urgently arrange a new date, and all that made him ill at ease. Because expressing his feelings intensely and hurriedly would make him seem like a teenager, but not alluding to them at all would make him seem cold, and he'd much rather avoid the latter.

He went back in and opened the cupboard where he kept the medicines, looking for a painkiller for his headache. It was full of the bottles of cough syrup and the boxes of pills, antibiotics, analgesics and indigestion tables with which Dulce always self-medicated, in fits and starts and to excess. When she felt unwell, she always took a remedy that proved useless, as she never dealt with the causes of her discomfort: she would take cough mixture but still smoke two packs a day; or she would take something for an upset stomach, but not stop eating the fruit she liked so much or the sweets that had upset her stomach in the first place... *There are still so many of her things around; it's so difficult to empty, clean, and erase all traces and detritus left by a woman in a house where she lived for ten years. Ten years! You look at the sell-by date on a box of pills and think how distant that month seems, you're sure you'll use the pills before then, but time goes by too quickly and the pills expire, and what was once good for you is now good for nothing, for nothing, for nothing, a useless product,* he thought.

He put two aspirin in half a glass of water and, as they dissolved, got a bag and threw everything into it that was unusable or expired. The cupboard ended up almost empty. The knowledge that he would never get back anything he'd just thrown away filled him with a gentle sadness, quite different to the fits of pain and hatred that a similar action would have provoked a few weeks before.

Despite his emotional ups and downs, he wanted to believe that if he was emptying himself of so much from the past it was because he was in some way making room for something newer and better. He had gathered enough courage to let go of memories and to wait, without too much impatience or planning or uncertainty, and see what happened. A relationship like his with Rita, which in the summer would have been unthinkable, now seemed possible and in time perhaps it would become as necessary as his love for Dulce had been. *Because Rita is partly responsible for this new calm,* he thought. He lit up another cigarette thinking he'd taken too long already. He dialled her number.

'Hi, I was about to call you,' said Rita in a voice that suddenly erased all of his fatalistic suspicions from before.

'How was the trip?'

Rita started telling inconsequential anecdotes about the weekend, dwelling on small family details, calling the family members by their names as if he knew them, as calm and natural on the phone as she would be face-to-face, which showed a complete trust in the person she was speaking to. Listening to her, Julián Monasterio had the feeling that, with her, he would leave behind the desolate pessimism that made him expect bad news from every quarter. Listening to her speak to him like an old friend, in a voice that drew him into the personal life of her family without any reservations, he thought that his life needn't be an endless series of misfortunes, and that he might find moments when happiness would open out with the sudden splendour of a remote, wonderful landscape seen from a mountain top.

'And you?' she asked. 'What have you been up to?'

For a second he was tempted to answer: *I just missed you*, but he refrained, for it wasn't true, even if it wasn't entirely false, either. He felt clumsier and slower than her in his reactions, and over the past few days he had worried, as he had about the first night they spent together, that this was all an experiment, suspecting that experiments in love always ended up scalding the less cautious.

But hearing her again on the phone, he realised how much he wanted to see her. And he said to himself that if it was precisely that detail that differentiated love from simple physical attraction – the continuity of feelings whether the other was present or absent – then he wasn't in love with Rita. His emotions were too tied to how near or far she was, were not as autonomous as those strong passions that seem to exist independently of the distance, the will or the circumstances of the person who experiences them. And so his replies were vague. He'd worked in the shop, had spent time with Alba, taken her to the pool, and done some housework.

'Do you want to meet tomorrow?'

'All right. Around nine?'

'Yes.'

They agreed on the place and said goodbye.

The flat was dark now, with no other light than what came in from the streetlights through the blinds. He leaned back in the armchair, lit up another cigarette and put his feet on the coffee table, savouring that peaceful moment in the dark and remembering Rita's words. He felt as if she'd returned the precious gift she had given him a few days ago and which he had misplaced with his hesitation, his doubts, his nervousness. Receiving it a second time, Julián Monasterio had the impression that the relationship might prove so important that it would alter his future, his plans, the way he lived.

He put the cigarette out just as the butt was about to catch and closed his eyes, sinking into a deep, joyful calm. Thanks to the aspirin he no longer had a headache. He must have dozed off for a few minutes and didn't know how his memory brought back the image of the escalator, the great labyrinth of black conveyor belts that emerged from dark basements, rose and crossed each other in the air until they disappeared into the unreal, mountainous background, as in some surrealist pictures in which human forms look insignificant beside the grandeur of objects. From where he stood he could make out fragmented bodies, though without bloodstains or signs of violence: a row of heads advancing without any expression of pain, like pumpkins on a factory conveyor belt, or a succession of legs which receded until it stopped where two belts converged and, in crossing, looked like scissors, or a line of women who became increasingly shorter, although no change was noticeable in the height of the conveyor belt, as if they were being sliced down. He too got on one of them, moving towards a deep black funnel spinning on itself and swallowing everything, though now he no longer felt he was being pulled in the wrong direction. Or at least in that dream, he could not see the final destination. Then he felt it all stop suddenly, and everything, the conveyor belts and the transported figures, came to a halt in an unfathomable silence, as if some invisible and powerful being had flicked a switch and brought the world to a standstill.

17

What could the law do to him if he was already dead? He'd lied about the events of that night and now wasn't sure they wouldn't find out. But even if they did, what further harm would that do him? He lifted his eyes from the path he was clearing and looked at the road again, waiting for a car to appear. Whatever might happen couldn't be worse than what had already happened. Peace would not come, whatever the case.

In the four years since the death of his son there had been moments when he thought he could forget everything: one morning, having ploughed around the fallow field a hundred times in the tractor, followed by a flock of white egrets that landed on the furrows to devour the unearthed worms, his tiredness, the monotony of the work, and the noise of the engine plunged him into a daze that made the outside world disappear; or a particular sunset through the trees, enveloped in the smell of the ripe fruit under a sky of reddish clouds that seemed to have been set alight by the top of the volcano. But the pain soon returned. A pain he could not reduce to thought and, therefore, could not fight with ideas, words or the comfort of other people. He reckoned he'd live for another thirty years, and was sure his grief would remain with him until the last minute, feeding on the strangest stimuli. The last School Council meeting and the review of the previous administration had made him remember every detail of the death of his son with unbearable clarity.

And then, how could he have gone straight back home and missed such an opportunity, the two of them all alone, without witnesses to interfere and calm the intensity of his hatred and contempt? How could he go back to the farm in silence – where everybody wished he would stay – when a change of headmaster had been effected during that meeting that would surely bring about other changes? Perhaps Corona would not keep the post from which he'd orchestrated his son's expulsion?

He'd seen the director of studies and De Molinos linger a few moments in the bar, and he went out with the other teachers, leaving the group of parents by the bar to their inexhaustible capacity for pointless criticism, for censuring the school administration, the excessive holidays the teachers enjoyed, and their tendency to shirk their responsibilities: it was the eternal litany of complaints that they never dared express out loud or make public in any official way. He knew where Corona lived. He had followed him once. He arrived before him and waited in the hallway of the building, repeating to himself the words he'd put off saying for so long. And a few minutes later, when he saw Corona's large, obese figure at the door against the light from the street, he moved away from the wall and reached out to turn on the light. He enjoyed Corona's surprise, the fear clouding his eyes. '*You.* What's going on?' said Corona. At first he didn't reply, but stood there looking at him in silence for a minute or so, letting him feel the unease and the fear that something irreparable was about to happen and that there was nothing he could do to stop it. The timer-lights went out and he reached out again to hit the switch. When he turned, Corona had taken a step back towards the door, and was wringing his fat white hands as if they were covered in something, probably sweat or dirt. 'But what's going on?' he asked again, and there was a plea in his words, but also a fear so palpable you could almost see it, as if his words were underlined with the red ink they liked to use so aggressively to correct mistakes in their pupils' workbooks. He looked at him in silence. He was in no hurry to respond and dispel his fear. There were energetic, masculine footsteps outside, approaching along the pavement. Corona turned his head slightly, hoping they would stop at the door and someone would come in to interrupt the situation. But the footsteps went past, and once they were inaudible, Saldaña murmured: 'I remember my son every day. Tonight, at the school, more intensely than ever.' He fell silent again, thinking how strange it was to be telling Corona – the very person he held responsible for his son's death – something he never told anyone. 'It was nobody's fault. It was a tragedy, it was nobody's fault,' he heard him reply. The light went out again, but now he didn't switch it back on immediately, for he too was waiting for something to happen, any movement that would make it easier for him to start hurting Corona. 'Everyone at the school is very sorry about how it all ended,'

Corona insisted from the darkness, as if he couldn't bear both the silence and the dark and spoke for a response, to gauge if Saldaña had moved any closer. Or perhaps Corona was only trying to diminish his personal responsibility with that 'everyone'. And of course it was true, Saldaña thought then, that he was not solely responsible, that it had been many people who had his son at their disposal over those years, teaching him what he should have learned and didn't for five hours a day – so many hours which made up so many days and weeks and months and years and all wasted. But at least one of them, the one most directly involved, should suffer some pain and humiliation in the name of the others, all of those who'd thought he could endure anything because he was a peasant whose fate was to feed the town, and have dirty hands and a body toughened by labour. He knew this was the image they expected from him: a peasant dressed in corduroy whose highest aspiration in life was to get his picture taken with the well-fed pig or huge stud bull he'd won a prize for at a country fair.

He switched on the light again and waited a few seconds. He was pretty sure that, if he asked, Corona would kneel down and let him do as he wished. He stepped forward and saw him put out his arms to protect himself. When the light went out again, he hit Corona with an open hand, one humiliating blow, not very strong or violent, only humiliating. Then he stood still for a moment, listening to him breathe in terror, leaning against the wall a metre away, and expecting another blow.

Suddenly, though, all this seemed grotesque to him. The cure for his pain was not to be found here, either. Vengeance and its strange accomplices – violence, injury, sordidness, shame, even blood – was a tasteless, certainly unpleasant dish, whether it was served cold or not. He fumbled for the door handle in the dark, turned it and went out into the street without looking back.

And Corona had concealed the whole incident, because a few days later neither the lieutenant nor that tall detective had asked him to confirm it. No one referred to that encounter in the hall, and he too remained silent. From that moment on he understood that Corona had chosen to hide his humiliation, even at the risk of being added to the list of possible suspects. Fine, let him do that; let him prolong the anxiety of feeling himself watched and suspected. At least till everything was solved, if it ever was.

As he bent down again and drove the hoe into the ground, he felt the painful pull of a muscle in the back of his thighs, as if a rope drew tight down his back, and ended in a hook sunk behind his knees. They'd started to swell and sometimes seemed reluctant to hold him upright. Besides, now the cold was returning – every now and again he heard the loose wire of the lightning rod moving in the wind against the wall of the house behind him – the pain was increasing. He ignored it and carried on digging. For a few days he'd again been experiencing the strange impulse to recover the garden. After the death of his son he had abandoned it, as if it were obscene and irreverent to tend to the colourful splendour of the rosebushes, the clumps of hydrangeas and the borders planted with wisteria, lilac and geraniums, when his heart was still in mourning. The area of the garden, from the gate to the house, had been accumulating so many weeds, shrubs and remains of dead flowers that one day he almost went over it with the plough and razed the whole thing, turning so many seasons' work to dust. Now, however, he wanted to restore it and felt ashamed of his destructive impulses. Flowers had never been incompatible with the dead; on the contrary, they seemed their best companions, the best sign of respect. He was becoming indifferent to whether the harvest was bigger or smaller, and sometimes he surprised himself by thinking that a rose will always smell sweeter than an apple, a bunch of lilacs will always be prettier than a cob of corn, that a poppy will always shine brighter than an ear of wheat. There was something in the fragility and ephemeral nature of flowers that made him prefer them to the tougher crops. He told himself that, even when you cut them and they die, flowers give the best of themselves, their most delicate scent, whereas all farmed crops – grain, vegetables, fruits and legumes – decay in an explosion of dust, rottenness, worms and mice. How many hours, stolen from other tasks, he'd put into that splendid garden which had, nevertheless, died in a blaze of glory when he abandoned it! In contrast, rock rose, goosefoot, weeds, grass and reeds grew by themselves, resisted both hot and cold weather and, without any help, grew stalks as sturdy as spears or sharp as thorns. The world, he would tell himself, is not made for sensitive beings; only the tough ones endure the painful bite of the pest, the stain of mould, the stoning of hail, brackish waters, and the abandonment of their owners.

When he lifted the hoe for another blow he saw a terrified earthworm trying to bury itself in the soil with lamentable slowness. He picked it up and placed it on the palm of his hand. Then he remembered the poisonous mark of claws on the cold, lean thigh, and felt as if his own were being branded with a hot iron. He touched the worm's cold, gleaming and tender back, and bent down to place it on the loose earth.

'Now go, do your job,' he told it, watching the small brownish body wriggle into the soil with fear and determination.

Why had his son done such a thing? What resentment had compelled him to take the shears from the house, and cut some skin off the dog because of his lack of experience? Why he had committed that act of savage cruelty would always remain an unanswered question. He had taught him not to mistreat any living creature, to respect the life that pulsed around him, believing that anyone who intentionally hurts a defenceless animal comes very close to harming a fellow human being. And he thought his son had learned this lesson and taken it in, for he never saw him being cruel to any animal. He thought his son had established a healthy, natural relationship with animals, based not on fear, but on caution where necessary; without disgust, but also without worship. From an early age he'd tried to instil in him the duty to avoid pointless sacrifices – never stepping on a snail, touching a butterfly's wings, cutting off a lizard's tail, or crushing a bird's small skull – for with each animal sacrificed one was losing an ally for when the genuinely dangerous animals came along. And his son seemed to have learned that and at times even reprimanded his father for a moment of carelessness. So why such hatred towards Corona's dog, why such viciousness? Unless the hatred was not directed at the dog, and the animal was only the vicarious victim of his hatred for someone else, someone invulnerable to him.

He heard the noise of an engine coming round the bend and lifted his head again, waiting. First he saw a greenish bonnet, then a shiny windshield behind which nothing could be made out, and finally the whole car, with its green-and-white stripes and roof lights – though they were off. He thought it moved too slowly or with caution, as if it was floating forward, without realising it was his own impatience that slowed the minute unbearably and froze it in a kind of mirage heightened by the greasy shimmer of the road.

The car veered slightly to negotiate the entrance, stopped in front of the gate and the lieutenant and two officers, one of whom was a woman, got out.

He stretched his back trying to forget the pain and stuck the hoe in the ground. The earthworm was already hidden in the soil.

As the lieutenant opened the gate and walked in with the other two behind him, he heard the door of the house open behind him. He turned and saw his wife looking at him with her still fearful eyes, whose lids started flickering as soon as a stranger appeared on the farm. Their younger son was beside her. His only son.

'Go inside, and take the boy.'

'What do they want now?'

'Go inside. With the boy.'

He only half-heard what the lieutenant was saying to him, quickly and impatiently, as if he'd been waiting a long time to do it, but he understood the intent from a few words and legal formulae he knew from the television – arrest, lawyer, right to remain silent. They needn't have bothered; he knew what they were coming for. He also noticed the lieutenant stopping one of the officers using a pair of handcuffs that had suddenly appeared in his hands as if by magic. They would let him say a few words to his wife – who had reappeared in the porch – but he refused the offer and, flanked by the two officers, made for the car.

⤴

He wasn't afraid at all. What could the law do to him if he was already dead? How could they harm him any further? He was used to being alone, with the country patience born of waiting for a seed to blossom or a fruit to ripen, and so didn't even get impatient after three hours locked up in that room without any windows or mirrors, and with only a grille in the door through which no one had yet looked. A metal table and three chairs were the only furniture. Underneath his chair there was a blackish circle of soil that had fallen from his boots as it dried. Every now and then, he heard a noise outside: the engine of a car, echoing footsteps that might have been approaching or receding, the gurgling of a toilet and, once, the pensive caw of a crow. But he wasn't impatient or afraid of anything. He was only slightly curious about what they knew and why they'd taken so long to come and get him.

The door opened and the two officers who'd accompanied the lieutenant came in. The woman, who had some papers in her hands, sat in front of him, but the man stood leaning in the doorway, looking him over. He seemed to expect a scythe or a hoe to emerge from the clods of earth. His collar was unbuttoned, as if it were too hot, and he had rolled up his sleeves, displaying a pair of forearms strengthened from exercise. He came away from the door and pulled the remaining chair over to a corner. He looked like a boxer just before a fight.

'Where's the pistol?' he said, in a voice that was too loud for such a small room.

'What pistol?' he replied, not knowing what he was talking about.

The officer shook his head resignedly.

'You're not leaving this room until you tell us where it is, or until we find it. Take your pick. Either you tell us and we finish this quickly, or we send in some bulldozers to tear up everything on that shitty farm of yours until it looks like a desert. I bet you've buried it under a fruit tree.'

He was indifferent to the threat and looked at the officer with such coldness that it was not even scorn. He didn't care about the farm, because he didn't care about anything. For a long time now he got up every morning with the feeling that it was all an unstoppable tragedy and that any movement he might make to avoid it would in fact bring him closer to the final act. He wasn't attached to anyone, not even his wife and his remaining son. His heart was dead, and the image of his crops and fruit trees laid waste was not strong enough to wake him from his emotional indifference. Only when he thought about the borders of the garden he had been digging that day did a fleeting sense of unease flicker through his mind.

'Where's the pistol?' the officer insisted.

'I don't have a pistol. I've never had one,' he replied. It was absurd, for a pistol would have been useless for anything he might have wished to do.

'Let's start at the beginning,' the woman put in.

She read to herself, very quickly, a few lines from the papers she had on the table, as if she'd been studying them for the last three hours and wanted his help in rectifying a mistake in them.

'In your first statement you said you went straight back home, without stopping anywhere.'

'Yes.'

'But that's not true. You didn't go home after leaving the bar,' she said very slowly.

'I lied,' he replied. In spite of the apathy with which he took his own interrogation, he noticed the woman tense up, and the man shoot a restless look at him from his corner.

'OK. You lied. We're going to forget you said that. And that'll be that,' she explained. With the papers in front of her and a simple ballpoint pen, she looked like a student taking notes. Not even the greenish shirt of the uniform dispelled that young, harmless air. *As if she were a lawyer*, he thought, recalling the suggestion the lieutenant had made on the farm the first time, *someone who, for a bit of cash, would be unconditionally on your side.*

'Where did you go when you left the bar?'

'I walked to his house and waited in the hall for him to arrive. I know where he lives. I'd followed him before,' he replied tiredly. If they'd come for him, then they knew the answer.

'Who?' Now the woman seemed confused.

'Who? Well, Corona.'

'You mean Larrey,' corrected the man from the corner.

'Larrey? No. Why him? If there was someone worthy of respect that evening, it was Larrey.'

The man started to stand up, but the woman gestured for him to stay put.

'Fine. You waited for him in the hall. What happened next?'

'Didn't he tell you? Isn't it why you've come for me?'

'We want you to tell us.'

He detected how quickly she replied, her eagerness to know, and the memory of the man going on about a pistol for the first few questions made him suspect that her kindness concealed a trap.

'I hit him.'

The two officers fell silent, too surprised to react, and in that silence he thought he heard the rustle of clothes outside the half-open door. Without raising his voice, he went on:

'Once. In the face. With an open hand,' he said, and then, with the confidence of someone whose memories will not betray him, he added, 'like they hit children.'

'Who's "they"?'

'Teachers.'

'Teachers don't hit anyone anymore in this country. Neither do we. That was all a long time ago,' replied the woman, not very firmly, looking at her colleague, who was still in his corner, with his shirtsleeves rolled up to his elbows, his legs slightly apart and his shirt unbuttoned.

'They hit my son. Although not in the face, they hit him very hard,' he said.

The woman looked at him again, not even trying to hide her surprise at the turn the conversation was taking, but expecting him to use the word 'kill' at some point and make the final statement that would explain everything. She'd gone over the file many times; it was the first real assignment the lieutenant had given her and her partner, though she knew not a lot could be expected from Ortega except quick and effective assistance when action or violence was needed. She'd gone over the statements again and again, trying to find a contradiction, or possible motives, and gone through all the private and public information available on each one of Larrey's acquaintances, information that was sometimes so detailed Larrey's friends would have found it strange that the Guardia Civil were in possession of it. And she remembered perfectly what she'd read about Saldaña's eldest son, who had been expelled from school, and the tragic end to which that punishment had perhaps led. Although they had taken note of the story, never wholly discarding it, neither she nor the lieutenant had believed there was a motive in it, for Larrey had never been involved in that conflict. And perhaps there wasn't, she thought, for she felt that the man in front of her, with his coarse hands and muddy boots, was telling the truth. After the murder, they'd gone to interrogate him and he hadn't once hidden his hatred of the school and its staff, an old, stubborn and even sordid kind of hatred, more akin to the primal and direct rural violence with which people like him reacted to offences, than to the concealment, deceit and delayed revenge that seemed to have been employed against Larrey.

'You hit Corona in the hallway of his building,' she repeated with the insistence she'd been taught at the academy – you should repeat every question several times to make sure no nuance escaped, no thread remained loose or lost in mystery; insist, but never push too hard straight away; remember it's as easy to fall short of the mark as to overshoot.

'Only one blow. In the face. With an open hand. Like they beat the children,' he repeated without defiance or regret. 'Just one blow for him to feel the fear.'

'And what did Corona do?'

'He stood there, breathing heavily in the dark, leaning against the wall. Like a frightened animal.'

He realised they had fallen silent again, not knowing how to carry on. The woman looked at him as a woman does at an old man or a small child: not someone from whom she expects a sudden outburst of violence. He suddenly felt certain what kind of image he presented: a man who embodied all the limitations of a peasant, a dull, surly, dirty human being, with higher life expectancy than average, and an ability to do physical harm that was difficult to control, but was neutralised in that room: precisely the image of the farmer he'd tried to escape from. When he'd gone to live in the country he was conscious of the risks, but he was sure he'd enjoy the isolation without being deprived of the privileges of the city. He'd imagined a balanced future in which he would use the plough as skilfully as a computer, the hoe as skilfully as a pen. He'd tried to reconcile both worlds smoothly, without coming to the extreme of those African tribal chiefs who have their picture taken barefoot, wearing the tunic and bone necklaces of their tribe, but also a bowler hat and a gold Rolex. Living in the country might be hard, but it became a luxury if one took along everything the city jealously guarded within its walls for itself.

'And what did you do afterwards, that evening?' asked the woman.

'Then I went back home.'

'You went home? No you didn't,' said the man. His elbows rested on his knees and he looked at him attentively, his head leaning forward, gauging Saldaña's ability to lie.

'What did you do when you left Corona?' the woman repeated.

He was a bit disappointed that she too insisted on that question, but he still had the presence of mind to reflect that her job would make her disbelieving.

'I went back home. It was late.'

'Of course you did. But before that you went round to the school. You weren't finished yet, and now that you'd started settling old debts, you thought you might as well carry on. You saw the gate was open, went in and shot Larrey. Now, where's the pistol?' the man repeated.

Saldaña looked at him for a moment before turning his gaze to the woman, refusing to talk to someone who didn't seem to listen to what he was being told: he'd been watching everything the whole time and yet had learned nothing.

'Did you put it in the safe the next day?'

Now he really didn't know what he was talking about. Not that he cared, for he was indifferent to, and sometimes didn't even understand, anything that fell outside the black circle of his pain and his memories. He felt like a man struck by lightning: as he lay there burnt upon the floor, did it matter which cloud the blow had come from? He made an effort to reply:

'I don't know what you're talking about.'

'You don't know what I'm *talking* about! Don't you know you have a safe in the bank, either? What do you keep inside it? The pistol? Or are you going to tell me next year's seeds keep better there?'

The officer had left his corner and was behind him. He could hear his voice bouncing off his back, but didn't turn to look at him. The hours of waiting, the interrogation, the insistence, the threats, hadn't softened him. Not even the kindness of the woman, who was now looking at him again as someone does a child or an old man.

'Shall we start from the beginning?' he heard one of them say, but it no longer mattered who had spoken.

All of a sudden the woman got up from her chair, picked up her papers and left him alone with the man.

⌒

The lieutenant was sitting in the corridor, on a bench near the half-open door. When he saw her appear, he stood up and led her to his office.

'It wasn't him,' she said when they were alone.

'Peasants!' the lieutenant sighed. 'Always so complicated. I'd rather have a criminal hardened by a thousand interrogations than one of these sullen, stubborn farmers. Threats are as useless with them as promises to forget. They keep quiet for hours or repeat the same thing over and over, not caring if you believe them or not, not defending themselves, as if they don't care about either freedom or prison.'

'I don't think it was him,' she qualified, out of respect for the lieutenant's rank, but still in a confident tone. 'When we asked him about the pistol he looked surprised, as if he didn't know what we were talking about. Like a cow would look at a train going by.'

'Of course it wasn't him! I'm sure Corona will confirm he was waiting for him in the hall that evening. A man like Saldaña doesn't make up a story he doesn't even know will be useful as an alibi.'

'Shall I call Corona?' she suggested now that her partner was not there. This whole investigation had brought her closer to the lieutenant. The fact that they'd both thought about the same problems for those few weeks had created an invisible current between them, a camaraderie like the one between two soldiers who don't know each other but who keep watch together on the same front line.

'I've already sent for him. He won't be long.'

'And if he confirms it's true?'

'Then we'll be back where we started. We'll have wasted our time looking in the wrong place.'

She was aware that her own disappointment, although intense and disheartening, was not as great as the lieutenant's, for in this job failure was always proportionate to rank. At the end of the day, she had only followed orders and had done it with discipline; no one would demand anything else of her. But that was still no consolation. At her most optimistic she had imagined she and the lieutenant would solve a mystery that everyone else – including Ortega – was too slow to solve. And now that Saldaña had totally undone all of her hypotheses, going back to the start was not just a waste of time.

'Shall I tell Ortega to stop?' she asked.

'No. Let him carry on for a while. Maybe Saldaña will get his act together and learn he can't go around hitting people whenever he feels like it.'

18

Even Ernesto, who always stayed away from the stories, comments, reports and slander that circulated in Breda, greeted him with a remark about the news that had excited the city: the previous afternoon, a certain Saldaña had been arrested in connection with the teacher's murder.

'Did you know him?' asked Julián Monasterio. Ever since the detective had called him to tell him that Saldaña was the only person with a link to the school who also had a safe-deposit box in the bank, he had repeated his name so often that by now it almost seemed familiar. Yet he didn't know anything else about him.

'No.'

'Why would he do it?'

'He's the father of an ex-pupil. They say the boy was expelled and eventually committed suicide. There are stories of drugs. They're talking about revenge.'

'And how did they work out it was him?' he insisted, trying to find out if anything else was known about the pistol and its owner, if the lieutenant had kept his side of the deal with Cupido.

'There are so many different versions that probably none of them is true. That he surrendered himself. That his wife came forward. That they found the pistol on him.'

Julián Monasterio sat at his desk, unable to concentrate on his work, waiting for a call from the detective confirming or denying the rumours. He'd come to trust Cupido so much that he wouldn't be sure of anything until he heard the details of the events from the detective's own lips – the arrest, the interrogation, the possible confession. But he didn't want to call him in front of his employee. Unable to keep still, he went out to buy the papers and read them over a coffee. He turned to the crime pages hoping to find four columns of coverage, but there were only a few lines reporting the arrest and referring readers to future issues for more news. Larrey's murder was topical again, having been swallowed by other equally ephemeral news, without any useful lesson having been learned that might prevent someone else making the same mistake.

Two young men sitting at the bar were discussing the latest rumours with the waiters concerning a gun buried under some rosebushes and a boy who had overdosed.

'Any news?' he asked. He, of all people, feigning ignorance; he, who could have told them all about where the pistol had come from, its weight and balance, what it felt like to hold it.

'Sure. Every hour something else turns up.'

'And?'

'They've released him. I saw him leave the station myself about an hour ago. He hadn't shaved, and was wearing country boots covered in mud and was looking very tired. He walked to the square and got a taxi. Some people even waited for it to come back to ask the driver where he went. He went back home.'

'So why did they arrest him?'

'No one knows. Someone said they'd found the gun on him.'

Julián Monasterio went over to the phone booth and dialled the detective's number; he knew it off by heart by now. Cupido had talked to the lieutenant a few minutes ago and he confirmed what the man at the bar had said: Saldaña was innocent and had been released.

'And now?'

'Back to square one,' he heard him sigh, no doubt as nonplussed as he was. After a silence, as if he owed him an explanation, Cupido added: 'Don't worry about the money. It doesn't matter now. The main thing is to catch the person who's got the pistol.'

Cupido seemed to have guessed his thoughts, as if between them, a seller of virtual reality and a private investigator welded to only the most tangible of facts, ran a current of intelligence that went beyond the initial commercial exchange of 'my money for your work' that had brought them together.

'I'll have to talk to the lieutenant again and look at the list of the bank's clients. Perhaps we were too rash when we found a familiar name. I'll call you as soon as I have something.'

They said goodbye and, although he hung up reassured by the detective's words, when he got back to the shop he was struck by a new worry: If the real murderer knew that they had arrested Saldaña because he was a client of the bank, he would immediately work out that the Guardia Civil were on the right track to the gun and, therefore, hot on his heels. How would he react then? When the murderer had stolen the pistol, he had probably looked at the papers in the safe, at the ledger with the name of Julián Monasterio on it. If the murderer felt threatened, would he try to implicate him in a way he couldn't even imagine?

Once again he was afraid of seeing himself involved in a conflict whose first victim would be his daughter. And, aware of his selfishness, though unable to regret it, he realised that, in the grip of his own anxiety, he was almost indifferent to the fact that a man had been murdered.

⁓

That evening, Julián Monasterio left Alba at his sister's and went to Rita's flat, as they had arranged on the phone, though they hadn't decided what to do. In a very short time they'd become so comfortable with one another that they didn't need to plan distractions or excuses to meet, for their mutual company was beginning to be enough.

He found her in stay-at-home clothes – a jumper and worn jeans – and she didn't seem too keen on changing and going out. Outside, the autumn was blowing cold gusts, but the flat was warm and comfortable and invited indolence.

Rita took a sheet of paper out of the folder she always carried to school and showed him a drawing.

'Guess who did it?'

Julián Monasterio had never paid much attention to his daughter's drawings, but he instantly recognised it as hers. The pool at the centre with her bathing in a red bikini was unmistakable.

'Of course,' he replied.

'You've come out really well,' she said pointing at his tall, upright figure in the foreground, but didn't mention anything about the exaggerated tear ducts.

She sat next to him on the sofa and placed her hand on his shoulder to look at the drawing together. Julián Monasterio breathed in her smell, which now wasn't mixed with her usual perfume or residue from work. It was a more personal, intimate fragrance, the smell that emanated only from her skin and remained there when all the other smells had disappeared. Ignoring the drawing – he felt Rita wanted to tell him something about it, something they'd inevitably have to discuss, but which could wait for a few moments – he leaned back on the sofa and, regarding the room from that angle, had the feeling for the first time that he was not a stranger there. He felt at one with all the details of the decor, suddenly adjusted to her world and the pace of that world, in which everything was a bit slower than in the hustle and bustle of his life. Lying there, he let a feeling of calm and simple happiness take hold of him that was not at odds with the forceful intensity of the desire he felt growing inside him: the spontaneous touch of Rita's hand on his shoulder carried an unsuspected erotic current. Lost in the details of the drawing, he understood that desire needed neither dazzling words, nor risks and adventures, nor dangerous rivers, nor wild animals, nor seeing immortal sunsets in faraway cities, as he'd sometimes believed when thinking of Dulce. The most intense passion was here too, in the peace of a flat with no secrets, lying together on a sofa while the hi-fi played Schubert. *A love story is itself such a daring enterprise that it doesn't need tributary risks,* he thought.

'But you're not listening to me,' said Rita, pretending to be annoyed at him.

If lately his life had been marked by an absence of calm and the ease with which his memories assaulted him, now he seemed to see these memories from above, like a child on a balcony looking at a rabid dog barking at him from the street. That night they made love in a deeper, slower and more sensual way, for they were already so comfortable with each other that heroics weren't necessary. It was enough to be normal and happy. Their contentment made their words light and unimportant, and only when references to Saldaña appeared on his side of the conversation, to his arrest and later release, did their tone become a little heavier. They were both linked to Larrey's death, in very different but equally binding ways, and neither could think of him without feeling pain or guilt.

'Sometimes I think we'll never know who did it. Or why,' said Rita. 'It doesn't make any sense.'

'Did you know him well?'

'Very well. Although I think he knew me even better. What about you?' she asked suddenly.

'Did I know him?'

'Yes.'

'No, I don't think I ever saw him.'

'He was one of those good men that this country full of awful people sometimes produces: he didn't envy anyone, didn't want to hurt anyone,' she explained. Her words would have seemed theatrical if they hadn't been tempered by the firmness and sincerity of her tone; even a naturally sarcastic person would have found it difficult to mock them.

They were in bed, Rita with the sheet up to her armpits, in that gesture of modesty that so many women cannot help even having opened and offered the most intimate part of themselves. They lit up a cigarette. As she told him more about Larrey, an expression of sorrow he'd never seen before appeared on her face. She stumbled trying to reproduce some of his phrases exactly, smiled with sadness as she remembered a story, and even had to fight back tears.

Julián Monasterio listened to her in silence. He felt uncomfortable, for he – the legitimate owner of the gun – was partly responsible for her loss. An ambiguous responsibility, halfway between culpability and innocence. Still, Rita's words elicited a sort of shame that pressed his back into the pillows. Up to now, whenever he'd heard talk of Larrey, it had been from people like the detective, the civil guards, his employee – people who hadn't known him – or reports in the news which praised him as they do any innocent person who dies violently and prematurely. But until that moment he had not seen him as an individual.

Rita had slipped towards him and had her head on his chest, so he couldn't see her face. They were silent, waiting for the shadows to lift. For a second, he thought of telling her everything he knew, of confessing his involuntary role in the tragedy, but immediately he considered it too cruel and gratuitous to put it into words. There was nothing he could do now; it was all out of his hands. So the fleeting impulse of sincerity was followed by an even stronger one of caution. What was he going to tell her for? How could he explain that the hands that now caressed her had, a few weeks previously, caressed the pistol, seduced by the beauty of its shape, the coldness of the metal, the balance of its weight? How could he dissociate the caress from the moment he'd held it, how not to imagine the distant smell of cartridges on the fingers that touched her thighs?

Of course he couldn't tell her, and he feared his silence would become a block of ice between them that would never entirely melt. He feared that quiet point of friction that hid deep beneath their mutual happiness, in the same way that some pleasant-tasting foods will hide a noxious smell which is only discovered when a long-sealed pot is accidentally opened one day.

'What's wrong?' asked Rita, lifting her head as if, with her ear to his chest, she had noticed a sudden change in his heartbeat.

'Nothing,' he said, smiling unconvincingly.

'I shouldn't have mentioned all this.'

'Not at all,' he replied. 'Knowing what's worrying you brings me closer to you.'

But for the rest of that night any other conversations they started seemed weighed down and quickly died out, lacking the lightness which happiness had sometimes given their most insignificant words.

⌐

He had declared his earnings for the third quarter and, as always, had to update the ledger he kept in the safe at the bank. He hadn't been back since the gun had been stolen. He had avoided it, fearing his worries would resurface, and had dealt with the bank on the phone, over the Internet or by sending Ernesto. But now there was no way round it.

He copied the undeclared portion of his earnings on to a disk, deleted it from the hard drive and went to the bank with a wad of notes and his security key.

The manager greeted him as cordially as ever, without letting on, by a single gesture or comment, that when he'd received a court order requesting a list of customers with safe-deposit boxes, he had thought of him.

He walked him to the door of the vault, gave him the bank key necessary to open the safe, and went away, leaving him on his own. Going in, Julián Monasterio had the usual feeling of claustrophobia and sense of being in a cave full of traps, secrets and hidden treasures. Everything was as he'd left it in the safe: the disk and the ledger, the pouch containing the *arras* and his father's jewellery, and the small leather purse with the two million. Like the last time, only the book with the gun was missing. He closed his eyes and stood still for a few seconds, going over each and every movement of that day. After all this time, he still hoped for a light that might be cast on a forgotten detail. He was tense, like someone buried alive trying to discern where the light draught he feels on the back of his neck is coming from. But that fleeting draught did not blow again. He took the disk with the quarterly declaration and the roll of new notes from his briefcase. He couldn't stop himself touching the cold gold of the *arras* and looking at his father's small things again. He thought of Rita and chose a small tiepin to wear for her the next time they met.

Then he locked the safe, first with his key, then with the bank's, and double-checked that everything was where it should be and that he hadn't made a mistake or forgotten anything. He went out and said goodbye to the manager. He was almost at the door when he got that feeling again – a light draught on the back of his neck – that despite all his care and effort he was still forgetting something, that there was something different from last time that would not make itself known.

And then, struck by a painful revelation, he stopped dead still as his hand grasped the stainless-steel door handle. It wasn't that he was forgetting a material possession, an object. In fact, in order to avoid another mistake, he had recalled that day's movements so precisely that now, as he was leaving, he had almost looked back as if to take the hand of his daughter, who had been waiting for him outside the vault. But Alba wasn't there now. She was at school, maybe with Rita, in that pleasant room that didn't seem a part of the rest of the rough building. And that memory had so many consequences, shook him so much that, before any other sensation, he felt an intense spasm of pain. For only now did he realise that his daughter, who gazed at everything with her big fearful eyes, who knew how to remain so quiet and still among adults that she became nearly invisible, must have seen from her deep armchair who – a man, a woman, or a man and a woman – was waiting by the door to the vault while he was in there. And if she had seen them, Julián Monasterio was sure she'd be able to recognise them.

He hurried along the street wondering how he hadn't thought of his daughter before, when he'd gone over what had happened that morning so many times. And he knew the answer was in that first unequivocal decision to keep her away from all his problems: it had also raised a barrier that had automatically cut any link between them. He had always ensured that no news of the wreckage of his life should reach the girl's eyes and ears. He could bear the accusation of being a careless father for having taken her to the bank with him, but not that of being a bad father.

Now he was assaulted by doubts over what to do. If he told anyone what he'd just remembered, Alba would inevitably be involved in this horrible business. Even if he kept it from the lieutenant, the detective would still want to speak to her; he might even ask her to identify someone. It wouldn't be at all pleasant.

He was walking by a phone booth and at that moment took a decision. He'd had enough of dithering. To go on hiding, in a way that contaminated every one of his actions, from his relationship with his daughter to his best moments with Rita, would probably be more counterproductive for Alba than to confront it once and for all. He wanted to provide security and shelter for his daughter, but he couldn't do it while he himself felt weak and unprotected. He took some coins from his pocket, dialled the number and waited to hear Cupido's voice.

⌣

Cupido and Julián Monasterio arrived at the school gate together, a few minutes before morning classes finished.

The detective felt a bit out of place among the groups of mothers. He didn't and would never have children, so this was a particularly strange world to him, one in which women played a role that was quite different from the one he was used to: once through the gate, they seemed to shed any suggestion of sexuality, of flirtatiousness. Almost none of them wore any make-up that could be considered a weapon of seduction, or was dressed provocatively, or gave off a scent that turned his head. On the contrary, the playground seemed an extension of their domestic and family territory. The maternal instinct – which was unknown to him and whose intensity he could not imagine – prevailed, wiping out everything else.

The bell rang loudly and there were a few expectant seconds, all eyes fixed on the wide gate, until the first children started appearing and, seeing their mothers, rushed into their arms.

Presently they saw Alba. She was carrying a cardboard butterfly she'd made in class which she showed her father, proud of her work. She didn't ask why he'd come to pick her up instead of Rocío – lately he did it quite regularly – but she looked at Cupido enquiringly, almost distrustfully.

'He's a friend of mine. His name is Ricardo,' he explained. 'Why don't you give him a kiss?'

Cupido bent down, kissed her first, and offered his cheek to the wet touch of her lips, while he smelled soap, glue and eraser shavings.

Julián Monasterio decided it would be better to go to neutral ground, a cafe or a bench in the park, where what they had to ask her wouldn't seem too official or serious. A few minutes later, when they were sitting at a table and Cupido had gone over to the bar to order, Alba asked him in a low voice:

'Does that man work with you?'

'No,' he replied. 'He's a friend of mine and I've asked him to help me find a very important thing that I've lost.'

'A very important thing?'

'Yes.'

'What kind of thing?'

'A book,' he answered. Without looking, he saw Cupido come back with their drinks, sit down in silence and listen attentively.

'Is it a book of stories?' Before starting a new sentence she seemed to need to understand the previous one properly.

'One with lovely stories. But you have to help us, too. If we find it, I'll read you one every night.'

'OK.'

'I think I left it behind at the bank, one morning we went there together. Do you remember?'

'The day I got lost on the ramp in the supermarket.'

'Yes, that day. Do you remember I went into a room to put some things away?'

'Yes,' she answered, the 's' whistling slightly through her toothless gums.

'And you waited for me outside, sitting in a big armchair,' he explained, helping her remember, sparing her any unnecessary words, leading her gently to the final questions.

'Yes.'

'Do you remember when I was inside, someone else arrived who wanted to go in and had to wait for me to come out?'

The girl looked silently at her father and then at Cupido. She didn't seem to be hesitating, but rather gauging the need to tell her father something he must have known better than she did.

'Do you remember if there was someone waiting?'

'Yes.'

'Who? A man, a woman?'

'A man and a woman.'

From his jacket Cupido took the photographs of Saldaña that had appeared in the local paper the previous day.

'Is this the man?'

Alba looked at the clippings and answered promptly:

'No. He wasn't old.'

'Did you know the man?'

'Yes.'

'Do you know his name?'

'No.'

'But you've seen him again?' asked Cupido.

'Yes.'

'Where?'

'At school, sometimes when we leave in the afternoon.'

'Does he work there?' asked Cupid in a calm voice.

'I don't think so. But sometimes he's there.'

'And if you see him this afternoon when I come to pick you up, would you be able to point him out to me?' asked her father.

'Sure.'

The two men looked at each other, confident and hopeful in what they were hearing, because the girl was at that age when children are old enough to separate reality from fantasy, but still too young to tell a lie on purpose, whether maliciously or with the intention of pleasing the grown-ups.

19

By heart, he knew how a lump of lead becomes a bullet: the exact path of the trigger and how much pressure you can exert without the hammer striking; the precision of the strike at the centre of the bore, which in this pistol eliminated the possibility of mechanical failure; the instant deflagration of gunpowder – that mixture of cellulose and nitrates which gets compressed inside the case for two thousandths of a second to produce a formidable expansion of gasses, propelling a piece of metal forward at a speed of four hundred metres per second.

By heart, he knew its serial number and, without looking at it, he caressed it gently with the tip of his index finger, whispering happily:

'F, N, zero, five, five, three, seven.'

By heart, and even blindfolded, he could assemble and dismantle it, identify any one of its thirty-two pieces, and recognise any alien bolt or spring that might be placed among them, no matter how similar they might look to the real thing.

By heart, he knew its weight, its colour, its sheen of bluing which prevented oxidation, its texture, how warm it got when it was fired, the shape that gave concrete expression to its balance and beauty.

Well. Now that he'd have to use it again, he needed to oil it and replace the cartridges missing from the clip. On the previous Sunday – when his shots could be mistaken for hunters' – he had practised again, in a secluded spot where no one might surprise him. He hadn't touched it until the day of Larrey's death, and afterwards he didn't have a chance to be alone to reload it. This would be the last time before he lost it forever in the waters of the Lebrón.

He covered the kitchen table with a clean woollen cloth and on it placed the pistol, the silencer and the box of cartridges. Then he brought out the pot of oil, a cleaning rod, and a piece of cloth. He surveyed everything before sitting down, checking nothing was missing with the attention to detail of a surgeon checking his instruments before an operation.

It was half past one in the afternoon, so he had over two

hours. Without hurrying, he opened a bottle of beer and downed half of it in one swig. He always ate alone. For a few years that solitude had upset him: either he had no appetite for what his mother left him – the same food she used for the tapas and snacks at the bar – or eagerly devoured it with his hands, ignoring all rules of hygiene or decorum, wiping his mouth on his sleeve like a fly cleaning its legs. He'd eventually got used to it, and now sometimes found it difficult to eat in another's company, adjusting to their pace, using a napkin before drinking, not forgetting the table manners he'd not been reminded of in a long time. Since the age of ten, it had only been on very few occasions – an illness, a celebration, a day during the holidays – that he had shared a table with a member of his family. At ten he'd been left to his own devices. His parents had bought a bar and forgotten about everything else. His father served wine and beer with a professional demeanour whose precision he'd always admired – the twist of the bottle at the last moment to avoid spilling a drop, altering the tilt of the glass under the tap to get a good head – always with a feigned smile, faking that diligence, loudness and good humour – 'Two beers over here!' 'Tripe coming right up!' – which regulars seemed to like so much. Meanwhile, back in the kitchen, his mother took care of the tapas and snacks with similar enthusiasm, now and again poking her head through the hatch in her clean cap, to check on the fun outside, or check the level of the trays, or deliver a steaming dish of chips, meat or entrails.

Years ago, the couple of times he'd dared reproach them for having left him on his own so much, their replies had always been identical and spoken in unison. Receiving the same firm speech from both of them, he realised how pointless it was to complain. They said they couldn't look after him at that time of day as lunch was the busiest time in the bar: the best time for filling up the till that paid for his clothes, his food, his pocket money; it was the time customers left their jobs hungry, thirsty and tired, and didn't care about the price, as long as they got quick, clean, efficient and good-humoured service without having to wait, without the beer being warm or the tapas stale and disgusting, without staining their elbows on a dirty, greasy bar.

But that time wasn't just the busiest at the till; it was also the moment when the bar earned its reputation for the rest of the day. Spain wasn't like abroad, where he had been born and where they'd lived as emigrants for a few harsh years. In other countries, cafes and pubs earned their reputations from continental breakfasts or good cocktails, or from the artists and writers who hung out in them, or the women who drank there regularly. Here in Spain, a bar – they would tell him, one on each side, surrounding him – is made or broken between lunchtime and the siesta, that stretch of time when people toast, with a beer and tapas, the work they've just finished, and toast the break that's just starting. It's the defining moment. In Spain, a bar may serve the best coffee and have the best decor, it may be immaculately clean and play the best music, but without good tapas it will never succeed.

This was the way they always shut him up, and he resigned himself to his loneliness. It was then that he understood he would have to get anything he may need on his own, without any help. By the time he was twelve he'd learned how to lie successfully, how to hide his thoughts and deceive. Knowing that tears were pointless, he never cried again.

After a few years, the situation was reversed. Now it was he who wanted to be alone, and grumbled whenever an illness or some other circumstance kept his parents at home. He'd discovered the advantages of independence and the privilege of having walls and a roof at his sole disposal five years before his legal independence. He sometimes invited over his schoolmates – not friends, he didn't have any real friends – who seemed envious of so much freedom. He would come and go without anyone setting him limits or schedules, had no arguments when he chose a violent TV station or turned up the volume on music videos. He had rummaged through all the drawers in the cupboards and knew his parents' little secrets, how much they'd saved and how miserable they'd been during the years they had been abroad, their physical ailments, their vulgarities and their whims. At home he could do anything he liked. He'd lost his virginity in the bed where he slept every night, to a transient neighbour in the same building, a married woman of whom he had wonderful memories, only clouded by the suspicion that all the older women he'd been close to had used him – delicately and tenderly, no doubt, but never taking him seriously. Later there had been other girls who had loved him or pretended to love him, and who never surprised him.

At home, discreetly and secretly, he had done every act condemned in a provincial town like Breda, where breaking rules of good behaviour makes a permanent stain. And he knew that his reputation as a good boy came from that secrecy. Let his parents stay in the bar forever, filling up the till with beer-stained notes, and celebrating their cult of tapas. As well as the benefits of his inheritance, he also had a few years left to enjoy that happy autonomy.

All the separate pieces were laid out on the cloth now, and he started going over them, cleaning, oiling, sliding his fingers along the metal. He liked the garage smell that drifted off the kitchen table. It made him feel like a specialist handling sophisticated precision instruments whose utility and purpose no one else knows.

When the pieces were separate they looked as if, once assembled, they would make a very large gun, almost impossible to hide in your jacket. But that was an illusion. The end result was a medium-sized but very powerful pistol, whose size belied its calibre, and which, when fired, was deadly even at a distance. When the bullet hit him, Larrey, with all his height and strength, had collapsed like a rag doll. Only when Larrey fell and he heard his moans did he suspect his mistake. Then, hitting the switch with his elbow, he had turned on the light in the office and confirmed it, but without feeling much anxiety or bewilderment. Fortunately, he had the presence of mind to leave the light on and draw the blinds (covering his hands with a tissue), so that he erased all evidence that might point to an accident or a mistake, and everyone would follow the wrong lead. Because of course it wasn't Larrey he'd come looking for. Larrey was the only teacher he liked, a guy who didn't give orders – get me a ream of paper from the shop, clean that vomit on the stairs, make these photocopies, tidy up that cupboard, go to the tobacconist's and buy some stamps – and who called him by his name when they bumped into each other and not by the name of one of the previous objectors. In some of his classes on the track he'd helped Larrey put up the bar for the high jump, measure the sandpit, carry the base of the horse and the mats. Sometimes he even thought he would like to have been one of his pupils.

But although he'd pulled the trigger, he didn't feel guilty, and blamed the whole thing on Nelson instead. In every conversation he'd heard on the evening of the election, most teachers felt sure he would be the next headmaster. So he should have been the one in the office a few hours later. What was Larrey doing there in the dark, what was he looking for? And wearing that suit. He had always, always seen him in a tracksuit, except on that evening, when Larrey had decided to wear clothes that, in the darkness of the office and with their similar physique, had led to his mistake.

〜

If he had the chance, it wasn't often that he could resist the voyeuristic pleasure of listening to others when they didn't know they were being listened to. He had heard so many things over the school intercom that, if he had to, he could bring to light enough secrets and dirt and misery to cover all the blackboards in all the classrooms in shit. He only had to be alone in the office – when he was asked to copy out a list on the computer or was left there to answer the phone – and to press the button for each classroom to hear what went on in them, the noise of children or a private conversation. That gadget, originally designed to contact others and save time and legwork along the corridors of a large building, could become an efficient means of monitoring the teachers and, of course, of espionage.

And it was over the intercom, last term, when he'd pressed the button of the Speech Therapy Office, that he'd heard gentle words, a disturbing silence he imagined filled with caresses, and the click of a kiss. Blood flooded into his face, and he experienced anger and a sort of hatred, that was partly directed at her, but mainly at Nelson, whom he could only see as the more experienced rival, skilled and self-sufficient, and so complacent that he didn't spare a thought for someone he must regard as a child. How he'd hated him. Of course he'd hated him! Hatred was what generated that excess of energy, hatred kept him in shape, stopped him from shrivelling up like the rest of them.

During the following weeks he would spy on them from afar,

as they talked in the playground, or said hello in the morning, as if they hadn't seen each other since they'd left the school the previous day, or as they went up the stairs between two lines of pupils, their steps so synchronised that he wondered how it was possible that no one else noticed. He felt an uncontrollable anger when he saw how smug they were in their secret; when despite his age he could have given them lessons on hiding and dissembling. Sometimes he felt like shouting out loud what was going on, or pointing his finger at the clues no one else could see.

He thought he'd been in love with Rita. He'd missed her terribly after she left Breda for the summer. During those hot months he felt like the third member of a *ménage*, while the other two had taken off for a glorious tour of the world. But when term started and he saw her again and wanted her, he promised himself that this time he wouldn't let them treat him like a child.

The situation, however, didn't improve: he'd known, since the first day of September, that Nelson was running as a candidate for headmaster. If he won – and everyone predicted he'd defeat De Molinos's blind faith and self-confidence – the power and prestige would make him look even stronger compared to a simple conscientious objector whose only advantage was his youth. It was on one of those early September days, when term had started for the teachers but not for the pupils yet, that he decided what he would use one of the bullets in the gun for.

He knew now that if he had not had the pistol he wouldn't have thought of killing. He knew now that having a gun in your hands will lead you to use it, and that what was once a fantasy, with a gun, passes easily from the realm of the fantastic to the realm of the possible. Weighing up a cartridge, he had started noticing the enormous fragility of the human body, the great number of bones, entrails, glands, arteries and organs on which the impact of a bullet is fatal. How easy it would be to hit a target on the one third of the body surface that makes death feasible! How flimsy the skin was! The skin that you caress, kiss, lick and bite is so fine that it cannot protect life from a sliver of lead and antimony.

He finished adjusting the pieces and clipped the loaded magazine into the butt of the pistol. Then he reached out and aimed at the beer bottle he'd just drunk and left on the hob. His hand was steady: he was calm, and calmness would be an invaluable ally in a couple of hours. Even if he had only one arm and only one eye and half of his organs, he was sure he'd be able to hit a man-sized target thirty metres away. How nice it was to have a gun! He felt powerful and, even better, felt that no one could harm him; that while holding it his body was invulnerable and his arms were filled with strength, as if the pistol produced an energy that charged his muscles. *It is weapons that conquer and subdue the world,* he told himself. *A rose could never win a battle; but with a pistol a determined man can achieve anything.*

He put it underneath his jumper, and had the same feeling of power he'd experienced the first time he held it, a little while after leaving the bank. That morning he had agreed to go with Mari Angeles to get some jewels out of her parents' safe that she and her mother were going to wear to a baptism. In the vault there were several empty safes with their doors half-open. Peering into one of them he'd come across what no one would have believed possible: a purse full of money, a pouch containing coins and some dull, old-fashioned masculine jewellery, a computer disk, a notebook with a name and a weird surname, Monasterio, and an old, very heavy book. Seeing the open safe, Mari Angeles begged him not to touch anything, anxious about the camera on the ceiling, but he assured her that it was off. As she opened hers, he took out the book, and lifting the cover, discovered its contents: pistol, silencer and a small square box full of ammunition. Without his girlfriend noticing, he shut it, shoved it into his trousers under his shirt, and went back to what she was saying. She was so glad that he showed such enthusiasm for the pearl necklace, the earrings and the sapphire brooch she would wear when they got married – as if he had accepted the new butcher's shop that his hypothetical in-laws had offered to buy them as a wedding present – that she didn't notice what he was carrying against his stomach. How easy it had been to take the book with the pistol in it, an object he'd dreamt of so many times.

It wasn't until later, after a few days went by and the local press – which scrupulously published an account of all the reported crimes – didn't make any reference to the robbery, that he wanted to see the owner's face. He had only seen his back when the man left the vault. Then he started wondering why he had hidden the gun, why he didn't report it missing, what he did for a living, who he was. In the telephone directory he found several entries for Monasterio, the surname on the notebook. But his curiosity went no further until a day in early September when he found himself alone in the office, typing out a list of students handed to him by that old gossip, Julita Guzmán, and he came across the surname again: Monasterio Pina, Alba.

Once again he was surprised at how easy it was to move around the school, on this occasion to get some confidential information from the school registration records. The girl's father was called Julián, a name that he remembered perfectly once he saw it. The mother's name was also there, both their ages, occupations, address and telephone number. And most importantly, a picture of the pupil.

It was a small, passport-size photograph, which made him shiver when he remembered where he'd seen her before: the girl had also been at the bank that morning, sitting in one of those armchairs in the lobby, no doubt waiting for her father. He'd been surprised to see her there on her own, so small, almost engulfed by the leather seat, looking around her alertly, as if she feared an attack at any moment. Ever since he'd recognised her in the picture he'd tried to avoid her class, or meeting her in corridors, for he suspected that, in the same way as he had, the girl might remember him waiting outside the vault.

However careful he was, it had been impossible not to bump into her sometimes when she left in the afternoons. And she had never shown the least sign of having recognised him, never looked at him with curiosity or as if she were startled. To her he must have been just another of the many adults who were at the school for reasons a six-year-old doesn't even try to comprehend. And so, until this morning, he had come to believe that the danger had passed.

Until the collection of circumstances that made him mistake Larrey for Nelson, he'd always thought that chance was on his side. And by chance he didn't mean the one random possibility in a million that determines a game, but something more personal and dramatic, the kind of chance that comes with the flip of a coin: heads or tails, now or never, black or white, up or down, left or right; the kind of chance that permits no going back, no draws or any alternative but total victory or total defeat. He'd summoned it many times in previous years, had forced it to help him and it had always been on his side: heads, now, white, up, right. On this afternoon he was confident it still was on his side: it was chance that a few hours earlier had made him see, from a window, the tall detective and the girl's father waiting for her outside.

In early October Nelson had once again rostered him for afternoon shifts, so he could help check and move any material or equipment necessary for extracurricular activities: sports, languages, music, painting, drama... However, he was sometimes required to do a morning shift instead. And today he'd had to go with a teacher on a school trip to an exhibition of smells and perfumes, so he had the rest of the afternoon free. If he was careful not to be seen – and he'd managed to get the key to the boiler rooms – no one would be able to say they'd seen him at school at all that afternoon.

20

At five, Cupido and Julián Monasterio were waiting for Alba to come out again. In a few minutes, the girl was possibly going to identify the man who, accompanied by a woman, had gone into the vault after her father. They waited discreetly behind the groups of mothers, containing their impatience. Julián Monasterio was smoking nervously, his index finger tapping repeatedly on the cigarette, keeping the ash short, anxious about this moment he had tried so hard to avoid, when his daughter would have to point her finger at a man. In an attempt to calm him down, the detective had told him that there was nothing to be afraid of, that they were the ones who had the advantage. But he couldn't help feeling afraid. He couldn't keep his feet still, as if the ground were burning and an unbearable heat was coming through his shoes.

All the children had left except for a couple of stragglers who eventually ran out, but they had not yet seen Alba. They went over to the gate and spoke to the caretaker:

'We haven't seen Alba Monasterio come out. First year.'

'Hold on a moment.'

They saw him walk off along the corridor and come back a minute later with her tutor, Matilde Cuaresma, but without Alba, which was terrible. Julián Monasterio had spoken once to this woman, and only to hear that his daughter was a difficult pupil.

'We were just phoning you to see if she'd arrived. A woman told us she wasn't there, but that she might be with you, with her father.'

'How do you mean?'

'We believe your daughter's run away again. She must have gone when the whole class goes to the bathroom. We thought she must have gone home, like that other time. Hasn't she turned up?'

'No, but has anything happened in class?'

'On the contrary. She's beginning to be more at ease with the other pupils.'

'Alba hasn't run away,' he responded, with such tension in his voice that Cupido put a hand on his arm to calm him.

'Maybe you missed each other on the way. Please, come with me and we'll call again.'

They went to the headmaster's office and the detective stood by the door. Inside was only Julita Guzmán, stamping papers and filing them away in folders. Julián Monasterio dialled the number of his house, spoke briefly to Rocío and promptly hung up.

'My daughter has not run away,' he repeated, but by now anxiety had given way to fear. 'Where's the headmaster?'

The secretary reacted to those words; she pressed the caretaker's number on the intercom and asked him and Moisés to go and look for Nelson. Over the loudspeaker they heard the caretaker say he would have to find him on his own, as the objector was not in that afternoon. He had done the morning shift.

'Was anyone absent from work today?' asked Cupido. He'd remained silent until then, but now he understood he was the only one who knew what to do.

'No one is missing today,' replied the secretary as if she was reading a war dispatch. 'We're all here.'

'Call Moisés.'

'But Moisés is not a teacher,' she said. She looked at the detective and still hesitated for a few seconds, beginning to understand why he was there, surmising that his request not only involved Alba, but that the girl's disappearance was linked, in some dark and terrible way, to Larrey's death. She went over to the phone, checked a list of numbers tacked on a cork noticeboard and dialled carefully; she couldn't stop her finger shaking.

'No answer,' she said after several seconds.

'Where does he live?' Julián Monasterio asked. They wouldn't solve anything in the office and he could barely breathe in there while his daughter was being held somewhere, terrified, waiting for him to come and get her, to rescue her from some isolated, deserted place – a cave perhaps – which he imagined covered in the bones of animals. With a shudder of horror, he couldn't help thinking that in Breda people were still killed out in the country, that barbarism still avoided the centre of town.

'I think we should talk to the headmaster about this,' said Matilde Cuaresma.

'Of course. But we haven't got time to wait for him right now. Where does Moisés live?'

The secretary fetched a diary and gave them the address. As they were leaving she stopped them.

'If you can't find him there, I think you should try the farm of the girl he's going out with. It's very near El Paternóster.'

With her characteristic accuracy, she drew them a map with directions showing how to get there.

⤳

At least she hadn't screamed. She wasn't one of those girls whose hysterical shrieks at the sight of an insect or at the slightest knock in the playground had been so unbearable to him during all those months. Neither had she screamed when he'd made her come out with him through the boiler room, and offered almost no resistance when he told her they were going to see her father who was waiting for them outside, although it was quite likely she hadn't believed it.

Now she was at the back of the shelter, her hands tied behind her back, not because he feared she might run away, but to stop her tearing off the tape he'd stuck over her mouth. Only her big frightened eyes were free to move, but they were not shedding tears.

He'd lived alone for a good part of his life and had been forced to make decisions without anyone's help or advice. In that solitude and secrecy he had understood that some acts of cruelty were inevitable because there was no one around to delegate them to. He didn't like what he had to do now, either – erase that unbearable gaze from those eyes – but it was inevitable. If, in his attempt to kill Nelson, he had willingly fought a duel with chance, now it was simply a matter of defending himself and surviving. Once the girl disappeared, no one else would be able to identify him. He was getting tired of this whole business he had started because of a woman he didn't care about anymore. Everything he'd done for her had been pointless. The day he went over to her flat again, Rita had shouted at him, humiliating him, refusing to give him any convincing explanations for her disdain – the same hateful entitlement to silence that every older woman claimed over him. Now he needed rest; he needed to leave behind the sound and fury of the last few months. In a few weeks he would finish his community service at the school and would be free from all those teachers who couldn't live without ordering people about, and from the six hundred children who never stopped screaming and flailing their limbs. He wanted to forget them all and think of this year as an extra school year he'd been forced to repeat. Once he was finished here, he'd spend a few months alone with Mari Angeles, perhaps making her happy sometimes, since he knew how to so easily. He might even consider helping the future in-laws at the butcher's and learn the trade: how to rig the magic scales, how to sharpen the fearsome hatchets and knives, to cut chops and steaks, to remove the entrails without their dark juices spoiling the rest of the meat. And he might even agree to marry her, although he knew she would never be beautiful. At times, when he saw her naked, he couldn't help thinking she was like one of the cuts her father sold: opulent and generous in weight, with abundant blood wherever there was an open wound, with rosy-coloured skin, and showing the same lean and fat streaks as the pieces on the plastic trays under the harsh light of the spots – touching her was like touching raw meat. But prudence told him, too loudly to ignore, that hiding behind her was the most intelligent thing he could do right now. The moment when the fun stopped had come far too quickly. Growing old meant chaining yourself to a tool, he thought, and in the end, his was a butcher's knife.

He wiped his earth-covered hands with a handkerchief and noticed that the cramps from digging the hole had passed. The ground had hardened since the end of the summer, and was without any vegetation. Still, he'd found a spot between two large rocks and had made a deep hole there that he would later cover with stones, to avoid anything unforeseen. No one would ever find her, the sheep and the pigs would cover all traces of smell, all tracks, and he'd never be caught.

He took the pistol out of his belt with his clean hands. He didn't want the child to suffer any more, so with his back to her, so she wouldn't see anything, he started carefully screwing the silencer on. Everything would be short and clean. Then, before turning towards the shadows, he heard the engine of an approaching car.

21

A strong wind had been blowing for the last two days, a relentless, troublesome wind that seemed intent on stripping the trees and only stopped from time to time to contemplate its effects on the bare branches and the leaf-covered ground. But this morning it had finally subsided and the air was filled with a fresh, clean peacefulness; the last clouds scudded high across the sky and sunshine streamed through the gaps between them. At last he'd be able to go for a spin.

Whenever he finished a difficult case, he liked to devote the following day to a long, tiring bike ride. In the morning he put on his cycling gear, filled a bottle with water and another with glucose and stuffed the back pockets of his jersey with snacks and high-energy bars. Once he was ready, he went out on a route that he had planned meticulously the night before – not that he always followed it, letting himself drift when he felt like it – feeling that, for seven hours and one hundred and thirty kilometres, the exertion, the sweat and the wind beating against his face and chest cleansed him of the words and lies he'd accumulated during the investigation. In those final excursions, it seemed to him that – like the tortoise that draws its head inside its shell, crosses through a dark hole in the ground, shakes itself and manages to emerge clean – he left the latest episode of misery and evil definitively behind him. It was as if he returned to the obscurity and the anonymity he'd emerged from for a while. If he had to tell someone – whether in person or in writing, whether in a letter or in a hundred-thousand-word novel – what he'd been up to for the last four weeks, he knew he would barely figure in the closing pages, that Larrey and Moisés and Julián and Alba Monasterio would have more weight in this story, for the culprits and their victims are always more interesting and human and believable than the heroes; his clients always came before him, an obscure, lonely private detective, after all; the feelings, emotions and anxieties of the soul always came before what was a pretty monotonous criminal intrigue. His job was to be like the catalyst necessary to trigger a particular chemical reaction, whose role is forgotten as soon as it serves its purpose, and he would have rejected, with an ironic smile, anyone's suggestion that he should give himself a more important part in the story.

In fact, the moment he guessed that Moisés had kidnapped Alba, he had called the lieutenant and handed the whole operation over to him, so all the laurels and prestige of rescuing the girl, as well as the resolution of Larrey's murder, went to Lieutenant Gallardo and his two subordinates, in particular the officer who, 'risking life and limb', in the words of the hackneyed prose of the local press, 'gunned down the kidnapper with two shots'. Cupido wasn't interested in those kinds of violent actions. He wasn't afraid of them, but he wasn't interested.

It was hard enough to come through unscathed, not to feel utterly disgusted every time he came into contact with squalor and hatred. He had confirmed once again that neither wars, nor a mafia, nor any other kind of criminal activity based on economics or power was necessary for people to do harm or to kill. He had confirmed once again that the warring feelings rotting inside the human soul claim more victims than any other cause. In the Western Europe he lived in, so well-armed against plagues, natural disasters and uncertainty, where there were no wars and no prospect of them in the near future – which realised the astonishing utopia of a generation of men and women able to live their whole lives without ever hearing a bomb explode – military service was no longer compulsory. And so it was ironic and disquieting that someone who had officially chosen not to touch a weapon was the very one harbouring enough hatred to pull a trigger.

He'd nearly finished getting ready when the phone rang. It was Lieutenant Gallardo.

'Yesterday I paid your client a visit. Julián Monasterio. In his shop. To tell him he should have handed in the pistol that very first day, but that it was all in the past now and he didn't need to worry. No one will ever know where that objector got it from. A bloody conscientious objector!'

'Thanks,' said Cupido, understanding that neither of them had eliminated compassion from their daily job, and it was this that kept alive the strange friendship between a lieutenant of the Guardia Civil and a private detective.

'His daughter was with him. The girl. He seems like a good

father. And a good man,' he added in a low voice, aware that these words were not expected from him or his position.

'He is. And I think he'll never have anything to do with guns again.'

'I hope so. Speaking of which, you can come round to pick up your gun licence any time. It's been renewed. I hope you'll never have to use it, either,' he said before ringing off.

It was rare that he experienced such a strong protective feeling for a client as he did for Julián Monasterio; it was rare he was so sure that the person who hired him was innocent, so he was glad to contribute to his happiness. Yesterday he'd seen him taking a walk with the teacher and his daughter, and in their slow, lingering steps, which were neither escaping anything nor trying to get anywhere in particular, there was a calm that even he found reassuring, as if they were unwittingly offering him an act of faith, the certainty that, in spite of everything, it was still possible to find something good and valuable in a profession dominated by gloom and evil.

He should get going now. He finished dressing and went down to the garage to get his bike. He mounted and, pedalling unhurriedly, it wasn't long before he left the town behind – a term that was used less and less and was gradually being replaced by 'city', as if the older term was a little archaic and not very prestigious.

He felt in good shape. There was hardly any wind, and in the sky the sun's rays penetrated the clouds with unexpected intensity. He changed up a gear and pedalled more determinedly towards the hill, which looked like a painted backdrop, with mounts Yunque and Volcán as the main feature. Hardly any cars went by, and there was no sound. Whenever he stopped pedalling for a short stretch downhill, all he could hear was the swift susurrus of the tires spinning along the tarmac. The land shone with the ochre patches of autumn. As he carried on uphill, the red mane of the vineyards gave way to the woods adjoining El Paternóster. And there, before reaching the dense, dark and unsettling wall of greenery of the reserve, a light breeze blew over the red and orange leaves of oak and chestnut trees, making them look as if they were on fire. Now he was growing older, these natural changes could move him as much as a woman changing her dress.

He finished digging the borders in the garden he had abandoned a few days before. The ground was now turned and fertilised, good for earthworms and seeds, the clods of earth broken up and the dead roots unearthed; everything was ready for planting new flowers. But that wasn't his to do anymore.

He slung the hoe over his shoulder and went towards the house, feeling a mild, familiar pain in his knee. It was only mid-morning. As usual, his wife had gone to work in town, and had taken their son to school, so she wouldn't be back for a few hours yet. He was alone, and felt hollow and tired of resisting the temptation of the noose. He needed a sleep so long that on waking there would no longer be any reason for sorrow around him. He felt he'd suffered more in the last four years than in the preceding forty-eight of his life.

He yanked free the cable of the lightning conductor, which had come loose from the ground and had been flapping against the wall and demanding his attention for a while. Now he knew what it meant. The other end of the cable slithered down from the roof like a snake, hitting him lightly across the face. He checked how slippery it was, and its strength from the combination of plastic and copper. It would take his weight, no problem.

He went into the house and, without once looking into the living room, at the pictures on the fireplace and everything he left behind, went down the stairs into the cellar. The fruit he'd picked over the last month hung from the roof beams: melons from a reed-rope, strings of beans, garlic, grapes, peppers, chilli and laurel. On the floor, heaped on a tarpaulin were figs, apples, potatoes and quinces. The mixture of scents coming from the different ripening fruits created an intense, sickly-sweet smell in the cellar.

Before, when all the members of the household had lived and were hungry, they picked many of the fruits hanging on the trees, shiny without artificial help, plump like coloured light bulbs – the whole farm lit up by the glow of pears, peaches, cherries and apples. Those reserves of food lasted until Christmas. Yet in the last couple of years, although the crops had dwindled and they kept little for themselves, they ended up throwing a good part of it away, uneaten by them and their younger son. Dried fruit became impossibly hard to swallow; it felt like the pears and quinces had turned sour, grapes left a smoky taste in their mouths and cherries left their mouths full of stones. When his elder son had lived that never happened; when he had lived the harvest never seemed sufficient. Before he'd started to die he would come home full of energy, always hungry, and if dinner was late, he would go down to the cellar and take whatever fruit he liked. But in the last couple of years such a big store made no sense.

Very slowly, almost fondly, he tied the slipknot and made sure it slipped properly before slinging it over one of the roof beams.

⁓

'In the name of the Father, in the name of the Son and the Holy Spirit.'

'Amen,' replied all the children after crossing themselves, as they always did when class finished.

She knew she shouldn't say prayers outside religious studies, and even less if, as was the case now, there were three children who didn't take that subject. That gesture, the sign of the cross at the start and the end of a lesson, was an imposition on the children and was against the rules. But she was not ready to give it up, for in performing it she was sure she was erecting a barrier that protected her work from outside evil. Everyone – teachers and parents alike – knew it was her only requirement, and Nelson hadn't said anything to her when he took up his position, nor had the parents of the three students come in to complain.

However, that silence unsettled her as much as a formal complaint. She was beginning to suspect that Nelson's indifference was that of a man confident in his beliefs, who ignores the words of a fanatic and refuses to get into an argument, much like the condescending way people will humour idiots, or tolerate the little ways of the old. The three pupils who didn't take part in her religious classes weren't exactly from one of those loud, dirty, ignorant and marginalised families that despises any gesture redolent of the sacristy, but – as had been Marta's case – were excellent pupils: clean, diligent, clever, whose desertion irritated her more than if they had been mediocre. She could bear some of her soldiers going over to the enemy, but not her most brilliant generals. What was happening to the world when it was the best, the most industrious and best-educated, the least violent, who disregarded the Word with such indifference, not with hatred or scorn or anger, just indifference? It was the dreadful consequence of having made the subject optional.

Thinking about all this, the frequent disjunction of religion and behaviour, she sometimes came to the conclusion that some people, even without any spiritual guide, are nobler, kinder and more just than many of her most pious fellow Catholics. Then she would reflect that it is not your religion that matters so much as the way you follow its precepts.

But these phases of tolerance didn't last long and she soon reconstructed a direct line from Mount Sinai to Breda. She thought herself too old to call into doubt what she'd held true for so long, to change her reasoning and beliefs without also experiencing some mental crisis, and so she stubbornly went back to basing her conduct on the inflexible order of the catechism. She would imagine herself then as a vestal who keeps the sacred flame of devotion burning, while outside the barbarians get drunk, copulate and blaspheme.

The children left the class one by one, and she went over to the office to finish some filing. Nelson wasn't there, and De Molinos's presence there seemed a bit strange, as he'd avoided the office since he'd been replaced. He was standing still, looking out of the window, with his hands crossed behind his back, a characteristic pose for him, a gesture from the seminary he couldn't help, even when talking to someone, as if he was hiding something or concealing a stump. He even kept his hands behind him when telling pupils off, though then they didn't seem to conceal anything: then, it reminded Julita Guzmán of some of her own teachers who had seemed intensely threatening in that pose, as if at any moment they could extend their hand to hit a face, without the pupil being able to guess from which side the blow would come.

Without his previous rank, he now seemed old and weak, and she had to restrain a surge of pity. She made a noise with her chair to let him know she was there.

'Oh, it's you.'

'Yes,' she replied, her head lowered, fearing that the sense of shame and betrayal she felt would be obvious, for since staying on as secretary she was overwhelmed by it every time she came near him.

'And Nelson?'

'Down at the town hall. He had a meeting in the afternoon with a councillor about developing extracurricular activities. He wants to expand them,' she explained, thinking he would like the small deference of being given information before everyone else.

'Then could you give him a message when he comes back? I'll be a bit late tomorrow, by a couple of hours. I've got an appointment with the doctor,' he said.

'Anything serious?' she asked kindly.

'No. Just a check-up,' he replied dryly.

She felt a flood of loneliness when De Molinos went out of the office. No matter how much she complained about her job, the school kept her alive and alert, it was her world, the only place where she met her fellow human beings. And although, like one of those second-rate court painters who understood and painted hounds and horses better than the monarchs in all their pictures, she was obviously incapable of communicating with those who played the main role here – the children – she wasn't unable to establish friendly ties with some of her colleagues. For years De Molinos and his wife, Matilde Cuaresma, had been two of her most convivial workmates, those with whom she reminisced and told stories, discussed physical ailments and intrigues, and shared secrets about acquaintances or the children's parents. Without husband, children, or family, now she didn't even have them anymore.

↩

It was terrible: none of his best ideas had come from a conversation with someone he worked with; not one of his projects was the result of a collaboration. If, at some point, he'd believed that as headmaster he'd be able to establish a better working relationship, even a closer friendship, with the rest of the staff, he'd been wrong. It was the other way round. Although the new position had satisfied his vanity by lifting him one rung above his colleagues, it had left him alone. In less than a month he had realised that solidarity and comradeship are delicate, wild fruits, which only grow away from the contaminants of power.

The more open ways he'd tried to introduce, his kindness and his desire to reach decisions, if not unanimously, at least after a general debate, had done nothing to reduce the distance growing between him and his colleagues. He'd abolished De Molinos's old rigidity, once accused of running the school like an army camp, but no one seemed particularly grateful. He hadn't even been able to avoid the contempt of the person he liked most. In fact, he hadn't spoken to Rita alone since then, and knew now there wouldn't be another chance. He'd seen the girl's father waiting for her outside, and then all three had gone off together.

Just as it was at the beginning, only Mozart was left. He went into the study and closed the door, fearing his wife would come and disturb him; he spoke so much at school, made such an effort to be kind to people, that at least at home he could indulge in an hour of solitude and silence.

But that afternoon he didn't feel like playing; he didn't even get the clarinet out of its case. Humbled, convinced of his own insignificance, he just put on a record and admired how transcendent a few seemingly frivolous bars could prove in the hands of a true creator. Lying on the chaise longue, he closed his eyes so as not to be distracted by anything, convinced that mankind received this music without having done anything to deserve it.

⌐

'Come on, get in.'

He opened the door and pulled on the lead a bit. The puppy didn't want to go in, no doubt afraid of the medicinal smells of the house and the long corridor ahead. He nudged it gently with his foot and closed the door. It walked forward a bit, stopped again and, as if on cue, urinated before anyone could stop him.

'Don't be disgusting!' he scolded, but not severely. There would be time to teach him where he should sleep, where he should eat, and what was forbidden inside the house.

'Have you got someone with you?' called his father from the living room.

'Yes.'

He came to the door and showed him the puppy. He hadn't named it yet. As with Bruno, he didn't want to rush things until he found the right one.

'Another dog?'

'Why not?'

After Bruno's brutal death, he thought he would never have another animal. But a few days ago the school's caretaker had shown up with two cocker spaniel puppies bred by a relative of his who couldn't find any buyers. He didn't want to keep them and didn't dare abandon them, as the latest – and constant – news of feral dogs attacking children had made people careful. The caretaker would keep one and was offering the other to anyone who'd have it.

He'd thought about it for a day, and the next morning had made his decision. Since Larrey's murder had been solved – and also since the suicide of the person who'd slapped him in the face – it seemed all those painful episodes lay in the past and had brought a period of his life to a close. Suddenly, the reasons for his unhappiness had begun to seem old and irrelevant.

Now he would have to get used to living with no project or hope other than staying alive, without the possibility of a career change, with not much happening except alternating a visit to the hairdresser's and the brothel every fortnight. That cinnamon-coloured puppy brushing against his feet would not be a bad companion.

'Petra's broken a plate again.'

'It must have fallen.'

'No. I think she breaks them on purpose. Soon we'll have nothing to eat on.'

'Don't worry about the plates, Dad. I'll buy some more,' he replied in a conciliatory tone.

'She thinks she can do anything she likes because we're both men. If your mother was alive, she wouldn't allow so many liberties,' he insisted.

'That's not true, Dad, come on!'

Now that everything else seemed to have calmed down, it was particularly annoying that such stupid things should cause tension in his own house. His father's complaints struck him as more obsessive every day. Everything seemed wrong to him, he got angry over the smallest detail or delay, and even the Nembutal was beginning to lose its effect as a tranquilliser, so he'd stopped worrying if, some nights, he put two or three too many drops in the glass. Of course, he was still his father, and he still felt a gut-wrenching pity when he saw how the cancer was eating away at him, as furiously as a fire devours a dry log; when he looked at his face, whose eyes were sunk into their sockets as if something were drawing them in from the inside; or when he looked at his head, sunk so deeply between his shoulders that he seemed to be missing a few vertebrae. Still, every day it became harder to cope with his demands. He would sometimes tell himself that a terminally-ill person, even his father, had no right to hurt others, as if his illness were their fault. And so he would sometimes imagine his death, a sweet death like he'd seen in the movies, a book or a photograph dropping from someone's hands as they lie still in an armchair as if asleep.

〜

He woke up startled in the armchair where he'd dozed off. It was happening too often: resting his head for moment when he came back from school and losing consciousness for a few minutes of turbulent dreams.

He screwed up his eyes and yawned deeply. Then he opened them, but was still in a daze amidst the shreds of a nightmare in which someone made him cut down a wood with just a pair of secateurs. On the wall in front of him hung two portraits, of himself and his wife. He focused his eyes on the year, 1978, and the painter's signature, Alcántara. Those paintings had been his gift for their tenth wedding anniversary, but also an attempt to adopt the traditions and privilege of the Cuaresmas. No one in his family had ever been immortalised by a painter. All he had were some dull black-and-white photographs, without signatures or dates or any indication of who the person in the picture was. But the Cuaresmas had sat before an easel for several generations, wearing that arrogant expression born of noble ancestry and money. However, to him these portraits had the false sheen of counterfeit coins, the excessive shine that contrasted pitifully with the cracked oil paint of the older ones. Looking at his face he suspected that his portrait wouldn't stay on the wall for too long, and that as soon as he died it would be consigned discreetly to the attic.

His wife appeared at the door to tell him:

'I'm going to my sister's. I haven't seen her for a few days.'

'All right. You don't need to take the keys. I won't be going out.'

Since he'd lost the headship and no longer had to attend meetings, he had too much time on his hands. But he didn't know what to do with it. When classes ended, he put on his jacket and left the building almost without saying goodbye to anyone. Although he had cursed his job many times and was looking forward to retirement, he was beginning to wonder whether he wouldn't miss it. He'd known people who had spent forty years wanting to have a break and get away from the children, but who, as soon as they'd reached it, felt paralysed, barely able to move their arms, as if they'd broken their collarbones. They suddenly realised that the thing they moaned about so much was the one thing that had made them tolerably happy. And despite the longed-for rest, the day they discovered that was the day they started to die. People whose jobs consist of being listened to and obeyed couldn't adjust to a situation of inactivity and oblivion in which no one listened to or obeyed them.

Of course, he wouldn't suffer such fits of professional nostalgia. But he suspected that in a gentler though equally pertinacious way, he would miss a job to which he had devoted forty years of his life, and in which, despite all its difficulties, it was still possible to stand up for discipline, logic and order against the generalised onslaught of chaos.

⏝

'Eight o'clock?'

'OK.'

'Are you coming here?'

'I'd like you to come to mine.'

She smiled, though she knew he couldn't see her. The invitation pleased her; she'd been expecting it for a while and it seemed that, with that invitation, everything between them became clear and transparent.

'Would you like to?' she heard him ask, as she had stayed silent for too long. But silence only created greater intimacy between them.

'I'd love to.'

'Eight o'clock it is then. We can go to the cinema from here.'

She had sometimes been afraid of becoming one of those women who has so many loves because none of them is true. But she didn't consider herself loose, even if last term she'd been with two very different men, one of them married. She wasn't one of those women prone to having affairs with any man they like. What happened was that her relationships, for reasons she didn't quite know, ended up being problematic in one way or another. She didn't have the ability some of her friends had of sleeping with ten different men without anyone – at least none of the men – knowing, their lives and bodies being left with little more than a hazy memory of pleasure. No. Because of her personality, none of her relationships disappeared into oblivion or stopped mattering five minutes after ending.

Now she was strangely sure that everything would be all right with him. She couldn't imagine anywhere in the world where one couldn't follow the other, or any reason for insecurity or scepticism. From their first date she had discovered how far their problems became simpler when they were together. Of course, in time difficulties would appear that they would need to overcome, but it would be the same with any man. What couple was so perfect that one has never hurt the other, or felt that they were not receiving as much as they gave, or sometimes wanted to escape the stifling atmosphere that can arise in any relationship?

↬

'I can't catch it with any of these programmes,' said Ernesto. 'I don't know where it's hiding.'

'Let me try.'

Julián Monasterio sat in front of the computer and started typing codes while his assistant, looking over his shoulder, followed his movements attentively. Long columns of passwords, numbers and signs appeared on the computer screen, incomprehensible to anyone who wasn't an expert in its mysterious insides.

Every now and again he stopped to think, read the information and deleted or added something else, only to pause again, like a hunter in the woods who stops to observe the reactions of his prey after each movement. He hated people who created viruses, not so much for the nuisance and setbacks they caused at work, as for how they knowingly brought chaos and conflict into others' lives, remotely and anonymously. Also, for how gratuitous the destruction that came from their mechanisms of damage and confusion: their creators gained no benefit from driving computers mad, and making words that had once been clear and simple, fit for communicating ideas, desires and feelings, into indecipherable hieroglyphics.

'It's there!' he exclaimed, pointing to a line of letters and numbers which looked no different from the others. 'There's our little gatecrasher, right inside.'

He inserted a CD-Rom into the hard drive and typed a few more instructions, nodding to each of the messages that appeared on the screen.

'That's it. Won't bother us again,' he said at last, giving the seat back to Ernesto.

'You've got to tell me how you did it. I got lost at one point.'

'Tomorrow. I'm in a hurry now. I'm almost late. You can close up,' he said, putting his jacket on.

He'd arranged to meet Rita to take Alba to the cinema, and didn't want to be late for either of them, or for any rush to disturb the calm that had surrounded him in the last few days. Now at last everything was solved, and the future didn't look like a wall he had to climb only to find shards of glass at the top. He no longer owed anyone anything. The tragedy of the pistol, once set in motion, had ended in the best possible way for him. Besides Cupido and the lieutenant, no one knew where the objector had got the gun. Neither did Rita, of course, and she never would, for he realised how fond she'd been of Larrey and feared that telling her would cast a shadow between them for ever. He told himself that at their age, a man and a woman who meet and decide to carry on together will always have secrets in their past they cannot reveal without risking their relationship. He didn't trust women who grew up without making any mistakes and so could, by the same token, be equally indulgent towards himself. And for the rest, if love demands hard work and force of will, then he was willing to work very hard. He knew how much he could do for a woman he loved.

As for Alba, he hoped that that afternoon wouldn't leave any irreparable scars. There were signs that this terrifying experience, having taken her to the depths, might actually help her rise back up to the light. Now he understood it wasn't physical violence his daughter had feared most, but the unhappiness and disquiet of feeling lost. Compared to that fear, nothing else could come close.

He arrived home and put his key in the door. Rocío was waiting for him and left soon after.

Alba ran towards him down the hall, and he bent to give her a kiss. When she smiled, he saw the fleeting blur of white in her gums. Surprised and hopeful, he kneeled down, held her face in his hands and tilted it towards the light. With his thumbs, he gently pulled her lower lip to check it wasn't just a breadcrumb or some milk or yogurt. No, there it was. The incisor was beginning to cut through after so many months. He touched it with his index finger and felt the tiny point.

'Bite down a little,' he asked her.

She clenched her jaw and Julián Monasterio screamed and fell backwards exaggerating the pain in his finger.

'You've got another tooth!' he exclaimed, hugging her. 'You can't bite people anymore, you're a big girl now.'

They were cheek-to-cheek and he felt his daughter laugh. He stayed there for a while, overcome by a feeling of happiness and relief. Then he stood up and said:

'Let's go and get changed. Rita will be here any minute.'

As he tied the laces of her trainers, he remembered an old riddle his father had told him thirty years before.

'Do you know which creature has the most teeth?' he asked her very seriously.

'The lion.'

'No.'

'The crocodile.'

'No.'

'The shark.'

'No.'

'The wolf.'

'No.'

'The dog!' she exclaimed, beginning to get impatient.

'Still no.'

'Come on, tell me!'

'The tooth fairy!'

Alba frowned for a few moments, confused, and all of a sudden let out a great happy laugh that sounded like a miracle.